Street Banditz

Street Banditz

C. J. Hudson

www.urbanbooks.net

Urban Books, LLC
300 Farmingdale Road, N.Y.-Route 109
Farmingdale, NY 11735

Street Banditz Copyright © 2020 C. J. Hudson

ISBN 13: 978-1-64556-081-4
ISBN 10: 1-64556-081-3

First Trade Paperback Printing October 2020
Printed in the United States of America

10 9 8 7 6 5 4 3 2 1

This is a work of fiction. Any references or similarities to actual events, real people, living or dead, or to real locales are intended to give the novel a sense of reality. Any similarity in other names, characters, places, and incidents is entirely coincidental.

Distributed by Kensington Publishing Corp.
Submit Orders to:
Customer Service
400 Hahn Road
Westminster, MD 21157-4627
Phone: 1-800-733-3000
Fax: 1-800-659-2436

Prologue

"Bulletproof" Bobby Walker and Michael "Red" Roberts sat in Red's 2018 snow white Escalade in front of Kim's Wings. Puffing on a blunt, they peered out the window. On a stakeout, both men were trying to catch up with Juice, a petty dealer from around the neighborhood, who copped from them from time to time. It was Juice who had beaten Red out of $200 two weeks ago by paying for some product with counterfeit bills.

Juice had run into Red at a bar, and when he saw that Red was slightly inebriated, he decided to make a quick come-up. He was supposed to go out of town the next day, but some personal business caused him to delay his plans. That delay was just enough time for Red to discover that he'd been had.

When Red leafed through his money the following morning, he became enraged. After informing his cousin Bobby of the funny money, the two of them conducted a search-and-destroy mission for Juice. Then, as luck would have it, the two of them decided to stop and get something to eat, and it was there that they spotted Juice's money green old-school Chevy Impala.

"Yo, wassup, cuz? You wanna cash this nigga's chips in or what?" Bobby asked while rubbing the barrel of a black 9 mm.

"It all depends on if this muthafucka got my money. If he comes up off them ends, then I might just pistol-whip his bitch ass. But if not, hey, I'll holla at that nigga when

I get to hell." From their vantage point, they could see Juice standing at the counter, getting ready to gather his order.

"He's getting ready to come out," Red said with excitement. "Go ahead and jump in the back seat while I creep on this fool."

After getting out of the front seat and sliding into the back, Bobby chambered a round, looked at Red, and nodded. Red trained his eyes on the front door of the famous wing spot. He remained in his truck until Juice had exited Kim's. Since Juice was parked on a side street, he had to turn his back to the other vehicles parked in front of the place. This worked out in Red's favor. As soon as Juice turned his back and headed for his car, Red snuck up behind him and jammed a TEC-9 in his ribs.

"Sup, nigga. 'Member me?"

Juice froze, cursing himself for not following his first mind and sending one of his boys out instead of going himself. He knew that Red would be looking for him, so he chose to stay holed up in his homie's house until it was time for him to leave town. However, the grumbellies changed his itinerary and caused him to leave the safe confines of his hideout spot. His girl, who knew what he had done, begged him to stay in the house and have something delivered. But the fearful look in her eyes caused his pride to flare up.

"Fuck Red," he'd screamed. "If that nigga wanna see me, then he can come and see me!" Although his mouth spoke the tough words, his heart said something totally different. He knew how Red gave it up, and he wanted no part of him. Red was a cold, ruthless, drug-dealing murderer who was working his way up the cocaine food chain and would kill his own mother before he let her beat him out of a dollar. The fact that he was only five feet eight inches tall with a "short man" complex made him that much deadlier.

People thought that he was called Red because of his skin tone, but in reality, his sister had given him the name because of his love of the long-running show *Sanford and Son*. Despite his age, he was a huge fan of the late Redd Foxx.

"Yo, Red, what the fuck?" Juice asked, trying to act surprised that Red was rolling up on him.

"Don't be acting all surprised and shit! Like you don't know why the fuck you getting dealt with," Red spat, jamming the gun deeper into his side. "Walk yo' bitch ass over there to that truck!"

For one second, Juice thought about running, but from what he knew about Red, he wouldn't get far before a hot slug was put in his back.

"Move, muthafucka!"

"Okay, I'm going."

When they got to the truck, Bobby opened the back door and waved Juice in with his pistol. No sooner had Red gotten in the driver's seat and pulled off than Juice started trying to offer an excuse.

"I didn't even know that dough was funny money, man."

Red yanked over to the side of the road. Turning around slowly, Red stared at Juice with cold, dark eyes. "If you didn't know that the money was funny, how did you know that was what I picked yo' bitch ass up for?"

Juice almost pissed on himself when Red started screaming at him, raining spittle on his face. "Where the fuck is my damn money?"

Juice stuck his hand inside his pocket so quick he almost punctured the bottom of it. "I got it for you," he said, handing the bills over. All the while, Bobby kept his gun trained on Juice's forehead.

Red looked at the money and smirked. Even though he'd told Bobby that if Juice paid him, he was only going to pistol-whip him, he knew from the second the words left his lips that it was a lie. Juice had violated him, and for that, the repercussions would be more severe than a simple pistol-whipping.

As Red counted up the money, Bobby hauled off and slapped Juice in the mouth with his gun.

"What the fuck was that for?"

"That was for thinking you could steal from us and get away with it, muthafucka!"

Juice opened his mouth to say something, and Bobby hit him again. Blood flew from Juice's mouth and landed on the edge of the windowsill. "And that was for whatever stupid-ass shit you were about to say outta yo' mouth just then!"

Juice slumped over semi-conscious and laid his head on the window.

"You want me to throw this half-dead muthafucka out into the fucking street?"

"Nah. I got a better idea for this nigga," laughed Red.

Crushed-up beer cans, smashed cigarette butts, and other forms of debris littered the old softball diamond behind the Thurgood Marshall Recreation Center. Once a place where youths went to live out their LeBron James and Mike Trout fantasies, the center now lay dormant because of city-wide budget cuts. Neighborhood residents and local tenants loudly voiced their displeasure over the move, citing a guaranteed increase in drug activity and violence if the center were to close down. Ignoring the people's concerns, the mayor closed it down anyway. Within six months, crime had increased by 55 percent. By the time the mayor realized that he'd made a huge mistake, he was well on his way to being voted out of office.

Sitting in the parking lot, clutching his weapon, Red was in deep thought. It was only seven short years ago that he was on the inside of the now-vacant building, dreaming of highlight-reel dunks and all-net jump shots that he would make when he went to college. But when everyone around him experienced growth spurts and he didn't, Red knew that it was time for a different game plan. Knowing that he wasn't a nine-to-five type of guy, Red hooked up with some of the local knuckleheads from around the way and started slinging rocks on the corners of Hough. A year later, he graduated to selling weight and had been on his grind ever since.

"What the fuck we waiting for, dawg?" Bobby asked, breaking his train of thought.

"Just thinking about something. A'ight, pussy-ass nigga, get the fuck out," he yelled at Juice.

"Come on," Juice started to beg. "You got ya money. Ain't no need to—"

Crack!

Before another word could leave his mouth, Bobby slammed the butt of his gun into it for a third time. Six of Juice's teeth were dislodged from his gums and took up residence in the pit of his stomach.

"Get the fuck out," Bobby ordered.

Juice staggered out of the truck, holding his mouth. A stream of blood ran from his palm to his elbow. After all three of them had exited the truck, Red and Bobby walked Juice over to the softball field.

"Stand right here," Red told him, pointing toward home plate. "You know I been looking for yo' ass for two fucking weeks? That's fourteen punk-ass days!"

Red didn't even give Juice a chance to plead for his life as he pointed the TEC-9 at his chest and squeezed the trigger. As a symbol of how long it took him to find Juice, Red held the trigger for a full fourteen seconds. By the time he released it, Juice's body looked like ground-up hamburger meat dipped in red paint.

"Out at the plate," Bobby yelled, gesturing with his thumb like he was an umpire. Everyone in the hood knew about the fast one that Juice had tried to pull on Red, and this would serve as a reminder to all that if they fucked with Red's money, they would surely meet their Maker.

Chapter 1

Bobby Walker sat in the interrogation room with a smirk on his face.

"What the fuck is so funny, eggplant?"

"You and yo' silly-ass partner. Y'all ain't got shit on me, so y'all might as well let me the fuck out of this bitch."

Detective Brian Stone glared menacingly at Bobby. If looks could kill, Bobby would be lying in a casket. Stone wasn't just pissed because of Bobby's cavalier attitude. That was just part of it. He was also upset because he knew Bobby was right. They didn't have anything to hold him on. At least, not anything serious. The lightweight possession charge against him would only serve to piss the DA off. She'd told Stone not to come back to her with petty shit. She was up for reelection, so she wanted something that was going to stick on these gangbangers and put them away for a while, not just some little slap on the wrist.

Stone's partner, Detective Eugene Dryer, stood behind Bobby, playing the bad cop. Every ten seconds or so, he would blow cigarette smoke at the back of Bobby's head.

"What's up wit' yo' partner blowing smoke at the back of my fucking head? You know how much them bitches be charging to twist my shit up?"

Dryer laughed so hard that he almost choked on the Winston in his mouth. "You mean to tell me that you actually pay for your hair to look like a pile of shit?" he said. "Boy, you're crazy as hell!"

Bobby immediately stood up and turned around. "Who the fuck you calling 'boy,' peckerwood?"

"I'm calling your black ass a boy," Dryer shouted. "A man would help himself in a situation like this."

"No, a man would tell you to suck his dick, so suck my muthafucking dick, pig."

All the color drained out of Dryer's face as his body trembled. Bobby looked at Dryer's balled-up fist and smirked.

"I wish yo' ass would," he said, taunting Dryer.

Stone quickly stepped between Bobby and his partner. "Look, Robert," he said, trying to defuse the quickly escalating situation, "we don't even want you. We want that piece of shit murdering-ass cousin of yours."

Bobby sat back down and threw his Timberland boots on the interrogation table. "Let me get this straight. Y'all mean to tell me that y'all busted me for smoking a joint 'cause y'all want me to sell out my own flesh and blood?"

"We ain't asking you to sell anybody out," said a cooled-down Dryer. "We just want you to tell the truth and help yourself."

"Okay, here's the truth, the whole truth, and nothing but the truth. I don't know what the fuck y'all talkin' about! Now, if y'all ain't gonna arrest me, I'm out of this muthafucka. I feel like getting my dick sucked today. Hey, Dryer, you got a daughter?"

Rage filled Dryer's eyes as he rushed toward Bobby in an attempt to do him some serious bodily harm. Stone grabbed his partner in a frontal bear hug and held him at bay.

"You son of a bitch!" Dryer yelled. "You keep fucking with me and I'll find out if your ass really is bulletproof!"

Bobby laughed all the way out the door.

***

Since Rite Aid was only a couple of blocks down and across the street from the precinct, it took Bobby just five minutes to jog there. By the time he reached the parking lot, his side was hurting him from giggling so hard. He didn't know if Dryer had a daughter, but seeing the look on the cop's face was priceless.

After buying a pack of Newports, Bobby walked out of Rite Aid with the cancer sticks in his pocket and a forty-ounce of Olde English 800 tucked under his arm.

"Fuck," he yelled as he scratched off a losing lottery ticket.

Bulletproof Bobby looked like a darker version of John Henton with braids. He'd earned the nickname two years ago when he was shot by rival drug dealers from the west side of Cleveland. The doctors said that it was a miracle he survived given his slender frame.

Throwing the scratch-off ticket on the ground, Bobby headed over to the Subway restaurant next door. Before he took two steps, a raspy baritone voice called out to him.

"Yo, man, pick that shit up! The fuck you think this is?"

Bobby looked around to see if anybody else was standing there.

"Yeah, I'm talking to you, throwing shit all on the ground and shit!"

Bobby looked at the short, five-foot six-inch security guard with thick, wavy hair and dark brown eyes, and he lost it. He laughed so hard that he almost threw up. "Who the fuck is yo' short ass talking to like that?"

"I'm talking to yo' litterbug ass!" replied the guard.

"You betta take yo' rent-a-cop ass back in the fucking store before you catch a headache! 'Cause the only thing you're gonna get out here is fucked up!"

"What? I'll beat yo' ass like you was one of my bitches."

"Knuckle up then!" Bobby said as he threw his hands up.

"You ain't said shit!" The two combatants circled each other in a feeling-out process when, all of a sudden, the security guard shot a lightning-fast jab to Bobby's left shoulder and followed that up with an even faster right cross.

"Ah, shit!" screamed Bobby, grabbing his shoulder. "What the fuck is wrong with you? I ain't know you were gon' hit my ass for real."

"Oh, my bad," the security guard, whose name was Hank, said. "But yo' ass was laughing a little too hard over there. What's good with you?" he asked as the two embraced.

"Not much. About to hit up this Subway over here. Five-oh had a nigga hemmed up for like three hours and shit. You believe them muthafuckas tryin' to get me to roll over on Red?"

"What? Fuck them pigs," Hank said as he fired up a Newport.

"I see you still got them skills," said Bobby, still rubbing his shoulder.

"Listen," Hank bragged as he started shadowboxing, "I got skills to pay the bills, ya heard?"

Five years ago, Henry "Hank" Blue was Cleveland's boxing sensation. He was so good, in fact, that some experts predicted that he would make the U.S. Olympic team. But that was before a scandalous groupie set him up. Upset at Hank for screwing her but not liking her enough to make her wifey, a neighborhood sack chaser named Sharia cried rape. Hank was so pissed that he broke the girl's jaw and ended up doing two years in the joint for felonious assault.

His defense lawyer tried to argue that it couldn't be felonious assault because Hank didn't have a weapon, but the prosecutor reminded the judge that Hank was a boxer and, by law, his fists were lethal weapons. While in jail, Hank worked out religiously. When he finally did get out of jail, his body resembled that of a bodybuilder. If he had resumed his career, there was little doubt that he would've made a big splash in the boxing world.

But unfortunately for the boxing community, Hank had no interest in climbing back into the ring. The only thing on his mind was making money, which was why he hooked up with Bobby and Red. Even so, he was as dangerous as ever, because no regular street dude could come close to matching his skills.

"You want something back from Subway?" Bobby asked.

"Naw, I'm straight. I betta get my ass back inside before I end up slapping the shit outta my bitch-ass boss."

"A'ight, I'll holla. Peace."

Bobby strolled over to Subway and ordered a cold-cut twelve-inch sandwich. After flashing a knot and flirting with the cashier for a few minutes, he walked out of the restaurant confident that the next time he saw her, he would definitely be able to get her number. He would've stayed and tried to get it then, but because the cops had him hemmed up for three hours, he was already late getting to the house of one of his girls. After that, he was supposed to meet up with Red and help him cook up a quarter key of cocaine. He knew Red was gonna be pissed, but he would just tell him that 5-o held him longer than they really had. The way the Cleveland Police liked to fuck with minorities, he thought, Red would more than likely believe him.

Chapter 2

Tammy sat at her kitchen table, twirling a pen in her right hand. The only thing brighter than her smile was the sunshine peeking through her curtains. After working two jobs nonstop for a year, she'd finally saved up enough money to further her education. Given her financial situation, Tammy was more than eligible to receive government assistance. But her stubbornness and strong urge to be independent caused her to strongly object to any form of aid from Uncle Sam. Everyone, including her little brother, Hakim, and her best friend, Ivory, thought she was a fool to turn down free money, but Tammy didn't see it that way. *How the hell is it free money when you have to pay it back with interest?* she reasoned.

Although her mother was proud of her for sticking to her plan, she did wonder at first if Tammy had the willpower to finish what she started. So when Tammy told her mother that she was going to fill out an application to attend college, her face lit up like fluorescent lights. It was only community college, but Janice Green acted like her daughter had just been accepted into Harvard. Truth be told, Janice couldn't care less if it was a community college, trade school, or just learning how to do hair. She wanted her daughter to have some form of higher education. At the very least, with a higher education, she could support herself and not have to depend on a man to take care of her. Janice had made that dreadful mistake when she was younger, and because of it, she'd spent the last seven years of her life struggling in a workforce she wasn't prepared for. In her opinion, the only good thing that came out of her ex-husband, Mark, running away with another woman was that it taught her daughter to never trust a man.

At least, Janice thought it was a good thing. The last thing she wanted was for Tammy to get sidetracked because of some no-good, nappy-headed thug with his pants hanging off his ass. The way Tammy looked, she had reason to worry. Tammy was 19 years old, but if you paid attention to just her body and not her face, you'd swear that she was 23. She stood an even five feet seven inches tall. She had a small waist and thick Beyoncé-type hips. Her blemish-free skin was the color of honey. Her light brown eyes often fooled people into thinking she wore contacts, but that was nowhere near the case. She had a Rihanna-style haircut that she kept fresh to death. There was a rumor going on around the hood that Tammy was still a virgin, but that wasn't quite true. Although she wasn't the promiscuous type, Tammy had been dug out a time or two. But if the locals wanted to think her goodies were uncharted territory, she definitely wasn't going to discourage them from letting the thought dwell in their minds.

Still, the neighborhood dogs came at her like a pack of wolves, only to be quickly shot down. Tammy was on a mission. She was determined to succeed. She had seen far too many people fall victim to the streets, either by getting themselves killed or getting married to the streets with no possibility of divorce.

After Tammy finished filling out her application, she put it in an envelope, put a stamp on it, and put it into the mailbox. She returned to the kitchen just in time to see Hakim rummaging through the refrigerator.

"Fuck! There ain't shit in here to eat," he fussed. "Yo, sis, let me borrow five dollars so I can go to Subway and get me a five-dollar footlong."

Tammy vigorously shook her head from side to side. "Hell nah," she spat. "Yo' ass don't like to pay back. You betta hook up with some of the damn Frosted Flakes in the cabinet."

"What?" he said with a screwed-up face. "Don't nobody want no fucking cereal."

"Yo' ass gonna just be hungry then," she said, matching his tone. "'Cause I can't help you."

Just as Hakim was about to plead his case, Tammy's cell phone rang. After listening for a few seconds, Tammy said, "I'll be there in a few." After slapping her cell phone shut, Tammy slipped into her sandals. "Tell Mama that I went over to Ivory's house and I'll be back later on."

"Fuck that," he said, still angry that she wouldn't lend him $5. "I ain't telling Mama shit! You want her to know where you at, tell her ya damn self!"

"Whateva," Tammy said as she rolled her eyes and walked out the door.

For Tammy, one of the benefits of having Ivory as a friend was that Ivory had her own apartment. It was only a one-room studio apartment, but it served its purpose well for when Tammy just wanted to get away from her mother and little brother and just chill.

After Ivory buzzed her in, Tammy got on the elevator and rode it to the third floor. During the ride up, a tall, lanky, young dude with numerous tattoos stamped on both forearms tried to engage Tammy in conversation. His hair was braided into tight cornrows. He had light brown eyes and a thin mustache connected to a goatee. He might as well have been talking to himself. Tammy stared straight ahead as if she were in the elevator alone. Feeling slighted, the young man mumbled, "Fuck you," under his breath as Tammy stepped off the box and continued on her way.

As she approached Ivory's door, Tammy just smiled and shook her head. Loud Jay-Z lyrics blasted from Ivory's apartment, making it impossible for anyone trying to sleep to catch some z's. A frown fell across her face as she turned the doorknob and walked right in. Time and time again, she had warned Ivory about leaving her door unlocked. As soon as she stepped through the door, the pungent smell of weed hit her in the face like a Floyd Mayweather jab. The impact gave her an instant contact high.

"Damn, bitch, you're getting blazed up in here," she coughed. "And why the hell do you keep leaving your door unlocked? Someone's going to come up in here and clip your ass one day."

"I left it open because I knew your ass was about to walk through the door," Ivory shot back. "Plus," she said as she reached between her brown suede couch cushions and pulled out a black .38 snub-nosed revolver that looked like it had seen better days, "I wish a muthafucka would run up in here tryin'a pull a damn heist. I'll put some lead in their asses."

"Please," Tammy laughed. "That raggedy-ass gun probably won't even shoot."

"Word? It won't? Let's find out, tramp." Ivory wrapped both of her hands around the instrument of death and pointed it in Tammy's direction.

Tammy froze. "Don't play with me like that," she said fearfully. "What if that thing goes off?"

"Then yo' ass just a dead bitch, ain't you? Now stop dissing my shit," Ivory said, sticking her gun back between the cushions.

"Whatever," Tammy said. She didn't like Ivory waving a gun in her face and made a mental note to tell her about it later. But for right now, she just wanted to kick back and chill. "What do you have to drink in here?"

"There's some Absolut in the cabinet, but I ain't got no cranberry juice. You gonna have to run to the store if you wanna get your drink on."

"What do you mean, *I'm* gonna have to go to the store? Yo' ass is gonna be drinking too. You betta bring yo' ass on."

Rolling her eyes, Ivory got up, grabbed her knockoff Gucci purse, and headed toward the door.

Chapter 3

The second the traffic light turned red, Tammy and Ivory sprinted across the intersection at 105th and St. Clair. This particular light was notorious for malfunctioning and had caused numerous accidents in the last few months. It wasn't until a 3-month-old baby was killed in a head-on collision between a Honda Accord and a beer truck that the city finally decided to fix it. It was funny how a multimillion-dollar lawsuit could cause that effect. Still, people in the area were cautious.

"Girl, you betta hurry yo' ass up," yelled Ivory. "You know how this light be tripping and shit."

"I thought they fixed this damn light."

"Are you willing to take a chance on that shit? Fuck around and yo' ass will be roadkill."

"Slow your long-legged ass down."

"Keep up," Ivory said, laughing.

A full three inches taller than Tammy, Ivory had pretty, light brown skin and beautiful brown chestnut eyes. Her hair was silky black and pulled back in a ponytail. She was the spitting image of Tyra Banks in the movie *Higher Learning*.

Tammy noticed that Ivory kept looking across the street at the Rite Aid pharmacy. "What the hell do you keep looking over there for?"

"You know I'm s'posed to be at work today. I'm trying to make sure don't nobody see my ass."

"Work? I thought you told me on the phone that you were off today."

"No, I told yo' non-listening ass that I called off today."

The two young women quickly made their way back to the cooler.

"Looks like they're all out of cranberry juice," Tammy said with a frown.

"What? Where the fuck they do that shit at?" Ivory fussed. "Run the fuck outta cranberry juice at a damn grocery store."

"Shit happens," Tammy said, shrugging her shoulders. "Fuck it then. I'll just get this orange-mango juice."

Ivory twisted up her face. " I bet that shit nasty as fuck."

"Then your ass doesn't have to drink it," Tammy shot back.

Before Ivory could utter a comeback, she was startled by a light tap on her shoulder. She turned around and was immediately disgusted by what she saw. "Fred, take yo' ashy-ass hands off me," she screamed.

"Damn, it's like that?" her coworker asked while holding his hands up in surrender mode.

"Nigga, it's always been like that."

Fred Howard and Tammy had been working together at Rite Aid for the past six months. From the first day he worked with her, Fred had made it his life's mission to get between her legs. The fact that she was repulsed by his mere presence did nothing to dissuade him. He tried everything, including offering to pay her rent, to get a crack at her goodies, but nothing seemed to work. Now, in his mind, at least, he had her right where he wanted her.

"Yeah, whateva," he said. "I thought yo' ass called in a sick day. You don't look sick to me."

"You know what? You need to mind your own fucking business, midnight."

Tammy started laughing so hard she almost busted a gut. There was no secret as to why Ivory called him midnight. Fred was short, fat, and extremely dark. His skin looked like wet, shiny coal. Embarrassed and angry, Fred stormed off without saying another word.

"You betta stop talking to that nigga like that," Tammy said, still laughing.

"Fuck that nigga. I wish he would try to start some bullshit. I'll have Darnell stomp his fat ass."

"Darnell? I thought y'all broke up last week."

Ivory looked at her like she had lost her mind. "Come on, you know how that shit goes. We break up to make up."

"I guess y'all do," Tammy responded.

When they got to the checkout counter, there was an old lady at the front of the line, counting out dimes. Ivory took one look at the total and went berserk.

"Ah, hell naw! I know damn well y'all ain't gonna let twenty muthafuckas stand in this one line while she counting out all that damn change! Why don't y'all open up another damn line or something?"

"Stop all that damn hollering," an embarrassed Tammy whispered.

"This shit is ridiculous," Ivory screamed, ignoring her friend's pleas to quiet down.

Tammy thought about walking off and leaving Ivory in the store by herself. She hated when her ghetto-acting friend made a spectacle of herself in public. By the time they got ready to pay for the juice, another line was opening up. Ivory looked at the cashier who had opened up the line, and she popped her lips.

"You can pop yo' lips all you want," the cashier, who was an older lady, tried to whisper, but she said it a little too loudly.

As soon as she heard the words, Tammy tried to hurry up and pay for the juice. She knew from past experience that Ivory was not going to let that slide.

"What the fuck did yo' old ass just say? Not only will I pop my lips, I'll pop yo' ass!"

Tammy then grabbed Ivory by her arm and pulled her taller friend out of the store. "Do you have to act a fool everywhere we go?"

"You know that was some bullshit! Them muthafuckas done that shit on purpose!"

"You know what? Let's just get the hell out of here before we get arrested for disturbing the peace," Tammy said.

As both young ladies started walking across the street, Tammy looked and saw Fred and another gentleman standing in the Rite Aid doorway. Fred seemed to be pointing in their direction. She held her breath for a minute but exhaled when she realized that Ivory hadn't noticed.

Nancy sat in her latest chocolate boy toy's passenger's seat, bobbing her head to Lil Wayne. She had just gotten off from work, and due to working a twelve-hour shift, her bouncy blond curls were now string-straight. Nancy wasn't your typical white girl. From her light blue eyes to her cantaloupe-sized tits right down to her beach ball–sized ass, Nancy was a knockout.

"What's up? You got any more blow?" she asked, sniffing air into her nose.

"More blow? You high as the clouds now!"

"I'm not high, Mike."

Mike looked at her like she was three shades of crazy. From the second she hopped into his car, Nancy had been trying to snort up every drop of cocaine he had. Mike had about a quarter of an ounce of cocaine left, and there was no way in hell he was going to let Nancy snort up all of his product. Besides, it was almost time for Nancy to work off her debt, and the last thing he wanted was for her to get too high and not be able to service him.

"Nah, I ain't got no more," he lied.

"That's really too bad," she said as she reached into his lap and squeezed his dick. "Because I was gonna let you do all kinds of nasty things to me tonight."

Mike damn near crashed his whip as he thought about all the kinky things that Nancy might be willing to do just to get another taste of powder. A wicked thought popped into his mind as he made a left from 79th onto Wade Park. "You know, I might be able to cop some from a friend of mine. How much money you got on you?"

"About four funky-ass dollars."

"Nah," he said, shaking his head from side to side. "That ain't gon' get it." When Nancy didn't say anything, he decided to push further. "That's a shame, too, 'cause he be having that primo shit."

Nancy's mouth started to water as she thought about the good coke she would be missing out on if she didn't find a way to make this happen. "You can't get him to give it to you on credit?" she asked.

"Hell nah! I owe that muthafucka money now!"

Nancy took a deep breath and dropped her head. "Maybe we can work something out," she whispered in a voice that was barely audible.

A sly smile crept across Mike's face. Nancy wanting to get even higher than she already was gave Mike the green light to try to get her to let him and his homeboy run a train on her.

As Nancy sat back and closed her eyes, she couldn't help but reflect on how she'd let her life slip this far. Nancy D, as she liked to refer to herself, grew up on Lakeshore Boulevard in a suburban area of Cleveland, Ohio. She was an only child and was only 8 years old when her mother was killed at the age of 36 by a drunk driver. Her father became all she had. It took Nancy almost a year to climb out of the deep depression she'd sunk into.

It didn't make it any better that her father was a workaholic who rarely had any time for her. People close to Nancy tried to tell her that working fourteen hours a day was just her father's way of coping with her mother's death, but in Nancy's eyes, he should have been there for her. He was all she had. By the time she was 15, Nancy was rebelling against her father in the worst way. Staying out past her curfew was the norm. Smoking weed was a way of life for her, and the friends she had started hanging out with were nothing short of hoodlums. Although she had first started having sex when she was only 13, it wasn't until she was 17 that she received her first real orgasm.

True to her rebellious nature, Nancy had snuck out of the house and hooked up with some friends from her neighborhood. They had gone to a house party that eventually turned into a coed slumber party. With them was a black dude she had never met before. He was the cousin of one of her friends. She thought he was cute, but he ignored her pretty much the whole night. Determined to make him notice her, Nancy made it her business to dance with him every chance she got. She made sure to grind her ample ass on his crotch, and she even "mistakenly" touched his dick a few times. Knowing what time it was, the dude proceeded to sneak her upstairs. After licking her clit until she exploded three or four times, he climbed on top of her and pounded her guts until she passed out from the pleasure. From that day forth, a white man couldn't do shit for her. To her, if the dick wasn't black, then they could have it back.

"Okay, we're here," Mike said, breaking her out of her once-upon-a-time daydream.

Nancy got out of the car and slowly walked her way to Mike's friend's apartment. Knowing what the deal was, as soon as she got inside the door, she was taking her clothes off.

Chapter 4

By the time Tammy left Ivory's house, it was almost one o'clock in the morning. The two longtime friends laughed, argued, made up, and laughed some more as they talked over old times with each other. Ivory developed a slight attitude when Tammy told her that she was getting ready to leave.

"Leave? You always wanna hurry up and go when we're having a good time," Ivory said as she folded her arms and pouted.

"Please! I have to be at work at ten o'clock in the morning! I'm not trying to get fucked up all night with you and miss my damn money!"

"Oh, okay," Ivory said, shrugging her shoulders.

After smoking two blunts and downing half a bottle of Hennessy with Tammy, Ivory was extremely horny. She laughed when she thought back to how Tammy had played her once again.

"That bitch only drank one glass of this shit," she said as she looked at the bottle and laughed. Tammy had always been a light drinker. Every time they got together, it would take her three times the amount of time to drink one glass of liquor as it took Ivory to drink three. Ivory never noticed until after Tammy was long gone.

Ivory walked over to the kitchen table and picked up her cell phone. Heat radiated through her body as she thought about her boyfriend, Darnell, and how she wanted to slobber him down. Ivory and Darnell had been together for the past two years. Their on-again, off-again relationship had its share of ups and downs, but through it all, she had his back, and he had hers.

Darnell was a high school basketball star who dropped out when he injured his knee and it was obvious that no one was going to offer him a scholarship. His grades were already subpar, and the fact that he'd torn the anterior cruciate ligament in his knee all but snuffed out the free ride he was counting on. Darnell knew that he wasn't going to get to college on his grades alone, and with a baby already on the way, he decided that he needed to make some money, and fast.

When the job he had wasn't paying enough for him to take care of his seed, Darnell turned to selling drugs as a way to make ends meet. He wasn't a kingpin by any means, but he did make enough bread to live comfortably and break off to his baby mama to stay out of the courthouse. He only kept his job to make it look good.

Feeling especially naughty tonight, Ivory hung up the phone before Darnell could answer. Then she went to her closet and took out the black trench coat that Darnell had bought her for her birthday. With a devilish grin on her face, Ivory stripped down to her birthday suit, ran to the bathroom, and jumped in the shower. After getting herself cleaned up, Ivory rubbed coconut-scented lotion all over her body, splashed some perfume on, and wrapped the trench coat around her naked body. Ivory grabbed the keys to her 2005 Ford Taurus and headed out the door on a mission to get her freak on.

When Ivory pulled up in Darnell's driveway, she was surprised to find it empty. She had talked to him earlier in the day before she'd hooked up with Tammy. He assured her that he was tired from making moves all day and he was just looking to relax. That was one of the reasons she'd chosen not to bother him for the day.

Shrugging her shoulders, Ivory backed out of his driveway, drove down the street until she found an empty spot and parked. She reached into her glove compartment and took out the key to Darnell's apartment. She'd secretly had it made a year ago and would go over and snoop around from time to time when she knew that Darnell would be out of town. He may have been good to her, but he was still a man, and Ivory didn't trust any men.

Ivory let herself in and glanced around the house. Except for a few things moved around, everything looked like it did the last time she was over at Darnell's house. Even though she had consumed a large amount of liquor throughout the day, Ivory still felt the urge to sip more alcohol. She didn't want to drink too much and end up passing out before she got a chance to get her some dick, so she made sure to fix herself a light drink.

After mixing the Hennessy and Coke, Ivory took off her trench coat, sat down on Darnell's couch, and crossed her legs. She sat there for a full ten minutes, sipping her drink before deciding that she could set the mood better in the bedroom. The three-inch heels that she had on click-clacked across the floor, making a loud echoing sound as she entered Darnell's sleeping quarters. Once inside, she sniffed twice, just to see if there was a hint of sex in the air.

I'm being silly, she thought, shaking her head. *Hell, if I did smell sex, it's probably the lingering scent from Darnell blowing my back out a couple of days ago.*

As she sashayed her way over to the bed, the liquor kicked in even more. Her pussy was on fire as she lay back onto the bed and fingered herself. She was so hot that it didn't take long for her to reach her first orgasm. But masturbating only gave her a small sense of satisfaction. Ivory craved to feel Darnell inside of her. She thought about calling him again but resisted the urge. She wanted this to be a total surprise.

As the effects of drinking half the night finally caught up with her, Ivory hurried to the bathroom and sat down on the toilet just in time. Relief surged through her body as piss shot out of her bladder. After wiping herself, Ivory was just about to flush the toilet when she heard the front door slam.

Knowing that she would not be able to get back to the bedroom in time to lie back down on the bed, Ivory jumped in the shower and pulled the curtain closed. She knew from past experience that Darnell almost always went to take a leak as soon as he came in the house, so the only way for her to keep the surprise alive was to hide.

Right on cue, Darnell walked in, unzipped his pants, and emptied his bladder. Feeling the urge to sneeze, Ivory started to panic. Before she could get her fingers to her nose . . .

"Achoo!"

Darnell's head snapped around so fast he almost caught whiplash. With his eyes trained on the shower curtain, Darnell reached behind his back and took out his 9 mm pistol. With one hand, he aimed. With the other one, he pulled back the shower curtain. Surprise and shock registered on his face as Ivory stood there, looking like a sex goddess.

"Surprise, baby," she said, seductively licking her lips. "I see somebody's glad to see me." Ivory's eyes were now glued to Darnell's dick. Things had happened so fast that Darnell had forgotten to put his penis back inside his pants. Nervously, Darnell started to put his tool back into his pants.

"Oh, no you don't," Ivory said. With the grace of a ballerina, Ivory leaped out of the shower and got down on her knees. Before Darnell could protest, Ivory grabbed his meat and stuffed it into her mouth.

"Oh, shit," Darnell moaned in pleasure. It felt so good to him that he forgot all about the company waiting for him in his bedroom.

"Darnell, baby, hurry up," a voice called from the bedroom.

Ivory stopped in mid-suck. "Who the fuck is that?" she yelled.

"Huh? Who?"

"Don't play with me! Who the fuck is that calling you?" Ivory asked as she got up from her knees. When Darnell didn't answer, Ivory bolted through the bathroom door and sped toward the bedroom.

"Ivory, wait! Hold up! You said that we were through after our last fight," Darnell yelled to her as he ran after her.

"I always say that shit," she yelled back to him. When Ivory reached the bedroom, she found a light-skinned girl with short, spiked blond hair sitting Indian-style on Darnell's bed.

"Bitch, what the fuck you doing in my man's bedroom?"

"Excuse me? Who the fuck you think you talking to?"

"I'm talking to yo' ass! What the fuck you doing in my man's bedroom?"

"Yo' man? Please! He wasn't yo' man when he was finger fucking me at the movies tonight!"

A slick smile crossed Darnell's lips as Ivory's mouth hung open. Before Darnell could stop her, Ivory stormed across the room and grabbed the smaller woman by the throat. The woman responded by scratching Ivory on the face. This only served to piss Ivory off even more. While squeezing her neck with her left hand, Ivory drew back and punched her in the face with her right. The girl's arms went limp as the force of Ivory's blow dazed her. Ivory got off two more punches before Darnell ran over and pulled her off the girl.

"Get off me! Get the fuck off of me! I'm gonna beat the brakes off that bitch!"

"Nah, ma, what you gonna do is take yo' ass home!"

"What? You kicking me out over some bum-ass bitch you just met?"

"Fuck you," the girl screamed from across the room. The way she flinched when Ivory lunged at her was a clear indication that she didn't want any more of Ivory.

Darnell grabbed Ivory by the waist, picked her up, and carried her into the hallway. "You need to calm the fuck down!"

"Fuck that! How could you do this shit to me?"

"What the fuck are you talking about? As I recall, the last words you said to me were, 'Nigga, we through,'" he said, imitating her. "Was I supposed to just brush that shit off like it didn't fucking happen?"

"I'm just saying," she said with tears running down her face, "we break up all the time."

"Yeah, we do! And that's the fucking problem! This 'break up to make up' shit is getting old! That's high school shit, and my prom has long been over with! I ain't got time for these little punk-ass games! I'm out here every day throwing rocks at the penitentiary, trying to get it in not only for myself, but for yo' ass too! So unless you stop actin' so fucking juvenile, I suggest you find you a new nigga, ya feel me?"

Just then, the girl who was in the bedroom stormed past them. "You know what? I ain't got time for this love triangle bullshit! Call me when you get rid of this ho!" She made it out the door just in time as Ivory's shoe crashed up against the door.

Darnell just smiled slightly and shook his head. All of a sudden, his smile faded. "Wait a minute. How the fuck did you get in here? I know damn well I locked that damn door," he said, looking at Ivory sideways.

"I climbed in through the window," she said, spitting out the rehearsed lie with no problem. "As you can see, I was trying to surprise you."

Ivory twirled around to give Darnell a good look at her body. Amid the confusion, Darnell had stopped noticing that Ivory was naked. Darnell then scooped her up and carried her into the bedroom, where he made love to her well into the next day.

The constant beeping of Tammy's alarm clock sounded like fireworks going off in her head. Finally, after not being able to take it anymore, she reached over and hit the snooze button. She had just drifted back off to sleep when it started beeping again. This time she turned it completely off. Fifteen minutes later, it went off again.

"What the fuck? I know I turned that damn thing off."

"You did. I turned it back on and reset it . . . and watch your mouth in my house, young lady," Tammy's mother chided her.

"Oh, I'm sorry, Ma. I didn't even know that you were in the room."

"Mm-hmm. Don't you have to be at work at ten o'clock?"

"Yeah. I'm going to get up in a minute," she said as she lay back down and covered her head with the pillow.

"You betta get yo' behind up, come downstairs, and eat this food I cooked."

Even though she didn't feel like it, Tammy knew better than to question her mother when she said something. Janice Green was old school when it came to child-rearing. She wouldn't hesitate to slap Tammy or Hakim in the mouth if they ever made the mistake of disrespecting her.

Tammy rolled out of her bed and staggered down the hall toward the bathroom. Hakim bumped her as he walked past her on his way to the kitchen.

"Watch it, asshole."

Hakim gave her the finger and kept walking. He was obviously still upset that she wouldn't lend him $5.

After getting washed up, Tammy headed downstairs and sat at the opposite end of the table from her brother.

"Hakim, do you have to work today?" his mother asked as she set the table.

"Yeah, unfortunately."

"What do you mean, unfortunately? In these hard times, you're lucky to even have a job."

"This job ain't paying me nothing. I can't even buy a pair of tennis shoes with the little bit of money they paying me there."

Janice waved her hand at her son's complaints and walked back to the stove. She always made sure that her children ate before she did.

"Yo, sis, you should've seen the shoes Mike had on when he came into the store two weeks ago. Then he bought two more pair that was just as nice."

"I guess you've forgotten what Mike does to get the money to buy those nice shoes," Janice reminded her son.

"Maybe I should be doing what that nigga doing then. That way, I can keep some money in my pocket."

Crack!

The last word had barely made it out of his mouth when his bell was rung from a spatula upside the head. The one thing in this world Janice hated was drug dealers. In her mind, if a drug dealer could spend all that time hanging out on the corner selling drugs, he could just as easily be holding down a job. "Have you lost your damn mind talking about selling drugs in my house?"

Hakim jumped up with his fists clenched at his sides. Janice responded by grabbing a butcher knife off the counter. Afraid that she was about to lose her only sibling, Tammy jumped between Hakim and her mother.

"I wish yo' ass would hit me! I'll bury your ass right next to your father!"

As soon as the words left her mouth, Janice instantly regretted it. Although she was still bitter about her husband leaving her, she knew that it was wrong to talk about her kids' father that way. Hakim slammed his fist down on the table and stormed out the door.

"Hakim, wait," Tammy said, running after him. Catching him just before he reached the curb, Tammy put her hand on his shoulder. "She didn't mean it."

"Get the hell off of me," he screamed.

Tammy just stood there feeling helpless as her brother headed off down the street. She prayed to God that he was going to work.

Tammy sat on the bus quietly, thinking to herself. She was in her own world as thoughts of her younger brother dominated her mind. The last thing she wanted was for him to get tangled up in the web of the streets. They were cold, ruthless, and above all, heartless. The streets didn't care that her only sibling was only 17 years old. They didn't care that he had a bright future ahead of him. The streets had no pity for the innocent. They had even less for the African American male. And then, when the street's cousin, crack, entered the neighborhood, it was a wrap.

Death became the street's not-so-silent partner as young black after young black suffered violent deaths. Tammy struggled to fight back the tears that threatened to fall from her eyes. It split her heart in half to see the direction her brother was headed in. She'd known all along that he was unhappy at the amount of money he made at Foot Locker. Since his grades were in decent shape, she had hoped that she could talk him into following in her footsteps and attending college. But seeing the anger in his eyes and hearing it in his voice about being broke led her to the conclusion that he was leaning more toward learning lessons in crack than learning lessons in the classroom.

Although Tammy knew her brother was wrong for coming sideways at his mother, she wished like hell that her mother hadn't hit him. Hakim was going to hold that against her, and Tammy was going to have to find some way to smooth things over with her brother and mother.

Tammy stepped off the bus at Richmond and Monticello and made her way into Richmond Town Square Mall. After a brief stop at the food court to grab a few napkins, Tammy headed to her job at the JCPenney department store.

She took the napkins and dabbed the corners of her eyes. The last thing she wanted was for her nosy coworkers to start asking a bunch of questions. After clocking in, Tammy walked to her assigned work area and took a deep breath. She knew that she had to put her game face on in order to do her job competently.

Besides, she still wanted to do her job to the best of her ability. She owed them that much. She'd learned through the grapevine that they had been planning on laying her off, but Tammy begged them to let her stay on the job, at least part-time. She explained to the manager that, since she was going to be going to school, she needed this job to keep a few dollars in her pocket. By the time she got to the part about how she had saved for a year to be able to go to school, he told her that she could stay there as long as she wanted. It didn't hurt that he was also a product of the inner city, so he sympathized with young black kids trying to make something of themselves. Tammy had quit her other job two weeks ago, so she desperately needed to keep this one.

Tammy looked around at all the clothes that she was responsible for sorting. Only after she started working did she realize how tired she really was. Staying out until one in the morning was taking its toll on her. *Wait a minute.* She paused as a sudden thought occurred to her. *Where the hell is Nancy? She's supposed to be helping me sort through this shit.*

Tammy grabbed the phone off the wall. She had every intention of dialing the supervisor's extension and inquiring about Nancy's whereabouts. But before she could dial the number, Nancy walked in looking like death warmed over. Her normally bouncy curls were scattered all over her head. Her eyes were red and slightly sunken into the back of her head. Her skin, which was usually smooth and vibrant, was ashy. Tammy started to go off on her until she looked at Nancy a little more closely.

"What the hell happened to you?"

"Don't even ask," Nancy said, holding up her hand. "I had a long-ass night."

"Well, I'm glad your ass finally decided to show the fuck up for work. Separating all this shit is a fucking headache."

"Shit, I barely made it in here. I started to call the hell off," Nancy responded. "I'd rather be anywhere but here today."

Tammy looked at her watch and noticed that Nancy was over an hour late. The more she thought about it, it dawned on her that Nancy had started being late more and more often. She had also been calling off quite a bit, so if she felt as bad as she said she did, Tammy didn't know why she just didn't call off today as well.

Before she got a chance to question Nancy about it, the boss peeked in and summoned Nancy into his office. *Uh-oh,* Tammy thought. *She's about to get her ass chewed out.* Tammy felt bad for her friend. Knowing Nancy the way she did, she knew there was something she wasn't telling her.

Nancy came back out, laughing like she had just heard the funniest joke in the world. Tammy was beyond confused.

"Uhhh . . . what's up, girl?" she asked.

"Mr. James is a trip. He just asked me to coordinate the company picnic."

Tammy was so flabbergasted she couldn't even offer a response.

Chapter 5

Hakim stormed into the employee locker room at Foot Locker and plopped down on the bench. He was furious at his mother for hitting him. Although he was out of bounds for even talking about selling drugs in her presence, he still felt that he was much too old to be physically disciplined by her. For the better part of ten minutes, he sat there trying to calm down before going out on the floor to start his shift.

He'd worked as a salesman at Foot Locker for almost a year. Even though he'd gotten a couple of raises since then, the money he was making was still chump change. Buying one pair of tennis shoes would wipe out most of his check, even with his employee discount.

"Hey, youngblood, you working today?" his boss, Jay, asked him.

Hakim glanced at the clock on the wall and noticed that his shift started five minutes ago. "Shit," he said as he opened his locker and took out his Foot Locker shirt. Frowning as he put it on, Hakim shook his head. He never understood why they were forced to wear the zebra-styled shirts.

Seeing the agitated look on Hakim's face, Jay walked over to him. "You okay?" he asked.

"Yeah, I'm straight. I'm just dealing with some bullshit going on at home, that's all."

"Well, don't let it get you down. We all go through shit at one time or another. Let's go get this money," he said, leading Hakim out onto the floor.

The second Hakim walked through the door, his eyes lit up. The store was packed. *Damn, it ain't been packed in here like this the whole ten months I been working here.* Doing a few quick calculations in his head, Hakim figured that he could make a killing on commission if he hustled hard enough. His smile grew even wider when he looked up and saw who was walking into the Foot Locker store. Before anyone else could beat him to the punch, Hakim sprinted across the floor and up to Red to offer his services.

"Yo, wassup, Mike?"

Red shot him a death glare. "What you call me, li'l nigga?"

"Oh, my bad, Red."

Hakim, like everyone else, knew that Red did not like to be called by his government name in public. He was paranoid that way. Hakim had slipped and called him Mike only because it was fresh in his mind after referring to him as Mike when he was at home earlier.

"That's more like it," he said, giving Hakim a pound. Red knew of Hakim through Hakim's girlfriend's sister. The two met one day when Red showed up to pick her up and saw Hakim sitting there on the couch, making googly eyes at her sister. Although there wasn't much conversation, Red took a liking to the young lad and told him that if he ever needed anything, just holla at him. This, of course, was mostly just lip service. Red didn't really expect Hakim to call him on it, and so far, he hadn't. "You still banging Chanel's li'l sister?"

"Nah, we broke up three weeks ago," Hakim said, dropping his head. The wound was obviously still fresh in his heart.

Picking up on Hakim's sorrow, Red placed a hand on his shoulder. "Hold ya head up, my dude."

When Hakim lifted his head, he stared directly into the coldest set of eyes he'd ever seen in his life.

"Lesson number one: don't ever let a bitch break you to tears. Bitches come a dime a dozen. If one starts tripping, slide on to the next one. If the situation starts getting too emotional, back up off that bitch. Feel me?"

Hakim nodded his head absently.

"Good. Now, enough with the small talk. What the fuck y'all got new up in here?"

Hakim had been waiting for this. After showing Red the latest kicks, Hakim sat back and waited for him to dig into his pockets.

"Ya know what? Give me that whole row. Size eleven."

Hakim's smile widened as he looked at the row Red was talking about. It had about ten pairs of shoes on it, and not one pair cost less than $80. As fast as he could, Hakim ran to the back and gathered Red's shoes. By the time he'd finished carrying all the shoeboxes to the counter, he felt like he had been working out at the gym for about three hours. His eyes got as big as beach balls when Red reached into his pocket and pulled out a wad of hundreds.

"Damn, I need to be clocking dough like that," he shrieked.

After paying for his shoes, Red gathered up the two large bags that contained his shoes and headed toward the exit. He suddenly stopped and turned around. Then he opened his mouth as if he were going to say something to Hakim. But just as quickly, Red shook his head, signaling that he had changed his mind, and left.

Ivory rolled over onto her back and stretched her arms over her head. It took a few seconds for her to realize that Darnell wasn't lying next to her. She didn't have to wonder where he was for long as the strong scent of pork sausage attacked her sense of smell. Her eyes popped wide open as her mouth watered. The growling sound of her stomach reminded her that she hadn't eaten anything since before she was with Tammy the previous day. After going to the bathroom to relieve her bladder, Ivory made her way down the stairs and into the kitchen.

For a minute, Ivory just stood in the doorway and smiled. Her sex box got hot and moist as she stared at Darnell's shirtless body. His deep, dark chocolate skin and well-toned physique had her wanting to devour every inch of him.

As if he had a sixth sense, Darnell spoke without even turning around. "I see you finally decided to get up," he said, working a spatula with chef-like magic.

Ivory was caught completely off guard by his innate senses. "Yep. I see you got it smelling good up in here," she complimented him. "What are you cooking?"

"Sausage omelets for me, cereal for you," he said, pointing toward the Cap'n Crunch cereal box on top of the refrigerator.

"What? Yeah, right, boy. You betta quit playing," she said, laughing. Ivory took a seat at the table and waited to be served. She couldn't wait to dig in. She knew from personal experience that Darnell's cooking skills were on point.

Darnell grabbed two plates out of the cabinet, scooped the breakfast delights out of the skillet, and placed them on the plates. When he turned around to walk toward the table, Ivory could see his hard-on trying to poke through his boxers. "I see somebody wants some more of the good-good this morning."

"Shit, baby, I'm always down for the good-good."

"This mean we back together again?" Ivory asked. With all the drama that unfolded the night before, they didn't get a chance to finish their conversation.

Darnell set Ivory's plate down in front of her, took his seat across from her, and sighed. "Look, if we gonna be together, then let's be together. Like I said last night, I ain't got time for the dumb shit."

"I'm sorry. I don't wanna break up. I just be mad when I be saying that shit."

"Well, the next time you say it, yo' ass betta mean it," he said, giving her a stern look. Darnell wasn't about playing games. He was about his paper. He didn't mess with the powder but sold weed by the pound.

Ivory felt as if she were being scolded by her mother. She knew right then that she would have to learn to control her temper. Darnell had just made it clear that the next time she acted like she wanted to break up, he would be sure to make it permanent.

After another steamy lovemaking session, Ivory asked Darnell to run her up to her job so she could pick up her check and see what schedule she was working the next week.

"Didn't you drive over here?"

"Yeah. So?"

"So what's wrong with you driving yo'self up there?"

"Oh, come on, baby, please," she whined.

"I got some shit that I need to do in a few, so you just gonna have to drive yo'self."

Ivory responded by grabbing his forefinger and putting it in her mouth. She closed her eyes and seductively sucked on it, rolling her tongue over it. "If you take me, I'll give you a special treat when we get back."

Darnell didn't know if he had any more nut in him. Ivory had damn near drained him dry. Just in case he did, he accepted her offer, thinking that he'd be a fool to turn down such a proposition.

After getting showered and dressed, they hopped into Darnell's gold tricked-out Oldsmobile Cutlass. They both nodded to Tupac's old jam, "Toss It Up." Getting as comfortable as she could, Ivory leaned the leather bucket seat back and put her feet up on the dashboard.

"Get ya fucking feet off my dashboard! You know betta than that bullshit!"

Poking out her lips and folding her arms, Ivory pretended that she was mad. Darnell saw right through it and egged the situation on by reaching over and placing his hand between Ivory's legs.

"Don't touch my coochie," she said, slapping Darnell's hand away.

Darnell cracked up laughing as he turned into the Rite Aid parking lot. Ignoring the handicapped parking sign, Darnell yanked into the spot reserved for people in worse health. "Yo, hurry up, ma. Like I said, I got moves to make today."

Ivory hopped her long legs out of the whip and high-stepped into her place of employment. The minute she walked in, she noticed her coworkers looking at her strangely.

The fuck wrong wit' these bitches?

"Sup, Ivory," the girl at the front register greeted her.

Ivory noticed the weird look on the girl's face but ignored it. "Sup, Cookie. Is that the schedule you looking at?"

"Uh . . . yeah."

"Pass it here then. Let me see how many hours they got me down for next week."

Hesitantly, Cookie passed it to her. Ivory looked at the schedule, then at Cookie, then back at the schedule. A woman who was ready to pay for her items cleared her throat in an attempt to get Cookie's attention. Ivory mean-mugged the woman for several seconds before looking back at Cookie.

"How come my name ain't on the fucking schedule? Never mind! I'll find the fuck out myself," Ivory screamed when Cookie didn't answer her fast enough.

Ivory stormed past her and marched up to the store manager's office. She pounded on the glass door so hard it threatened to shatter. Ivory peered through the door and saw three people sitting in the office. When none of them got up to answer the door, Ivory took this as a sign of disrespect and started pounding harder.

The manager, whose name was Cassandra, finally got up and opened the door. "Why are you banging on this door like you're crazy? Have you lost your mind?"

"Damn all that! I wanna know why I'm not on the schedule next week," Ivory spat.

Not wanting to make a scene in front of the customers, Cassandra asked Ivory to step into the office. The security officer and Fred, both of whom were in the office, stepped out. Fred smirked as he left.

"The fuck you laughing at, you fat muthafucka?"

Knowing that he would get the last laugh, Fred ignored her and kept it moving.

After closing the door, Cassandra wheeled around and got in Ivory's face. "Let me tell you something, Ivory. If you want to keep working here, you had better learn to control that funky temper of yours," Cassandra warned.

Not wanting to lose her job, Ivory started to calm down. The fact that Cassandra had used the phrase "if you want to keep working here" told her that she still had a job.

"I'm just saying, Cassandra," she said, finally lowering her voice, "how come I ain't on the schedule?"

"You're not on the schedule because, apparently, you don't want to work."

"What? What the hell gave you that impression?"

"You."

A confused look fell across Ivory's face. Then it hit her. Fred. *That fat muthafucka musta run straight back here and told that bitch that he saw me at the store.*

"How the hell are you going to call off sick and then be across the street laughing and giggling with one of your friends? Maybe a week off will remind you that you work for Rite Aid and not the other way around."

Ivory was so mad she wanted to smack Cassandra in the face. She didn't trust herself not to do it, so she turned on her heel and walked out of the office, slamming the door in the process. Once again, Fred smirked when she walked past him. This time, Ivory couldn't control herself.

"You know what? I know yo' fat ass told Cassandra that you saw me at the store yesterday! Why can't you just mind yo' own fucking business, you rusty bastard?"

Cookie and a few of the customers doubled over in laughter at Ivory's insults. Fred, clearly embarrassed, decided that he wasn't going to let her do this to him two days in a row.

"I don't know what the fuck yo' problem is, but if you don't stop coming at me sideways, I'm gonna fuck yo' skinny ass up!"

"You ain't gonna do shit to me, you bitch-made mutha-fucka!"

By this time, Cassandra and the security guard had made their way over to where the commotion was. "Fred, go wait in my office, right now," Cassandra yelled. When Fred didn't move, the security guard walked over and placed his hand on Fred's shoulder.

"Come on, man. It's not worth all this."

"Yeah, you betta listen to that rent-a-cop! Don't get fucked up trying to show out," Ivory screamed. The security guard ignored Ivory and continued looking at Fred.

Cassandra grabbed Fred by the hand. "Listen to him. It's not worth it."

"It damn sure ain't worth it," Darnell said. He had come in to see what was taking Ivory so long. As soon as he heard loud screaming, he didn't have to wonder who the guilty party was. "'Cause if you put your greasy-ass hands on my woman, fat boy, I'm gonna shave fifty pounds o' bacon off ya back."

Fred made a move toward Darnell but was stopped dead in his tracks when he heard the familiar click that everyone in the hood was aware of. Darnell wasn't stupid, though. No one saw the gun under his coat, but it didn't take a genius to know that he had one.

"You got something you wanna say, Mr. Security Guard?"

"I just don't wanna see anybody get hurt in here."

"Then y'all betta take his ass on somewhere." Cassandra and the security guard led Fred to the manager's office.

"What about my damn check?" Ivory screamed.

"They haven't come in yet. When it gets here, we will mail it to you."

Right then, Ivory knew that her days of working at Rite Aid were over.

Chapter 6

Shortly after returning home to drop off his purchases, Red hit the road again. This time he was on his way to meet up with Bobby. They were supposed to meet with a few of the local knuckleheads who wanted to cop some weight from them. Red dipped in and out of traffic on I-90 west. His patience grew increasingly thin as every driver on the road seemed to want to follow the speed limit today. "Muthafucka, come on," he yelled out the window to an old white lady driving a beat-up Ford Escort. He was nowhere near late, but he knew that Bobby was probably already there, and the last thing he wanted to hear was his cousin bitching at him about tardiness.

Red smiled as he thought about the come-up that he and his cousin were about to stumble upon. They stood to make a cool $60,000 on this sale if everything went according to plan. He was thinking so hard about the cash that he almost missed his turn. Red got off at the Eddy Road exit and hung a left. After crossing St. Clair Avenue, he decelerated. He had no plans of getting stopped at this point and letting some cop fuck up his paper. Red hung a right at the stop sign. As soon as he pulled into the parking lot of the Bump Taylor football field, he saw Bobby looking down at his watch.

"You gon' be late to yo' own damn funeral," Bobby said, frowning.

"No, the fuck I ain't, 'cause I ain't showing up at that bitch." The two cousins laughed and gave each other a pound.

"How long we have before these muthafuckas get here?" Bobby asked.

Red looked at his watch and saw that they had about fifteen minutes before the buyers got there. "We got a few. Let's burn one."

"Now you're talking my language," Bobby said as he reached into his pocket and took out an already-rolled blunt. "You really think these stupid muthafuckas gonna try this dumb-ass shit?"

"I wouldn't doubt it," said Red. "If the info I got is on point, I think the shit is pretty much guaranteed." After passing the blunt back and forth twice, Red spotted a black Lexus pulling into the parking lot. He got on his phone and dialed a number.

"What you got for me?" He listened for a minute before spitting out, "That's just what the fuck I figured! Dirty muthafuckas!"

Red hung up the phone and looked at Bobby. With a look and a nod, Bobby knew just what Red was getting at. Bobby quickly chambered a round in his 9 mm. Red already had his .45 Desert Eagle off safety and tucked on the side of his hip. The black Lexus came to a stop about twenty feet away from where Red's and Bobby's whips were parked. When the doors opened, three militant-looking brothers with bald heads and camouflage army fatigues jumped out and started walking toward them. One of them was carrying a black duffle bag that was supposed to contain the buy money. However, based on the research done by Bobby and Red's team, Red knew that was far from the truth.

"Showtime," Bobby sneered.

"Yo, what it be like, homies?" the shortest of the three asked. "Y'all ready to handle this business?"

Without saying a word, Bobby reached down on the ground and picked up a brown briefcase. Looking around carefully, he opened it just wide enough for the buyers to see what was inside.

"Y'all got the dough?" Red asked.

"Yep, right here." One of the men reached into the black duffle bag, but before he got the chance to pull the pistol that was hiding inside of it, his head exploded like a watermelon.

"Shit," one of the men screamed when he saw his partner's brain hanging out of the side of his head. The two surviving men took off running. A hail of bullets followed them as they scrambled to get to their vehicle. The man who was the driver took two in the back as he tried to jump in the driver's seat. The other man dove inside the back of the whip. He didn't know that his man behind the driver's seat was shot until he looked up and saw the agony on his face and the blood pouring onto the seat from his back. As fast as he could, he tried to crawl over the seat so he could get away.

Meanwhile, Red, Bobby, and the man they had stationed behind the bleachers, whose name was Ray-Ray, descended upon the car like vultures. By the time the man was able to push his dying partner out of the way in order to execute a getaway, the three killers were upon him. In a matter of seconds, the car resembled Swiss cheese.

Bobby and Red had done their homework and learned that the three dudes they were going to do business with were setting them up. In fact, they had set up the last three crews they were supposed to do business with. They had also learned that they carried a black duffle bag, and when the exchange was supposed to be made, they pulled out guns, wet the crew up like a car wash, and robbed them. Red and Bobby were ready for it.

Chapter 7

When Tammy left work, she was as tired as she had been in a long time. She was also agitated that Nancy wasn't much help. All she did all day was brag about how their boss entrusted her with overseeing the company picnic. Tammy was glad that she wasn't asked, but she did wonder why Nancy was given the responsibility. She wasn't the most organized person in the world. If she didn't know any better, she would think that Nancy and the boss were screwing around.

She quickly shook it off and started thinking about her mother. She still hadn't had a chance to tell her that she'd filled out the enrollment application for school. She'd meant to tell her at breakfast, but the incident between her and Hakim had ruined the moment.

After about ten minutes of waiting for the bus, Tammy figured that she had time to run across the street to Arthur Treacher's and get something to eat. She was so busy at work that she hadn't had time to eat anything. Taking her chances and running across the street on a red light, Tammy hurriedly dodged the vehicles coming from both directions and made her way into the restaurant. By the time she ordered her food and walked out, the bus was fast approaching the bus stop. "Shit," she yelled as she started an all-out sprint. The bus's doors were closing just as she arrived at the steps.

"Wait! Hold up!"

The bus driver rolled her eyes as she opened the door and allowed Tammy to get on. After paying her fare, Tammy ignored the mean-mugging she received from the driver and walked to the back. Not feeling like hearing the lies and uninteresting conversations of the other patrons on the bus, Tammy slapped her headphones on and tuned in to iTunes.

As the soulful sounds of H.E.R. massaged her ears, Tammy drifted to her own world, which consisted of a white picket fence, a husband, two children, and a dog. Although she rarely saw any semblance of this in the real world, Tammy still believed that, outside of the hood, it existed.

She was so lost in her thoughts that she almost missed her stop. Tammy hopped off the bus and walked toward her house at a fast pace. She felt bad about not telling her mother that she had filled out the college application. After all, it was one of her mother's dreams to see one, if not both, of her children go to college. She had meant to tell her when she got home from Ivory's house the other night, but it was so late when she got in that her mother was already in a deep sleep.

The closer Tammy got to her house, a strange feeling started to come over her. She almost felt like she was walking into some kind of trap. When Tammy reached her house, she noticed a car in the driveway that she had never seen before. Thinking that it was probably just one of her mom's friends with a new whip, Tammy didn't think anything of it. She just shrugged her shoulders and walked up on the porch. Tammy was so tired and worn out that she dropped her keys twice.

After almost dropping them a third time, she finally managed to slide them into the lock. Just as she was about to yell out and alert her mother that she was home, she walked into the house and stopped dead in her tracks.

First, she listened. Then she shook her head vigorously from side to side. Her ears had to be deceiving her. Tammy eased through the living room and stopped short of the kitchen. Her heart pounded as she leaned her head into it. Her eyes almost popped out of her head at what she saw. There her mother was, bent over the kitchen table, getting hit doggie style by a man she had never seen before.

As fast as she could, Tammy ran back out the front door, holding her stomach. She didn't know or care if her mother heard her slam the door when she left. She just wanted to get as far away from the scene as possible. She made it one block before throwing up all over the concrete. The image of her mother getting her freak on was too much for her to wrap her mind around. After wiping her mouth with the back of her sleeve, Tammy took out her cell phone and called Ivory.

"Hello," Ivory sleepily answered the phone.

"Girl, wake yo' ass up! I'm on my way over there, and please roll a blunt, 'cause I just saw some shit that's got me all fucked up!"

Before Ivory could get any details from her, Tammy had hung up.

Hakim walked out of Foot Locker with mixed feelings. Although he was happy about Red buying so many shoes, thus ensuring that his commission would be large, he also envied the wealth that enabled Red to do it. Hakim knew that the college route his sister chose would never work for him. He simply couldn't see himself holding down a regular nine-to-five gig. He liked fast money. The only reason he even got a job in the first place was to keep his mother and sister off his back. He'd always promised himself that, the first chance he got, he was going to en-

ter the dope game. He also knew that if his mother ever
found out, she would not hesitate to throw him out of the
house. Still, he didn't care. Hakim was more than willing
to live on the streets and hustle if that meant becoming
the modern-day Nino Brown.

Hakim walked to the bus stop and plopped down on
the bench, shaking his head. He hated the fact that none
of them—he, his sister, nor his mother—had a car.

"This some bullshit," he mumbled to himself. Before he
could get too comfortable, a shiny black Dodge Charger
pulled up to the bus stop and blew the horn. When the
passenger's side window rolled down, the sounds of Lil
Wayne boomed throughout. Hakim squinted to see who
was in the car.

"Hakim! What the fuck you doing at a bus stop?"

"Oh, shit, is that my nigga Rick?"

"The one and only! Where the fuck you headed?"

"I'm headed to the house! I just got off of work, and a
nigga tired as fuck!"

"Shit, nigga, hop in! I'll give you a ride to the house!"

It only took Hakim a split second to decide whether to
roll with Rick. For right now, this was as close as he could
get to being a real baller. He laughed at the thought of
his mother, knowing that she would have a fit if she knew
that he was riding around with a known drug dealer.
Rick wasn't big time yet, but he was definitely on his way.
Right now, he was playing the block and copping product
from Red, but he had bigger aspirations.

The minute Hakim's ass touched the black leather
seats, a charge went through his entire body. Goosebumps
rose up on his body as he stared at the walnut-grain dashboard and navigation system. A blunt burned in the
ashtray as Rick noticed how Hakim was admiring his
whip. "You getting it in, huh?"

"I'm eating," Rick said with a shrug of his shoulders.

"It look like you doing more than eating to me."

Sensing the envy in his friend's voice, Rick smiled. From the time they were in junior high school, Rick and Hakim had always had a friendly rivalry. They competed in sports, getting girls, and everything in between. Now that Rick was getting it in the trap, he was a step ahead of Hakim and was savoring the moment.

"What you been up to?" Rick asked.

"Just chilling, wondering what the fuck a nigga gon' do after I graduate next year. I got a li'l job at Foot Locker, but that's short money. I'm trying to figure out how to make some long paper."

Rick picked up the blunt, took a pull, and passed it to Hakim. It didn't take a rocket scientist to figure out where Hakim was going with his statements. But Rick was selfish. He had no intention of putting Hakim up on the dope game for fear that he might start making more paper than he was.

Seeing that Rick wasn't going to throw him a lifeline, Hakim reached for one on his own. "You think you can plug a nigga in?"

When Rick didn't answer, Hakim grabbed the volume knob in the car and turned the music down.

"Yo, nigga, what the hell wrong wit' you? That cut was the shit."

"I asked you if you could plug me in," Hakim said. He strongly suspected that Rick had heard him the first time, but he didn't want to accuse his buddy of ignoring him.

"Into what? The dope game? I don't know about that one. I don't know if you cut out for this hustle."

Hakim instantly developed an attitude. With his butter light skin turning red and his hazel eyes glaring fire, Hakim turned and looked Rick directly in his face. "What you saying, huh? You think I'm some kind of pussy or something?"

"It ain't nothing like that. And I definitely don't mean no disrespect, but this game here is for the treacherous at heart, for the larcenous type of muthafucka, and you just don't strike me as that type."

Hakim was pissed. Beneath Rick's words, what he was really saying was that he thought Hakim was soft. At least, that's the way Hakim took it. What he didn't know was that Rick's reluctance to put him on had nothing to do with him being soft. The truth of the matter was that Rick feared the competition. He was a greedy, selfish individual who wanted to make every dime he could for himself. He was terrified that if he did pass Hakim the hustle torch, Hakim would pass him in the dope game, and he wasn't trying to take that chance.

"Nigga, listen," Hakim said, continuing to state his case, "I can be any type of nigga when it comes to getting paper."

Rick ran his hand across his goatee as if he were in deep thought. "Let me holla at the dude who plugged me in and see what he has to say, a'ight?"

"Yeah, a'ight. Good looking out on that," Hakim said with a half-smile. From Rick's body language, Hakim knew that he had less than a snowball's chance in hell of getting put on by him.

After letting Hakim hit the blunt for the second time, Rick dropped him off at home. As soon as he pulled off, the conversation that had gone on between them about putting Hakim on would pass through him like gas through the ass. He had no intention of putting Hakim on, at least not with his connect. The only way Hakim was going to ever get into the dope game by his hand would be when he was running his own operation. Rick had desires to be the next big thing in the drug industry. His ambitions had him making moves from Cleveland to New York. Unfortunately, the power move that he had researched so hard to set up was against seasoned professionals.

As Hakim hopped out of Rick's whip, he threw up the peace sign. At that moment, Hakim knew there was little hope that Rick would put him in the game.

Hakim walked through the living room and straight into the kitchen. With his arms outstretched over his head and his eyes closed, he yawned a tired yawn. He'd lived in this house for so long that he didn't even need his eyes to be open when he walked through certain parts of it. Hakim knew that Rick was probably bullshitting him, but the hustler in him was desperately hoping that he wasn't being sold a dream.

Hakim was hungry as hell. The blunt he smoked with Rick had given him a severe case of the munchies. He walked toward the refrigerator and made it as far as the table when he suddenly stopped in his tracks. His nose wrinkled up as he sniffed the air twice.

"Ah, hell nah. I know damn well Tammy ain't been fucking in here!"

Reaching on the side of his hip to retrieve his cell phone, Hakim walked back into the living room. He did a double-take as he saw a strange man leaned back against the couch, asleep. A light snore emitted from his nostrils as Hakim stood there stunned for a minute. Thinking that he was there for Tammy, Hakim's blood started to boil. *The fuck this ancient-ass nigga doing fucking around with my sister?*

"Yo, nigga, who the fuck is you?"

The man was so startled that he sat straight up. His face was a mask of confusion as he wondered who the angry young man was who stood before him. Groggily and sleepily, he looked around the house. The last thing that he remembered was Janice telling him that she was going to run to the store right quick and asking him if he wanted something back.

"You betta start coughing up some info! Is yo' old ass up in here fucking my sister?"

Before the man could answer, Hakim started yelling for Tammy. With his six-foot, 200-pound frame serving as an intimidator, Hakim stared the much smaller man down.

"I'm gonna ask you one more time, and after that, I'm gonna commence cracking yo' muthafucking head! What the fuck you doing in my house?"

The man was a shade under five nine and was clearly frightened by Hakim's threat. Much to his delight, Janice came walking through the door.

"Ma, who is this old dude Tammy got lounged up in here? And I think she left him in the house by himself, too, 'cause I don't think she here."

"He's not here for Tammy. He's here for me."

"You?"

"Yeah, me," she said, offended at the way Hakim was looking at her. Janice walked over to the couch and handed the man a pack of Newports. "Sorry it took me so long, Steve, but the line was out the door."

Hakim just stood there with an amazed look on his face.

"Oh, I'm sorry. Where are my manners? Steve, this is my son, Hakim. Hakim, this is my friend Steve."

As Steve got up to shake Hakim's hand, Hakim suddenly remembered the smell that he'd experienced in the kitchen. At that moment, it occurred to him that it had been his mother in the kitchen screwing and not his sister. He immediately got sick at the thought of his mother having sex. Backing up from Steve like he had the plague, Hakim ran up to his room and slammed the door.

"You are lying! You are fucking lying! I know damn well that you didn't catch your old-ass mother getting her back blown out," Ivory yelled.

"Yes, the fuck I did, and that shit was disgusting as hell!"

Ivory doubled over on her couch in laughter. Tears rolled down her face. When she looked up, she saw that Tammy wasn't smiling. "Please don't get brand new! You know good and damn well if this shit were the other way around, you wouldn't let me live it down."

Tammy started to smile a little. "Yeah, you're right. But the shit was just so disgusting. I told you that shit made me throw the fuck up!"

"Whatever," Ivory said, still laughing. "How the fuck you think yo' ass got here?"

"I know that! That doesn't mean I want to see that shit, though!"

"Here ya go, homegirl," Ivory said, passing her an unlit blunt. "You need this shit right here."

Tammy took the weed-filled cigar paper, grabbed a lighter from the table, and set fire to the tip. After holding it in for a longer period of time than usual, she blew a cloud of thick smoke into the air.

"Girl, does yo' mom know that you smoke weed yet?"

"Hell no, and I want to keep it that way."

"Yo' ass betta. Remember how the fuck she looked at me when that dime bag dropped out of my pocket that time?"

"I remember." Tammy then looked at Ivory strangely.

"What the hell you looking at me like that for?"

"Because it just occurred to me that it's your fault I started smoking this shit in the first damn place."

"My fault? How the fuck is it my fault?"

"Don't you remember when we snuck out of the house and went to that party? You were messing around with that nigga Donnie at the time, and he gave us a ride. Y'all was smoking weed on the way there, and because I didn't want to try it, you said that when we got to the party, you were going to tell everybody in that piece that I was a square."

"Well, shit, yo' ass was a square," Ivory shot back. "But I wasn't gonna say nothing to nobody. I just said that to scare you into doing it," Ivory admitted as she took the blunt from Tammy and took a hit.

"Conniving-ass bitch," Tammy said, shaking her head. Before she could cuss Ivory out for her deceitful ways, her cell phone went off. Looking at the screen, she saw that it was Hakim. She started not to answer it, but something in her gut told her to do so.

"Yeah, what's up, Hakim?"

"Yo, sis, where you at? You not gonna believe what the fuck I ran up on when I got to the house today."

Tammy's mouth almost dropped to the floor. *I know damn well that my mother is not being so reckless that she is getting caught by her son. It's bad enough that I walked in on that shit.*

"What happened?" she asked, playing dumb.

"When I got home from work today, some old mutha-fucka was leaned the fuck back on our couch asleep and shit. At first, I thought that he was some sugar daddy yo' ass was seeing. But just when I was about to put the heat to his ass, Mama showed up talking about he was there to see her."

Tammy was speechless. She was still stuck on the fact that Hakim thought the man was there to see her. "Hold up. Did you say that you thought that old-ass dude was there to see me? What the hell is wrong with you?"

"Well, shit, I didn't know."

Tammy looked over at Ivory, who had been eavesdropping on the entire conversation. Ivory covered her mouth in a lame attempt to conceal her laughter. "What are you laughing at?"

"You and yo' dysfunctional-ass family."

Tammy bit her tongue. She started to go there with Ivory, but knowing her past issues with her family, she let the comment slide, although she made a mental note to check Ivory about the snide remark later.

"Listen," she said, getting back to her overly excited brother, "don't worry about it. As long as Mama's all right, everything's cool."

"But I ain't never seen this cat before, have you?"

"Nah, but I trust Mama's judgment. I can't see her bringing somebody around the house who's gonna do us harm. Just be cool. I'll be there in a little bit." After hanging up with Hakim, Tammy walked over and snatched the blunt back out of Ivory's hand. "Let me get that. Your ass is babysitting."

"Yeah, whatever."

"Oh, by the way," remembered Tammy, "I need you to get me some pads with yo' Rite Aid discount. It's almost cramping time, girl."

Ivory's smile slowly faded.

"What? Don't tell me you hit your discount limit again."

"It ain't nothing like that. Check this shit out. Darnell took me up there earlier so I could see my work schedule."

Tammy rolled her eyes and popped her lips.

"Annnyway," Ivory said, after staring at Tammy for a minute, "can you believe that they had the nerve to take me the fuck off the schedule?"

"What the fuck did you do for them to do that?" Tammy had an idea. The moment she looked over at Rite Aid when she and Ivory were coming from the store, she just knew that was going to come back to haunt her friend.

"That bitch-ass nigga Fred must've gone back and told my supervisor that he saw me at the store after I called in sick that day."

"What the fuck does that nigga have against you?"

Ivory looked at Tammy like she had two heads. "What the fuck do you think? That nigga wants some of this pussy, and I won't give him none."

Tammy shook her head. "Typical ho-ass nigga," Tammy spat.

"Tell me about it. Then when I got ready to leave, the punk-ass nigga was giggling like a bitch. I couldn't take it no fucking more! I cussed his bitch ass out. Then the muthafucka acted like he was gon' do something until Darnell came in and checked his ass. And when I asked my supervisor about my check, she was like, 'We gon' mail it to you.' It don't take a fucking genius to figure out that they're firing my ass."

"Damn, that's fucked up." After hitting the blunt once more, Tammy stood up and headed toward the door. "I got to go. I better get home and see what's up with my moms and brother. They got into it this morning, and I know what happened earlier left a bad taste in his mouth."

"A'ight, I'll holla."

Tammy left, hoping that she wouldn't have to referee when she got home. But one thing was for sure. Janice Green was going to have to tell her who the hell this new man in her life was.

Chapter 8

Nancy's face scrunched up from the pain of Samuel James's ten-inch dick as it reshaped her womb. She loved black dick, but what her boss was doing to her was borderline torture. The two of them had been screwing on a regular basis for quite some time now, and Nancy had always found it enjoyable. But today, for reasons known only to him, Samuel wanted to rearrange her insides. Tears streamed from the corners of her eyes as Samuel hammered her guts. With her legs resting on his shoulders, Nancy resembled a sideways V. Nancy looked at her boss with pleading eyes, silently telling him that she couldn't take anymore. But instead of showing mercy, Samuel thrust himself deeper into her sex cave.

The sock that Samuel had stuffed in her mouth prevented her from screaming. The store had long since been closed, but he didn't want to take the chance of someone coming back and hearing him banging Nancy's back out. Just when Nancy thought she was about to pass out, Samuel's body jerked, and he released a stream of semen inside of her. Exhausted, he fell to the side of her on the floor. Nancy lay there for a moment, stunned, and wondering why he'd chosen to punish her this way.

She glanced over and noticed that he wasn't wearing his wedding ring. *Maybe he's mad at his wife and took that shit out on my pussy.*

Arching her back so she could get a good look at his face, she stared into his eyes and saw nothing. His blank expression told her that his mind wasn't even in the room. It seemed as if he were a hundred miles away. Nancy quickly stood up and put her pants back on. Every movement hurt as she tried to hurry up. The last thing she wanted was for him to get hard again and pummel her pink walls even more. After getting dressed, Nancy briskly walked toward the dressing room door. She looked back one more time and saw the same blank stare that she'd seen five minutes earlier. With pain slicing through her vagina at every step, Nancy walked out the door and headed for the bus stop.

By the time Tammy got home, Steve was gone. Hakim was still in his room with his door locked. He hadn't come out since he'd realized that it was his mom and not his sister who was in the kitchen getting her freak on. Apparently, the thought of his mother having sex sickened him, and he would rather, for the time being, just be left alone.

Tammy walked into the house to find her mother sitting on the couch in her pink satin robe watching television. As soon as she laid eyes on her, thoughts of her bent over the table, getting serviced flooded her mind. It took everything in her not to throw up again.

"Hey, Ma," she said, trying to avoid eye contact.

"Where you been? I was just about to call your cell phone. Did you have to work overtime or something?"

"I was just chilling with Ivory."

"Hmmph," Janice said, twisting up her lips. Although she had never tried to pick Tammy's friends, she didn't like her daughter hanging out with Ivory at all. In her mind, she was a bad influence on Tammy because she smoked weed. Little did she know that her daughter smoked more weed than half of the neighborhood.

Tammy was very careful not to let her mother find out that she got high. It would kill her if she did.

"What, Ma?"

"I don't know why you keep hanging out with that girl. You know damn well she smokes marijuana. Hell, I wouldn't be surprised if she's smoking something else."

"Ivory ain't like that. Besides, she's been a real good friend to me, and she has always shown you respect."

Janice couldn't deny that. Even though Ivory was as hood as they came, she did have the good sense to act civilized around her. The only way she found out about Ivory smoking weed was when a twenty sack dropped out of her jacket pocket while she was visiting one day. Janice got so mad that she told Ivory if she ever brought drugs into her house again, she would flush them down the toilet.

"Yeah, well, I just think you could hang out with a better class of people." Just then, Hakim came walking down the stairs. "Well, well, well, look who decided to come out of hibernation," Janice said.

"Whatever. Yo' boyfriend still here?"

Janice glared at him.

"You got a boyfriend now, Mama? When did this happen?" Tammy teased.

"It happened a while ago, and the only reason I didn't bring him around you guys earlier was because I wanted to make sure he wasn't some kind of nutjob."

Nah, you just wanted to make sure the nigga could fuck, Tammy thought.

Janice then walked up to her son and pulled him close to her. After hugging him tightly, she looked into his eyes. "I know you miss your father. And I'm sorry about the comment I made earlier this morning. But no matter what, you have to respect me. So don't you ever, as long as you are black, talk about selling drugs in my house again." She paused to let the severity of her words sink in. "Now, as far as the man you met in here earlier, Steve, he has been nothing but a perfect gentleman to me so far. I know he's not your dad, but he works for me."

Don't you mean he works on you? Tammy thought.

"You want me to be happy, don't you?" she asked Hakim, looking directly into his eyes.

Hakim nodded solemnly.

"What about you, Tammy? Are you okay with this?"

"Mama, if you're happy, then we're happy," she answered. The three of them engaged in a group hug. Tammy thought long and hard about telling her mother that she saw her getting her rocks off in the kitchen earlier. She would never tell her that in front of Hakim, but once he was out of sight, all bets were off. Before she could decide what she was going to do, the doorbell rang.

"I got it," Hakim said as he made his way toward the door.

While he was gone, Tammy figured that she would say something to her mother about her indiscretion. The last thing she wanted was for Hakim to walk in and catch his mother getting screwed. She was only 42 years old, so her freak light hadn't gone out yet, but still, she was going to have to be more careful.

"Mama, I need to talk to you about something."

"What's on your mind, baby?"

"Well, earlier today—"

"Ya friend is back," Hakim said as he came walking back into the room.

Steve followed him with a nervous look on his face. "Uh, I forgot my cigarettes."

"Hakim, do Mama a favor and go get that pack of cigarettes out of my room. I took them upstairs earlier this evening." While Hakim ran the errand for his mother, Janice took the opportunity to introduce Steve to her daughter. "Steve, this is my daughter, Tammy."

"Nice to meet you," Steve said with a smile. He stuck out his hand so that Tammy could shake it.

The minute his skin touched hers, a chill ran through her body. She cocked her head to the side. "Don't I know you from somewhere?" she asked.

"I don't think so," he said, looking at Janice with a confused look on his face.

Tammy continued to stare at Steve for a brief moment before shrugging her shoulders. "Sorry. I must be thinking of someone else."

Tammy then said good night and walked up to her room in deep thought. She racked her brain as she closed her door behind her, thinking that she was sure she had seen Steve's face somewhere before.

When Nancy woke up the next morning, her womb was so sore that it hurt her to even move. Her legs felt like jelly. When her cell phone buzzed, she looked at it, saw that it was her job, and gave it the finger. She decided on the bus ride home from work the night before that she wasn't going to go to work the next day. She knew that Tammy was off and that they were going to be shorthanded, but she gave less than a fuck about that. All she wanted to do was lie around the house and rest her aching clit. Then, when she thought she was properly healed up, she would give Mike's friends a call and see if he wanted to make a deal so she could get some more blow.

With great difficulty, Nancy crawled out of bed. Her growling stomach called to her for some much-needed nourishment, but with the way she was feeling, cooking was definitely not an option. Not that she had much to cook anyway. Her cocaine habit kept her refrigerator hollow. When Nancy started doing cocaine, she, like every other addict, was only a casual user. But as her urge to get high strengthened, her willingness to be responsible weakened. Pretty soon, she was using bill money to support her habit. In order to keep from getting evicted and still be able to get high, Nancy started prostituting her body for product.

After taking a painful piss, Nancy walked to her kitchen and almost passed out when she saw her father sitting at her kitchen table reading a newspaper. Sitting on the table in front of him was a bag from McDonald's. Nancy glared at him as he smiled back at her.

"What the hell are you doing in my house?" she asked with scorn. She didn't even bother to ask how he got in, because in his line of work, he could easily access a residence.

"Now, honey, is that any way to talk to your father?" he shot back.

"Father? Oh, is that what they're calling what you are nowadays?"

The comment stung him, but Nancy didn't care. In her eyes, he had put her through so much pain and disappointment throughout the years that she would never be able to catch up. She still got pissed off thinking about how he'd disappointed her on her sixteenth birthday. She was supposed to have a birthday party, but at the last minute, he canceled it because he wanted to spend the night with some tramp. Seeing the pain in his eyes gave her a small sense of satisfaction.

"Come on, honey, let's not fight. Here, I brought you some breakfast."

Nancy slowly and reluctantly reached down and picked up the bag. Under normal circumstances, she would not have accepted anything from him. No gift he bought would ever be able to make up for the early years of abandonment. But with hunger pains hitting her like a Mike Tyson jab, she had little choice. Nancy's father then jumped up and walked around the table.

"Have a seat," he said as he pulled the chair out for her. After she sat down, he went back around the table, sat down, and smiled.

"What are you smiling about?" she asked.

"I was thinking . . ." he started. "Remember when you were ten years old and we took you to the zoo? They were giving free elephant rides that day, and we stood in line for an hour and a half just so you could get a ride."

The memory from yesteryear brought a slow smile to Nancy's face. "Yeah, I remember."

"You were scared at first, but when that boy who was smaller than you went before you, you arched your back up and decided that no kid that small was going to outdo you."

Nancy let out a slight chuckle. The thought of that day brought a little joy to her heart. It was one of the few times she could remember when her father actually had time for her. Another happy thought went through her mind.

"What about the time we went to Cedar Point and got on that roller coaster? You tried to act brave, but I could tell that you were scared."

"Scared? I wasn't scared," her father said.

"Oh, please. You were screaming louder than I was."

For the next twenty minutes, Nancy and her father caught up on old times. It was twenty of the most enjoyable minutes of Nancy's life. That was, until her father's cell phone rang. As soon as he finished the conversation, he pressed end and looked at Nancy. She immediately knew what was about to happen and got mad.

"Let me guess. Your ass is about to leave, right?"

Nancy's father rubbed his brow. He'd known all along that Nancy would react like this when it was time for him to leave. Never mind the fact that they hadn't seen each other in three months. Forget about the fact that the nature of his job prevented him from being the father Nancy so desperately wanted and needed. The father who was around all the time.

"I'm sorry, but yes, I do have to go."

Nancy then let out a disgusted laugh. Shaking her head, she got up, walked to her bedroom, and slammed the door.

Chapter 9

Tammy was sleeping peacefully in her bed, dreaming about R&B singer Usher. Just as they were about to climb into bed together, her mother threw open the bedroom door and yelled into her room.

"Tammy, get the damn phone!"

Still half asleep, Tammy reached over and picked up the cordless phone sitting on her nightstand. "I got it." When Tammy was sure that her mother had hung up the phone, she spoke. "Hello?"

"What you doing?" Ivory asked her.

"I was asleep until your silly ass called and woke me the hell up. Why the hell did you call the house phone anyway?"

"I called yo' cell phone first, but it went straight to voicemail."

Tammy got up and looked around. After a few seconds, she spotted her phone on her dresser. It was unplugged, so she knew instantly that her battery was dead. "Damn," she whispered to herself. She plugged it in and then plopped back down on her bed. "My damn battery is dead," she told Ivory.

"Oh, no wonder. Hey, what you doing later today?"

"Shit, I don't know. Why?"

"I want you to roll up to Rite Aid wit' me and pick up my check."

"I thought they were going to mail you your check."

"Cookie called me this morning and told me that they came in today. I'm going up there to get my damn ends."

"You're crazy," Tammy said as she started laughing.

"Crazy, my ass. I'm serious as a fucking heart attack. Them muthafuckas ain't never gon' say my shit got lost in the mail."

"That's a place of business. They wouldn't do anything like that."

"I ain't taking no damn chances with my dough. You rolling with me or what?"

"I guess so. I don't have anything to do today."

"Even if you did, you betta cancel that shit. You know we down for each other."

"Yeah, yeah. I'll call you in a couple of hours."

After hanging up, Tammy went back to sleep, hoping that she could continue her romantic dream with a singing superstar.

She woke up exactly one hour later. She didn't bring it up when she talked to Ivory earlier because she didn't want to give her crazy friend any ideas, but she hoped like hell that Ivory wasn't going up to Rite Aid to start some bullshit. The last thing she needed was to be caught up in some dumb shit before she started school.

This thought made another cross her mind. She still hadn't told her mother that she had filled out and sent back the application. She made a mental note to do that before she walked out of the house.

After taking a quick shower, Tammy jogged down the stairs and went into the kitchen. She cringed as the thought of her mother and Steve quickly ran through her mind.

"What the hell is wrong with you?" her mother asked when she noticed the look on her face.

"Huh? Oh, nothing. I was just thinking about something. Where is Hakim?" she asked.

"He told me that he was going to the gym to play basketball."

"Oh. Well, there's been something I've wanted to tell you for the last couple of days, but things have been getting in the way of me doing it." Tammy walked over to the sink, where her mother was washing dishes, and grabbed her by the hand. "Come and sit down for a minute."

"Oh, my God, you pregnant, ain't you?" Janice asked with wide eyes.

Tammy stood there in shock for a second and then burst out laughing. "No, Mama, nobody's pregnant. At least not me."

"Oh, okay then," Janice said with a huge sigh. "Well, if you not expecting, what is so important?"

"Weeell, I just thought I should let you know that I applied for school the other day."

A large smile fell across Janice's face. Tears formed in her eyes. To her, this was a dream come true. "Oh, baby, I'm so proud of you," she said as she wrapped her arms around Tammy's neck and squeezed so tight Tammy couldn't breathe.

"I'm not going to be going anywhere if you keep hugging me like this, because I will be dead."

"I'm sorry. This is just such a happy day for me. One of my children is doing something that I never got to do. I gotta tell somebody," Janice screamed. With her hands shaking, she ran to the phone and picked it up.

Tammy just shook her head and smiled. No doubt she was about to brag to all of her friends that her daughter was about to go to college. Tammy then remembered that she had left her cell phone in her room. Making a mad dash up the steps, she went to her room to retrieve it and saw that she had a missed call.

"Oh, brother," she said, rolling her eyes. Knowing that it was Ivory, she dialed her number.

"Where the hell you been?" Ivory asked without so much as a hello. "I been calling yo' ass for the last fifteen minutes."

"First of all, I was talking to my mother, if that's okay with your ass. And secondly, you haven't been calling for the last fifteen minutes, because I only see one missed call."

"'And secondly,'" Ivory teased Tammy about the way she talked. "Why the hell you gotta be sounding so proper all the damn time? Yo' ass is from the ghetto just like me."

"Whatever. Don't hate because I know how to pronounce my damn words."

"Yeah, whatever," Ivory said, laughing. "You still going up to Rite Aid with me to pick up my check?"

"Yeah, I'll ride with you. How soon will you be here?"

"I'm on my way now."

"All right. I'll see you in a minute then." Tammy hung up with Ivory and went back downstairs to tell her mother that she was about to leave. When she got back in the kitchen, her mother was still on the phone, bragging like she had won the lottery.

"I'm about to go to the store with Ivory. I'll be back in a little while."

"Yeah, okay," her mother said, frowning. Her dislike for Ivory was once again evident. "Oh, by the way, your job called. They asked me to tell you to call them. They said it's important."

Tammy spat out a laugh. "Yeah, right," she said and headed out the door to wait for Ivory.

She knew exactly what her job wanted, and they would have to find another sucker today. Every time Tammy's job called her, it was because they wanted her to come to work because someone else didn't. Tammy wasn't falling for it today, though. All she wanted to do this day was kick back and have a little fun. The weather was nice. The temperature was seventy-three degrees with a slight breeze and made Tammy think about going back into the house to get a light jacket. Before she could make a decision, however, Ivory came screeching to a halt in front of her house. Tammy just shook her head at her friend's reckless driving style.

"You really need to learn how to drive," she said once she got inside the car.

"Whatever," Ivory said, pulling off as soon as Tammy's door was closed. Tammy tried to gage Ivory's mood as the two of them engaged in idle chitchat. She wanted to see if Ivory was in hood mode. Ivory seemed a little too calm for her, so she decided to lay it down to her.

"Okay, look, Ivory. Go in there, get your check, and let's roll the fuck out. I don't have time to be calling my mother to bail me out fucking around with your hotheaded ass."

"What? Girl, ain't nobody on that shit. Yo' scared ass. As long as they give me my muthafuckin' ends, there won't be a problem."

"I don't know. I still think maybe you should've let them mail it to you."

"'Should've,'" she said, mocking her proper-talking friend.

"What the fuck ever," Tammy said.

"And fuck that! I'm going up there to get my damn money."

Five minutes later, Ivory pulled into the pharmacy's parking lot and jumped out like she owned the place.

"Damn, girl, you're getting out like you're about to go in there and rob the place or something," Tammy commented.

Ivory ignored her statement and kept walking. Her long legs didn't miss a beat as Tammy had trouble keeping pace with her. Ivory walked into the store and once again spotted Cookie. She walked over to the register, where Cookie was working and tapped her on the shoulder. When Cookie saw that it was Ivory, she looked toward the office. Then she leaned over to Ivory and whispered in her ear.

"Girl, you better go 'head in there and get yo' shit. Cassandra's passing them out now, so if you go in there right now, she can't talk no dumb shit about they didn't come in."

"Did the bitch say I was fired or just suspended?" Ivory asked.

"I ain't heard her say shit about it."

"Okay. Let me go in here and get my paper. Thanks."

While Ivory walked over to the office, Tammy and Cookie engaged in light conversation. They only knew each other through Ivory when Tammy would come up to Rite Aid and see her from time to time.

When Ivory got to the door, she peeked in and saw Cassandra reaching into a large manila folder. She then pulled out a check and handed it to Nathan, the pharmacist who worked in the back. Before they even realized she was there, Ivory burst through the door like she was on a SWAT team. After a few seconds of silence, Ivory looked at the folder and crossed her arms.

Acting as if she had no idea why Ivory was there, Cassandra hunched up her shoulders and said, "What?"

"The fuck you mean, what? I want my damn check!"

"Ivory, I told you the other day that we would mail you your check."

"Oh, you got a bitch like me fucked all the way up! I didn't mail no muthafuckin' hours up in this piece. Y'all ain't about to mail me no damn check! You just gave this nigga here his paper in his hand, but you gon' tell me that I have to wait for mine?"

Seeing trouble brewing, Nathan hurriedly ran out the door.

"Ivory, that's a common procedure when—"

"When what?"

Cassandra was about to let it slip that she had indeed fired Ivory. Knowing how quick-tempered she was, Cassandra would have much rather sent it to her in the form of a registered letter than tell her face-to-face. But now that Ivory was there, she had no other choice but to tell her.

"Because of you calling off from work under false pretenses, combined with you pretty much showing your behind in here yesterday, the company feels that they have no other alternative but to let you go."

"The company, huh?" Ivory said, smiling. She had been at Rite Aid long enough to know that her supervisor was feeding her some bullshit. Cassandra and Cassandra alone did the hiring and firing, and Ivory knew it.

Cassandra got nervous as Ivory started taking off her earrings. She almost pissed on herself when Ivory got up in her face. She wanted to call security but didn't want to let Ivory know that she was partially afraid of her.

"You know what? I kind of figured that I was gonna get fired for what happened in here yesterday. But the least you could've done was be a woman about it and tell me that you were firing me and not hide behind the damn company. Now give me my muthafuckin' check before I stomp yo' ass in here!"

Knowing that her options were limited, Cassandra reached into the folder and took out Ivory's check. Ivory didn't even wait for her to offer it to her as she snatched it out of her hand. Ivory then turned and started to walk out of the office. She was just about to push the door open when the colored glass revealed Cassandra giving her the finger from behind. Ivory's head spun around like in *The Exorcist* in an attempt to catch Cassandra dirty. Cassandra had already put her hand back down, but the reflection was good enough for her.

"Oh, so now you wanna disrespect me, huh?"

Before Cassandra could utter an excuse, Ivory hauled off and punched her in the face. Cassandra dropped to the floor like a rock, hitting her head on the cushion of the chair. Ivory then spat on her and walked out. By the time she got twenty feet away from the office, she heard Cassandra yelling for security on the loudspeaker. Not wanting to be detained by the rent-a-cop until the real police got there, Ivory picked up the pace.

"Come on, girl, let's get the fuck outta here," she yelled to Tammy.

"Ah shit, what the fuck did you just do?" Tammy screamed, following closely behind her. The two of them jumped in the car and peeled away, with Ivory laughing the whole time.

"I knew it! I fucking knew it! I knew your ass was going to start some damn trouble," Tammy fussed.

"I didn't start shit! I just finished the muthafucka," Ivory stated with pride. "What's that in your hand?" she asked Tammy.

"They're invitations to Cookie's birthday party. But I don't know if I wanna go with your crazy ass."

"Look, I wouldn't've done that shit if the bitch hadn't tried to disrespect me. She got what she fucking deserved. And now I need a damn drink," Ivory said as she headed to the nearest Arab store to cash her check. For the second night in a row, the two friends sat back and got blazed.

Chapter 10

Bobby and Red sat next to each other on the couch, holding Xbox 360 controllers in their hands. The two had been lying low ever since murdering their would-be robbers the day before. It was a cool-down tactic they always employed after performing such a heinous crime. In their presence was Ray-Ray—the sniper who they had posted up behind the bleachers—Hank, and Ray-Ray's cousin, Dennis, who had just been released from prison.

Dennis was definitely violating his parole by hanging out with felons, but like most of the thugs from the hood, being away from the homies was never an option. Also, like a lot of convicts passing through the system, he had adopted the teachings of Islam and become a Muslim. He scrunched up his face at Ray-Ray, who was eating a rib sandwich from B&M Barbeque.

"If you knew what the fuck I knew about that pig, you wouldn't be eating that shit," Dennis told him.

"Look here, Malcolm X, don't start with that bullshit. I ain't no damn Muslim, so don't be telling me about that dumb shit. I'm getting my muthafucking grub on."

"I'm just trying to educate yo' ignorant ass. That pig animal is nasty as fuck."

"That's why it's washed off before it's cooked, nigga," Ray-Ray retorted.

"Yo, man, you gon' have ta chill out calling me the *N* word."

"Yeah, whatever."

"Both of you muthafuckas shut the fuck up," Bobby yelled. "Don't y'all see a nigga trying to concentrate ova here?"

"Yeah," Red chimed in. "Let this nigga concentrate. I don't want no excuses when I get finish digging off in his ass."

"You wish. I'm the *Madden* star up in this piece."

"That game's garbage," Red spat as he shook his head in disgust. "Ray-Ray, put something in the air."

"You ain't said shit." Ray-Ray reached into his pocket and pulled out an extra-large blunt.

"Damn, nigga, you trying to get high for days off that shit," Bobby said.

"I don't play wit' it." Ray-Ray beamed.

"Oh, shit. I gotta roll," Dennis said. Hanging around his buddies was one thing. But when they started smoking weed, he wanted to be nowhere in sight. He'd learned firsthand how second-hand smoke could cause someone to fail a drug test, and the last thing he wanted was to be locked back up on a humble, especially when he wasn't the one doing the smoking. "Ray, you wanna give me a ride to the house?"

Ray-Ray looked at him like he was from Mars. "Now?"

"Yeah, man, now," Dennis said through gritted teeth.

Ray-Ray mistakenly took the way he said it as Dennis being disrespectful, and he lashed out. "Muthafucka, you crazy!"

"You know I can't be around this shit!"

"Look here. You know damn well how we get down. What the fuck you think we was gon' do when we got together, play *Monopoly?*"

"But—"

"But my ass! Now, the way I see it, yo' ass got three choices," Ray-Ray said. "You can sit here and wait until I'm ready to leave, catch the muthafucking bus, or call

Allah and see if He can come and get yo' non-pork-eating ass, 'cause I ain't ready to go."

And with that, Ray-Ray fired up the weed and took a pull.

Dennis stormed out the front door in a huff. "A'ight, muthafucka," he mumbled under his breath.

"Damn, Ray, that was some cold-ass shit to be doing to ya fam," Bobby said, laughing.

"Man, fuck that nigga. Cousin or no cousin, he knew we was gonna be getting blown when he came up in here."

After the four thugs passed the blunt around once, Hank asked Red, "Don't you got a bitch who work for that Rite Aid on 105th?"

"Yeah. Matter of fact," he said as he looked at his watch, "she oughta be here in a few. I got her bringing me a twelve-pack tonight 'cause I knew we was gonna be chilling and shit."

The four remaining thugs went about their business, oblivious to what was about to happen next.

Dennis got on the elevator, mad as hell. Even though Ray-Ray was his cousin, there was no way he was going to allow him to disrespect him that way. He'd tried unsuccessfully to remove his family from the equation but figured since his cousin wanted to show off in front of his friends, then he was on his own. Dennis opened up his cell phone and dialed. When the person on the other end answered, he made two statements.

"I'm on my way. Get ready."

After the elevator doors opened, Dennis rushed out and ran right into a sexy light-skinned tenderoni. She had a peacock weave in her head that was blond blended with blue and red.

"Damn, nigga, watch where the fuck you going," Cookie screamed.

Normally Dennis would wild out at a female talking to him in that manner, but since he was on a paper chase, he decided to take the high road. "My bad," he apologized as he knelt down to help her pick up the beer cans that had fallen out of the now-torn box. Since it was only torn at the top, Cookie could still carry it by holding it from the bottom.

"Yo, you still there?" the caller on the other end asked.

"Yeah. Hold up a second."

Cookie could clearly hear the person on the other end on the phone. She could even hear what they were saying. Content to mind her own business, Cookie continued picking up the cans until she heard the word "rob." Then, when Dennis mentioned apartment 3C, Cookie immediately put two and two together. Dennis was so preoccupied with his conversation that he never heard Cookie inadvertently whisper, "Oh, shit." After Dennis helped her put the rest of the cans of beer into the box, Cookie thanked him and hurried to the elevator.

Dennis wondered why her attitude went from shitty to docile in a matter of minutes, but he shrugged it off and went to meet his partners in crime.

Rick's moment of opportunity had finally arrived. He was mere minutes away from making a major come-up. His plan was to run up inside Red's spot, rob him, and kill whoever was there. Nodding to the sounds of Tupac, Rick loaded his black 9 mm pistol. He was dressed in all black with a ski mask rolled up on top of his head, waiting to be pulled down. Rick had been copping product from Red and Bobby for a little over a year now. All along though, he knew the day would come when he would want to get rid of them both and take over as the major supplier in the Dawg Pound city.

What better way, in his mind, than to get rid of them permanently and make a come-up in the process. His getaway vehicle was a stolen DirecTV truck that his accomplice, Bear, had ripped off only an hour earlier.

"You ready to go get this chedda?" he asked Bear, who was sitting in the passenger's seat beside him.

Bear, a hulk of a man who stood six feet four inches tall and weighed in the neighborhood of 275 pounds, simply nodded. A smile was something that hadn't been seen on his face in quite some time. A former car thief, Bear was also an expert at picking locks. He needed a quick payday to ward off loan sharks. He had twenty-four hours to pay them off, or they were going to kill his mother. Rick flinched as the back door opened, and Dennis slithered into the back seat.

"The hell you jumping for, scared-ass nigga? I told you that I was on my way back down."

"Everything set up right?" Rick asked, ignoring Dennis's statement.

"I told you that it was on the phone."

Rick took a deep breath and then turned around to face Dennis. "You sure you wanna go through with this shit? That is yo' fam up there."

"Man, fuck that clown. I tried to give him an out, and he wouldn't take it. And like I told you before, that jackass ain't no blood kin to me. We just cousins by marriage."

Rick just stared at him for a few seconds. He honestly didn't know if Dennis was going to have the heart to bust something if shit got thick, and he was going to make sure it did. What Rick hadn't told Dennis was that he planned on killing everyone in the house who wasn't taking part in the plan. He concluded right then that if Dennis wanted to go down in flames with Bobby, Red, and Ray-Ray, then he would surely send him to meet his Maker.

The plan to rob Red and Bobby was devised in a bar by a chance meeting between Dennis and Rick. Dennis had sat down beside the younger Rick, and while throwing back shots of liquor, the two discovered that they had a few things in common. It was purely coincidental that both of them had connections to Bobby and Red. Rick had figured that it would be the perfect time to try to make a come-up off the two drug dealers.

Rick's mind snapped back to the present as Dennis started rapping along with the Tupac track. He reached up under the seat and grabbed two more pistols and handed one to each man. Bear then reached under the passenger's side seat and took out a small black bag, which contained his lock-picking tools. Rick gave both men a sinister smile as he looked up into the darkening skies.

"A'ight, y'all," he said with malice in his voice. "Let's do this."

The three of them hopped out of the truck to go meet their destiny.

Cookie stumbled off the elevator and headed down to the cool-down apartment where Red was. All she could think about was getting to her lover before the whole robbery thing could go down. Cookie was no fool. She knew that Red was smashing plenty of women. But as long as he kept them out of her face, she wasn't going to worry about it. Plus, the money and gifts that he was tricking off on her more than made up for his lack of monogamy in her eyes. The last thing she wanted was for someone to get the drop on Red and take him out. Her heart pounded furiously as she got to the door. She knocked on it twice before Ray-Ray snatched it open and looked at her like she was crazy.

"Oh, my bad, Cookie. I thought you was my silly-ass cousin who just left outta here."

"Nah, uh, I think I just passed him. What did he look like?"

"Big, black, ashy-looking muthafucka."

Damn! I gotta let Red know what the fuck is going on. I didn't know that nigga was Ray-Ray's cousin! Cookie walked over to Red with a long stride.

"Here's the beer you asked me to bring. You want me to take it in the kitchen for you?" Before Red could even answer her, Cookie was running into the kitchen with the box of beer under her arm.

"Damn, hello to yo' ass too, Cookie," Hank spat. He knew Cookie from having done security at the Rite Aid where she worked.

Five seconds later, she called Red into the kitchen.

"Shit, man, the fuck this bitch want?" he asked no one in particular. "Pause the fucking game." Red walked into the kitchen with a frown on his face. "What? Don't you see I'm playing the fucking game?"

"I just thought you should know that I bumped into Ray-Ray's cousin on the way up here. He was in such a hurry that the nigga knocked this beer outta my damn hand. But check this shit out. While he was helping me pick it up, I overheard his phone conversation. Somebody on the other end of the phone was talking about robbing you and shit."

Red was quiet for a minute as he thought about Ray-Ray. Although Ray-Ray acted like he didn't give a fuck about Dennis, Red couldn't be sure that he would turn his back on him if some serious shit jumped off.

"Did you hear him say when this shit supposed to go down?" Red asked.

"Pretty soon. I heard him say, 'Get ready.'"

Red had to move fast. He didn't want to have to kill Ray-Ray, so he devised a plan to get rid of him before anything jumped off. He quickly walked back into the living room. Reaching into his pocket, Red took out a knot of money and peeled off $200.

"Yo, Ray, I need you to do me a favor. Take the Benz, run over on Hough, and pick up some smoke from Tone. I forgot I told that nigga I was coming through there earlier."

Bobby immediately knew something was up. He and Red were just discussing how they had to check Tone about selling them some garbage weed the previous week. He knew that until Red had a chance to talk to Tone, there was no way in the world he would ever buy anything else from him.

Ray-Ray hurriedly jumped on board with Red's request. He'd been begging Red to let him push the black Mercedes ever since Red bought it a month ago.

As soon as Ray-Ray walked out of the house, Bobby asked Red what was going on. Red quickly explained what Cookie had told them. Then he looked at Cookie. "Strip," he said.

"Huh?"

"You heard me. Strip."

"In front of your friends?" she asked with a look of shock on her face.

"Cookie, just do what the fuck I told you to do."

Reluctantly, Cookie started taking off her clothes. Bobby and Hank stood there mesmerized by the firmness of Cookie's body. Red went over to the CD player and put on some old-school Jodeci. As the sounds of "Freek'n You" eased through the speakers, Red walked over to Cookie and whispered instructions in her ear. Cookie nodded and sat in a beige recliner that faced the door. She grabbed a pair of sunglasses off the table and slid them on. After hearing three beeps from the alarm system, Red turned the doorknob on the front door and cracked the door slightly.

Then he ushered Bobby and Hank into the coat closet next to the front door. What Dennis hadn't counted on was that Red had that door wired in case someone tried to break in, and he always kept it locked. Only he and Bobby could open it without setting off the beep, and if someone else did, it was because they were up to no good. Red grabbed three bats that were lying in the corner of the closet. Although he had every intention of killing them, he would do so at another time. His sick mind was already thinking of ways to make the violators suffer.

"These muthafuckas never learn," Bobby whispered. Red just shook his head.

The three hoodlums eased up the back stairwell with dollar signs dancing their heads. They were praying that no one came out of one of the hallways and inquired about their intentions, but if so, then so be it. Rick had already decided that no one was going to stop him from getting paid, and if anyone tried, he was going to let his pistol make love to them.

"This fucking ski mask is making my damn face itch," Dennis cried.

"Stop crying like a little bitch, and bring yo' ass on," Rick remarked.

Dennis's dark black pupils stared through the ski mask. He wanted to crack Rick on the back of the head for talking to him that way. He made a mental note to check his ass later, after they got paid. All three men crept down the hallway until they came to the door with the emblem 3C on it.

"You sure this is it?" Rick asked, hearing the soft sounds of Jodeci seeping through the door.

"Hell yeah, I'm sure. I just left the damn place, remember?"

Rick looked at the door and smiled. "This muthafucka slipping," he said when he noticed that the door was ajar.

It never even crossed Dennis's mind that it could be a setup. If he had thought for a second, he would've realized that he was the last one out of the door and he had closed it.

"Y'all ready?" he asked. "On three," he continued, not waiting for them to say if they were indeed ready. "One, two, three!"

The three goons burst into the place, only to find Cookie dancing naked with her back to them. They were so captivated by her performance that they all started walking toward her. Anticipating them being there, Cookie spread her legs sexily, bent over, and allowed her palms to touch the floor. She looked between her legs and saw that they were in a trance, marveling at her body.

From her angle, she couldn't see Red and his thugs come out of the closet, but she did hear the sickening sound of bones being broken. Dennis, Rick, and Bear hit the ground with a loud thud. Bear was the only one of them still conscious, but Hank took care of that with another swing of the Louisville Slugger. The three men then dragged each man to the elevator and took them down to the basement of the building. It took them ten minutes to bound and gag their would-be jackers. Red then looked over at Bobby and smiled. *It's times like this that make me glad I bought this building,* Red thought.

Chapter 11

Detectives Dryer and Stone stood over the deceased Joshua "Juice" Wiggins and shook their heads. For the first time since he'd was a rookie cop seeing his first dead body, Dryer was on the verge of throwing up. Murder was vicious enough. But overkill was downright sinister, and this was the definition of overkill.

"What do you think, partner?" Stone asked.

"Oh, there's nothing to think about. This shit here is definitely personal. Hell, the first two shots were probably enough to put ol' Juice out of his misery. The bullets that ripped through him after that were just to prove a point."

Stone nodded his head, indicating that he and his partner's thinking were along the same lines.

"Let's hurry up and examined this scene and get the fuck away from here. I need a fucking drink," Dryer said, disgusted.

"Who in the hell could have done this to a man, and why?"

"I don't know about the why part, but I'm pretty sure I know the who," Dryer said.

"Oh, yeah? Who?"

"I'll tell you when we leave here. Now let's get this shit done."

Detective Dryer sat at the bar with a somber look on his face. The murder scene he was called to was one of the worst he'd seen in his entire career. Although he couldn't prove it, he was fairly certain who the murderer was.

"You know this looks like some of our boy Red's hand-iwork."

"Jesus Christ, Eugene, we don't even have any leads on the killing yet, and already you're fingering him."

"I don't have to have any evidence to know that prick was the one responsible," Dryer said, slamming his hand down on the bar. "I'm tired of that son of a bitch getting away with murdering innocent people in my damn city!"

"Innocent? That nigger we scraped off the ground in the back of Thurgood Marshall Recreation Center was a convicted drug dealer, rapist, and thief. Some people would say whoever killed his ass did the world a favor."

Dryer stared at his partner.

"I'm just saying," Stone said, throwing up his hands.

"All right. What about the time that old woman who had come forward and said that she would testify that she saw Bobby leaving the scene of a murder was found with her brains blown out and her tongue sliced off? Now it was clear to everyone with a brain that Red was warning people to keep their mouths closed."

Stone knew that Dryer was right. But the last thing he wanted was to arrest Red and Bobby for such a serious crime and then have to let them go on a technicality. "I hear you. But we don't want some slick-talking-ass law-yer to get them off because we didn't go by the book."

Dryer leaned back on the barstool and rubbed his face. Deep in his heart, he knew that his partner had a legiti-mate point. If they were going to make something stick on Red and Bobby, then they were going to have to get in-disputable evidence on them. He knew from experience, though, that getting evidence on the two drug-dealing killers would be easier said than done.

Chapter 12

The next morning, Ivory was treated to a surprise from Darnell. He came over early and took her to breakfast at Bob Evans in Mayfield Heights. On the ride up there, Ivory told him about how she had gotten fired from Rite Aid and about how she had punched the supervisor in the face. She didn't want to tell him but figured that if she got arrested, she was going to have to call him anyway. She knew she wasn't going to call Tammy. Tammy was her girl, but she knew that Tammy had saved up a lot of money to attend school, and she didn't want to put her in the position of tapping into her education money.

"What? You fucking jumped on a supervisor? What the hell is wrong with you? Why you gotta be so damn ghetto all the time?"

"What the hell was I s'posed to do, just let her ass disrespect me?"

"How, Ivory? How did she disrespect you? Did she say something about your height? 'Cause we both know how you hate to be teased because yo' ass is tall."

"No, she didn't," Ivory said, getting agitated. "She gave me the finger, so I right crossed her ass," Ivory said, throwing a punch at the air.

"And what if she'd had yo' ass arrested, then what? What the fuck would yo' ass have done then?" Ivory didn't answer because she knew where Darnell was going with his statement. But instead of letting her off the hook, he answered for her. "I would've had to bail yo' ass out, that's what!"

Ivory couldn't say a word. She was pissed that he'd thrown it in her face like that, but she couldn't dispute the fact that his money would've been spent on her bail. Darnell pulled into the parking lot and parked. The frown on his face told Ivory that he was upset about the situation.

Oh, well. I'll just suck the nigga off later. He'll be a'ight, she thought as she got out of the car. As soon as they got into the restaurant and sat down, Darnell's phone rang.

"Damn, who in the fuck is this calling me this early?" Irritated, Darnell snatched the phone off of his hip and looked at the screen. His mood changed instantly when he saw who it was.

"Yo, what's up, dawg?" Darnell listened intently for a few seconds before smiling and nodding. "Where you at right now?" he asked. "Oh, cool then. I'm up here at Bob Evans. Come on up."

"Who was that?" Ivory asked. The last thing she wanted was for someone to intrude on their quality time. Besides, she wanted to hit him up for some cash and knew there was no way he was going to break her off if someone else was around.

"Just an associate of mine. Look, I gotta run to the bathroom right quick. If a light-skinned dude with a short Afro comes in here looking for me, come get me."

"Come get you?" she asked, snaking her neck. "I ain't coming in no damn men's bathroom to get you."

Darnell glared at her. He wanted to clown her and remind her of the time she followed him in the bathroom of a bar and gave him head in one of the stalls, but he refrained from it. "Look, ain't nobody asking you to come in the fucking bathroom. All I need you to do is yell inside of it, a'ight?"

Darnell didn't even wait for an answer as he headed toward the back. It was at that moment that Ivory discovered she'd left her cell phone in Darnell's car. She looked across the table and saw that he had left his car keys on the table. Feeling naked without her phone, Ivory picked them up and started to get up.

"Are you ready to order yet?" asked a skinny-looking woman with her hair wrapped up in a bun.

"Not yet. My boyfriend is in the bathroom, and I have to run back out to the car for a minute."

The woman rolled her eyes and walked away. Dismissing her with a raised middle finger, Ivory hurried to the car to get her phone. She opened the door and looked on the seat, but she didn't see anything. She then reached her hand up under the seat and felt for her phone. She couldn't feel anything, so she leaned down and looked. Not only did she see her phone, but her eyes got moon big as she also spotted a large bag filled with weed.

"What the fuck? That nigga told me that he ain't have no more weed," she fussed. "Lying muthafucka." As fast as she could, Ivory closed and locked the car door. A few seconds later, a car pulled up beside her, and a man fitting the description of the one Darnell described to her hopped out.

"What, the muthafucka didn't want to get his hands dirty?" the man asked, mistakenly thinking that Ivory was there to make the deal for Darnell. "You got the smoke?"

"Uh, Darnell had to go to the bathroom. Let me go get him," she said as she started to get out of the car.

"What? Go get him? Nah, sweetheart, I ain't got that kind of time. Tell that nigga I'm gonna get up wit' him later." The guy then stroked his goatee and thought for a second. "You know what?" he said as he leaned into Darnell's ride while taking a folded brown paper bag out of his pocket. "Just put the shit in here."

Before Ivory could say a word, he threw the bag into her lap and reached into his other pocket. He then took out a roll of money wrapped in a rubber band and tossed it to her. Ivory just sat there frozen.

"Damn, girl, hurry the fuck up! I gotta go!"

Without a second thought, Ivory reached up under the seat and took out the bag of marijuana. She then stuffed it into the paper bag and handed it to him. After the man jumped back into his car and pulled off, Ivory nervously walked back toward Bob Evans, wondering where the hell Darnell was. By the time she got back to her seat, Ivory was a nervous wreck. Although she smoked weed faithfully, she wasn't a drug dealer, and the whole episode had her slightly shook. A few seconds later, Darnell came running back toward the table.

"I gotta run to the car. Damn, I hope I ain't missed this nigga," he mumbled to himself. "This deal is worth five grand."

"He's gone," Ivory said.

"Gone? What you mean he gone?"

"He left."

"What?"

Darnell grabbed his phone and immediately started dialing. After the phone went to voicemail, he slammed it shut and jammed it back on his hip. "Fuck," he said a little louder than he wanted to. He ignored the stares of the other patrons in the restaurant and plopped back down into the seat.

"Don't worry about it, baby. I took care of it."

Darnell narrowed his dark pupils on Ivory. "What do you mean, you took care of it?" he asked.

"Well," she started, "I left my phone in the car, and when I went back to the car to get it, he pulled up beside your car. He said he didn't have time to wait for you and was about to leave. So instead of letting you lose out on getting that dough, I stepped in and handled that shit for you."

"How the hell did you know where I had my shit at any muthafucking way? Was you snooping through my damn car?" he whispered in anger. Just as Ivory was getting ready to defend herself, Darnell's cell phone went off.

"Hello," he answered with his eyes still trained on Ivory.

"Damn, nigga, where the fuck was you at? You lucky you got a down-ass broad like that on yo' team to handle business for yo' ass when you in the damn bathroom takin' a dump. 'Cause if you didn't, yo' ass woulda just missed out on five Gs."

"Hold on for a second." Darnell held the phone to his chest so that his customer, Dwight, couldn't hear him. "Give me my damn money," he snarled at Ivory.

"You could've said thank you to a bitch." Ivory reached into her pocket and pulled out the wad of money.

Darnell quickly took it and stuffed it into his pocket. "Dwight? You still there?"

"Yeah, I'm still here."

"I'm sorry about that shit, man. A nigga just had to take one of them monster dumps, though."

"It's cool. But peep game, though. I'm gonna probably need more in a few days. Think you can handle that?"

"Just holla at me. I'm sure we can do some type of something," Darnell said, not wanting to say too much of anything on a cell phone.

"Bet. But you need to treat yo' bitch to dinner or something. She stepped up for you for real."

"I'll keep that in mind. I gotta go. I'm gonna get up with you later."

After hanging up with Dwight, Darnell just stared at Ivory for a minute. Just as he was about to speak, the waitress came back and asked them if they were ready to order. Apparently, she'd gotten tired of waiting on them and wanted to know if the bickering couple was now ready to eat.

"Are you guys ready to order now?" she asked.

"Yeah, we ready."

After they ordered, the two continued to stare at each other. Ivory folded her arms over her chest and gave Darnell a defiant look. She honestly didn't know what he was so upset about. If it weren't for her, his ass would've lost out on quite a bit of money. If anything, he should've been breaking her off a nice piece of bread.

After the staring contest lasted a full ten seconds, Darnell reached back into his pocket and pulled the money out. Then he peeled off $500 and handed it to Ivory. "Good looking out on that."

"Thanks," Ivory said as she took the money.

"Something wrong?" Darnell asked when he saw the look on Ivory's face.

It wasn't that Ivory wasn't appreciative of the bread that Darnell had just broken her off with. She just felt that since she did all the work, she deserved a bigger piece of the pie. "Nah," she lied.

As the two of them sat there enjoying their meal, Darnell seethed. The last thing he wanted was for Ivory to find out what kind of money he was making while grinding. Now she was going to stay in his pockets.

Meanwhile, Ivory was thinking that since she didn't have a job anymore, maybe she could get her hustle on and make some money by slinging weed packs. She smiled as she thought of the quick cash she could make. She also thought of all the weed she could smoke if she had her own to sell. She would talk to Darnell about it later and see if he would put her on.

Red walked into the IMG jewelry store with mixed emotions. He hated spending money on women, but it was Cookie's birthday. Deep in his mind, he felt it was enough that he was throwing her a party. He was spending a mint on the hall, DJ, and food. But Cookie had been begging him for the last three months for a diamond bracelet. Red smiled. The things that he was doing for Cookie would probably get him two weeks of the nastiest sex he could imagine. He just hoped that she would bring some friends to the party for his crew.

Red peered inside the glass case. He took one look at the bracelet and shook his head. Cookie had dragged him down to the store twice in an attempt to get him to get it for her.

"Good afternoon, sir. May I help you with something?"

Red looked up at the shapely saleswoman. His eyes lingered on her size-six hips and her jet-black weave that she had pulled back in a ponytail. Her skin was light brown in color, and her eyes glistened like glass polished with Windex. If he weren't there to buy his main bitch a gift, he would have definitely tried to crack for her phone number. Red figured that she must've been a new employee since he didn't see her there the two times Cookie brought him there. He made a mental note to try to get her digits the next time he came in.

"You sure can, Ms. Tasha," Red answered, reading the name tag pinned to her shirt. "How much is that bracelet right there? I'm thinking about buying my mother an early birthday gift," he lied.

The saleswoman picked up the bracelet and examined the price tag. "This particular bracelet right here is twenty-seven hundred dollars."

"Price is no object," Red said, waving his hand as if he didn't know what the price of the bracelet was.

"Okay. Let me just ring this up for you, put it in a gift box, and you can be on your way." Red continued to admire her frame as she punched numbers into the cash register. "With tax, your purchase comes to $2,900.16."

Red reached into his pocket and pulled out a knot of money. He slowly peeled off thirty $100 bills and laid them on the counter. The look in the woman's eyes told him that she was impressed. Red wondered how long it would take and how much he would have to spend to get between her legs.

"Here is your change, sir."

As Red took his change, he rubbed her hand gently. The woman blushed and quickly looked around to see if anyone was looking.

"One day, I hope to meet a girl I can spoil with gifts like this," he said to her.

"I have to go, sir," she said as she walked off, blushing and smiling. "You're going to get me into trouble."

Red smoothly walked out the door feeling that it was just a matter of time before he was blowing her back out.

After jumping back in his truck, Red took off down the street. Before he got to the corner, he was dialing Bobby's cell number. "Time to take care of that little situation that ran up on us earlier." Red then hung up and smiled as he thought of the intense pain that he was about to cause his would-be jackers.

As Red got close to Richmond Road, he spotted a police car. "Fuck," he screamed as he was caught by the light. The police car coming from the opposite direction turned in front of Red's truck. The officer mean-mugged him as he passed. As the officer turned his head to look back at the road, Red gave him the finger. While sitting at the light, waiting for it to change, Red spotted a thick hottie sitting at the bus stop.

Normally, Red wouldn't have given a second thought to a white girl, but the girl's body was banging so loud it couldn't be ignored. *Damn, that bitch thick as fuck,* Red thought as he eyed the girl hungrily. He quickly rolled down his window before the light could change, and he went into mack mode.

"Hey, baby. What you doing out here in this heat? This shit can't be good for your pretty skin."

"You talking to me?" Nancy responded.

"Hell yeah, beautiful. Why don't you let me give you a ride and get you outta this heat?"

"How do I know that you not gonna take me somewhere and try to do something to me?" she asked flirtatiously.

"I ain't like that. I won't do nothing to you that you don't want me to do."

Nancy stood up and switched her way over to Red's truck. Red hit the automatic locks and stared at her with lust in his eyes as she got inside. He ignored the blows of various horns as he tried to get a peek under the blue jean miniskirt that Nancy was wearing. But while he was trying to see Nancy's goodies, she was looking at his Rolex watch, diamond-encrusted necklace, diamond-filled pinky ring, and hustler-style clothes, and she knew automatically that she was in the presence of a baller.

"Where you headed to, pretty lady?"

"Work. I work at JCPenney at Richmond Mall."

"Is that right?" Red asked as he tried to figure out the best approach to try to get some ass. From the looks of Nancy, Red figured that she was a sack chaser. He just needed to know what her price would be to give up the good-good. "What time you get off? Maybe we can kick it later on."

"Around seven," she said with wicked intentions in her mind. "And since I ain't got shit else to do, I will be glad to hang out with a nice-looking man like you."

After giving Red her phone number, Nancy got out of Red's truck and walked toward the mall. Just because she knew he was looking, she put a little extra shake into her hips.

Damn, that bitch got a body like a sista. I can't wait to rip a hole in that pussy.

Chapter 13

Stars danced in front of Dennis's eyes. A blackout seemed inevitable as the pain in his right foot reached new heights. A wicked smile fell across Red's face. With a cigarette dangling from his lips, Red raised the aluminum baseball bat high over his head. Then he paused for a few seconds to let his sadistic intentions take hold of his victim's mind. Although Bear and Rick were still tied to their respective chairs, they would not have been able to move even if they were free. They were both far too paralyzed with fear. A half-second before bringing the bat down, Red looked at Rick and smiled. Bobby let out a satanic laugh as the bat came crashing down on top of Dennis's big toe. No sooner had the sound left his mouth than it was cut short by a right hook courtesy of Hank's deadly hand. The impact of his punch instantly broke Dennis's jaw.

"Shut up all that bitch-ass hollering! Don't nobody wanna hear all that sucka-type-ass shit," Red scolded. After taking a long drag off of his Newport, Red blew smoke directly into Dennis's face. "Did you actually think that you was gonna pull a fucking heist on me?"

Red backhanded Dennis so hard his pinky ring left a two-inch gash across Dennis's cheek. Red ripped the duct tape off Dennis's mouth, causing more pain. Tears flooded Dennis's eyes as he began to beg for mercy.

"Oh God, please, man, don't kill me! I'm sorry, I'm—"

"Shut the fuck up," Bobby screamed. "Don't ho up now!"

Red knelt down in front of Dennis. He was so close that Dennis could smell the cheeseburger he had for lunch. "I guess you trying to eat out here, huh? Is that why you tried to fucking rob us? 'Cause you hungry out in these streets? Well, you know what? I'm gonna feed yo' bitch ass!" Red got up, walked over to a table, and grabbed a large roll of duct tape. "I'm gonna teach you bitch-ass niggas what happens when you try to rob me!"

"Come on," Dennis continued to plead. "Think of my cousin. It's gonna fuck him up if something happens to his family."

Red, Bobby, and Hank all started laughing at the same time.

"Ray-Ray ain't even yo' blood cousin, and he don't like yo' punk ass anyway," Bobby told him.

Red walked over to Dennis, tore off a large piece of tape, and wrapped it around Dennis's eyes and head. "Open yo' mouth, muthafucka! Since yo' ass is hungry for cheese, I'm gonna feed yo' ass something that's close to it!"

Dennis was scared to death. He didn't know what Red was about to do, but he knew that it wasn't going to be pleasant. Still, whatever it was, it seemed like following Red's orders was the only way he was going to get out of this. Hank snickered as Dennis obeyed Red's order and opened his mouth.

"Wider!"

Dennis's jaw was killing him. It was going to be a monumental struggle for him to open his mouth as wide as they wanted him to. Slobber and blood ran out the corner of his mouth as he agonizingly stretched his mouth open.

Red went back to the table and picked up a small white box. He quickly walked back over to Dennis, opened the box, pulled out the small rodent that was in the box, and shoved it into Dennis's mouth. Before Dennis could react, Red slapped a piece of tape on his mouth. With his hands tied up, Dennis was powerless to save himself from the horror. He desperately shook his head from left to right in a vain attempt to free the tape from his lips. With nowhere else to go, the small white mouse traveled down Dennis's windpipe and became lodged.

The three goons looked on in sadistic satisfaction as Dennis's body shook violently before slumping over in the chair. When Bobby looked over to where their other two future victims were, one had passed out while the other one's bowels had released.

"Nasty muthafucka. Bobby, shoot both of them mutha-fuckas in the head, and let's roll the fuck up out of here," Red ordered.

Tammy walked out of JCPenney a tired young lady. After hanging out deep into the night with Ivory for a second night in a row, all she wanted to do was go home and fall face-first into her bed. She was almost to the bus stop when a car pulled up next to her. She did a double-take and remembered that it was the same car Steve had been driving.

"Hey. You need a ride?" he asked in a way that made Tammy's skin crawl.

Just as she was about to tell him no in a not-so-nice way, Ivory pulled up blowing her horn. "No. Thanks. I already have a ride."

The look on his face said that he was none too pleased with the way Tammy blew him off. Steve screeched off with an attitude as Tammy got into Ivory's car.

"Who the fuck was that?" Ivory asked.

"That's the nigga who was screwing my mother when I got home that day."

"Whaaattt? That's ol' sweet back, huh?"

"That muthafucka gives me the fucking creeps. I swear I think I've seen that nigga somewhere before." The two rode in silence for a few seconds before Tammy suddenly realized something. "Whoa, wait a minute. How the fuck did that nigga know where I worked?"

"And what the fuck is he doing here to pick you up?" Ivory chimed in.

Tammy opened her cell phone and called her mother. When Janice answered, Tammy didn't even bother to say hello. "Ma, did you tell Steve where I work?"

"Uh, hello to you too, missy. And yes, I told him."

"Why would you do that?"

"Calm the hell down. I was just telling Steve how you had to catch the bus home, and he offered to pick you up. I didn't think you would mind someone giving you a ride home. I would think you would be grateful."

"I just met this guy. What makes you think I want to get in a car with someone I barely know?"

"I know him. He's my boyfriend, and I would appreciate it if you started showing him some respect. Don't think that I didn't notice how you came in last night and spoke to me without speaking to him."

Tammy was speechless. It had been a long time since her mother had gotten mad at her. *How the fuck is she going to try to check me over some nigga she just met?*

"And since you don't seem to have anything else to say, I'm about to hang up." Without even saying goodbye, Janice hung up in her daughter's face.

"What the fuck?" Tammy screamed while looking at her cell phone. "She hung the fuck up on me!"

"You messing with her dick," Ivory teased her.

"That shit ain't funny!"

Ivory just shook her head and smiled. The second she heard Tammy use the word "ain't," she knew she had struck a nerve. "Damn, my bad. Don't get all sensitive and shit. I was just playing wit' yo' ass."

"I know. I'm sorry. There's just something about that muthafucka that rubs me the wrong damn way. Thanks for coming to pick me up, too. I really didn't feel like riding the damn bus today."

Ivory looked at her like she was crazy.

"Why the hell are you looking at me like that?"

"Yo' ass don't need to smoke no more damn weed. Don't you remember, girl? You asked me to come pick you up today."

"Oh, that's right. I totally forgot."

"That old muthafucka got yo' head fucked up like that? You betta keep an eye on that nigga then. He might be one of them tag-team niggas."

Tammy gave Ivory a strange look. "What the fuck is a tag-team nigga?"

"You don't know what a tag-team nigga is?"

"No. That's why I asked."

"That's a damn shame. Yo' ass ain't up on shit. A tag-team nigga is a muthafucka who likes to try to fuck both the mother and the daughter. You know. Tag-team in that coochie."

Tammy's mouth fell open in shock. " I wish that muthafucka would try some bullshit like that on me! I'd have Hakim stomp a mudhole in his muthafucking ass!"

"That old nigga gon' fuck you and Hakim up," Ivory instigated.

"You've got me and my baby brother fucked all the way up if you believe some shit like that! We'll bury that muthafucka in Lake Erie!"

"I know that's right," Ivory agreed while giving her friend a high five.

"I just can't shake the feeling though that I've seen his face somewhere before "

"You sure it wasn't at the free clinic?" Ivory cracked.

"Oh, you got jokes? You're the only one around here in need of penicillin shots."

The two friends laughed long and hard as they continued to make fun of each other.

"What's up wit' yo' bad-ass li'l brother, anyway? What he been up to?"

"You said it right the first time. Being bad as fuck. He hasn't said too much since my mother went upside his head with a spatula. I think it hurt his feelings more than anything else, though. You should've seen my mother's face when she hit him."

"What she hit him for?"

"I didn't tell you? That silly-ass boy had the nerve to say something about selling drugs! In her house!"

"Whaaattt? I know that li'l nigga done gone crazy the way yo' mom feels about drugs."

"I know, right? But what really fucked him up was when she told him that she would bury him right next to our father."

Ivory shook her head. "That's some foul-ass shit to say right there."

Tammy shrugged her shoulders. "I guess she thought that when he jumped up, he was going to hit her or something."

"I doubt that shit. That nigga ain't crazy."

"Yeah, but you know how mothers are. They always think their kids are trying to test them."

"Is your brother fucking yet?" Ivory asked out of the blue.

"What? I don't know, and why the hell are you worried about some shit like that?" Tammy asked with a raised eyebrow.

"Calm yo' ass down. I was just asking. When the fuck did you get so sensitive?"

"Hummph, whatever," Tammy mumbled as she cut her eyes toward her friend. There was something in the tone of Ivory's voice that didn't quite sit well with her. Knowing that her friend had been around the block a few times, the last thing Tammy wanted was to fall out with her over her brother.

It wasn't that she thought Ivory wasn't good enough for Hakim. But Tammy knew that with Ivory's experience and looks, she would have Hakim wrapped around her finger in no time. She definitely didn't want to lose her best friend because she hurt her brother.

As Ivory continued to drive, Tammy noticed for the first time that they had passed her house and were coming up on Superior Avenue. "Where the fuck are we going?"

"To Hot Sauce Williams on 123rd. I figured I'd treat your broke ass today."

"Broke? I'm hardly broke. You know how much money I've saved for college?"

"That shit's for school. I ain't talking about shit that you can't spend."

"Anyway," Tammy said, ignoring her friend's comment, "what's up with the birthday party Cookie is having?"

"Oh, it's gonna be Tizzano's Party Center tonight."

"Tonight? When the hell were you going to tell me?"

"I just told yo' ass."

"Whatever. Hey, can I bring somebody?" Tammy asked, thinking about Nancy.

"Who?"

"Nancy."

"Who the fuck is Nancy?"

"My coworker."

"You talking 'bout that dusty-looking-ass white girl you introduced me to the last time I came to your job?"

"Yeah. Girl, she's cool people."

"I don't know about that one. I'm gonna have to ask Cookie about it."

"Well, just get back to me and let me know what she says."

Ivory yanked so hard into the parking lot Tammy was thrown into the passenger's side door.

"Damn, why are you pulling up in here like you're the police?"

Ivory smiled and ignored her, and the two women entered the restaurant. Fifteen minutes later, they walked out of the place with Tammy shaking her head.

"I don't know if I would eat that. Not the way you talked to them folks for taking so long."

"Please. I wish I would find out one of them bum bitches did something to my food. I'll come back up here and stomp a mudhole in that ho's ass."

Tammy laughed hysterically at her friend. She knew from experience, though, that Ivory meant every word she said. "Why does your ass always have to . . . What the fuck?" Tammy stopped dead in her tracks.

"What? What's wrong?" Ivory asked. Ivory followed her friend's stare. Her gaze finally came to rest on the handsome young man across the street. With him stood some of the neighborhood's most notorious young drug dealers. Without waiting for the light to turn, Tammy stormed across the street. People yelled and cursed as cars narrowly missed each other trying to avoid her. She ignored them and continued on her mission toward a blowup. As soon as the light changed, Ivory was right behind her.

"What the fuck is wrong wit' you? You trying to get yo'self killed or something?" She, too, was ignored as Tammy gorilla stomped across the concrete sidewalk.

"Hakim!" she screamed when she got within ten feet of him. Hakim heard her but chose to ignore her, which only fueled her anger. "Hakim! Boy, I know you hear me talking to you!"

The fact that her baby brother was ignoring her made her furious. She reached up with her right hand and tried to grab his shoulder. She tried to spin him around, but he responded by snatching his arm away from her.

"I know you hear me! What the hell are you doing out here on the corner with these damn thugs?"

The other three hoodlums looked at each other as if they had no idea who she was referring to.

"Damn, sis, chill the hell out! Ain't nobody doing shit!"

"Chill out? What the fuck is that in your hand?" Tammy asked when she noticed him trying to put his hand behind his back. Right on cue, one of the thugs slipped behind Hakim and took the bag of rocks out of his hand.

"I saw that shit," Ivory screamed. "Stop covering for his ass!"

"You need to mind yo' muthafucking business," one of the tatted-up thugs spat. He wore an unpleasant scowl on his face, and his thick braids protruded through the doo rag he had wrapped around his head.

"Li'l boy, I'll slap the shit outta yo' ass out here," Ivory threatened.

"And I'll beat yo' muthafucking ass out here too," the thug responded with a threat of his own.

"Let's do this shit then," Ivory said as she started taking off her earrings. Hearing Ivory call him little again caused him to become incensed. She was at least four inches taller than he was, so it was no surprise that he would take exception to it. He took a step toward Ivory but was stopped in his tracks by Hakim.

Hakim wasn't stupid. He knew that if Ivory got into it with the thug, his sister was going to get involved. He also knew that the thug was strapped. In his mind, there was no sense in all three of them going to the morgue.

"Dru, I got it. Ivory, you need to be cool. This ain't even none of yo' business."

"Anything that involves my girl is my business!"

"Yo, my dude, you betta check that broad before I put some heat to her ass!"

"Whateva, nigga!"

"What the hell are you hiding, Hakim?" Tammy asked, dismissing every other statement that was being uttered.

"Ain't nobody hiding shit! Take yo' ass on somewhere!"

"You think I'm stupid? I know what you call yourself doing out here, and trust me, there are better ways to make a living."

"Yeah, right. You mean by going to school like you?" Hakim asked as he spat out a laugh.

"Go to school?" Dru repeated as if the idea of higher education were something to be ashamed of.

"Yeah, school, you li'l ignorant bastard!" Ivory shouted.

"Ignorant? Fuck you, bitch!"

"Oh, I got yo' bitch, nigga," Ivory spat as she set her bag of food down.

"Yo, sis, you and Ivory need to take y'all asses on wit' that dumb shit!"

"You know what? Cool! Maybe I'll just go home and tell Mama what the hell you're doing out here! How do you think she will feel about that?"

"I don't know, maybe the same way she would feel if she knew yo' ass was smoking weed on a regular fucking basis! Now what?"

Tammy was shocked. Not only had she kept her habit a secret from her mother, but she was almost positive that she had kept it from Hakim, until now. She didn't want her mother knowing that she smoked weed, but in her mind, keeping her brother out of the streets was more important than her mother getting mad at her.

"You know? Whatever! I'm telling her as soon as I get home!"

"I don't give a fuck what you do! Just get the fuck out of my face!"

Before she could stop herself, Tammy hauled off and slapped Hakim in the mouth.

"What the fuck is wrong with you? Don't you ever put yo' muthafucking hands on—"

Slap! Hakim couldn't get the last word out before Tammy slapped him again.

"Ooh, she slapped the nigga again," one of the other thugs said.

Purely out of instinct and embarrassment, Hakim backhanded Tammy to the ground.

"Dayyumm, that nigga just slapped the shit outta his sister," said an innocent bystander who just happened to be waiting to get served. Hearing the word "sister" brought Hakim back to his senses.

"Oh, shit, sis. I'm sorry! I'm sorry," he repeated as he reached down to help her up.

"Get the fuck off of me!"

Ivory gave him a death stare as she helped Tammy up. The two of them walked back across the street and hopped in Ivory's whip. Tears formed in the corners of Tammy's eyes as she watched her baby brother start down the wrong path of life. Her jaw had already started to swell and was aching off the charts. But the pain shooting through her face was nothing compared to the pain of losing her brother to the streets.

"Why the fuck does she get to leave early?" asked one of Nancy's coworkers.

"First of all, watch your damn language in here. This is a place of business, not the street corner you're accustomed to. Secondly, because I said so. Now get back to work before I send you home permanently."

"But that's not fair, Mr. James. Whenever we get slow around here, she's always the one who gets to go home early."

"Let me tell you something," he said, stepping into her space. "I don't have to justify or explain to you why I make the decisions that I make around here. Now, I'm going to say this only one more time. Get back to work!"

Nancy smirked at the hater as she stormed by. She had informed her boss earlier in the day that she was going to have to leave early. But when he told her that there was too much work to be done and, therefore, she would not be able to leave, she decided to pull her trump card. Mr. James had no idea that, during their last screwing session, Nancy was secretly taping him on her cell phone. At first, he just laughed and told her that it could be anyone's voice on the recording. She agreed but then told him that she was willing to bet her paycheck that his wife would recognize the voice. She then laid down the law to him as far as what she expected to get away with, not to mention that she had plans to extort a few bucks from him from time to time to support her habit.

Looking at her watch, Nancy saw that she had forty-five minutes before she was actually scheduled to get off. After her growling stomach reminded her that she hadn't eaten anything all day, she decided to stop at the food court and get some nourishment. Thirty minutes later, she saw Red slithering through the mall with a few bags from Diamond's Men's Wear in his hand, talking with another man. As they got closer, Nancy could overhear their conversation.

"Why the fuck you keep asking me the same ol' shit? He yo' cousin. How the fuck should I know where he at?" an irritated Red ranted.

"I'm just asking 'cause Shavonda been bugging the shit outta me the last few hours. Plus, it ain't like that nigga to disappear and not say shit to nobody," Ray-Ray said.

"For the last time, I don't know where the fuck that nig-ga at, so stop sweating me about that bullshit! Oh, shit, what's up, baby girl?" he asked when he spotted Nancy at a nearby table.

"Nothing. Just waiting for you, big daddy. Hello," she said to Ray-Ray when she noticed him gawking at her.

"What's happening, sweet thang? My name is Ray-Ray, but you can just call me Sugar Ray," he said, trying to get his mack on.

"Why?" Nancy asked.

"Why what?" he responded with a strange look on his face.

"Why should I call you Sugar Ray? Is it because you're sweet like candy, or is it because you stick and move like 'Sugar' Ray Leonard?" Not only were they impressed with her quick wit but her knowledge of the legendary boxer as well.

"Take yo' pick," Ray-Ray said without missing a beat. "Whicheva you prefer."

"Ay yo, let's roll the fuck out,'" Red interrupted. "I got a party to go to tonight and a lot of shit to do before I start to get ready."

The three of them walked out of the mall and got into Red's truck. Ray-Ray twisted up his face as Nancy walked straight to the front passenger's side door, opened it, and hopped her thick frame into the front seat. He was about to say something, but Red silenced him with one of those looks that said there was a plan in motion. Truth be told, Red had forgotten all about telling Nancy that he was go-ing to pick her up. Since he now knew where she worked, Red figured that he was going to get the pussy sooner or later anyway, so in his mind, there was no need to rush it. He was basically at the mall to get some new shoes and clothes.

As soon as Red turned onto Monticello, he reached into his ashtray and picked up a half-smoked blunt. "Here, fire this shit up," he said, passing the icky back to Ray-Ray. In the rearview mirror, Red saw that he was still bent out of shape about having to sit in the back. Red just smiled, reached into his console, and pulled out a bag filled with cocaine. He closed the bag back up and set it on top of the console. Out of the corner of his eye, Red saw Nancy lick her lips. Subconsciously, she started sniffing like she was trying to keep snot from coming out of her nose. Nancy tried in vain not to look at the pure white cocaine. Red looked in the review mirror at Ray-Ray. He, too, was now smiling because all of a sudden, he realized what Red was doing.

"You okay over there, baby girl?" Red asked.

"Huh? Oh, yeah, I'm okay."

"You sure?" he asked, trying to bait her.

Nancy looked at the bag, then at Red, and then back at the white devil and sighed heavily.

"What? You want some of this?" Red asked, knowing full well what the answer was going to be.

Nancy, who was smart enough to know when someone had her figured out, decided to answer the question truthfully. "You know I do," she said with her eyes still glued to the bag.

"I would love to help you out, but to be honest with you, this ain't even my shit. This shit belongs to my buddy Ray-Ray back there."

Nancy's head snapped around so fast she almost caught whiplash. She was now looking straight into Ray-Ray's face as he took another puff of the blunt. "Sugar Ray, can I have some of your candy?"

"I don't know about that. That kind of candy is expensive. How much money you got on you?"

Nancy had heard this line before. Unbeknownst to Ray-Ray and Red, Nancy had been through this many times. This wasn't the first time she'd had to give up some ass or suck some dicks to get high, and it damn sure wouldn't be the last.

"Well, actually, I'm kind of broke right now, but I'm sure we can work something out," she said, licking her lips.

Red pulled into the parking lot of a corner store that he knew sold liquor. "Ay yo, I'll be back in a second. I'm gonna run in here and get a gallon of Cîroc."

As soon as Red got out of the truck and went into the store, Nancy got out of the front seat and made her way into the back. When Red came back, he wasn't surprised to see Nancy's head in Ray-Ray's lap, giving him a supreme blowjob. Ray-Ray's eyes rolled to the back of his head as Nancy worked her magic. "Mmmmm," she moaned as she tried to suck the skin off of his dick in anticipation of her powdered gift.

"Shit!" Ray-Ray yelled as he came deep down her throat. No sooner had she lifted her head up than Nancy was reaching for the white lady.

"Not so fast, baby girl. You obviously know how this game works, so after you rest ya jaws and we get to my place, you can get ready to work with a real monster," Red told her.

"Can't I have just a little?" Nancy asked, feening.

Red reached into his console once again and took out a mirror. He opened the bag, scooped out a small amount of powder, and placed it on the mirror. After giving Nancy a dollar bill, he watched as Nancy rolled the bill up into a tube, held the mirror up, leaned her head down, and sniffed the cocaine up into her nostrils.

Nancy lay back and smiled as the powerful drug took hold of her bloodstream. "That's what the fuck I'm talking about."

While Nancy floated up to cloud nine, Red continued to stare at her thighs, anxious to get her home so he could get up in some white girl pussy.

Chapter 14

Meanwhile, just off Interstate 271, Bobby was holed up in the Marriott with a pretty brown-skinned hottie he'd met after they'd taken care of the three fools who had made the fatal mistake of trying to rob him and his crew. Although the girl was doing a nice job of sucking him off, Bobby's mind was otherwise occupied. For as tough and ruthless as Bobby was, the one thing that he was missing in his life was love. Bobby may have grown up in the streets, but he was the product of a stable home. His father was a postal worker, and his mother was a librarian. When Bobby was younger, he was a very respectable young man with a passion for writing. He was well-mannered and respected females.

All that changed when he turned 15. After hearing their parents arguing over their father's suspected infidelity, Bobby's older sister, Robin, took him to the store to get him away for a while. When they returned, it was to a deathly silent house. Robin, getting an eerie feeling from the moment she stepped inside the house, told her brother to wait downstairs while she went upstairs to make sure everything was okay. Seconds later, her ear-splitting screams caused Bobby to run upstairs. When he got there, his life was turned upside down. The nightmarish scene that awaited him would haunt him until his dying day. He nearly threw up at the sight of his parents' brains hanging out the side of their heads. There was so much blood spilled that it had started to seep through the cracks in the wooden floor. While his sister screamed and cried, Bobby stood there in shock as his mother and father both lay on the floor, dead from gunshot wounds.

It was ruled a murder/suicide. With his sister being 21 years of age at the time, he was never in danger of being placed in foster care, but from then on, Bobby started hanging out more with his cousin Red. Although he loved his sister, Bobby saw his cousin as a role model. Red was the only other male in his family whom Bobby had a connection with. The two of them hadn't seen each other much before the incident, but their bond became stronger afterward. Soon after, he started selling drugs in order to keep money in his pocket. Robin tried in vain to keep him from falling victim to the streets, but the lure of fast money, shining jewelry, and easy women was too hard to resist. No one, including his sister, could ever give him a satisfactory answer as to why his mother had taken their father's life and then decided to take her own. But the one thing he did hold on to was the memory of the good times that their family used to have together.

He would often smile when he thought of all the fun his parents had as a couple and how they seemed to genuinely love and care for each other. He promised himself that, once he grew up, he would have that same kind of relationship that his parents had. Robin, on the other hand, had seen much more than Bobby had. She and her mother were very careful to keep it from Bobby that their father was abusing their mother physically and mentally. In Bobby's eyes, his father could do no wrong. He was the best father in the world. He would always make time for Bobby and had never ever hit him. That's why Bobby thought he was the best thing since sliced bread. All of the ugly things that were going on behind his back had been hidden from him. As a result of his mother's and sister's love for him, they shielded him from his father's beastly ways.

"You like that, baby?" the girl asked, breaking Bobby's train of thought. "Cum for me, baby. Cum for mama."

The girl continued to try to suck the semen out of Bobby's penis. Bobby grabbed the sides of her head and started thrusting in and out of her mouth as if it were a vagina. "Fuck," he yelled as he released a sea of swimmers down her throat. The girl made gulping sounds as her stomach was filled with liquid babies. Then she fell to the side of the bed, wiped the excess cum from the corner of her mouth, and placed it on her tongue.

"Mmmm, baby, you taste sooo fucking good," she said, as she swallowed the last drop. "I'll be back in a minute. I gotta go to the bathroom."

While she was in the bathroom, Bobby lay back on the bed and wondered if he would continue to fuck hood rats or if he would ever find that special someone.

"What? Girl, I know you ain't gonna make a bitch go to the party by herself," Ivory said. Even though she knew it was a possibility that Tammy would change her mind about going to the party after getting smacked by her brother, she was hoping that she wouldn't.

"If you think that I'm going to any kind of social outing with my face swollen, you must be crazy. I can't believe that muthafucka hit me!"

"Okay, I'm not taking up for him, but you did hit him first."

"That's because he called me out of my damn name!"

"Stop yelling at me!"

"I'm sorry. I don't mean to take this shit out on you."

"Look at it this way," Ivory said as she continued to try to get Tammy to go to the party. "If you stay at home, the only thing that's going to happen is that you and yo' brother gonna get into it. Wouldn't it be better if you just got out of the house and had some fun instead of being there and arguing with Hakim?"

Tammy thought about it for a second. "I still don't know. I'll have to look in the mirror to make sure I'm presentable."

"Well, go 'head then. I'll hold on."

Tammy set the phone down and got up off her bed. She walked over to her bedroom dresser and fearfully looked at herself in the mirror. She turned her head to the left and then slowly to the right. Although she was still experiencing some pain, her face was not quite as swollen as she thought it was originally. She had thought that it would continue to swell, but amazingly it had stopped.

"It's not as bad as I thought it would be. I thought it was really going to swell the hell up, but so far it hasn't."

"Then pick you out some clothes and let's party."

"Yeah, whatever. Did you call Cookie and ask her if I could bring Nancy?"

"Oh, yeah, she said it's cool, as long as she don't try to hit on her man. Hey, what did your mom say to you when you got home? She still pissed at you or what?"

"I have no idea. She's not even here. When you dropped me off, I walked into the house and expected her to trip, but she wasn't here. Then I found a note that said she was going to the movies with Steve."

"Steve, huh? You on a first-name basis with that nigga already?"

"Fuck no! I was just calling the asshole by name, that's all. I'm going crazy, though, wondering where I've seen his ass before."

"I wish I could help you out, but I didn't get that good a look at him when I picked you up from work the other day."

"Well, it'll come to me sooner or later. What time do you want to leave for this party?"

"I don't know, probably in a couple of hours. It's eight o'clock now, and I damn sure don't wanna be the first bitch in the damn door."

"That's cool. That will give me time to call Nancy and see if she wants to go."

"Damn, you ain't called her ass yet?"

"Uh, no. I was waiting to see if Cookie would say that it was all right first."

"Oh, yeah, my bad. Must be the weed."

"Uh-uh, heifer, don't blame it on the good herb. I smoke weed just like you do."

"Yeah, yeah, whatever. Just be ready in a couple of hours, tramp." Ivory laughed and hung up before Tammy had a chance to respond.

Ivory had just hung up with Tammy when she heard a knock at her front door. She rolled her eyes as she walked toward the door, wondering who it could be. She wasn't expecting anybody, so it annoyed her that someone had just popped in on her without calling her first. She opened the door and smiled when she saw Darnell's handsome face standing in front of her.

"Hey, baby, what you doing here?"

"I gotta go out of town for a few days."

Ivory's smile instantly became a frown. With Darnell out of town, her refrigerator empty, and only $500 to her name, Ivory wondered how she would make do.

"Don't worry," he said as if he were reading her mind. "I'm gonna give you some more money before I leave."

"It ain't just about the money," she lied. "I'm gonna miss you." She walked up to him and kissed him passionately on the lips.

"I'm gonna miss you too. But I gotta make this trip. I got some important business to take care of up in New York. Here," he said, handing her a black bag that was slung over his shoulder. Then he reached into his pocket and gave her a cell phone. "Do not use this phone to call anybody. If it rings, answer it. I done already told my dude that you may be handling business for me on this end."

Darnell opened the bag and revealed the ten pounds of weed inside. Immediately Ivory started thinking about all the weed she was going to be able to smoke. Knowing exactly what she was thinking, Darnell figured he'd better nip this in the bud right now.

"Get that fucking look off your damn face. This weed is for selling, not for you and yo' weed-smoking-ass home-girl Tammy to smoke up. That shit is on consignment, which means it ain't paid for yet."

"I know what the fuck consignment means. You think I'm stupid or something?"

"What? Ain't nobody call you stupid. Quit tripping."

"Annnyyway, I can't smoke none of it?"

"Hell nah! That's business weed! Here," he said, reaching into his other pocket and pulling out a smaller bag. "This is for you to smoke."

Ivory's eyes lit up as she gazed at the near-half pound of weed that was staring her in the face. "If that ain't enough for you and ya weed-smoking friend, then shame on y'all asses. Use that scale at the bottom of the bag to weigh the shit up if you happen to get a call from some-one who wants to cop some smoke."

"Okay."

Although Ivory may have thought that Darnell was showing her that he trusted her, in all reality, he had told his clients to call only if it was absolutely necessary. While he trusted Ivory to take care of one or maybe two transactions at the most, he in no way was going to put a lot of trust in her with any more than that.

"A'ight, I gotta roll. It's like a nine-hour drive from here to New York."

"Don't be going up there messing with them New York hoes either."

"I'm going up there on business. Ain't nobody thinking 'bout no muthafucking pussy."

"Yeah, right," she said. "But just in case you forgot who got the best pussy around," she said as she grabbed his belt buckle and pulled him in the bedroom, "I think I should remind you."

As soon as they got into her bedroom, Ivory dropped to her knees and unzipped Darnell's pants. After getting him nice and hard with her dick-sucking skills, she stood up and took off her clothes. Then she pulled him onto the bed and allowed him to enter her. The two had wild sex for an hour before Darnell finally convinced her that he had to leave and take care of business. As soon as he walked out the door, Ivory started scheming on how she could sell the weed and keep the money.

Nancy stood in her shower with her head hanging in shame. But no matter how long she stood there, no amount of soap or water could wash off the dirty feeling that was attached to her. What started off as a simple way to escape reality quickly turned into a full-blown addiction. Tears mixed with the water from the showerhead as Nancy contemplated getting herself some help. The more she thought about it, the more she seemed to be following her mother's path. Nancy wasn't the only one affected by her father's absence in her life.

It drove her mother right into the arms of a slick-talking heroin dealer. Not wanting to relive her painful past, Nancy shook off the hurtful memories of catching her mother giving oral sex to her dealer, and she stepped out of the shower. She had to fight to hold back the tears as she walked to her bedroom. Each step was more pain-ful than the last as she walked toward her bedroom. She had no idea when she accompanied Red to his place that he and Ray-Ray were going to play ping-pong on her vagina. She thought that she would give another quick blowjob and get paid for services rendered. But instead, the two thugs commenced blowing her back complete-ly out, which in turn left her walking extremely funny. Without even drying off, Nancy fell backward onto her bed.

She had almost drifted off to sleep when her cell phone rang and snapped her back from the land of the snoring. She had no intention of answering it until she looked at it and saw that it was Tammy. Tammy was one of the few real friends she had, so there was no way that she was going to jeopardize losing her friendship. Although she didn't feel like it, she answered.

"Hello?"

"Hey, girl, what's up? What are you doing tonight?"

"I don't feel like doing a damn thing except lying around the house and being lazy."

"Come on now. It's Friday night. Let's go out and have some fun."

"I just don't feel up to it," Nancy said, trying to get out of going anywhere.

"So, you're going to make me fly solo, huh?"

Now Nancy felt bad. Tammy had always been there for her, and now that she was asking for a favor in return, Nancy felt like shit because she didn't want to go.

"Tell you what. Give me an hour to catch a nap, and then we can kick it," Nancy said, praying to God that her sore coochie had healed enough by then. "Where do you want to go?" she asked.

"A friend of a friend of mine's man is giving her a birth-day party, and I got invited. I asked her if you could come along, and she said that it would be okay."

"Are you sure?" Nancy asked. "The last thing I wanna do is start trouble."

"All we're going to do is go there, score some free drinks from the wannabe ballers, and chill."

"Well, okay, if you're sure it's gonna be okay."

"I'm sure. We'll pick you up in an hour."

"We?"

"Yeah. Me and Ivory. Hell, you know I don't have a car."

"Who the fuck is Ivory?"

"My best friend. You know, the real tall chick who comes up to the job to see me sometimes? I introduced her to you the last time you were up at the store."

"Oh, okay. Well, let me get my nap on so I won't be sleepy as hell when you guys pick me up."

"All right. Be ready in an hour."

After hanging up with Tammy, Nancy set her alarm clock for an hour and fell asleep. An hour later, her alarm went off, and she jumped out of bed and ran to the bathroom. She had already taken a shower before she went to sleep, so all she had to do was get freshened up and dressed. She didn't know what kind of party to expect, so she went to her closet and took out one of her sexier outfits. She got dressed just in time, as she heard a horn blow seconds after applying the last coat of her lipstick.

"I'm telling you, Tammy, if yo' girl don't hurry the fuck up, I'm leaving her ass. I know she hear this damn horn."

"People in East Cleveland can hear that loud-ass horn," Tammy cracked.

"Whateva! I know she betta bring her trick ass on!"

Tammy cut her eyes at Ivory. "Please don't embarrass me by calling my friend out of her name."

"Ain't nobody gon' embarrass yo' prissy ass! You just betta make sure that yo' white friend don't make the mistake of calling me a nigga! 'Cause if she do, it's gonna take the whole Cleveland Police Department to pull my foot out her ass!"

"She's not going to call you anything but your name."

"Better not."

Tammy rolled her eyes again as Nancy walked over to the car and got in the back seat.

"Hey, what's up, girl," she said to Tammy.

"You, girl. You remember my friend Ivory."

"Hello, Ivory. How you doing?"

"I'm straight. Ready to get my party on. You bitches ready to roll?"

"You damn skippy," Tammy shouted as she turned her head to the side and looked at Ivory.

"What happened to your face?" Nancy asked when she gazed at Tammy's face a little closer.

"I don't even wanna talk about that shit right now. I'll tell you about it later."

"Put something in the muthafucking air," Ivory barked.

"I hope you have something to put in the air, because I damn sure don't."

"Girl, you ain't said a damn thing." Ivory reached into her purse and pulled out a super-fat blunt.

"Gottdamn, how the fuck did you get all that weed inside that fucking blunt?"

"Don't worry about that! Just fire this muthafucka uuuppp!"

Tammy gladly took the get-high tree from her friend and blazed up. The thick aroma of marijuana smoke filled the air as Tammy blew smoke rings.

"You wanna hit this shit?" Tammy asked Nancy.

"Maybe later. I'm cool for right now."

Shrugging her shoulders, Tammy took another pull from the blunt and passed it to Ivory. With one hand on the steering wheel and two fingers around the blunt,

Ivory inhaled deeply. She closed her eyes as she let the smoke ooze out of her mouth slowly.

"Open your muthafucking eyes," Tammy screamed. "What the fuck is wrong with you?"

"I got this," Ivory said as she continued to blow smoke into the air. Ivory then took her phone out of her purse and dialed. "Yo, Cookie! We on our way, so get ready to get live, gurrll!"

"I hope they have some good food there," Nancy said. "I'm hungry as hell."

"You didn't eat before you left the house?" Ivory laughed.

"Hell no. I assumed that they were going to have some damn food there."

"Yo' ass betta hope so. 'Cause once I get there, I ain't leaving until the party ends." Ivory pulled her car into the parking lot. After checking themselves in the mirror a few times, the three dime pieces got out of the car and headed toward the party.

Fifty people were jam-packed on the floor as the DJ skillfully blended a collection of old- and new-school jams. Cookie was ghetto fabulous as she sauntered around the room, showing off the bracelet that Red had bought for her. With her hair swept in a bun, combined with the six-inch see-through stilettos she was wearing, Cookie stood out larger than life. After showing off for the have-nots, Cookie walked back over to the bar area where her mother sat with a solemn look on her face.

"Ma, you gon' sit here and sulk all night, or is you gon' tell me what's up with this attitude?"

Cookie's mother just shrugged, finished off her vodka and tonic, and beckoned for the bartender to bring her another one. Cookie just shook her head and walked away. She had no idea why her mother was acting like a total bitch at her birthday party, but she was close to the point of not giving a fuck. She wasn't going to let anyone ruin her night, and that included her mother.

A wide smile broke across her face when she saw Ivory and Tammy walk through the door. At first, she was puzzled by the presence of the white girl with them, but then she remembered that Cookie had said something about Tammy bringing a friend with her. Because Ivory provided very little information, she assumed that Tammy was bringing a man with her.

"What's up?" Ivory shouted from across the room. "I see you got a real hairdo this time instead of looking like a fucking peacock."

"Fuck you," Cookie said as she hugged her friend and former coworker.

"What's shaking? Happy birthday," Tammy said.

"Thanks. I appreciate it."

Tammy hoped that Cookie didn't expect to get a gift from her. She didn't know her all like that.

Cookie looked at Nancy, who already felt out of place. "Hey, girl, my name is Cookie. And who might you be?" she asked.

"My name is Nancy. Happy birthday to you."

"Thanks." After Cookie and Nancy had been formally introduced, Cookie turned her head and stared directly into Ivory's face.

"What the fuck you looking at me like that for?"

"Please," she said as she leaned back and folded her arms. "You know exactly why I'm looking at yo' ass like this. Where the fuck is my gift?"

"Gift? Ain't nobody bring you no muthafucking gift."

Cookie didn't budge. She knew damn well that her friend was just playing with her. Ivory couldn't even hold a straight face as she tried in vain to pretend as if she didn't have anything for Cookie. Finally, she burst out laughing.

"You know I got you," she said as she reached into her purse. Knowing that Red had probably bought her something that no one would be able to compete with, Ivory had decided to hook her up with some of the weed that Darnell had left her with. She figured that since she only took a little bit, either Darnell wouldn't miss it when he got back, or she could just short some fool if she got a sale.

Chapter 15

Tizzano's Party Center was one of the classiest spots in the city. Even though it was small, it was highly elegant with silk drapes and wall-to-wall Persian carpeting. Crystal chandeliers hung over the tables and glistened in the lights. Red had put out a pretty penny to ensure that his main woman was good and happy. As Cookie ran off at the mouth with her friends, Red and Bobby were both posted up in the VIP section, tossing back shots of Hennessy and smoking blunts. Hank was with them, but instead of drinking liquor, he was chugging back beers.

"You really went all out for ya girlfriend this time," Bobby said to Red.

"How many times I gotta tell you she ain't my damn girlfriend?"

"If she ain't yo' girl, then why you spend all this cheese on her ass?"

"'Cause the pussy is the booomb!"

Hank looked around and shook his head. "All this cheese for some muthafucking coochie?"

"Coochie on call, my nigga, coochie on call."

"Ain't that her over there?" Bobby asked.

Red squinted and stared in Cookie's direction. "Yeah, that's her ass. I don't know who the hell them thots are with her, though."

"Let's roll ova there and find out," Hank said. "One of them other hoes might feel like fucking."

As they made their way over to where Cookie, Ivory, Tammy, and Nancy were standing, Hank asked about the whereabouts of Ray-Ray.

"He said he was going to meet us here. The nigga probably still running around looking for his dead-ass cousin," Red laughed.

"Damn, that was cold as fuck," Bobby said.

"Man, fuck that bitch-ass nigga. He lucky I didn't torture his ass worse than I did, trying to rob a nigga and shit." As the three of them passed the bar, Red looked over to where Cookie's mother was sitting. She twisted up her face in an evil scowl and shot him the bird.

"The fuck up with Cookie's moms? She usually cool as fuck, but she actin' like a straight bitch tonight," Bobby said.

"Fuck that bitch! She just mad 'cause I told her ass she can't have none of this dick tonight!"

Bobby stopped dead in his tracks. "You fucking Cookie and her mama?"

"Hell yeah. Shit, I ain't gotta tell yo' ass everything."

"If that ain't some foul-ass shit," Hank said, shaking his head.

"Listen, pussy is pussy," Red rationalized.

The minute they got close to the three women, Bobby felt something stir inside of him. He looked at Tammy and unintentionally started to stare.

"Yo, what's shaking, Cookie?" Red asked as he walked up to her and slapped her on the ass.

"Nothing but ass, baby, nothing but ass."

Nancy's face became flushed as she eyed Red. Her pussy got sore all over again as she remembered the pounding that he and Ray-Ray had put on her.

"I heard that. Ay, who ya friends?"

"This here is my girl, Ivory. She used to work at Rite Aid. You don't remember her? She was there when you came and picked me up a couple of times."

"Nah, not really," Red said as he eyed Nancy. Red slowly shook his head from side to side to subtly let Nancy know to keep her mouth shut.

"This is Tammy, and her name is Nancy," Cookie said as she concluded the introductions.

"How y'all pretty ladies doing?" Red asked as he extended his hand toward the women. As he shook each woman's hand, he made sure that he held on to Nancy's a little longer than he should have.

Cookie quickly cut her eyes at Ivory as if to say, "Didn't I tell you not to bring this ho up in here if she was gonna try some bullshit with my man?"

Ivory looked right back at her as if to say, "Hey, your man is the one holdin' her damn hand."

"What's up with you, pretty lady? You want a drink or something?" Hank asked Tammy.

Tammy took one look at Hank and got a bad vibe from him. "No, thanks. I'll get something later," she said. Although she chose to ignore him, she was quite aware that Bobby was staring at her.

"You gon' blink?" Red asked Bobby when he, too, noticed how he was looking at Tammy.

"What? Man, what the fuck you talking about?"

"Muthafucka, please! Everybody standing here see yo' ass staring at her!"

Bobby gave Red a hard stare. He didn't like Red putting him on blast like that and made a mental note to check his cousin about it later. "Worry about yo' own muthafucking business," Bobby said as he walked off in the direction of the bar.

Tammy watched him move with swift grace as his long strides ate up the distance quickly. Her inner thighs became moist.

"You a'ight?" Ivory asked.

"Huh? Oh, yeah, I'm straight."

"Uh-huh," Ivory said, twisting up her mouth. "It look to me like you feeling him."

"I don't even know that dude."

"That's my cousin, Bobby," Red chimed in. "Want me to introduce you to him?" Red asked.

"Nah, I'm straight."

"Shit, if he wanted to holla, he would've stayed his ass over here," Hank hated.

"Damn, somebody in the hate zone tonight," Cookie joked.

"What the fuck eva," Hank said, waving her off. Red started laughing his ass off. He thought it was hilarious how the whole scene was unfolding. He was just about to fuck with Hank for being a hater when his cell phone went off.

"Hello? A'ight, I'm gonna be over there in a few seconds," he said after listening to the caller. "Be back in a second. One of my little dudes is having trouble with security."

"I gotta go to the bathroom," Tammy suddenly said. "I'll be back in a minute." Nancy, Cookie, and Ivory all looked at each other and smiled.

"Guuurrrl, you know damn well she was feeling that nigga," Cookie said, giving Ivory a high five. Nancy, obviously uncomfortable with Cookie's use of the N word, looked down at the floor and picked at her nails.

"You want something to drink?" Ivory asked Nancy.

Nancy looked around as if she couldn't believe that Ivory was talking to her. "Who?"

"The fuck you mean, who? You!" Ivory screamed.

"Oh, yeah, that's cool."

"Yo' ass gon' have to loosen up if you gon' be hanging wit' us," Cookie said as she turned and walked toward the bar.

"Cookie, go ahead," Ivory told her. "We gon' meet you over there in a minute."

"Where y'all going?"

"We going to the bathroom to get Tammy."

"A'ight. Just hurry the fuck up. I'm ready to get my party on wit' you hoes."

Bobby posted up at the bar and watched Tammy and Ivory walk into the bathroom. He was definitely feeling her, but the company she kept left a lot to be desired. He wondered if she was a loudmouthed gold digger like Cookie. Even though Bobby was grateful that Cookie had looked out for him and Red on the jack move that Dennis was going to pull, there was no doubt in his mind that if Red were just another hustler struggling to make a come-up, Cookie wouldn't have given him a second thought.

That's why he didn't feel sorry for her, knowing that Red was screwing everything under the sun, including her mother. Bobby looked down to the other end of the bar and saw that Cookie's mother still had an attitude. Bobby just shook his head disgustingly, thinking that she was getting exactly what she deserved. He knew that there were some trifling women around the way, but to be fucking your daughter's man behind her back was a new low, even for the skeezers in the hood.

Every few seconds, Bobby would look over at the women's bathroom door. He had already made his mind up that as soon as Tammy walked out of it, he was going to spit game to her. He ordered another shot of Pinnacle vodka and sipped it as he waited for her to emerge.

"Hey, baby," he heard a sweet voice call from behind him. To say that he was caught off guard was an understatement as a slim, dark-skinned honey slid behind him and wrapped her arms around his waist.

"Kat, what the fuck you doing?" Bobby asked his former lover.

"Don't act like you don't like it."

"You know what? Get yo' fucking hands off of me," Bobby yelled, snatching away from her. "I ain't got shit to say to yo' lying ass! You're lucky I don't put a bullet in yo' ass for that shit you pulled!"

"I know you ain't still mad about that bullshit from back in the day, are you?"

Bobby looked at her like she had lost her mind. "You muthafucking right I'm still mad about that shit! What muthafucka wouldn't be mad at a bitch who tells him that he has a child and then he finds the fuck out that the kid belongs to somebody else?"

"I'm sorry about that. But I really did think that it was your child."

"Get the fuck outta my face with that bullshit! How the fuck did you get in here any muthafucking way?"

"Uh, Cookie is my cousin."

"I don't give a fuck what she is to you! You've got five seconds to get the hell away from me, or there's gonna be a problem."

Kat stared at Bobby for a few seconds before she realized that he was serious. She slung her shoulder-length weave over her shoulder and stormed off. It took everything in Bobby not to run up behind her and smash her in the back of her head with his gun.

After finishing his drink, Bobby was feeling nice. He wanted to order another one but decided against it. The last thing he wanted was for Tammy to think he was a lush. Normally, Bobby didn't give a damn about what other people thought of him, but there was something about Tammy that made him want to impress her. Something that made him want to look good in front of her.

He absentmindedly brushed invisible lint off of his clothes as he got up to go over and wait by the ladies' bathroom. The moment his eyes zoomed in on Tammy, he clicked the safety off of his gun and power-walked over to her defense.

Just Ten Minutes Earlier

"What's the damn problem over here?" Red asked. He was quite annoyed that he had to leave the party to see about some dumb shit like a couple of his little workers not being able to get into the party.

"This dude tripping, Red! Talking 'bout he don't recognize us so he can't let us in."

"They straight, man. Come on in, li'l niggas," Red said as he turned around and led them into the party center. The two young thugs mean-mugged the huge bodyguard as they made their way inside. The bouncer simply looked at them and smirked. He couldn't care less who got inside the place as long as he got paid.

Once they got inside, Red tuned to both of them and held out his hand. "A'ight, cough that dough up. I know damn well y'all done made a killing out there this week. Give me my cut and show me that I can trust y'all."

Both of them dug into their pockets and pulled out knots of money. They each peeled off $2,500 and handed it to Red.

"That's what's up! Now I ain't got to kill you niggas about my cheese," Red said, laughing. "Oh, and tonight I'm introducing y'all to my partner, Bobby. We the only ones you answer to, got it?" Like lost little puppies, the two juvenile delinquents nodded their heads.

"A'ight, cool. Go 'head and have fun, but don't be on no bullshit tonight," Red said, pointing at the shorter of the two, knowing that he had a quick temper. Red walked away and left the two of them standing there like two scolded children.

"I'm about to go to the bathroom and fire this weed up," the taller one, whose name was Cedric, said.

"Lead the way, my dude, lead the way," his partner in crime said. They started walking toward the men's restroom, but in order to get there, they had to go past the ladies' restroom. They were just about there when they almost bumped into two young ladies coming out of the women's bathroom.

"Well, look what the fuck we have here," Dru said as he eyed Tammy and Ivory.

"Excuse me, do we know you?" Tammy asked. Because she was so focused on her brother earlier, she didn't really look at Dru when she approached Hakim.

"Oh, so now you bitches don't know who the fuck we is, huh? After talking all that bullshit earlier, now you hoes wanna get amnesia!"

"Nigga, who the fuck you calling bitches and hoes? What I said earlier today still goes, muthafucka! I'll still slap the shit outta yo' li'l short ass," Ivory screamed.

It took a minute for Tammy to realize that Dru was the same guy Hakim was hanging out on the corner with earlier. "Oh, you're the dude my brother was with earlier," she said.

"You know what? Seeing that you my dude's sister, I'm gonna give you a pass, but this other bitch is gonna have to be taught how to respect a G."

"Ay yo, we got a fucking problem ova here?" Bobby asked.

"Who the fuck is you?" Cedric asked.

"I'm asking the muthafucking questions up in this bitch! Now, like I said, do we got a fucking problem over here?"

"What you need to do is mind yo' punk-ass business before—"

Crack!

Before his sentence was completed, Cedric crumbled to the ground as a result of being smashed upside the head with the butt of Bobby's gun.

"You want some?" Bobby shouted to Dru.

"What the fuck is going on ova here?" Red yelled as he made his way through the crowd that had started to form.

"I don't know who the fuck this bitch-ass nigga is, but he need to learn some fucking respect," Bobby said.

"Get the fuck off me," Cedric yelled as Dru tried to help him up. "Yo, Red, I'm about to blow this muthafucka's brains out!"

"You ain't gonna do shit but stand there and bleed," Red said in a calm voice. He wanted to laugh but didn't want to embarrass the youngster more than he already was.

"This punk muthafucka hit me with a gun, and I'm s'posed to just take that shit? Fuck that shit!"

Bobby raised his gun in the air again. He was about to hit Cedric in the head again, but Red grabbed his arm. "Be easy. I got it."

Bobby lowered his weapon and tucked it into the small of his back. "Y'all a'ight?" he asked Tammy and Ivory.

"I'm fine. Thanks," Tammy said.

"Yeah, we good," Ivory said, noticing how Bobby seemed to be talking more to Tammy than to both of them.

"First of all, li'l nigga, you need to start learning who the fuck you be talking to. This here is my cousin Bobby. The one I've been telling yo' ass about."

Cedric's mouth fell open. "Oh, shit! This the Bobby you been telling us about?" Cedric asked while still holding his head.

Bobby turned his head and faced Dru, who was giving him a sinister sneer. Bobby quickly locked eyes with him, showing the young thug that his heart didn't pump Kool-Aid. A speedy knot had already begun to form on the right side of Cedric's forehead. Dru and Bobby stared at each other for what seemed like an eternity before Red intervened.

"Let's take a walk," Red suggested as he draped his arm around Dru's shoulder. "Look," he said once they got out of earshot, "I know you tight about my cousin slapping yo' homie with his hammer and all. I would be pissed off at that shit too. But the last thing you want to happen is to blow making all this easy paper with us because of a little misunderstanding. Feel me?"

Dru nodded. He was mad as fuck about what happened but didn't want to let his temper stop him from potentially making large paper. Red and Bobby were blood cousins, so if it came down to it, Red would have no problem cutting Dru loose. So, because of that circumstance, Dru decided to let it slide. But he swore to himself that he would never forget what Bobby had done.

Bobby stared at the back of Dru's head as Red hauled the youngster away. There was something about the way Dru carried himself that made Bobby want to aim his pistol and put a bullet through the back of his skull. He got a bad vibe from the youngster and, therefore, didn't trust him.

Hank, who had been at the bar trying to talk his way into the pants of a sexy redbone, came walking up cracking his knuckles. After breaking Dennis's jaw earlier, he was itching to show off more of his pugilistic skills.

"I heard some niggas at the bar talking about a commotion, and I just knew you niggas was involved," he asked Bobby.

"Nothing I can't handle. Some li'l BG got outta line, and I had to tighten his ass up."

"You okay?" Hank asked Nancy, who had been quiet the entire time.

"Yeah, I'm okay."

"You sure? 'Cause you looking kind of shook right about now. Come on. Let me buy you a drink." Before she could say yes or no, Hank had her by the wrist and was pulling her to the bar. After being shot down by the red-bone, Hank was more determined than ever to dig into some fresh pussy.

"I hope that nigga don't think that he gon' buy her ass a drink and not get me one too," Ivory stated as she hustled off to catch up to Hank and Nancy.

"Thanks again for helping a sister out," Tammy said. Someone had to break the ice, and since he'd stepped up and stopped Dru from attacking her and Ivory, she figured that she owed him one, so to speak. She normally didn't care for guys who wore braids, but Bobby's were nice and neat, which made him even more attractive in her eyes.

"Don't worry about it. I couldn't let that nigga mark up a pretty face like yours."

Embarrassed by his kindness, Tammy started to blush. There was something about his rough but gentle nature that appealed to her. She wasn't a fool, though. She knew that anyone hanging around Red had a bad side to them. Even though she had only seen Red a couple of times, she was well aware of who he was. She couldn't ever remember seeing Bobby, though.

"What's ya name, pretty lady?"

"Tammy. What's yours, handsome man?" she asked, trying to embarrass him back. It didn't work.

"My name is Bobby," he said as he took her hand and gently kissed it. "Nice to meet you."

Tammy was amazed at how Bobby had gone from a head-splitting gangster one minute to a soft-spoken ladies' man the next. She definitely wanted to find out what was lurking beneath the surface of his rugged exterior.

"You hungry?" he asked.

"A little."

"Cool. They got all kind of wings and chips and shit over there on the snack table."

When they got over to the table, the servers tensed up. They, too, like everyone else, had seen Bobby hit Cedric upside the head with a gun.

"Be easy," he told them. "We're just here to get our grub on, that's all."

Bobby smiled at them, and they relaxed. After their plates were filled, they went to a nearby table and sat down. They started talking and sharing things about each other's lives that strangers normally didn't share with each other.

"Fuck outta here," Bobby said when Tammy revealed to him that she could sing.

"I'm for real. I can hit high notes like Whitney Houston."

"Let me hear something," Bobby challenged her.

"In here?" she said, looking around.

"Yeah, why not?" he asked.

Tammy thought for a minute and shook her head.

"Scaredy-cat," he said as they both laughed.

Bobby was very impressed that Tammy was on her way to college. He liked that she wasn't the same as many other chickenheads and gold diggers who did nothing more than wait for a man to take care of them. He was enjoying their conversation so much that he decided to let her in on a little-known secret of his own.

"Not many people know this about me, but I like to write."

"For real? What do you write, rap songs?"

"Hell nah," he said, laughing.

"Oh, sorry. I didn't mean to offend you. It's just that everybody wants to be a rapper nowadays."

"Not me."

"What do you write about?" Tammy asked, now genuinely interested.

"I like to write stories."

"Stories?" Tammy asked in a confused manner.

"Yeah. Hood stories, about the type of stuff that happens around here in the hood."

"Oh, I see."

"But even if it were rap, so what?" he said, smiling. "Hey, you can't knock someone's hustle or the way they eat, know what I mean?"

Tammy made a mental note that he had used the word "hustle." That alone pretty much told her what he did for a living. She didn't like to stereotype people, but the way she grew up was if it walked like a duck and talked like a duck, then Aflac. She was just about to ask him what he did to make ends meet when Bobby reached into his pocket and pulled out a blunt. After seeing the surprised look on Tammy's face, Bobby just shrugged his shoulders.

"Hey, if you're gonna be hanging around me, you might as well get used to seeing a nigga hit the trees."

"And who said I was gonna be around you that much?" Tammy said sassily.

"Oh, I didn't mean to imply that—"

Tammy burst out laughing before he could even finish his statement. "I was just playing with you."

"Oh, I see you like to play games, huh?"

"Sometimes. It depends on what kind of games you're referring to," she sexily said.

Bobby's dick almost punched a hole through his pants. His eyes lustfully traveled up and around her model-type frame. Her smile could warm even the coldest thug's heart. "Girl, you betta quit playing before you start something that you ain't willing to finish."

"I'm willing to finish anything I start."

Although Bobby's penis was as hard as a piece of steel, he had been around women trying to spit game too long to not know when he was being tested. Every fiber in his being wanted to call her on her bluff and ask her to go to his place. But he was smart enough to know that, from her conversation, Tammy was not the type of girl who gave it up easily, and if his calculations were correct, she would be more than worth the wait.

"Pretty lady, we just met. Don't you think we should take things a little slower?"

"If you say so," she said. Inside she was as giddy as could be. If Bobby had invited her back to his place, she would have walked away from him in two seconds flat. But because he didn't, she planned on giving all of herself to him . . . when the time was right.

Meanwhile, Nancy and Hank had snuck off to a nearby closet. After talking to Nancy for a few minutes, Hank had figured her out completely. He kept a bag of blow on him just in case he ran into the type of jump off Nancy was. It took Nancy all of five minutes to suck Hank to an orgasm. As soon as Hank left her in the closet alone, Nancy started sniffing. When she came back out to the party, she was so high that she couldn't see straight. Tammy, who was enjoying her conversation with Bobby, made the mistake of thinking that she was just tired. When she saw her with her head down, she thought she was sleeping and let her stay there until the party was over.

After Ivory dropped Nancy off, she turned to Tammy and asked her how long Nancy had been getting high.

"Getting high? Nancy doesn't get high."

"You crazy! That ho was high as fuck! If you weren't sniffing up behind Bobby's ass all night, you woulda peeped that shit," Ivory said, laughing.

"First of all, I wasn't sniffing up behind anybody's ass. And second of all, we had to take a drug test to get hired at our job."

"So fucking what? Maybe she started getting high after she started working there, and the boss is covering for her ass." When Tammy didn't respond, Ivory kept on talking. "How many one-on-one meetings does she have with your boss? I've met that asshole, and I see the way he looks at some of the white women who go shopping there. I betchu he bonin' her white ass."

Tammy remained speechless while wondering how in the world a good friend of hers could be on drugs and she not know anything about it.

Chapter 16

After putting in work on the block for more than half the night, Hakim decided to head home. Unbeknownst to Hakim's mother or sister, Dru had been trying to get Hakim to join his crew for a couple of months now.

"When you ready to make some real paper, come holla at me," Dru had said to him. So three days ago, Hakim did just that.

"Does that offer you made me about making some real paper still stand?"

"My word is my bond. You damn skippy the offer still stands."

"Good. 'Cause I'm tired of pitching in the minor leagues. It's time to step my game up to the majors."

Dru rubbed his chin and nodded. "A'ight. I'ma put you down, but first, you gotta prove ya'self."

"What do I have to do?"

"I'm gonna have you post up on the block with my boy James and see if you got what it takes to make money in the jungle."

While Dru and Cedric attended a meeting disguised as a party for Red's girl Cookie, Hakim and James stayed on the block and got off as much work as they could. A smile crept across Hakim's face as he counted out $3,500 for a few hours of work. He handed the money to James, who, after peeling off $500 and handing it to Hakim, stuffed the rest in his pocket. Hakim thought briefly about asking James to give him a ride home but let it pass. He figured there was no way in hell James was going to leave the spot unoccupied with the way the fiends were flocking toward them. Hakim had to wait almost forty minutes for a bus to arrive.

"Fuck this shit," he said to himself. "As soon as I save up enough bread, I'm gonna get me a muthafucking whip." Hakim stepped on the bus, paid his fare, and headed toward the back of the bus. He hadn't made it halfway before a beggar started hounding him for his money.

"Excuse me, sir, but could you spare—"

"Hell nah. Get a fucking job." Hakim cut him off.

The beggar frowned and flipped Hakim off once his back was turned. Hakim was already pissed about having to catch the bus in the first place. The last thing he wanted or needed was for someone to be trying to siphon off his hard-earned dough.

During the ride home, Hakim thought about his sister. He hated himself for hitting her. For the most part, they had always gotten along, and to see her lying on the ground as a result of his hand made him feel like stir-fried shit. He made a promise to himself right then and there that he would do everything in his power to make it up to her. He felt the side of his face and smiled slightly.

"I shoulda known that she was gonna slap the shit outta me when I called her out of her name like that," he mumbled. "That's another thing I gotta apologize to her for."

Hakim understood why Tammy went ballistic, and he appreciated that she was trying to keep him out of trouble. But Hakim was fast becoming a man. In his mind, that meant doing whatever was necessary to eat. If he was making enough to live on and have at least some of the things he wanted, he probably wouldn't be selling drugs. But the little money he was making wasn't enough to buy him a decent pair of jeans, let alone name-brand shit.

Hakim knew that Tammy would never understand where he was coming from because she would never be able to see the world through his eyes. In less than six months, Hakim was going to be 18 years old. He was tired of sneaking girls in and out of his mother's house. If he wanted to continue to get laid, he would definitely need to get his own apartment. Hakim was in such deep thought that he almost missed his stop.

"Shit," he yelled as he pulled on the yellow cord. The bus driver glared in the rearview mirror at Hakim as he brought the bus to a stop. Hakim ignored his stare as he jumped off the rear entrance of the bus and headed home. He looked across the street and noticed his ex-girlfriend, Nikki, walking alone. *The fuck she doing out here this time o' night?* he wondered.

"Hey, girl, what the hell you doing out here in the wee hours of the morning?"

"Oh, hey, Hakim. Come here for a minute."

"Where yo' boyfriend at?" Hakim asked. "I'd hate to have to fuck his punk ass up out here."

"Ain't nobody here but me. Come on and walk me home."

Although he didn't feel like it, Hakim knew the dangers of the neighborhood, so he decided to be nice. He quickly dashed across the street. The second he got close to her, Nikki's perfume attacked his sense of smell, causing his dick to do a somersault.

"You still ain't told me what the fuck you doing out here this late."

"'Scuse me? Don't be talking to me like you still my man," Nikki said, rolling her neck.

"Oh, is that right? Then you need to be calling that nigga to walk yo' smart-mouthed ass home."

"You know you wanna walk me home. And to answer yo' question, I was going to that Arab store that stay open late."

"For what?"

"Damn, you nosy. I wanted to get a box of swishers, okay?"

"I was just asking yo' smart ass."

"Mm-hmm," Nikki said as she turned and walked away from him. Nikki was a chocolate-skinned honey with more ass than a strip club. Her long, flowing weave hung to the top of her ass cheeks. She sometimes wore gray contacts, which only added to her sex appeal. Hakim licked his lips as he watched his ex's hot ass leave smoke trails on the sidewalk.

"You never did tell me what was up with you and ya man."

"We broke up, okay?"

"Nigga couldn't hit that shit right, huh?"

"Why you say that?"

"I can tell. That nigga don't know what to do with no pussy."

"Oh, and I guess you know what to do with it, huh?"

"Stop fronting. You know I used to put a hurting on that thang."

"Whatever!"

Hakim then intentionally slowed down so that he could get a good look at Nikki walking. The sexy way she switched her ass was turning him on.

Before the two of them knew it, they were standing in front of Nikki's apartment building. Hakim opened the door for her to go inside and was almost knocked down by a charcoal black nappy-headed youngster. The young thug gave Hakim the "what's up" nod as he came out of the building, zipping up his pants. His smile almost blinded Hakim as the light from the lamppost caused the gold grill in his mouth to gleam.

"My bad," he said to Hakim. Nikki rolled her eyes and started walking up the stairs. Hakim followed her and wondered why her mannerisms seemed to change so suddenly. She was no longer walking like the sexy vixen she was a few seconds ago. Now she was stomping toward the apartment on a mission.

"Everything a'ight, Nikki?"

Instead of answering Hakim, Nikki picked up the pace. By the time Nikki got to her door, she was steaming mad. She opened the door and stormed in. Hakim wasn't sure what was going on, but he followed her in just the same. Nikki stopped dead in her tracks when she saw what was taking place on the sofa.

Sitting amid a cloud of smoke were Nikki's mother and sister sharing a crack pipe. Hakim looked around and was amazed at how different the place looked from the last time he was there. It was a far cry from the immaculately clean apartment where nothing was ever out of place. Now it was a disheveled mess with clothes strewn about the floor. Empty soda cans, beer bottles, and debris were everywhere. Nikki was so distraught that she just stomped into her bedroom and slammed the door. Even though they were not a couple anymore, Hakim felt he had to go and make sure that Nikki was all right.

"Nikki? You straight in there?" Hakim asked as he lightly knocked on the door. When she didn't answer, Hakim took it upon himself to walk right in. Nikki's room didn't look anything like the rest of the house. Surprisingly, it was neat and clean. Hakim stared at Nikki as she lay facedown on her bed, crying her eyes out. He walked over to her bed and sat down. He had no idea what to say or how to soothe her pain. He had seen plenty of people on crack before, but this particular situation hit close to home. It didn't matter to him that he and Nikki weren't together anymore. The only thing he saw was that someone he cared about was in pain. When he reached down to put his hand on her shoulder in an attempt to comfort her, she sat up.

"Hakim, I have something to tell you. I didn't break up with you because I liked someone else. As a matter of fact, there has never been anyone else."

"But I thought you had a boyfriend."

Nikki looked at him through tear-soaked eyes. "Tell me something. Have you ever actually seen me with anyone?"

Hakim racked his brain. For the life of him, he couldn't ever remember seeing Nikki with someone.

"Think back to how I broke up with you. I did it over the phone. I avoided you at all costs, and whenever you tried to call and talk to me, I would tell you or have my sister tell you that I had company. The truth of the matter is that when my mother and sister started smoking that shit, I was ashamed. I didn't want you to think that I was a piece of shit just because my family was strung out." Nikki laid her head on Hakim's shoulder and sobbed. "I'm sorry. I know I was wrong for dumping you, but I just didn't know what else to do."

"Don't worry about that," Hakim said as he stroked her hair.

"Do you think you can stay with me tonight?" she asked out of the blue. Hakim glanced toward the door. "Don't worry about them," Nikki said, reading his thoughts. "They probably won't remember what day it is by the time they get finished smoking their fucking brain cells away."

"A'ight. Let me go home and pack a few clothes," Hakim said, and he got up and walked out of Nikki's room. Hakim took one look at Nikki's mother and sister and shook his head. Although he knew that Red was the one to turn Chanel on to drugs, he wasn't dumb enough to tell Nikki. He liked Nikki but not enough to tell her Red's business and risk having to go toe-to-toe with the Cleveland drug lord.

After leaving Nikki's house, Hakim walked down the street, wondering how he was going to get out of the house so he could go back and spend the night with Nikki. The fact that he was almost 18 years old made no difference at all to his mother. School may have been out for the summer, but she wasn't about to let Hakim stay out all night for no good reason. Wanting to bang his ex-girlfriend damn sure wasn't going to be a good enough reason for her.

"Fuck it. I'll just tell her that I'm tired and that I'm going to bed. When she goes back into her room, I'll just sneak the fuck out," he mumbled to himself when he couldn't think of a lie good enough to get back out of the house.

Hakim had just reached the front of his house when Ivory pulled up. After looking through the windshield and seeing his sister, Hakim figured that now was as good a time as any to apologize. *Where the hell is she coming from this time of night?* he wondered. He walked up to the passenger's side door and waited for her to get out. He took a step back when he heard her pop her lips through the window. Tammy got out, rolled her eyes, and walked right past him. Hakim turned and looked at Ivory, who just shrugged her shoulders. Hakim then broke into a light jog in an attempt to catch up with his sister.

"Sis, hold up a minute."

"I don't want to hear it."

"Come on. We're gonna have to talk about the shit sooner or later."

"Well, it's damn sure not going to be sooner. And stop talking so loud before you wake Mama up."

When Hakim walked through the door, he noticed that his mother wasn't standing at the door or sitting in the living room, tapping her foot and looking at her watch. Since Tammy had made it clear that she didn't want to talk to him at the moment, Hakim left her alone and went upstairs to his room, thinking about Nikki. *This shit gon' be easier than I thought,* he said to himself. Hakim grabbed a blue Nike duffle out of his closet and packed it. He started toward the bathroom door but stopped when he heard the shower running.

The last thing he wanted to do was climb into bed with Nikki smelling like a sweaty rat, so he fell back onto his bed and waited. His dick started to throb as he day-dreamed about thrusting his manhood inside of Nikki's luscious walls. After ten minutes, Hakim got tired of waiting and decided that he would just take a shower at Nikki's place. He decided that he would just tell his mother that he got up early and went jogging. It was a weak lie but one that she might actually believe. Hakim hopped out of his bed and headed out of his bedroom. He did a double-take when he looked toward the bathroom and saw Steve standing at the door, trying to peek into it.

"Nigga, what the fuck you doing?" he said as he stomped angrily toward Steve.

Steve almost jumped out of his skin when he heard Hakim's booming voice. He'd been fantasizing about Tammy ever since her mother had introduced the two of them. Now here he was getting busted while looking through the keyhole trying to catch a glimpse of her na-ked. Steve quickly thought of an excuse.

"Huh? Oh, man, I . . . I had to use the bathroom, but the door is stuck."

"That door ain't been stuck all the years we been living here! Now all a sudden it's stuck? Get the fuck outta here with that bullshit-ass lie!"

Hearing the commotion on the other side of the door, Tammy quickly dried off, threw on her robe, and opened the door. "What are you yelling about?" she asked.

"That's what I would like to know," Janice chimed in as she made her way to Steve's side.

"Wait a minute. What the hell are you doing here at this time of night?" Tammy asked Steve.

"Young lady, what did I tell you about this being my house?" she asked Tammy as she pointed to her chest.

"Fuck all that! I just caught this nigga looking through the keyhole, trying to see Tammy naked!" Hakim yelled. "I'm 'bout to beat the blood out this bitch-ass nigga!"

In true cowardly fashion, Steve took a couple of steps back as Hakim stalked toward him. Janice stepped between them while Tammy continued to venomously glare at Steve.

"You are not about to beat nothing, and stop cussing in my damn house," Janice said to her son. Then she slowly turned to face Steve. "Were you trying to spy on my daughter while she was in the shower?"

"What? Hell no!" Steve then leaned in and tried to whisper in Janice's ear. "To be honest, I thought it was you, baby. I went downstairs to get a glass of water, and when I heard the shower running, I assumed that you had decided to take a shower," he lied. "I thought your kids were asleep, so I was going to come in there and give you some oral love."

"Oh God," Tammy said as she held her stomach. The thought of her mother having oral sex made her sick.

"You a liar," Hakim screamed.

"Hakim, what did I just tell you?"

Without saying another word, Hakim stormed down the stairs and out the door. He slammed the door so hard it almost shattered the living room glass. Janice shouted out after him, but Hakim was long gone. Then she turned her rage toward her daughter.

"You got something you wanna say? Let me tell you something, and you can relay this to your brother the next time you see his ass! This is my damn house! I have over here who the hell I want to have over here, and if either one of you don't like it, y'all can find somewhere else to stay!"

Tammy barely heard a word she said. She was in total shock that her mother chose to believe someone she had just met over her own son. With her mother still talking, Tammy turned, walked down the hallway, went into her room, and slammed the door.

Chapter 17

The buzzing sound of Ivory's cell phone woke her up from the scintillating dream she was having. She looked around her small apartment bedroom and frowned. This more than anything told her that the high-rise condominium she had been lounging in was only a figment of her alternate reality. Sleepily, Ivory wiped the crust from the corners of her eyes as she reached over to the nightstand and grabbed her cell phone.

"Hello?" Ivory became annoyed as she listened to the silence talking to her from the other end of the phone. "Hello?" she said louder.

"Yeah, can I speak to Darnell, please?" a female voice spoke through the phone.

Ivory instantly got an attitude. "Who the fuck is this?" she asked nastily.

"Excuse me?" the woman responded.

"You heard me! Who the fuck is this, and what do you want with Darnell?"

"You know what? I don't want shit," she said calmly. "But tell Darnell that if this is the type of person he is going to have on his team, then there is no reason for us to do business anymore. Goodbye."

"No! Wait! Fuck," Ivory screamed when she realized that the person on the other end had hung up the phone.

She fell back on the bed, thinking that she had just blown her chance at making some bread. Five minutes later, her cell phone rang. She immediately picked up the phone that Darnell had left her and tried to answer it. After putting it up to her ear and not getting any activity, she realized that it was her phone and not the one she had in her hand that was buzzing. As soon as she answered it, Darnell tore into her ass.

"What the fuck is wrong with you? Do you know how much money Marvin and his wife spend with me on a regular basis?"

"Who the hell is Marvin?" Ivory asked.

"Marvin is the guy whose wife you fucking disrespected when she just called you, that's who!"

"Look, I didn't even know who the hell—"

"You don't need to know who the fuck it is! All you need to do while I'm gone is handle business and stop actin' like a damn jealous-ass girlfriend! They gonna call you back in two minutes! Get yo' shit together, a'ight?"

Darnell didn't even wait for Ivory to respond before he hung up on her. Although Ivory knew that she was wrong, she was still pissed at Darnell for talking to her that way. She was tempted to call him back and cuss him out for disrespecting her, but the other cell phone buzzed, so she had to put it on the back burner.

"Hello?"

"You ready to talk business like you got some fucking sense now?" the woman whom she talked to before asked her. Ivory wanted to reach through the phone and snatch her ass through it. But since she knew that she needed to make some bread, she swallowed the smart comment.

"Yeah, I'm ready," she said.

"Good. Meet me at the Shoney's in Akron today at two thirty. Bring three."

"Akron?" Ivory asked. It never occurred to her that she might have to leave the city to make a sale.

The two women were quiet for a moment before the woman said, "Look, do you want to do business or not?"

"Huh? Oh, yeah, I'm sorry. Two thirty it is. I will be there."

"Cool. And, honey, let me give you a little free advice. If you are gonna be in this business, you can't be actin' like a jealous-ass wife. That shit will get you either knocked or killed. Think about it," the woman said before she hung up the phone.

Ivory looked at the phone and smacked her lips. "Who the fuck is this bitch to be trying to school me on the muthafucking game?"

She looked at the clock on her nightstand and saw that she only had a couple of hours before she was supposed to be at Shoney's restaurant.

"Damn, they ain't leaving a bitch no kinda time." Ivory quickly jumped out of bed and got in the shower. After getting dressed, she decided she needed a blunt to calm her nerves. She was about to head up Interstate 77 south on a mission to sell marijuana, so she needed a few good puffs to be in control of her emotions. She quickly rolled up a fatty and set fire to it. She took a good, hard drag and slowly blew the smoke into the air. She was just starting to relax a little when she heard a loud banging on her front door.

She started to ignore it but figured that she was about to leave anyway, so she might as well see who it was. After making her way over to the door and opening it, Ivory was greeted rather rudely by her landlord, Miss Tolliver, who walked right past Ivory without so much as a hello.

"Well, come the fuck on in," Ivory sarcastically remarked.

"Rent day, Miss Thang. You got my money?" Before Ivory could even start to make up a lie, Miss Tolliver pointed to the burning blunt that was now sitting in an ashtray.

"What the hell is that? I know damn well you ain't smoking weed up in here! That's a direct violation of your contract and grounds for immediate eviction." Miss Tolliver took out her cell phone and took a picture of the ganja before Ivory had a chance to remove it.

"What the hell did you do that for?" Ivory asked.

"Evidence, Miss Ghetto Queen."

Ivory started to panic. She remembered quite clearly the clause in her contract that called for immediate eviction if she were ever caught using drugs. "Wait, maybe we can make a deal or something," Ivory said.

"What kind of deal are you talking about? I know damn well you ain't trying to bribe me, 'cause you don't have the money to do that. Shit, if you did, you wouldn't be late on ya damn rent."

While Miss Tolliver was talking, Ivory was racking her brain trying to figure out how she was going to get her bitch of a landlord not to kick her out into the street. She had violated her rental agreement, and if she didn't come up with an idea that was to Miss Tolliver's liking, she was going to have to find another place to live. She was about to open her mouth and try to bribe her anyway with an offer of an extra $50 a month for her to forget that she ever saw the burning blunt, but she kept it closed when she noticed how the woman kept looking at it.

Ivory zeroed in on her eyes, and for the first time since she'd been there, Ivory saw something in them. She recognized it instantly. It was the look of a person who was feenin' for weed. Ivory looked at the blunt and then back at Miss Tolliver and smiled on the inside. She knew just what it would take to make Miss Tolliver forget about what she saw.

"Miss Tolliver, you looked kinda stressed. Why don't you come over here and sit down on the couch?"

Miss Tolliver gave Ivory a strange look and began to back away. Not wanting to let her off the hook, Ivory quickly ran beside her and grabbed her hand. "Hey, I don't play that shit. I'm strictly dickly," she said, still looking a tad nervous.

"What? Nah, I ain't like that. I'm just sayin' you look a little stressed, that's all. Here, take a puff of this, and all yo' troubles will disappear."

At first, Miss Tolliver hesitated, knowing that it was a very bad idea to be smoking dope with one of her tenants. But the strong scent and the powerful pull of the get-high stick was just too much for her to overcome. Ever so slowly, she held out her hand to accept the blunt. She looked at it for a second before transferring it from her hand to her mouth. Miss Tolliver closed her eyes and took a long pull. After holding it in for what seemed looked forever, she released the smoke into the air.

"Oh, yes, that's some good-ass shit," she said as the addictive herb did its thing on her system. "This don't mean you get a pass on the rent," she said with a silly smile on her face.

Ivory didn't care about that. For the moment, her only concern was that she still had a place to stay. "I was just hoping that, you know, you could forget about what you saw in here today."

"Is that right? Let me take another hit of this, and I'll think about it." Miss Tolliver took another pull so fast Ivory couldn't object even if she wanted to. "Tell you what," Miss Tolliver said. "I'll give you until tomorrow. But if you don't have my bread by then, all bets are off, and I'm reporting your ass."

"Wait a minute! Your ass just sat up here with me, smoking dope, and you still gonna put me out? Even though you were smoking weed too? That's fucking extortion!"

"I don't give a fuck what you call it! Either have my money tomorrow or get the fuck out."

Miss Tolliver got up and walked toward the door, smiling. She knew all along that if she had threatened to kick Ivory out and then acted as if she were feening for weed, she would be able to get a free high out of the deal. Ivory could have offered her an extra $200 a month and it would not have mattered. She wanted Darnell just that bad and figured that the only way she would ever have him was if Ivory was out on the street. She'd known for a while now that Darnell sold weed. She was just waiting for the right time to use it to her advantage.

As soon as she walked out and closed the door, Ivory smiled. She was one step ahead of her weed-smoking landlord. While Miss Tolliver was on cloud nine as a result of the potent marijuana, Ivory had slyly pressed the record function on her cell phone and recorded everything that was being said. Knowing that she would have the money later that day, she let Miss Tolliver's threat go unanswered and chose to save the recording for another day.

Chapter 18

Nancy woke up with her head in Hank's lap. His dick was just inches from her mouth. She staggered up from her couch, where the two of them had fallen asleep, and stumbled to her bathroom. The last thing that she remembered was Hank cumming in her mouth just before she sniffed a large amount of cocaine up through her nostrils. After relieving her bladder, Nancy walked groggily back to her bedroom. She was surprised to see Hank so wide awake after both of them had gotten high and screwed like dogs in heat for most of the night. Hank didn't touch cocaine, but he could smoke weed with the best of them. She sighed heavily when she spotted Hank's rock-hard dick trying to poke its way through the sheets. Nancy was tired. Her womb was sore and her back ached. In no way did she feel like being pounded on so early.

Sensing that Nancy was leaning toward not giving up the punanny, Hank reached down on the floor, dug into his pants pocket, and pulled out a small bag of cocaine.

Nancy's eyes widened as if she'd seen a ghost. The unspoken promise of giving her what she wanted—and, in her mind, needed—was all it took to ignore the pain radiating between her legs. Hank smiled as he pointed to his dick then to the bag of dope. Nancy understood exactly where Hank was going with his gesture.

"The dick for the dope, baby. You can't have one without the other."

Nancy closed her eyes slowly. She silently prayed that the Lord would push aside her sins and give her the strength to stand her ground against her addiction. An addiction that she now realized was growing by the second. Nancy opened her eyes and glanced at the clock. She had to be at work in an hour, but she hadn't showered or even picked out any clothes to wear yet. But none of that mattered at the moment. All she could think about was the escape from reality that was guaranteed with each snort.

"You know what? Fuck it. You taking too damn long," Hank snapped as he got out of the bed and put the dope back into his pocket.

"No!"

"Who the fuck you yelling at like that?"

"I'm sorry. I'm just saying you don't have to leave. I'll do what you want me to do."

Nancy slowly walked toward the bed. She fought hard to prevent tears from falling from her eyes. She couldn't believe that she had turned into a dopefiend who was selling her body to get high. Reaching out and grabbing Hank's rock-hard dick, Nancy lowered her head. As her mouth wrapped around the head of it, Hank stopped her.

"Uh-uh. Turn around and get on your knees," he commanded.

Nancy could already feel the pain. Her vagina already felt like it had friction burns. But the call of the hit was too powerful to resist. While Nancy was getting in position, Hank smoothly reached into his pants pocket again and pulled out a small tube of Vaseline. After squirting a small amount on his fingers, he rubbed the tip of his penis. Hank then rubbed his dick in an up and down motion against the back of her pussy.

"You wanna raise yo' voice to a brother, huh? Well, I'm gonna give yo' ass something to scream about!"

Nancy popped her lips. Although Hank's cock game had been on point, his length was nothing to brag about. She'd taken much bigger dicks before. Taking that as a sign of disrespect, Hank drove every bit of his seven inches into her asshole. Nancy howled like a wolf at the moon. It wasn't the first time that she'd experienced anal intrusion, but all the other times she'd known it was coming and expected it. This, however, was a complete surprise.

"Yeah, scream, bitch," Hank taunted her as he rammed into her anal cavity repeatedly. But Hank had severely underestimated Nancy's dick-taking skills. Over the years, she had learned how to take it up the ass like a porno star. Once the initial shock wore off and she loosened up, Hank's dick felt like a twig in a moon-sized crater. Nancy then clenched her cheeks up to make sure that Hank wouldn't last long. A few seconds later, it was all over as Hank emptied himself inside of Nancy. The last drop had not even entered her body yet before Nancy started looking around for the bag of dope.

"Where is it?" she asked.

"Hold up. I'll get it."

Hank had $500 in his pocket. There was no way that he was going to take a chance at getting his pocket picked. As soon as he got it out of his pocket, Nancy almost pulled his fingers off, trying to get at the drug. Hank just smiled as he lay back on the bed and lit a Newport.

"Why, God, why?" Nancy asked after sniffing twice.

Detective Dryer sat in his car, drinking a steaming cup of coffee. On top of trying to find evidence to arrest Bobby and Red, Dryer was hard at work attempting to repair the relationship he'd held so dear at one time. Wondering where it all went wrong, Dryer shook his head as he reached into his shirt pocket and pulled out a pack of

Marlboro cigarettes. Dryer held up the soft pack of cancer rolls and looked at them long and hard. He'd been promising himself that he was going to quit for some time now. The Cleveland Police had shitty insurance. If he ever developed cancer, he was going to be fucked. Dryer shrugged his shoulders, stuck the cancer in his mouth, and lit it. After taking a pull, Dryer let the smoke slide through his nostrils and out into the air.

Dryer looked at his watch and blew out a sigh. He was supposed to run up to Dunkin' and go right back to the precinct, but instead, his heartstrings tugged at him and pulled him in an entirely different direction. He was torn as to whether to get out of his car and walk up to the door or to just say fuck it, start up the unmarked black Crown Victoria, and drive away. Dryer finished the rest of his cigarette and flicked the butt out the window. He then reached into the large box of doughnuts and took out a chocolate-covered twister. Before he could stuff his breakfast of choice down his throat, his eyes zeroed in on two people walking out of the apartment building.

Dryer dropped his doughnut in disbelief. He looked at the slim black man, who seemed to be zipping up his pants, and became even more enraged. Dryer couldn't get out of the car fast enough. The box of doughnuts was knocked off the passenger's seat and onto the car's floor. The white woman who was with the black man snapped her fingers as if she had forgotten something and went back into the house. Dryer walked as fast as he could toward the black man.

Out of the corner of his eye, Hank saw Dryer coming toward him like a raging bull. Instinctively Hank reached for the pistol that was usually tucked in the small of his back. He grabbed nothing but air and then remembered that he had left his gun in his car. Hank then got in his boxing stance as Dryer got closer.

"Nigger, what the fuck are you doing with my daughter?" Dryer screamed at Hank.

"Daughter? What the hell are you talking about?"

Not even bothering to offer a response, Dryer swung wildly at Hank. Hank easily avoided Dryer's attempt to take his head off.

"What the fuck wrong with you?" Hank yelled.

Dryer then swung a wild left-handed punch at Hank. Hank ducked under the punch, sidestepped, and caught Dryer with a bone-crunching right hook to the ribs. Dryer crumbled to his knees. Hank drew back to finish him off just as Nancy walked back out of the house.

"Daddy!"

"Don't worry 'bout it, baby," Hank said. "Daddy got it all under control."

"Not you, Hank, him," she said, pointing at Dryer. "He's my father for real."

"What?" Hank said in shock as he looked at Dryer. Seizing the opportunity, Dryer, still gasping for air, quickly pulled his pistol from his holster.

"Daddy, no!" Nancy's pleas fell on deaf ears as Dryer aimed and shot Hank in the foot.

"Ah shit," Hank screamed as he fell to the ground. Dryer then struggled to his feet. As Nancy stood there in shock, Dryer smashed Hank on the top of his head with the handle of his .357 Magnum. Hank blacked out immediately, and Nancy was left standing there, begging her father not to kill him.

"Daddy, what the hell are you doing?"

"What the hell am I doing?" he screamed. "What the hell are you doing? You fucking niggers now?"

Embarrassed and stunned, Nancy ran back into the house and slammed the door.

"Open this door, Nancy! Open this damn door!"

Nancy ignored her father as she rushed back over to the nightstand, where Hank had left her a small amount of powder, and she began to snort. In a matter of minutes, she transcended to a world where she was the only inhabitant on the planet.

Bobby drove down the street with a huge smile on his face. He was in a good mood after meeting Tammy at Cookie's party and getting to know her. Although he knew that it wasn't any of his business to get involved in scuffles that didn't concern him, Bobby just couldn't help himself. When he saw a beautiful sister about to get strong-armed by two thugs, he felt like he had no choice but to step in and save the damsel in distress. He hoped that Tammy wouldn't be too upset with him for showing up at her house unannounced. After Tammy left the party, Bobby did a little palm greasing to find out where she lived. He gave Cookie $50 to find out her address. Cookie then went to Nancy and lied to her, saying that she was having another party on New Year's Eve and needed Tammy's address to formally send her an invitation.

Nancy smelled a rat and wanted to question Cookie as to why she couldn't just go and ask Tammy herself, but with Hank promising to get her high and screw her brains out, Nancy's priorities shifted.

With Tammy's address locked into his brain, Bobby pulled up in front of Tammy's place of residence. To calm his nerves, Bobby quickly fired up a blunt. When he felt that he was ready to face the storm, Bobby got out of his whip, walked up to the door, and knocked.

Tammy had tossed and turned all night. The fact that her mother had taken the word of a virtual stranger over her own children left her with an unsettling feeling. She was going to have to watch Steve's perverse ass.

"Shit!" Tammy yelled as she grabbed her head and shook it from side to side. It was killing her that she couldn't remember where she had seen Steve before. She was also worried about her brother. She had no idea where he was.

Although they had gotten into an altercation the day before, she was willing to put that on the back burner just to know that he was safe. She'd called and texted him no fewer than ten times, and he still hadn't responded. She knew that, even though Hakim was her brother, she would much rather he be somewhere up in some pussy than hanging out with his newfound friends. With attitude in tow, Tammy rolled out of bed. It didn't help her mood that she had to be at work in an hour and a half.

Even though she had taken a shower before she went to bed, the thought of Steve seeing her naked had her still feeling dirty, so she decided to take another one. She quickly walked out of the room and made her way down to the bathroom. The sweet aroma of bacon, sausage, pancakes, and maple syrup slid through her nostrils, causing her mouth to water. Tammy couldn't get into the shower fast enough. As fast as she could, she cleaned herself, rinsed the soap away, and dried off. She put her clothes on in record time as her stomach started to growl.

She had spent so much time talking to Bobby at the party that when Ivory was ready to go, she hadn't eaten a thing. Checking her watch, she had just enough time to grab a bite to eat and get to work on time. Tammy then hurried downstairs. She was beyond famished. The second she walked into the kitchen, her mood got instantly worse. With Steve sitting where Hakim usually sat, Tammy and her mother locked eyes with each other. Neither woman said a word as they stared at each other. Tammy finally broke the contest as she walked over to the cabinet and took out a plate. She shot Steve a death stare as she went over to the stove and fixed herself some breakfast.

When she sat down, her mother looked at her plate with a raised eyebrow. Tammy knew why, though. Her mother wasn't used to her having that much food on her plate, but as hungry as she was, Tammy wasn't going to have any problem finishing off the meal. At this point, she really didn't care if she was going to be late to work. All she wanted to do was eat. For several minutes, no one said a word.

"Have you heard from Hakim?" Janice asked, breaking the silence.

Tammy looked up into her mother's face and could tell that she was clearly worried about her son. "Nope," Tammy said, continuing to eat. After the way her mother treated them the night before, Tammy wasn't about to give her any sympathy.

"He could have at least called," Steve mumbled to Janice.

"And you could be minding your own damn business!" Tammy snapped. "You don't know me or my brother, so you need to attend to your own affairs!"

"Hey, all I'm saying is—"

"I don't give a damn about what you're saying! This is all your fault to begin with!"

"Okay, you two, that's enough," Janice said, although she was only looking at Tammy when she said it. "Steve is right. Hakim could have at least called me and let me know that he was okay."

Tammy looked at her mother like she had never seen her before today. *I can't believe she's defending this ass-hole again. Damn, is the dick that good to her?*

"Mom, are you serious? Do you even hear yourself right now? The way you acted toward him last night, we'll be lucky if he comes home at all."

Tears formed in the corners of Janice's eyes. Although she meant what she said about it being her house and that she could have anybody she wanted up in there, she never meant for her son to leave. She had hoped that he would just storm off and go into his room like he normally did when he got pissed off. She never thought that he would leave the house.

"Excuse me," she said as she got up from the table. Janice sniffled as she headed toward the bathroom to wipe her eyes.

While she was gone, Steve saw it as an opportunity to get closer to Tammy. "Look, I'm not trying to cause any trouble around here," he said to her.

"Oh, really? Is that why your perverse ass was peeping through the bathroom door at me?"

"As I said last night, your brother was mistaken. I would never do anything like that."

"Hmmph. We'll see. And another thing. Where the fuck do I know you from? I know I've seen you somewhere before."

"I don't know," Steve answered. "Maybe you saw me in the movies. People have told me that I look like Harry Belafonte."

"I don't know about Harry Belafonte, but I do know that I've seen your ass somewhere before. So why don't you just save me the investigative work and tell me where I know you from?"

Tammy watched as Steve got noticeably nervous. Tiny beads of sweat formed on his upper lip, but before Tammy could question him any further, Janice came back into the kitchen. Her eyes were red and slightly swollen. When Janice sat back down at the table, Tammy reached for her hand.

"Mama, I'm sorry. I never meant to—" Before Tammy could even finish her sentence, Janice held up her hand and cut her off.

"Don't even worry about it," she said with a slight attitude.

I don't know what the hell she has an attitude about, Tammy thought. *She's the one who chose to believe a damn man over her kids.* Tammy's head then snapped around at the sound of the door chime.

"Is that the doorbell?" she asked. "I thought it was broken."

"It was, but Steve fixed it," Janice said as she placed her hand on top of Steve's. Tammy rolled her eyes and let out a loud snort. Before she could get up to answer the door, Janice asked Steve, "Can you get that for me, honey?"

Tammy stared laser beams at Steve as he walked out of the kitchen with his head held high. "He's answering the door now? Why don't you just give his ass a set of keys and let him move the hell in?"

"I just might do that, Ms. Smart-ass, and make that the last time you cuss in my presence."

"Unbelievable," Tammy mumbled as she continued eating her food. She stopped in mid-chew as she heard a familiar voice asking if she was home.

"Who should I tell her is looking for her?" Steve pried.

Tammy jumped up from the table in a flash. Seeing the speed at which her daughter left the table, Janice followed her with a concerned look on her face.

"Hold up," Tammy shouted. "Why are you questioning someone who's here to see me?"

"I just thought—"

"Whatever you thought, it's none of your business who comes here looking for me! She's your woman, not me," Tammy said as she pointed at her mother. "So, tend to your business and stay out of mine!" Before Steve or Janice could respond, Tammy grabbed Bobby by the hand and led him off the porch.

"Where is your car?" she asked.

"My truck is right there," he said as he pointed to a blue GMC.

"Let's get in for a second," she said. As soon as they were inside, Tammy lit into him. "First of all, Bobby, I don't appreciate you showing up on my doorstep unannounced. And just how the hell did you know where I live anyway?"

"Whoa, pump ya brakes. Look, I'm sorry for just popping up like this. I just remembered from our conversation last night when you said that you had to catch the bus to work this morning. A queen like you shouldn't be getting on no damn bus."

Tammy's insides melted. As hard as she tried, she just couldn't suppress the smile that had made its way to her lips. "Thank you," she said, beaming. "But that still doesn't explain how you found out where I live."

"I did a little asking around for that info. Money talks and bullshit walks."

Tammy's pussy started doing cartwheels. She couldn't believe that Bobby cared enough about her after just meeting her to pay for her address. She was flattered that he wanted to pick her up and take her to work. So much so, in fact, that tears came to her eyes.

"You gonna let me take you to work or what?"

"Let me go and get my purse," she said, smiling.

Bobby watched as Tammy used smooth, graceful strides to make her way up the steps and into her house. He was tired and sleepy as hell but saw a great opportunity to get closer to Tammy by taking her to work. As soon as he dropped her off, he was going to go straight home and catch some much-needed z's.

Tammy was all smiles as she bolted up the stairs to get her purse. Bobby made her feel like a giddy schoolgirl. She'd only met him the night before, but there was something about him that made her stomach do backflips. After grabbing her cell phone off of her dresser, she looked at it and saw that she had a text message.

Sorry I haven't been answering my phone, sis. I just didn't feel like talking about what happened with Mama and her bitch-ass boyfriend last night. Just know that I'm okay.

Tammy's smile got even brighter. Knowing that Hakim was okay made her feel much better. Tammy ran back down the stairs and into the kitchen. She could almost feel her mother's eyes on the back of her head as she quickly emptied her plate and put it in the sink.

"I guess you're in a hurry," Janice said dryly.

"You know I have to work today."

"I don't know why yo' ass is rushing when you have that Snoop Dogg look-alike out there ready to give you a lift in his thugged-out truck."

Tammy ignored her mother's comment and headed for the door. She couldn't get out of the house fast enough.

"Where did you meet that thug?" Janice asked.

Tammy stopped dead in her tracks. She couldn't believe that her mother had the nerve to question her about Bobby when she kept her in the dark for so long about Steve.

"Let me see if I've got this straight," she said after turning and facing her mother. "You want to question me about a friend of mine when you tried to keep this dude a secret for so long?" she asked while pointing at Steve. "That sounds kind of hypocritical to me."

It took Janice all of two seconds to get all up in Tammy's face. "Did you just call me a fucking hypocrite? Who in the fuck do you think you talking to?"

Seeing the fire in her mother's eyes, Tammy backed up a little. "I'm not calling you anything. I'm just saying that your question sounds like a double standard to me. I have to go, Mama," Tammy said after seeing that her mother was getting angrier by the second.

After Tammy walked out the door, Janice went over to the window and peered out. She watched sadly as Tammy disappeared into Bobby's truck. She couldn't help but wonder if she was losing her children.

Seeing that she was upset, Steve walked over to her and wrapped his arms around her waist. "It's okay, baby," he whispered into her ear.

Janice then turned to him and looked him directly in the eyes. "Steve, I have to ask. Were you . . . I mean, is my son telling the truth about seeing you looking through the bathroom keyhole at Tammy?"

"I already told you that I didn't do no bullshit like that!"

"I'm sorry. It's just that Hakim sounded so convincing when he was talking about it."

"I can't believe this bullshit," Steve yelled. "You know what? I don't have to take this shit! I'm the fuck up outta here!" Steve headed toward the door, and just like he knew she would, Janice stopped him before he even came close to leaving.

"No! Please don't leave," she begged with tears leaking out of her eyes.

"If I'm gonna hang around here, you gonna have to start trusting me. I ain't got time to be arguing with you about ya fucking grown-ass kids! Either you control them muthafuckas, or I'm out!"

"Okay. I'll keep them outta your way."

With Janice down on her knees, practically begging Steve not to leave, he bent down to her level and kissed her on the lips. He then pulled her up by her arm and swept her off her feet.

"I'm sorry I made you cry, sweetheart," he said while nibbling on her earlobe. "Let daddy make you feel better." Steve then sat her on the kitchen table and spread her legs. He smiled when he saw that she didn't have any panties on.

"Wait, Hakim might come home," she said when his head dipped between her legs.

"So? Let his ass come," he said as he started licking around her pubic hair.

"No, I can't take the chance that he . . . Oooo shit!" Janice screamed in delight when Steve gently bit her clit. "Oh, my God, you gon' make me cum!" Just before she got ready to cum, Steve abruptly stopped.

"No, pleeeassse don't stop!"

Steve smiled wickedly as he unbuckled his belt. Seeing the lust in Janice's eyes, Steve slowed down. He wanted to make her wait. He wanted to tease her.

"Stop fucking teasing me!"

Steve laughed maniacally as Janice reached down and ripped his pants open. Her mouth watered as Steve's nine-and-a-half-inch dick sprang out. Before she met Steve, Janice hadn't had sex in over a year. She was sexually starved and deprived of satisfaction. So when Steve gave her the hammer for an hour straight, Janice fell face-first in love. Steve made her have no fewer than eight orgasms that night, and that fact alone gave him the power to tell her the sky was purple when it was blue.

"Give it to me, pleeassee," she begged. Satisfied with her pleading, Steve then grabbed her roughly by the neck and threw her on the floor. Janice screamed at the top of her lungs when Steve threw her legs on his shoulders and drove every inch of his man meat into her dripping womb.

"Ooohh, my God!"

"Shut up, bitch! You know you want this dick!" Steve yelled.

For the next fifteen minutes, Steve battered Janice's insides. When he got ready to come, Steve pulled out and squirted on her stomach. After rubbing Steve's babies into her skin, Janice collapsed onto her side with a satisfied smile on her face. With her passed out on the floor, Steve then went up to Tammy's room and went through her drawers. His dick instantly became hard again when he came across a pair of her Victoria's Secret panties. He put them up to his nose and sniffed. Then he put them in his mouth and started sucking on them as he masturbated right there on the floor.

Chapter 19

After waking up and feeling an arm draped across his chest, Hakim's eyes popped open. He looked up to the ceiling first and then to his right. It took him a minute to realize that he wasn't in his own bed. Hearing light snoring, Hakim looked to his left and saw Nikki lying there with a smile on her face. His memory of the night before slowly started to return. Nikki soon interrupted that thought as she ran her hand down his thigh and grabbed his dick.

"Good morning, baby," she said as she kissed his bare chest. "You ready to please me some more?"

As an answer to her question, Hakim reached down between her legs and rubbed her love nest.

"Hold up. I gotta go empty the tank. Then I'm gonna take a shower and come back in here fresh and clean for you."

Hakim slapped her on her ass as she slid out of the bed and started toward her bedroom door. While Nikki was in the bathroom, Hakim had time to reflect on what happened at his house the previous night. "I know Tammy and Mama tripping," he mumbled to himself. Hakim then picked up his cell phone and sent his sister a text message. Then he laid his head back on the pillow and tried to figure out the best way to get his mother to see that Steve was a snake. For one split second, he thought that he might have made a mistake and that maybe Steve wasn't doing what it looked like he was doing. He quickly slapped those thoughts to the side.

He knew for a fact that his eyes were not deceiving him. He knew one thing. If Steve ever hurt his mother or his sister, he was going to take care of him the thug way. Hakim's eyes got heavy as he waited for Nikki to come back into the bedroom. Still feeling slightly tired, Hakim let his eyes close, and he drifted back into slumberland. He was almost there when he felt something wet sliding up his thigh. Hakim smiled, knowing that Nikki was about to give him the ultimate treat.

He didn't get to enjoy her head-giving talents the night before, but if he remembered correctly, Nikki had one of the best head games in the hood. He moaned softly as she worked her magic. His toes curled as she let her tongue travel down to his balls. He damn near exploded when she took all of him inside of her mouth and sucked gently.

"Shit, girl, you was good before, but now you a straight-up thoroughbred with the head game," he said. With his eyes still closed, Hakim reached down and grabbed her hair. He skillfully guided her head up and down as she masterfully continued to deep throat him. Hakim tried hard to hold out, but he was no match for the profession-al head job that he was receiving. He smiled in satisfac-tion as he heard gulping sounds.

"Damn, baby, that shit was the fucking bomb."

"I know damn well it was."

The smile on Hakim's face was immediately wiped off. When his eyes popped open, he was shocked to see Nik-ki's mother between his legs licking her lips.

"What the fuck?" Hakim yelled.

"Shhh, nigga, you want my daughter to hear you?"

Hakim was shocked. In the back of his mind, he knew that when he grabbed the hair, it felt different, but he thought that is was due to her just getting out of the shower. He had no idea that it was her mother who had crawled between his legs to give him the business. And even though it wasn't his fault, he felt like shit. He had to admit, though, that Nikki didn't have shit on her mother when it came to the oral game. What he thought was an improvement in skills by Nikki was actually a lesson in fellatio by a vet.

"Did you like that shit?" she asked.

"What the fuck you doing? Yo' daughter is right down the fucking hall!"

"So muthafucking what? And you need to lower your damn voice before she hear yo' silly ass. And you didn't answer my question. Did you like it?"

"Hell nah," Hakim lied. "Get the hell outta here."

Nikki's mother just smiled. She knew Hakim was lying as soon as he opened his mouth. His moans of pleasure while he was getting serviced were proof of that.

"Yeah, right," she said as she walked around the bed and grabbed his hand. "But just so you know, the pussy is much better than the head."

Before he could resist, she put his hand between her legs and stroked her pussy with it. Both of them jumped when they heard Nikki walking back down the hallway. She quickly ran over to the closet and pretended like she was looking for something. When Nikki reached her room, she stopped dead in her tracks.

"Mama, what are you doing in here?" she said, adjusting the towel that was wrapped around her body.

"I was looking for my coat," she lied.

Nikki cocked her head to the side. "A coat," she repeated. "In eighty-degree weather?"

Nikki knew that her mother wasn't telling the truth. It would not have been the first time that her mother had pushed up on someone she was involved with.

"Look, Marie wanted to borrow it, okay?"

"Well, it ain't here! Why do you keep thinking that yo' clothes are in my room? Check your own closet!"

"Li'l girl, you betta stop yelling at me before I fuck you up. Don't let yo' little friend see you get embarrassed in here," she said as she walked out the door.

Nikki looked back Hakim, who was now covered up from head to toe. She wanted so badly to ask him if her mother had come on to him in any kind of way, but she didn't know if she honestly wanted to hear the answer. Instead, she crawled into bed with him and gave him her goodies. Hakim dug deep into her core, secretly wishing that he was test-driving her mother.

Red stood in front of the commode, trying to control the stream of piss that was rushing through his penis. He was hard as a rock and ready for round two with one of his old flames from the neighborhood, whose name was Beverly. Cookie was so drunk after her party that she couldn't put out if she wanted to. So after dropping her off, Red made it his business to visit one of the after-hour spots in the city, and he ran into Beverly. One thing led to another, and the two of them ended up in the same bed for the umpteenth time.

Beverly had sexed him from the time they got into the bedroom until they fell asleep. Still horny, Red went back into the bedroom and got between Beverly's legs. She moaned softly as he started doing his tongue thing. They were so into it that they never heard Cookie coming into the room.

"Oh, hell nah!" she screamed. "What the fuck is going on up in this bitch?"

Red jumped out of Beverly's vagina as if it were on fire. "Oh, shit," he said as Beverly grabbed the covers and tried to hide her naked body.

"Nah, bitch, don't try to cover yo' nasty-looking ass up now," Cookie yelled as she headed toward the bed.

"Bitch, who the fuck you calling—"

Beverly couldn't even get the last word out of her mouth before Cookie slapped her in it. Cookie then reached for a handful of her hair and dragged her to the floor. The two women punched, scratched, and kicked each other for what seemed like forever before Red stepped in and broke it up.

"Get off me, Red! Get the fuck off me," yelled Cookie as she tried to get at Beverly again.

Knowing that Cookie had gotten the best of her, Beverly was hesitant to continue the fight. "Yeah, you better hold that bitch," she said half-heartedly.

"Beverly, you need to roll out," Red said to her.

Beverly headed for the bedroom door but couldn't resist getting one good verbal dig in on Cookie before she left. "Thanks for the dick, big daddy. Whenever you want some good pussy, instead of that dry-ass shit you been getting, just gimme a call."

Cookie became enraged. She picked up a lamp from Red's table and slung it toward Beverly's head. Beverly had just closed the door when it smashed up against it and shattered.

"Girl, what the fuck wrong with you, coming up in here and tearing up my shit like you fucking crazy?"

"The fuck you mean, what's wrong with me? Nigga, what the fuck wrong with you, bringing some bitch up in here and fucking her in the bed where me and you get busy? What kinda fucked-up part of the game is that?"

"Ay yo, you need to calm yo' ass down up in here, yelling like you ain't got no damn sense!"

"Calm down? What the fuck you mean, calm down? I catch you in here fucking another bitch and you tell me to calm down? Fuck that!"

Before she could stop herself, Cookie hauled back and slapped the taste out of Red's mouth. For a very long minute, Red just stood there stunned. But as the shock began to wear off, Cookie knew that she was in trouble.

"I know you done lost yo' muthafucking mind now, putting yo' fucking hands on me like that!"

"I'm sorry. I didn't mean to—"

"Shut the fuck up," Red screamed as he backhanded her to the floor. As soon as the seat of her pants touched the floor, Cookie bounced back up and headed toward the stairs.

"Nah, bitch, don't try to run now! You wanted to act like a muthafucking man, so now I'm gonna beat yo' ass like a man!"

"Get the fuck away from me," she screamed as she started down the steps.

"Fuck that shit! I'm gonna show yo' ass what happens to wannabe tough bitches who think they can handle a nigga like me!"

Cookie ran for the door as fast as her legs could carry her. Red was right behind her with fire in his eyes. He was so mad that his light skin had turned his namesake.

"Come back here," he yelled. Just as Cookie opened the door, Ray-Ray came through it. Cookie almost knocked him down as she sprinted for her car.

"Damn, girl, what the fuck is going on here?"

"Ask ya boy! And while you at it, ask him about your—"

Bam!

Cookie ran face-first into an elderly woman walking down the sidewalk with a bag of groceries in her arms.

"You better run! I'm gonna beat yo' muthafucking ass when I catch you!" Red tried to run past Ray-Ray and get to Cookie, but Ray-Ray grabbed him and put him in a bear hug. "Get the fuck off me! I'm gonna beat the brakes off that ho!"

"Damn, Red, calm down. I know you ain't trying to go to jail fo' beating yo' bitch up."

Listening to Ray-Ray talk seemed to calm Red down a bit. "You right. I ain't got time to be paying money to get out of jail for putting the beat up on a bitch. Let's just go in here and smoke one."

The two friends walked back into the living room as Ray-Ray took a blunt out of his pocket. "What the hell went down up in here?"

Red cracked a slight smile. Five seconds later, the smile turned into a full-blown laugh. " I was up in here putting the dick on Beverly like only a nigga like me can, and Cookie's crazy ass bust up in here and start acting all loco and shit. She put the beat up on Beverly something terrible."

Red fell back on the couch and held his stomach. He was laughing so hard that Ray-Ray started laughing by association. A sudden thought flashed through Ray-Ray's head as he was giggling.

"What the hell was Cookie talking about when she told me to ask you about something?"

"I don't know what the fuck that crazy-ass broad was talking about. Hurry up and pass that blunt."

Ray-Ray tried to get the thought out of his mind, but something deep inside of him told him that Cookie had something to say that he might have been interested in hearing about. The strange look on Red's face when he asked the question gave him the impression that Red was not telling him something. He decided right then that he was going to use the fact that Cookie was pissed off at Red to get to the bottom of the situation.

Chapter 20

Dryer gingerly eased up the steps leading to the police station. His ribs were hurting him so badly he could barely breathe. He wasn't a doctor, but he could tell that they were severely bruised, if not broken.

"Damn, Eugene, what the hell happened to you?" one of his fellow officers asked.

Dryer, in no mood to answer questions about the incident, snapped viciously at his comrade. "None of your fucking business," he growled.

Stunned at his abrasiveness, the officer gave Dryer the finger. "Fuck you then, fat motherfucker. That's what I get for being concerned about your Krispy Kreme–eating ass."

Dryer contemplated apologizing but quickly decided against it. He knew from prior experience that an apology would have surely led to an inquisition of the incident. Shooting an unarmed African American was sure to bring mayhem to not only Dryer, but the entire Cleveland Police force as well.

The only things stopping that from happening were that Hank didn't know that Dryer was a cop and that Dryer had left the scene so quickly after it happened. This time it worked in the police's favor that no one wanted to get involved.

When Stone spotted his partner limping into the precinct without the box of doughnuts, he knew immediately that something was wrong. He silently cursed himself for not following his first mind and going with Dryer in the first place. Before anyone else in the busy station could see Dryer, Stone ran over to him and ushered him into his office.

"Jesus Christ, what the hell happened to you?"

Without answering, Dyer took a deep breath as he plopped down in a chair. Stone quickly closed the door to keep nosy onlookers away.

"I need . . . a glass . . . of water," Dryer said, coughing. As Stone rushed out into the hallway to get his partner something to drink, Dryer sat there seething. He took out his cell phone, got up, and slowly limped over to Stone's computer. Then he connected his phone to the computer and uploaded the picture that he had taken of Hank after hitting him in the head. He wasn't sure, but he thought he'd recognized Hank's face when the two of them were tussling.

After he was done uploading the picture, he ran it through the database and clicked known affiliates. The hair on the back of his neck stood up as Bobby's and Red's faces popped up. Knowing that he had shot one of Bobby and Red's associates gave Dryer a sick sense of satisfaction. "If I had known that you were a part of Red's crew, I would've killed your ass, nigger," he mumbled to himself. He sat back and smiled as he thought about the ear-piercing scream that Hank let out after being shot.

His temporary joy came to an abrupt end as he suddenly realized that his daughter was probably sleeping with the enemy. Dryer became nauseated as visions of Nancy getting screwed by a black man ran wild through his mind. He almost threw up at the image of her being on her knees, giving an African American a blowjob. And if that weren't enough to make him pass out, the thought of Nancy getting pregnant by a black man would surely do the trick. Pain exploded throughout his side as a result of Dryer slamming his fist down on the computer desk.

"Eugene, what the hell is going on with you?"

Dryer was in such deep thought that he never heard Stone reenter the room. "Nothing."

"That's horseshit," yelled Stone. "You leave talking about going to get some damn doughnuts but come back looking like you've been in a damn bar fight! Everybody out there, including our fucking boss," he said, pointing toward the door, "was wondering where the hell you were with the damn doughnuts! Now you can either tell me what the hell is going on, or I can just call the captain in here, and you can explain the shit to him! I'm your gotdamn partner, for Christ's sake!"

After Dryer broke down and told Stone what had happened, Stone just shook his head and stared at Dryer.

"I know, man, I know. It was a stupid-ass thing to do," Dryer conceded.

"First things first," said Stone, placing his hand on Dryer's shoulder. "We need to get you to the hospital to see about those ribs. It looks like you're having a helluva time breathing over there."

Stone walked over to Dryer and helped him up. He would just call his boss and make up a lie that would cover for both of them later. After Stone helped Dryer to the door, the two of them stood there and waited until the coast became clear. When they were sure it was, Dryer and Stone snuck out the back door.

"The fuck you keep asking me the same muthafucking questions for? Didn't I already tell yo' ass what happened?" Hank snapped at his girlfriend. He was so pissed at Dryer for shooting him and at Nancy for not letting him in afterward that he wanted to do nothing more than murder both of them. After Dryer hit him in the head with his pistol, Hank was dazed.

He figured that, after finding out that Dryer was Nancy's father, the best way for him to keep himself among the land of the living was to pretend that he was unconscious. As soon as Dryer left, Hank started banging on Nancy's front door. Two minutes passed before he realized that she wasn't going to open the door. With his foot bleeding badly, Hank had no choice but to call his girlfriend and tell her to come pick him up. By the time she got to him in his car, Hank was only semi-conscious.

"I don't know why you keep hanging around with Bobby and Red anyway," his girlfriend, April, said to him. "They ain't nothing but trouble."

"Look, when I want yo' muthafucking opinion on who to hang the fuck out wit', I'll give it to yo' ass! Now bring me another damn beer!"

"Beer? You know damn well you ain't supposed to be drinking no—"

"Stop badgering the fuck outta me, and bring me a fucking beer!"

"Fuck it then. Drink yo'self to death!"

April stomped off without saying another word. Based on the lie he had told her, April was under the impression that Hank had been running an errand for Red and got robbed. He may have treated her badly, but Hank was no fool. April wasn't a beauty queen by any stretch of the imagination, but the fact that she had Section 8 and was living rent-free was right up Hank's alley. And as long as he kept food in the house and slipped her some dick two or three nights a week, April put up with the mistreatment.

Hank wasn't about to take a chance on letting her know that he was screwing around on her, though. She'd always told him that if she ever caught him, that would be it. There was something in her eyes that told Hank that she meant what she said as far as that was concerned.

"Yo, bae, get the door," he yelled into the kitchen at the sound of a knock on the door. April mean mugged him as she passed him and set his beer on the table. Hank laughed at her and slapped her on her ass as she passed by.

"Quit fucking hitting me!" She rubbed her right cheek on the way to the door, trying to see if she could push away the stinging sensation. She opened the door and caught an instant attitude. Red and Ray-Ray ignored her usual eye-rolling and lip popping. Both men smirked as they walked past her without so much as a hello to her. They knew they were being disrespectful, but they honestly didn't give a damn.

"What the fuck happened to you?"

"It's like I told you on the phone. That muthafucking suicide mission you sent a nigga on."

Red and Ray-Ray looked at each other in confusion. When Hank called Red and told him that he needed to see him ASAP, he didn't tell him about what had happened. Sensing that his friends weren't catching on quick enough, Hank decided to get rid of April before she started asking questions.

"Yo, bae, you feel like going to the store right quick? I'm outta cigs."

Rolling her eyes at both Red and Ray-Ray, April walked out of the house and slammed the door.

"She salty as fuck," laughed Red.

"She'll get over it," said Hank as he turned up the bottle of Corona.

"Okay, what the fuck happened to you? And what the fuck you talking about a suicide mission that I sent yo' ass on?" asked Red.

"I just told her that shit 'cause I couldn't tell her what the fuck happened fo' real."

"Spill it then," Red told him.

"After I left the party last night with the white girl, we went back to her place and fucked half the damn night. Y'all was right! That bitch got a pussy like the Grand Canyon! I was trying my damnedest to touch the bottom of that shit, and I just couldn't reach it! Where y'all find that bitch at?"

"I told you that bitch was thorough. I picked her ass up at a bus stop. I didn't know that she knew Cookie and that other bitch Tammy. I was shocked as fuck when she fell up in that bitch. But the ho knew not to say nothing. It looks like she got some kinda game about herself."

"Tammy?" Hank scratched his head, trying to remember. "Oh, yeah," he finally said. "The bitch Bobby got all chivalrous with."

"Yeah, that's her."

Hank noticed that Ray-Ray wasn't saying anything. "What the fuck is wrong with you?"

"Just got some shit on my mind," Ray-Ray answered.

"Get to the part that got you looking all fucked up and shit," Red yelled. In his opinion, Ray-Ray was starting to act like a bitch, and he was getting tired of it.

"After giving that bitch a little bit of sniff to let me hit that pussy again the next morning, we was getting ready to go pick up some McDonald's and shit. As soon as I got out of the fucking door, this old white muthafucka attacked me! That muthafucka tried to swing on me, and y'all know that was the wrong thing to do!

"I hit ol' boy with a rib shot, and he folded like a bad poker hand. But here go the fucked-up part about the shit. When I was really getting ready to fuck him up, Nancy came back out of the house talking about Daddy this and Daddy that. Hell, after laying the pipe down the way I did, I thought the bitch was talking to me! Come to find out she was talking to that muthafucka! It was her father for real! I was shocked like a muthafucka! And while I was looking at that bitch, wondering what the fuck was going on, that muthafucka pulled out a piece and shot me in the fucking foot!"

"I see yo' shit all wrapped up and shit!"

"Then the muthafucka hit me in the head with the hammer! If I ever see that bitch or her ol' man again, they got to feel it!"

"You shoulda told us this shit on the muthafucking phone. You almost got yo' cover blown! Then yo' broad woulda been cracking yo' muthafucking head," Red laughed.

"Nah, I don't play that shit."

"I don't either. You girl gon' really hate my ass when her cousin tell her that she caught me screwing Beverly."

"You bullshittin'! You got caught screwing another bitch?"

"Hey, it is what it is," Red said in a matter-of-fact tone. "If the bitch don't like it, her ass can kick rocks. I got plenty of hoes who wanna kick it wit' a nigga like me."

Looking at his watch, Hank started to get frustrated. "Where the fuck is this broad at?" No sooner had Hank opened his mouth than April came strolling through the door. "Damn, it's about time. What the fuck did you have to do, make the damn cigarettes?"

Instead of arguing with Hank, April tossed the pack to him and walked straight to her bedroom. Once she got there, she immediately called her cousin Cookie. April wasn't as stupid as Hank thought she was. She knew instantly that there was something off about Hank's "getting robbed" story. While Hank thought that she was on her way to the store to buy him a pack of smokes, April was busy listening at the front door. She didn't have to go to the store because she had the Newports in her purse all along. She'd been pulling this trick on Hank for quite

some time now, and when the time was right, she was
going to put his ass out into the cold.

Armed with a pocketful of money and weed to burn,
Ivory smiled as she headed back to Cleveland. She had
just made a quick $5,000 and was itching to spend some
of it.

Although Darnell had told her that the weed she had
was given to him on consignment, she saw no harm in
treating herself to a few things. In her mind, she had
earned it. She thought about the many hours that she
had put in at Rite Aid the past few months, and she burst
out laughing. It would've taken her three months to
make this kind of bread at her old gig.

"I woulda been slinging weed a long time ago if I'd
known that it would be this easy to get paid," she whispered to herself.

Ivory jumped slightly at the buzzing of her cell phone
clipped to her hip. "Sup, bitch?" she answered when she
saw that it was Cookie calling her.

"Girl, you ain't gon' believe what the fuck happened! I
caught that no-good-ass man of mine in the bed wit' Beverly's trick ass!"

"What? I know damn well they didn't disrespect you
like that! I hope you beat the brakes off that ho!"

"You muthafucking right I did! I tried to kill that bitch!"

Ivory just shook her head. She'd heard through the
hood grapevine that Red was still messing around with
Beverly, but because she didn't have any proof, she chose
to keep her mouth shut.

"I need a fucking drink. I'm 'bout to head up to the bar.
If you get a chance, stop up there."

"Uh, Cookie, there's a million bars in the city of Cleveland. Which one you gonna be at?"

"The Honey Doo, on St. Clair. April gon' meet me up there too."

"I'll try to make it up there. I can't make no promises, though."

"Cool. I'll holla at you if you make it up there."

Ivory knew before she even disconnected the phone that she wasn't going to make it to any bar to hang out with Cookie. She didn't feel like spending her newfound wealth in a bar. There were only two things she was in the mood for: a fat blunt and a stiff dick. And since Darnell wasn't available, she was going to have to rely on her second source for the latter.

Chapter 21

Toi's eyes rolled to the back of her head as Darnell feasted on her sweet loins like they were the last meal he would ever enjoy.

"Right there, baby," she cooed as she grabbed the back of his head and pushed it in deeper. The two of them had been sexing each other down from the second they checked into the Aloft Hotel.

A twinge of guilt washed over him as he thought about Ivory. It quickly dissipated when Toi started grinding her pelvis on his lips. Darnell did care about Ivory. He just didn't love her. The story he had told her about going to New York on business had only been half true.

He was about to purchase thirty pounds of weed and a key of cocaine while he was there, but he was also enjoying the company of his chick on the side. Toi was the middle man who had hooked Darnell up with some major players in the dope game. They met at a rest stop in between Cleveland and New York during one Darnell's business trips. They clicked instantly. Every other weekend, Darnell would make a trip into New York just to see her.

During one such visit, Toi let it slip that her brother was the man to see if you wanted to cop some of the best weed from Manhattan to Harlem. Seeing an opportunity present itself, Darnell quickly let it be known that he was the top dog in Cleveland as far as weed went. He expressed how he would like nothing more than to hook up with her bother and buy from him, provided that the prices were right. Darnell had already heard about how the price of weed in New York was far cheaper than the prices in Cleveland. He figured that if he played his cards right, he could make a killing in no time. At first he was just using Toi to get to her brother, but along the way, he started falling for her. It didn't matter that he had a few women, including Ivory back in Cleveland. He would get rid of them all at the drop of a hat if he were ever forced to choose.

Toi wrapped her legs around Darnell's head and released a river of satisfaction onto his chin. "Ooooh, baby, that shit was the bomb," Toi said. Smiling like he had just won the lottery, Darnell slid up next to her and lay on his back. He was more than happy to please his newfound love. Feeling his dick stiffen, Darnell climbed on top of Toi and slowly eased inside of her vagina.

"Oh, yes, baby, yes," she moaned in ecstasy. When Darnell developed a good rhythm, Toi wrapped her legs around his waist and pulled him deeper inside. Darnell tried in vain to hold out, but Toi's loving was just too good to him.

"Oh, shit, baby, I'm 'bout to come!" Darnell's body shook with pleasure as he emptied himself inside of Toi. After cumming, he fell to the side of Toi and lay there, showering her with praise of how good he thought her sex was. All the while, she remained quiet. Darnell had been noticing for a while now that Toi wasn't as talkative as she was when they'd first met.

"You okay? You haven't been yourself lately."

"There's just something I have to do that I really don't want to do. I mean, it involves my job, but I might have to hurt someone I care about."

"If it's your job, then the person you have to hurt is just going to have to understand." It suddenly dawned on Darnell that, although he had known Toi a little over a month, he had no idea what she did for a living. *Maybe she's a supervisor and has to fire someone she's cool with.* "I don't know the ins and outs, so I'm not going to pry. But you said that it has something to do with your job, so I'm gonna assume that you have to give someone their walking papers. Am I right?"

"Something like that."

"If you have to fire someone, then you just gotta do what you gotta do. If they don't understand that, then fuck 'em! Now, I gotta go drain the main vein. When I get back, I want you to give me some of that good-ass head."

Darnell bounced off the bed, feeling like a king. He looked over at the satchel filled with weed and cocaine and felt like he was on top of the world. He had all the ammunition that he needed to pick up and leave Cleveland and lay roots elsewhere. He felt bad for Ivory, but she would just have to get over it. He liked her, but she was a drama queen, and Darnell knew it. He also knew that if he dealt with her long enough, she would eventually cost him either his freedom or his life.

He knew her well enough to know that no matter what he told her about the weed he gave her being on consignment, she was going to dip into it anyway. *Well, that's her problem. I just hope she can deal with the consequences.* Then he thought about all the fun he'd been having with Toi, and a knot formed in his stomach. He didn't know for sure since he had never felt the emotion, but it occurred to him at this very moment that he may have been falling in love.

After washing his hands, Darnell walked out of the bathroom on cloud nine. His euphoria was short-lived, however, when he looked up and saw Toi's face. It was devoid of emotion and as hard as stone. Gone was the smile that he had come to enjoy. Replacing it was an icy glare that chilled Darnell to the bone. His heart started beating at an accelerated speed as he froze in his tracks.

"What the fuck you doing? What the fuck is going on here?"

With her hands trembling, her eyes watering, and her voice cracking, Toi cocked the hammer back on the nickel-plated 9 mm pistol she held in her right hand.

"Darnell, I . . . I love you. And I'm sorry to have to tell you this. But you're under arrest."

Darnell's heart dropped to the floor as Toi pulled her shield out of her pocket and held it up.

Hakim staggered toward the bus stop like a tired marathon runner crossing the finish line. His legs felt like jelly and threatened to give out on him any second. Nikki and her mother had completely worn him out. As soon as he reached the bus stop, Hakim fell down on the hard wooden bench. His hair made a stain on the glass as he rested his head on the glass pane of the bus stop. Taking a deep breath, Hakim shook his head from side to side. The last thing he'd expected when he spent the night at Nikki's was for her mother to slobber his dick down.

Although he knew in his heart that what happened wasn't his fault, Hakim felt like shit anyway. He felt even worse when his dick started throbbing through his pants, thinking about the world-class blowjob that Nikki's mother had given him. Realizing that he hadn't eaten anything all morning, Hakim eyed the Rally's restaurant across the street. Then, after making sure that the bus wasn't on its way, he darted through the traffic and made his way inside. Hakim was hungrier than he thought, as he finished off one of the double cheeseburgers in five minutes.

As he unwrapped the second one, a young-looking woman with a small child came into the bus stop. Hakim became disgusted as he noticed the disparity of appearance between the two. The woman, who looked even younger than Hakim, was dressed very nicely. She had dark brown skin, and not one of her spiral curls was out of place. She had a diamond bracelet wrapped around her ankle and rings on each hand. The boy had on a dingy white T-shirt that looked more gray than its original color of white. His jeans were ripped and faded, and his Adidas sneakers were coming apart at the heels. To make matters worse, the boy's hair looked as if it hadn't been cut or combed in months.

On top of that, Hakim noticed that whenever a breeze blew through, the boy smelled like he was allergic to a bathtub. Hakim spat on the ground in disgust. For the life of him, he couldn't understand how some women could dress up and keep their hair and nails done but allow their children to walk around looking terrible. They didn't have a lot of money growing up, but their mother made sure that he and Tammy looked decent. It was then that Hakim suddenly realized that the young lad was staring at his grub. A half-second later, the boy's mother smacked him upside the head.

"Stop staring at other's people's food like you ain't never ate before!"

"But, Mama, I'm hungry."

"I told you I was gonna fix yo' ass some cereal when we got back home! Now shut the fuck up! I'm sorry, mister," she said to Hakim.

"It's cool. Li'l man ain't bothering me."

The woman smiled flirtatiously at Hakim. "What's yo' name?" she asked.

Hakim was grateful that her cell phone rang so he didn't have to answer her. Annoyed at her cell phone for messing up her groove, the woman popped her lips and snatched it off her hip.

"This shit betta be good," she spat into the phone without saying hello. "Canceled? What the fuck you mean, canceled? I'm only an hour late!"

This bitch is berserk, Hakim thought.

"Damn welfare muthafuckas make me sick," she ranted as she clipped her phone back onto her hip. "How the fuck they gonna cancel my appointment because I'm only an hour late? Hell, a bitch like me got shit to do!"

"But, Mama, I thought you told Uncle Tim that you didn't have nothing to do today."

Hakim flinched as the woman slapped her son in the mouth.

"Shut up telling my damn business!" Reaching into her pocket and pulling out a piece of paper and an ink pen, the woman jotted down her name and phone number. "Call me sometime," she told Hakim just before grabbing her son's hand and yanking him down the street.

The woman wasn't gone for five seconds before Hakim balled up the paper with her name and number on it and tossed it to the ground. "Trifling ho. She don't even know my fucking name and talking about call her," he mumbled. Two minutes later, Hakim hopped the bus and headed home.

The minute Hakim set foot inside of his house, he caught an instant attitude. The sight of Steve's size-ten feet resting on the coffee table where he sometimes set his snacks almost caused him to snap. Hakim looked around for his mother, but she was nowhere in sight. He was half expecting her to come at him with a stick the way he left the house the previous night. As Hakim stood there fuming, Steve laughed at the television. He was so engrossed in the show he was watching that he never even heard Hakim come into the house.

"Where my moms at?"

At the sound of Hakim's voice, Steve sat straight up. The sight of Hakim standing there with fire in his eyes had Steve completely shook. "Huh? Oh, I think she went to the store."

Without saying another word to Steve, Hakim went into the kitchen and opened the refrigerator. Not finding what he was looking for, he slammed the door so hard the light bulb inside blew. Pissed off, Hakim stormed back into the living room.

"Did you eat my fucking corned beef sandwich that I had in the fridge?"

"Huh?" Steve asked, looking around.

"The fuck you looking around for? I'm talking to yo' ass."

"I haven't touched anything of yours."

"You don't even live here! How the fuck do you know what's mine and what ain't mine?"

"Look," Steve said, standing up, "I haven't eaten anything in here since I got here."

Hakim could tell by the look on Steve's face that he was lying. He stared intently at Steve. Steve took Hakim's silence as a sign that Hakim was calming down. But nothing could have been further from the truth.

"And why didn't you call your mother last night? She was worried sick about you," Steve said, faking concern.

Hakim exploded. "What? Don't be questioning me on where the fuck I been and why I didn't call here! It ain't none of yo' muthafucking business why I didn't! You ain't got a fucking thing to do with what goes down between me and my moms, so you need to start minding yours! And another thing! You may have my mother fooled with all that nice-guy talk, but I know yo' ass ain't shit! And if I ever catch you spying on my sister again, my moms won't be able to stop me from breaking yo'

muthafucking jaw! You got that?" Hakim asked Steve as
he stepped into his face.

Although he was scared to death, Steve was determined not to let Hakim know it. He decided right then
that he was going to show Hakim that he was a man too.
"Look, youngsta. I told yo' ass before that I wasn't looking
at yo' damn sister! Now, if you don't believe me, then
that's yo' damn problem!"

"Who the fuck you think you talking to? My mother
ain't here to save yo' ass this time, so I suggest you stop
getting fly out the muthafucking mouth!"

"Whateva, Hakim! Like I said the first time, I ain't—"

Before he could finish his sentence, Hakim punched
him in the stomach. Steve doubled over in pain. He tried
to catch his breath and recover, but he wasn't fast enough
as Hakim maneuvered his way behind him and put him
in a chokehold. Steve gasped for air as Hakim increased
the pressure of the hold.

"Now what? Talk that bullshit now!"

Steve's face changed colors as he was on the verge of
passing out. He tried desperately to pry Hakim's arms
from around his neck, but Hakim was much too strong.

"Hakim! What the hell do you think you're doing? Let
him go," Janice yelled. But Hakim couldn't or wouldn't
hear her. His rage and hatred of Steve had taken over.
Hoping to get Hakim to let go of Steve before it was too
late, Janice quickly grabbed her cell phone and started
dialing.

Tammy sat quietly in the break room, eating her lunch.
She was trying to push back the smile forcing its way
to her lips. Even the drama surrounding her family life
couldn't spoil her mood. She was still feeling giddy about
Bobby picking her up from work. Out of the corner of her
eye, she saw her coworker Sharon walking toward her.

"Hey, Tammy. Have you talked to ya girl today?"

"Who?"

"Nancy's missing-in-action ass. She was supposed to be here thirty minutes ago, and now Mr. James's punk ass is telling me I can't leave until she shows up."

"He can't do that," Tammy said.

"Well, his ass is doing it!"

"You know that's some bullshit. He cannot make you stay past your regular shift."

"No, but his ass can cut my hours down next to nothing if I refuse. He did that shit to me last month when her ass pulled a no call, no show. That bitch must have some hellafied pussy or give vicious-ass head."

"What? Girl, please, they are not fucking."

Sharon laughed so hard at Tammy's naivete that she caught a cramp in her side. "You done fell and bumped yo' head if you believe some shit like that. Now, I know y'all cool and all, but you better open yo' damn eyes."

Sharon walked away, shaking her head. Tammy took out her phone and called Nancy. When the call went directly to voicemail, Tammy became slightly worried. She made a mental note to stop by Nancy's when she got off. Tammy was seriously starting to wonder about her friend. First, Ivory accused her of being on drugs, and now Sharon was talking about her and the boss sleeping with each other.

Before she could put her phone back in her pocket, it vibrated. Seeing that it was Ivory, she answered it before the third ring.

"Where you at?" Ivory asked without even saying hello.

"I'm at work. You need to come in here and fill out an application with your out-of-work ass."

"Yeah, yeah, whateva. What time do you go on break?"

"I'm on break now."

"Cool. Come outside in the parking lot right quick."

"For what?"

"Just bring yo' ass on."

Before Tammy could question her further, Ivory hung up.

"Damn, this bitch gets on my nerves sometimes," Tammy said to herself.

Looking at her watch, Tammy saw that she had about twenty minutes left for her break. She quickly bagged up the uneaten portion of her food and headed out the door. When she got outside, she looked around for Ivory but didn't see her. Like only a true ghetto queen would do, Ivory started blowing her horn as if she were in a parade. Tammy quickly ran over to Ivory's car in an attempt to keep her from making a bigger fool of herself.

"Why in the hell are you blowing your horn so damn loud?" Tammy asked as she hopped inside. The minute she closed the door, she caught a contact high. "I see you're getting blazed already," Tammy said.

"You damn skippy! I was supposed to go and get me some dick on the side while Darnell was out of town, but my side dude ain't answering the damn phone!"

Tammy looked at her friend in surprise.

"What? You thought that I was only gettin' it from Darnell? I don't know what the fuck he be doing when he be up in New York."

"You could've told me! I thought I was your girl."

"I ain't got to tell yo' ass everything!"

"Whatever," Tammy said. "Let me hit that before I have to go back to work."

Ivory smiled as she passed the blunt to Tammy. That was her whole reason for calling Tammy in the first place. She was a little upset that she wasn't able to hook up with her fuck buddy, so she found solace the only way she knew how. Smoking weed.

"Check this shit out, though. I just came from Akron and . . . bam," she said as she pulled out a large knot of money.

"What the fuck did you do, go down there and rob a fucking bank?"

"Hell nah! Darnell had me go down there and take care of some business for him."

Tammy raised her eyebrows. She had her suspicions of what "business" Ivory went to Akron to take care of. Still, she wanted to hear Ivory say it. "Business, huh? What kind of business?" she asked.

"I think you know what kind. Since he knew he was going to New York, he wanted to make sure that the money kept flowing down here."

"And he trusted you? Someone who has never sold drugs before?"

"Who the fuck else was he gonna trust? Besides, this shit easy as fuck. I just made five Gs in five fucking minutes."

"You'd better be careful. This shit don't sound too kosher to me."

"I got this," Ivory said as she took another puff.

"I have to get back to work," Tammy said while looking at her watch.

"A'ight. I think I'm gonna treat myself to a shopping spree," Ivory said while putting the money back in her pocket.

Tammy walked back inside the mall, wondering if her friend was getting in over her head. She'd only met Darnell a few times, but he didn't strike her as the type of man to let someone else handle his business. For him to do that, Tammy felt that he must have had something up his sleeve.

When she got back to her work station, she looked across the room and saw that Sharon had a very notice-

able scowl on her face. Figuring that it was because Nancy hadn't come in yet, Tammy took out her cell phone
and sent her friend a text message.

Nancy, where the hell r u? Aren't u supposed 2 b @
wrk? Call me wn u get this mssge.

Tammy didn't know what was going on but told herself
that she was going to get to the bottom of it when she got
off of work. Five minutes into the second half of her shift,
she received a phone call. She didn't recognize the number but answered it anyway.

"Hello?"

"I have a collect call from Hakim Green. If you wish to
accept these charges, please press one."

"Collect? What the hell is he doing calling me collect?"
she wondered. Slowly pressing 1, Tammy wondered what
other drama was about to creep into her life. "Hello?"

"Sis, it's me."

"Why in the fuck are you calling me collect on my cell
phone?"

"I need you to bail me outta jail."

"Jail? What the hell are you doing in jail? Does this
have anything to do with those thugs you were hanging
out with the other day?"

"Nah, nothing like that. Look, I don't wanna be in this
damn place no longer than I have to, so could you please
just get me outta here?"

"I am not getting you out of anywhere until you tell me
what the hell you are in jail for!"

"Assault!"

"Assault? On who?"

"I ain't got time to be going through this right now! The
CO is rushing me off the phone. It's gonna cost a thousand dollars to get me out. Go up in my room and look
under my mattress. I got the money there."

"Under your mattress? Where did you get a thousand dollars? Hakim! Hakim!"

Before she could get an answer from her baby brother, he had hung up.

Tammy ran upstairs as quickly as she could. Her boss didn't like it when she told him that she had a family emergency and had to go home, but she didn't care. The only thing she could think about was getting to her baby brother and getting him out of jail. She had never been to jail, but she had heard all the horror stories of being locked up. Lucky for her, Ivory was still in the mall when she got the call from Hakim and was able to give her a ride home. Ivory bombarded her the entire time with questions about Hakim being in jail. After convincing Ivory that she really didn't know anything except what Hakim had told her, she spent the rest of the ride wondering why Hakim had called her instead of their mother.

Trying not to waste any time, Tammy lifted Hakim's mattress and gasped when she saw a large roll of money bound with a rubber band.

"I knew this boy was doing something he didn't have any business doing," she muttered, shaking her head. Peeling off $1,100, Tammy stuffed it into her pocket and raced back down the stairs.

For the first time since she'd gotten inside the house, she noticed that her mother wasn't at home. She thought about calling her mother's cell phone but decided to wait until she talked to Hakim. She didn't know why her brother was in jail, and with the way things were going with her family, she didn't want her brother and mother getting into it again.

Tammy bolted out the door and jumped in Ivory's car. Ivory gunned the engine and fishtailed down the street.

"Slow the fuck down! I don't want to be in jail with my brother!"

Ivory ignored her and continued driving. By the time they got to the police station, Tammy was a nervous wreck. She tripped twice going up the steps, trying to get to her brother. She didn't even wait to see if Ivory was going in with her as she made a mad dash to the service desk.

"May I help you?" the overweight cop behind the glass asked with a disinterested attitude.

"I'm here to post bail for Hakim Green."

After shuffling through some papers, the cop told Tammy that it would be $1,050 to get Hakim released. After posting his bail, Tammy took a seat on the bench and waited for her sibling. Forty-five minutes later, Hakim came out looking wild.

"You okay?" she asked.

"Yeah, I'm straight," he said, laughing.

Tammy instantly became pissed. "What the fuck are you laughing about? Your ass just got out of jail, and you're standing here laughing like you've been vacationing to Hawaii or something."

"Chill out, sis, damn. You act like I been in Alcatraz."

Tammy just sighed loudly and shook her head. She knew that her brother was on a path of destruction, but she was powerless to stop it. "What the hell were you in jail for?"

"Mama didn't tell you?"

"I haven't seen Mama since I left for work this morning."

"She wasn't at home when you went to get the money?"

"No! Now tell me what the hell happened!"

"That punk-ass nigga Steve tried to flex up on me, and I put his bitch ass in a sleeper hold," Hakim said as he demonstrated his choking technique.

Tammy was speechless. She knew that Hakim didn't like Steve. Hell, she didn't either, for that matter, but she didn't think it would get that far. Nor did she ever think her mother would call the police and have Hakim arrested.

Reading her mind, Hakim nodded. "Yep," he confirmed. "Mama had me arrested."

"Hold up. Let me get this straight," Tammy said as she stopped walking. "You mean to tell me that our mother had you arrested? And put in jail?"

"Yeah, she did that punk-ass shit! All because she was trying to protect her ho-ass boyfriend!"

Knowing that her brother had a quick temper, Tammy decided to get the full story before jumping to any conclusions. "Just tell me what happened from start to finish." Before Hakim could get the first sentence out of his mouth, Ivory blew her car horn.

"Come on," she yelled out the passenger's side window.

Tammy grabbed Hakim by the wrist and pulled him to the car like he was a little kid.

"Stop pulling on me. What the hell wrong with you?"

Tammy ignored him as she continued to lead him toward the car.

"Damn, boy, what the fuck you done did?" Ivory asked Hakim when he got inside the car.

"I had to beat the brakes off a bitch-ass nigga I know."

Ivory burst out laughing. "Ah, hell to the nah!"

"I don't know why the two of you are laughing," Tammy scolded. "I don't see shit funny about this."

"'I don't see shit funny about this,'" Ivory repeated in a mocking tone. "I mean, damn, girl, you act like the boy been in Mansfield some damn where."

"I'm just saying, Ivory. I don't see anything funny about being locked up."

Ivory let the subject die. She knew that continuing to speak on it would only upset Tammy more than she already was. She glanced in the rearview mirror at Hakim, who seemed quite unfazed by the whole thing. His smug, roughneck attitude slightly turned her on. As soon as Ivory got three blocks away from the police station and turned the corner, she reached into her console and took out a half-smoked blunt.

"Is that the same one you were smoking on when I saw you earlier?"

"You know better than that. That muthafucking tree been burned to the ground."

Ivory lit it, inhaled a couple of times, and then held it out for Tammy to grab it. When she didn't take it, Ivory cut her eyes sideways and saw Tammy staring at her. Tammy jerked her head toward Hakim to indicate that she didn't want to smoke in front of him.

"I know you ain't trippin' 'cause Hakim back there. That nigga ain't thinkin' 'bout yo' ass. He done already told you he know yo' ass be smoking and shit, so you might as well stop frontin'."

When Tammy hesitated, Hakim reached. "Shit, if she don't wanna hit that tree, pass that muthafucka to me," he chimed in.

"Hakim!" Tammy yelled and snatched the blunt out of Ivory's hand before she had a chance to give it to him. "Ivory, what the hell is wrong with you?"

"The fuck you talkin' 'bout?"

"How you just gonna give my little brother a blunt right in front of me?"

A wicked frown formed on Ivory's face. She slowed the car down and pulled over to the curb. In her mind, her friend was being judgmental and a hypocrite. Someone had to put Tammy in her place, and she figured that she was probably the only one who could do it.

"Why the hell are you stopping?"

"Because I got something to say that yo' ass needs to hear."

Tammy folded her arms and rolled her neck. "Oh, is that right?" she asked.

"Yeah, that's right. First of all, I didn't pass yo' brother shit! I held it up for you to take, and you didn't. He reached up here on his own and tried to grab it. That's number one! Number two is that yo' ass is bein' a fucking hypocrite! Hell, yo' ass been smoking weed wit' me for a long-ass time! How you gonna try to check Hakim 'cause he smoke it too? Turn around and look at yo' brother, Tammy! He ain't no damn kid! He damn near grown, so you need to quit tryin' to baby him."

Without saying another word, Ivory pulled away from the curb and into traffic. The fact that Tammy didn't respond to her rant told her that she was at least thinking about what she had said.

Meanwhile, Tammy sat there with a somber look on her face. Deep in her heart, she knew that her friend was right. Hakim was growing up. He wasn't a child anymore. Needing an outlet in the worst way, Tammy put the mind blower to her lips and inhaled, hoping that it would somehow relieve the stress of the day. Tammy then leaned back, closed her eyes, and exhaled.

"Hakim, just tell me what happened, okay?"

"I ain't talkin' 'til you release that tree."

Reluctantly, Tammy passed the blunt to her brother. After taking a deep pull and blowing out, Hakim told his sister the whole story. By the time he was done talking, Tammy was livid. Ivory hadn't even come to a stop yet before Tammy was jumping out of her car and storming toward her house. Hakim and Ivory were right behind her. If something was about to go down, then Ivory was going to be there for her girl.

Tammy was surprised to see that her mother still wasn't home. "I don't where the hell she is, but me and Mama are going to have a talk when she gets here."

"You need me to stay with you?" Ivory asked.

"Nah, girl, I'm straight."

"But what if that nigga come back wit' her?"

"I'll slice his muthafucking ass up if he fucks with me."

"You know what? I don't even wanna see Mama right now. And I really don't wanna see that bitch-ass nigga she with. I got some shit I gotta do anyway, so I'm 'bout to be up outta this piece."

"Huh? Where the hell are you going, Hakim?" Tammy asked with concern.

"Ay yo, don't start this bullshit again."

Tammy started to say something but was cut off by Ivory. "It might not be a bad idea for Hakim to get away from here for a li'l while, Tammy. What do you think is going to happen if that asshole comes back here and they see each other? Not to mention, what if that nigga try to sneak up on Hakim?"

"I wish that bitch-ass nigga would," Hakim said, cracking his knuckles.

Ivory cut her eyes at Hakim and gave him a "nigga, I'm trying to help you out" look.

"Maybe you're right. The last thing I want is for something to happen to my bro," Tammy said as she playfully mugged Hakim upside the head.

"Yo, Ivory, you think you can give me a ride to the mall? I gotta explain to my boss why I missed work today."

"I got you, youngsta. But now that you ballin' and shit, you can kick in some gas money."

As soon as Ivory walked out the door, Hakim waved his hand at her. "I ain't givin' her ass shit."

"You'd better. She will put your ass out."

"Yeah, right," Hakim said, heading for the door.

"Hakim, please be careful," Tammy said with worry in her eyes.

"I'll be okay, sis." Just before he got out the door, Hakim turned to his sister and looked her square in the eyes.

"If you feel that you gotta talk to Mama about this shit, then that's cool. But don't say nothin' to that busta-ass nigga. 'Cause I swear to God, if he puts his hand on you, I'm gonna kill him."

Tammy stared back into the face of her sibling. It took less than a second for her to be convinced that he meant every word. While waiting for her mother, Tammy decided to call and check on her friend.

Chapter 22

Nancy woke up in a cold sweat. The last thing that she remembered was her father yelling at her on the other side of her door. For the life of her, she couldn't remember why, though. Nancy then got out of her bed and staggered to the bathroom. After splashing cold water on her face, Nancy looked in the mirror and noticed that her eyes looked glassy. She also saw that her once-beautiful skin was beginning to appear ashy. Her fingernails were becoming brittle and chipped. That's when she realized that she wasn't taking care of herself.

She was starting to resemble a cocaine zombie. Unable to bear looking at herself any longer, Nancy walked out of her bathroom and headed back toward her bedroom. On the way there, her stomach reminded her that she hadn't eaten anything in quite some time. Nancy took a detour and headed for her kitchen. After devouring a bowl of ravioli, she suddenly remembered that she was supposed to be at work.

"Oh, well," she said, shrugging her shoulder. "Too late now." Since she had the boss in her hip pocket, Nancy knew that nothing was going to happen to her. She also knew that her coworkers were going to be pissed, but she didn't care. She grabbed her phone off the table and saw that she had three missed calls and one text message. Before she could respond to Tammy's text, the phone vibrated in her hand. She no longer had to worry about calling Tammy back because it was Tammy on the other end of the phone.

"What's up, girl?" she answered the phone.

"What the hell do you mean, what's up? Where the hell have you been? Don't you know you were supposed to be at work today?"

"I was feeling sick. I talked to Mr. James about it, and he told me to just stay at home."

Although Tammy knew that Nancy was lying, she let it slide. She was just happy that her friend was okay.

"I'm still feeling kinda fucked up, though. I'm gonna just lie back down."

"All right, if you say so. Call me if you need me."

After hanging up with Nancy, Tammy said a prayer for her. Her gut feeling told her that Nancy was worse off than she was letting on.

April and Cookie had been sitting in the bar for hours, tossing back tequila shots. In between drinks, they were bashing their significant others. Several men had already tried to step to them, but with their attitudes on hate mode, the fellas didn't have a snowball's chance in hell of getting any play.

"I know one thing," Cookie spat. "I'm getting tired of that muthafucka cheating on me."

"You got that shit right," April concurred. "Hank think a bitch stupid, but I been hip to his bullshit for a while now. I'm just biding my time 'til I roll out on his ass. I been workin' on something that's gonna shock the shit out of him."

"I hear ya, but I'm on some get-back shit. I want some fucking payback for my feelings. That nigga wanna cheat on me? Well, two can play that muthafucking game."

April was so mad she could barely see straight. She had been faithful to Hank since the day they started dating. He had smooth-talked her into believing that the only reason he'd started cheating on her in the first place was because the other women were doing things in the bedroom that she wouldn't do. He'd told her that it was her responsibility to please her man in the bedroom by any means necessary. She'd even gone so far as to give him the ultimate gift for a man and allow another woman to come into their bedroom and participate in a threesome.

"I don't know about you, but I'm gonna get me some dick on the side tonight," Cookie proclaimed. "I'm tired of getting my feelings hurt 'cause that nigga wanna be a dog."

April thought about what Cookie was saying. She, too, was getting fed up with being the victim.

"And if you was smart, yo' ass would do the same," Cookie said as she reached into her purse and pulled out a pack of condoms. She reached over to April, opened her hand, and put them inside of it.

"What the fuck you gon' use?"

"Don't worry. I got an extra."

April noticed the sly smile on Cookie's face and shook her head. "You planned this damn shit, didn't you?"

"You damn right I did. The second you called me," she said, starting to laugh. "If them muthafuckas can have their fun, we can have ours. All we gotta do now is sit here and wait for these niggas to shoot their thirsty-ass regular. Shit, I need me some fresh dick anyway."

The two women gave each other a high five and ordered another drink apiece. After taking a sip of her drink, Cookie looked toward the door and saw a slightly heavyset chocolate-skinned man walking through the door. An evil grin slid across her lips. "How mad are you at Hank?"

"Pissed the fuck off is more like it," April snarled. "Why?"

"Because I just figured out a way to really get some payback on them niggas." Cookie then nodded in the direction of the door.

April looked and immediately started snickering. "You bad as fuck."

"Not yet, but I'm 'bout to be." Cookie got up and sauntered over to her mark.

Bobby woke up with a large smile on his face. His dick was rock hard, and pre-cum oozed from the tip. He'd just had the most intense erotic dream he'd ever had. Just to make sure that it was a dream and not reality, Bobby reached over to the other side of the bed and felt around.

"Damn," he uttered. Although he knew that it was a dream, he really wished Tammy were lying next to him. Bobby smiled as he thought about the conversations he and Tammy had engaged in since he'd met her. He was intrigued by her goals and liked that she wasn't just another hood rat from around the way. Tammy was the only person who knew that Bobby liked to write. He never told Red or any of his boys because he didn't want to hear the jokes that were going to come with it. He was serious about his writing and didn't want to subject himself to the negativity of his peers' responses. He didn't know why he told Tammy. He just felt like he could tell her.

Feeling extremely motivated, Bobby sprang from the bed. After taking a trip to the bathroom, he went back to his bedroom and picked up the half-smoked blunt that was lying on his nightstand. Then he went into his living room and sat behind the desk that held his notebook. With the remote control, he clicked on the CD player and pressed play to start the music pumping.

He decided to listen to a new artist from New York he'd been hearing about. After listening to the gravelly voice rain fire over the beat for a few minutes, Bobby lit the blunt and took a pull. He nodded as the rapper flowed with distinct New York flavor.

"Damn, that nigga's kicking some shit," Bobby said as he started writing. Because he couldn't type that well, Bobby wrote his stories down with the intent of having someone type them for him at a later date. As the music flowed through his ears, Bobby let his mind race through the city of Cleveland. With his mind cocked liked a semi-automatic pistol, the words effortlessly slid through the chambers of his thoughts, down the barrel of his arm, and out of his itchy trigger finger. The red pen he used leaked ink on the pages like blood. Bobby was in such a writing groove that he never even heard his phone vibrate.

By the time he put down his pen nearly an hour and a half later, he had written over a thousand words. Bobby's wrist was sore, but he felt good about being able to write as much as he did. A sudden thought occurred to him as he reached for his cell phone. After picking it up, he saw that he had missed three calls from Red. "His ass can wait," he said as he started texting Tammy.

Hey, I know it's l8 so I'm txtin u nstead of callin. I have smthin I wnt u to rd. Give me a call wn u gt the time.

Bobby didn't know if he was doing the right thing by letting Tammy read his work, but he did want to get someone's opinion about his writing. After sending the text, Bobby called Red to see what was so important.

"Where the fuck you been? I been trying to call yo' ass for the last hour."

"I was asleep," Bobby lied. The last thing he wanted to hear was Red talking shit to him about his writing.

"Well, I was trying to get a hold of you 'cause them niggas over that way wanted to get a little something-something. But don't worry 'bout it. I sent them two young niggas who was at the party to take care o' that shit."

Is this nigga smoking the shit we s'posed to be sellin'? How the fuck is he gon' send a couple of fucking rookies to take care of business? "You think that was a good idea to send those muthafuckas? We just met those niggas."

"*You* just met them niggas. I been knew what kinda work those cats wanted to put in. But check it. We still over here chilling if you wanna come through and smoke a couple of burnas with us."

Bobby thought about it for a minute. He was done with his writing session and didn't want to call Tammy so late, so he figured, why the hell not? "Give me about thirty minutes."

After hanging up with Red, Bobby hurriedly got dressed. On his way to Red's house, he figured he would stop at the store and pick up a box of blunts since they always ran out. Stopping at the first corner store he came to, Bobby quickly jumped out and headed inside. His thoughts drifted to Tammy as he was entering the store. Not paying attention, he bumped into an older cat making his way out.

"Hey, young blood, watch where you . . . Bobby? Is that you?"

"Ah hell nah, what's up, Tick?" Bobby spoke when he realized who he almost knocked down. "Where the fuck have you been hiding?"

"I been here, been there, been a li'l bit of everywhere," Tick answered. Tick was one of the originals from back in the day. Before drugs ravaged his body, he was one of the most sought-after hitmen in Cleveland. Anyone needing someone snuffed out, Tick was your man. He was a former Navy Seal who was well schooled in the art of assassination.

Back when Bobby was a young G, Tick came to his rescue one day when some older heads caught Bobby in the trap and tried to rob him. Tick came out of nowhere to save the youngster's hide. When Bobby asked Tick why he had helped him, Tick told him that he couldn't just sit by and watch three grown men beat up on a young dude trying to eat. Little did Bobby know that Tick himself had planned on robbing him that night and was pissed off that the other dudes had the same idea and beat him to the punch.

Bobby thanked Tick by hitting him off with a nice sum of cash for watching his back, but ever since then, he carried a pistol with him. Bobby looked at Tick and felt bad for him. The once-graceful features of a man who resembled Will Smith were now just a fading memory. Tick's skin was now ashy, and his hairline receded so much Bobby wondered why he didn't just cut it all off. He'd lost a good fifty pounds since Bobby had seen him last, and the teeth that used to be white were now on the other side of yellow, the ones that he had left anyway.

"Bobby, I hate to ask you this, but you think you can spare a few dollars for ya old buddy? I get paid next week. I can meet you back up here and square up wit' you then."

Bobby sighed and reached into his pocket. He knew that if he gave Tick money, he'd never see it again. Tick had pulled the same thing on him a little less than a year ago. But ever since Tick had saved him from getting robbed and catching a beat down that day, Bobby felt like he owed Tick, because that was the first time anyone other than Robin had looked out for him. Bobby knew, however, that he had to draw the line somewhere. If he didn't, then Tick would try to get money from him every time he saw him. Bobby gave Tick a stern look.

"I can't keep feeding yo' habit every time I see you. I love you like cooked food, but I ain't no ATM." Bobby peeled off two twenties and handed them to Tick.

"I know," replied Tick. "I appreciate it, though. I'm gonna pay you back, I promise," Tick said as he scurried away.

Chapter 23

Tammy sat in front of the television with one leg crossed over the other. She couldn't wait for her mother to get home so she could have it out with her. *No dick could be that good that you would have your own child locked up.*

After receiving the text message from Bobby, Tammy seriously thought about calling him back and asking him to come pick her up. Then she thought about her family situation and decided against it. This was one conversation that she and her mother needed to have.

Tammy needed to know where she and Hakim stood with their mother. Tears formed in her eyes as she wondered if her mother was actually going to put a man before her kids. Every indication that Janice had given her so far was that she was. Tammy wanted to brush it off as simple infatuation, but deep in her gut, she knew better. She didn't know what her mother saw in Steve, but she was definitely in love.

Tammy's attention turned toward the door as she heard the locks click. A plan to see where her mother's loyalty was quickly entered her mind. Janice walked through the door with a glow on her face. The look pissed Tammy completely off, but for the sake of her plan, she had to maintain her composure.

"Hey, Tammy. I'm surprised you're still up," she said with a fake smile on her face. "I thought you would be knocked out by now."

"I'm waiting up for Hakim. He texted me while I was at work and told me that he would be home today. I've tried to call him a couple of times, but he's not answering, and to be honest, I'm starting to get a little worried. You haven't heard from him, have you?"

As Tammy patiently waited for an answer, Janice stood there, trying to decide whether she should tell Tammy the truth or lie to her daughter. "No, I haven't," she said.

"Really?"

"Yeah, really."

"So, where's ya boyfriend?" Tammy asked as she turned her head back toward the television.

"He's at home, why?"

"Just asking."

Without saying another word to her daughter, Janice walked up the stairs, went into her bedroom, and shut the door. For a few seconds, Tammy sat there in shock. It was tearing her apart that her mother was choosing a man she barely knew over them. Tears flowed down her face as she turned the television off and stood up. Rage flushed through her body as she headed up the stairs and walked toward her mother's bedroom.

Ivory rolled over on her back, exhausted. She and her lover had just engaged in two hours of mind-blowing sex. "Damn, Hakim, that shit was the fucking bomb. I think I came about three or four times."

Ivory had never meant to seduce Hakim. On the way to the mall, she had to stop off at her house to pick up a blouse that she was going to return to JCPenney. Hakim asked if he could come in and use the bathroom. While waiting for him, Ivory figured she might as well fire up a blunt and get a few puffs in. When Hakim came out of the bathroom, she passed it to him. One thing led to another, and before they both knew it, Ivory was on her knees with Hakim's penis in her mouth.

Hakim felt bad for cheating on Nikki, but he couldn't pass up the chance to do something that he'd secretly wanted to do for a couple of years now. Ivory, however, had no such feelings of guilt. Since the dude she was going to see wasn't answering his phone, she felt quite satisfied that she was able to get herself some feel good.

All of a sudden, Ivory started laughing loudly.

"What the hell are you laughing at?"

"I was just thinkin', if yo' sister caught us fucking, she would kill our asses."

"Whateva. I'm a grown-ass man," Hakim bragged.

Ivory rolled her eyes. Hakim may not have known it, but Ivory was well aware of how Tammy felt about her brother.

Hakim looked at Ivory's naked body with lust in his eyes. Her legs were spread, and her neatly trimmed bush caused him to salivate. Licking his lips and rubbing his hands together, he grabbed his dick and walked toward Ivory in an attempt to get a second helping of sex, but he stopped dead in his tracks when his cell phone buzzed. Looking at the caller ID, he saw that it was Nikki.

"I gotta take this call right quick," he said, heading toward the bathroom.

"Take yo' pussy-whipped ass on then," Ivory said as she started fingering herself. Hakim's dick got so hard it became painful. "But if you want some more of this gold, you betta bring yo' ass back over here."

Hakim looked at his phone and then back at Ivory and laid it on the table. He smiled devilishly as he walked back over to Ivory's bed and climbed in.

With tears streaming down her face, Tammy stormed up the stairs. She couldn't get to her mother's room fast enough after the initial shock of her mother lying to her had worn off. Her mother had all but told her that Steve was more important to her than her kids were. Breathing fire, Tammy burst into Janice's room, screaming obscenities.

"I guess you weren't going to fucking tell me that you had Hakim arrested, huh?"

Janice looked like a deer caught in headlights.

"What? You didn't think that my brother was going to tell me what the hell happened? How the hell can you call yourself a mother when you're putting your own son in jail?"

"Let me tell your smart ass something," Janice yelled as she hopped off the bed. "You don't know what the fuck you're talking about, 'cause you wasn't here! Your brother was totally out of fucking line!"

Tammy decided to test her mother a little more. "So you're just going to let him stay in jail?"

"For the time being, yes! Don't worry, I'm gonna get his ass out in the morning!"

"Don't bother. I already got my brother out of fucking jail," Tammy said as she walked out of her mother's room and slammed the door.

"Then what the fuck you come in here talking that dumb-ass shit for?" Janice yelled through the door. "And I done told yo' ass about cussin' in my damn house! The next time you do it, find ya'self another place to live!"

As soon as Tammy got to her room, she slammed the door, fell down on her bed, and burst into tears. When she cried all she felt that she could cry, she picked up her cell phone and texted her brother. Then she called Bobby.

"What the fuck happened to yo' foot?" Bobby asked Hank as soon as he saw his friend.

"It's a long-ass muthafucking story," answered Hank as he tossed back a bottle of Heineken.

"I know yo' ass ain't dumb enough to drink when you takin' meds," Bobby said, laughing.

"Now you sound like my bitch! That's why I had to roll the fuck up outta that piece tonight. I got tired of hearing her fucking mouth about that bullshit."

"What the fuck she do, shoot yo' ass in the foot?" an amused Bobby asked.

"Didn't I just say that I didn't want to talk about the shit? And what the fuck yo' li'l ass grinnin' at?" Hank said, switching his venom from Bobby to Dru.

"Ain't nobody said shit to you," Dru spat back. He was getting tired of members of Red's crew disrespecting him. He made a promise to himself right then and there that the next time it happened would be the last. He and Ced had just dropped off a package that raked in major dough, but they were still getting treated like shit. At least he was. In fact, the more he thought about it, the more he realized that he was the one who was being mistreated. They barely ever said a word to Ced. *It doesn't matter, though. As soon as I get my weight up, I'm gonna assassinate them niggas and take over they spot anyway.*

As soon as his and Bobby's eyes locked on to each other, their stares hardened. Dru had in no way forgotten about the knot that Bobby had put on his head with his pistol, and Bobby knew enough about the game to know that he had to keep an eye on Dru. No one in the hood would ever let that kind of disrespect slide, and Bobby knew that. Whether Dru was now on the team or not, Bobby had to make sure not to get caught slipping around him.

"Leave that li'l nigga alone," Red said to Hank, breaking the silent stare between Bobby and Dru. "It ain't his fault you got fucked up by that old-ass white dude."

"What white dude?" Bobby asked as he turned serious. "Who the fuck we gotta go fuck up?"

"I don't feel like talking about this bullshit right now," Hank said in almost a pleading voice. "All I wanna do is kick it with my niggas and get drunk as fuck before I go home."

"Whateva," Bobby said as he grabbed a beer off the table.

"Bobby, let me holla at you in the kitchen for a minute," Red said to his cousin. After taking a swig of his drink, Bobby followed Red. When they got into the kitchen, Red's smile disappeared.

"What's up?" Bobby asked, seeing the tension on Red's face.

"Did you forget what the fuck we was s'posed to do tonight?"

Bobby scratched his head and racked his brain, trying to figure out what Red was talking about. "I don't know. What?"

"We was s'posed to cut the dope and bag the shit up into grams tonight."

"Shit," Bobby yelled. He had totally forgotten.

"I didn't want to say shit about it when I called you earlier, 'cause I didn't want them nosy muthafuckas in there eavesdropping on our conversation, but we can't be slipping like that. We gotta keep this product moving to keep the pockets fat."

"My bad. I didn't get a whole lotta sleep today. I got up early to take Tammy to work and—"

"Hol' up, man. What the fuck you just say? You was tired 'cause you had to get up early and take some broad you just met to work? What the fuck is wrong with you? Let me find out that you becoming one of them sucka-for-love-ass niggas," Red laughed.

"Never that," Bobby said, although he did like Tammy a little more than even he was willing to admit.

"Let's go blow some trees," Red bellowed as he gave his cousin a fist pound. The two of them walked into the living room, where Hank, Dru, and Ced were passing a blunt back and forth. Bobby and Dru mean-mugged each other as Bobby sat down on the couch.

"You two niggas just gon' stare at each other like a couple of bitches, huh?" Red asked when he noticed the tension between them. "Ay yo, there's a lotta money to be made out there, so I suggest you two muthafuckas find a way to get along, 'cause I'm placing them niggas under yo' watch, cuz."

"My watch? What the fuck do you mean, my watch? I ain't no muthafucking babysitter!"

"Ain't nobody asking you to be no damn babysitter! I just need you to look after these two niggas while they get their weight up. It's the least you can do for the operation since I had to bag all that shit up myself, seeing that you was on the muthafucking *Love Boat* and shit."

Dru started to snicker at Red's joke, but Red shot him a "shut the fuck up" look.

Before either of them could respond further, Bobby's cell phone went off. After looking at the screen and seeing that it was Tammy, he hesitated. He looked up at Red, who was staring directly in his face. Bobby knew that if he answered and Red caught on that there was a woman on the other end, his cousin would clown him mercilessly. *Fuck it. I can't fuck this nigga.*

"Hello," he said, easing the phone up to his ear. After listening to Tammy cry for a few seconds, Bobby no longer cared that Red was standing there. "Okay, I'll be there in a second," he told her. "I gotta roll," he said to Red when he disconnected the line.

"Roll where? Yo' ass just got here. Where the fuck you gotta go so muthafucking fast?"

"I got some business I gotta take care of."

"What kinda business?" Red asked skeptically.

"My business, ol' nosy-ass nigga!"

"Yeah, a'ight. Don't let me find out that you being a sucka for a bitch."

Bobby didn't like that Red called Tammy out of her name, but he kept walking, choosing to let it go . . . for now.

Chapter 24

"I don't think this is a good idea," Stone said. "The doctor told you to go home and relax, not go on a vigilante mission."

Dryer sat there stone-faced. After a few seconds of silence, he turned his head toward his partner and looked him square in the face. "You didn't see the smug look on that nigger's face when he walked out of that door, zipping up his fucking pants."

While Dryer sat there seething, Stone just shook his head. The last thing he wanted to be doing was sitting here on a daughter stakeout with his partner. He had a catcall he needed to make. "I'm just saying, there has to be a better way than this to go about it."

Dryer ignored his partner and continued to stare at the door. He didn't tell his partner, but he had every intention of shooting Hank in the face if he happened to walk out the door again. After about an hour of no activity, Dryer decided to come back another day. He made a solemn promise to himself that if he ever saw Hank again, he was surely going to kill him.

Stone dropped Dryer off at his house and, after making sure that his partner was okay, drove off. He felt bad that his friend was letting the thing with his daughter get to him the way that he was. The more he thought about the anguished look in Dryer's eyes, the more pissed off he became. He'd seen Dryer tear up on many occasions when talking about his daughter and wishing that the two of them had a better relationship. He'd also noticed the look in his partner's eyes when he dropped him off. He knew beyond a shadow of a doubt that if he ever caught Hank coming out of his daughter's house again, he was going to blow his brains out.

Feeling that he'd better warn Nancy about her father's attitude toward her actions, Stone drove back over to her house. He sat in the car for a few moments, wondering if he was doing the right thing by getting involved. Figuring that he'd better do it before he lost his nerve, Stone got out of the car and quickly walked up to the door. He saw that her door was ajar, so instead of knocking on it, he slowly pushed it open and walked inside. Stone made his way toward the living room.

"Hello? Nancy? You in here? I need to talk to you about—"

Stone's mouth dropped open, and his nostrils started to flare. Right on the floor in front of him was his partner's daughter on her hands and knees. With a giant penis in her mouth, Nancy was sucking for all she was worth. As he called out her name, Stone felt a lump growing in his pants.

"Nancy, what the hell are you doing in here?" Nancy and the guy she was blowing were enjoying it so much that Stone's words fell completely on deaf ears. After calling her name a second time and not getting any response, Stone became pissed. Ignoring the growing hard-on that was threatening to bust through his pants, Stone grabbed his gun out of his holster and walked up to the young black man who looked like he couldn't have been any older than 17. With one swing, Stone broke the young lad's jaw. Blood flew halfway across the room as the boy crumpled to the floor.

"What the fuck you doing with my partner's daughter, nigger?" Before he could answer, Stone pressed the gun up against his temple and cocked. Scared shitless, the boy pissed on himself. "Get the fuck out of here before I blow your fucking brains out!"

The young boy stumbled twice on his way to the door as a result of not being able to pull his pants up. Stone turned around to face Nancy, who by now had stood up and thrown her hands on her hips.

"What the hell are you doing busting in my damn place and pulling a gun on my company?" she yelled.

"What the hell am I doing? Nancy, what the hell are you doing? How would your father feel if he knew you were over here sucking some nigger's dick?"

"It's none of my father's business what the hell I do," she screamed with tears in her eyes. "Fuck, fuck, fuck! Now what the fuck am I supposed to do? How the hell am I supposed to get what I need now?"

Stone stood there with a confused look on his face. He had no idea what Nancy was talking about until he looked at the floor where the young boy had fallen while heading for the door. He looked back up at Nancy and saw her staring at the same spot. A smile broke out across her face as she headed toward the small bag that he'd dropped on the floor. Suddenly it all became clear to Stone, and the harsh reality made him sick to his stomach. Now he knew what Nancy had meant when she asked the question about getting what she needed. Before Nancy could get to the dope, Stone reached down and scooped it off the floor.

"No! Give that to me. It's mine," she screamed and lunged in his direction.

"Oh, so you're a fucking dopehead now?" Stone yelled as he held the bag up and out of her reach. With Nancy still trying to get at the bag, Stone pushed her down on the floor.

"This is going to kill your father," he said, shaking his head at her. As Stone turned to walk out the door, Nancy grabbed his leg.

"Wait, where are you going? Please give it to me! I'll do anything!" Stone tried to push Nancy away, but she held on to his leg.

"Nancy, let me go," he said in a low but firm tone. Nancy shook her head no as she frantically pulled at his pants. Her eyes then locked on to his crotch area. With blinding speed and before Stone could stop her, Nancy unzipped his pants and pulled out his meat.

"What the hell are you . . . Oh, shit," he moaned as she stuck his meat in her mouth. When Stone's hands fell to his side, Nancy eased the dope out of his hand. Stone was mesmerized by the intense blowjob that he was receiving from his partner's only child.

"Oh, my God," he mumbled as Nancy worked her magic. His toes curled inside his shoes. His body started to shake in anticipation of the nut that was fast approaching the tip of his dick. When she was sure that she had him right where she had him, she reached around and grabbed his ass. The move sent Stone over the top as he shot a river of cum down her throat. Stone then collapsed down on the couch and closed his eyes. He couldn't believe what he'd done.

He tried to convince himself that she'd caught him by surprise. But deep down inside, he knew that it was nothing but a lie. The way that Nancy had been on her knees, sucking off the young hustler, had caused his dick to harden instantly. While he was sitting on the couch trying come to grips with what he had just done, Nancy was sitting next to him, sniffing what was left of her brain away. After a few minutes, Stone got up off the couch and pulled his pants up. Without saying another word, he walked out the front door.

Chapter 25

Hakim got on the bus, went to the first open seat that he saw, and plopped down. His sexcapades with Ivory had left him weak in the knees. He shook his head and smiled to himself. *Damn, I been waitin' for a long-ass time to hit that pussy. That shit was juicy as fuck, too.*

His cell phone went off, but he ignored it. It had been going off ever since he climbed into bed with Ivory, but not once had he looked at it. He wasn't going to let anything interfere with getting a piece of ass he'd been thirsting for. Five minutes later, it rang again. Two minutes after that it rang again. Growing increasingly annoyed, Hakim flipped open his phone and shouted into it, "What?"

"Damn, nigga, what the fuck wrong with you?" James asked.

"Oh, my bad, man. I thought you was this broad who keeps calling me. What's up?"

"Where you at? Dru dropped off some work earlier, and I'm gonna need yo' help to get this shit off."

Even though Hakim didn't feel like standing out on the block, the thought of his pockets being filled with greenbacks gave his body renewed vigor.

"I'll be there in a few," Hakim said, thinking about the money he was going to make. Hakim then pulled the string, letting the bus driver know that he wanted to get off at the next stop. The bus had barely come to a complete stop when Hakim leaped off and headed toward the block where James was waiting for him to set up shop.

Hakim made his mind up right then that he wasn't going to leave the block until he sold every rock he had in his possession. He was halfway up the sidewalk when his cell phone popped off his hip and fell to the street. "Damn," he said as he had to stop running and reach down on the ground. Picking up his phone, he finally saw that his sister had texted him.

"I don't know what the hell she want, but I gotta go make this money. I'm just gon' have to holla at her later," he said, picking his pace back up.

Bobby pulled up in front of Tammy's house and parked. He didn't know why Tammy was crying the way she was on the phone, but just in case he had to handle shit like a real G, Bobby reached into his glove compartment and took out his 9 mm. He didn't know why, but in his heart, Bobby was willing to let his pistol smoke for Tammy. He shook his head, thinking about it because he knew that since he hadn't known her long, it would seem that he was sprung off of her, and they hadn't even slept together yet.

His head turned when he heard a door slam. He looked up on Tammy's porch and saw her lugging a large duffle bag down her steps. Being the perfect gentleman, Bobby jumped out of his truck, ran over to her, and grabbed the bag from her.

"You a'ight, li'l mama?"

"Yeah, I'm okay. I just have to get out of this house."

Bobby slung the bag over his shoulder and walked her to the car. Then he opened the door for her and guided her into the passenger's seat. After going around the truck and getting in, Bobby decided that he wasn't going to say anything unless she brought it up. He knew enough about women to know that sometimes they just wanted to be listened to. They didn't want any advice, nor did they want any snide comments. All they wanted was an ear to listen to them and a shoulder to lean on. After five minutes of silence, Tammy started to open up.

"You know, I will be so glad when I start school. That way I won't be in that house as much. I don't know what the fuck is up with my mother. She has fallen in love with a man she barely knows, and now she treats me and my brother like we're the fucking strangers!"

"Brother? I didn't know you had a brother."

"He's seventeen years old and hardheaded. I've been busting my ass to keep him out of these streets, but it looks like all of my prayers are falling on deaf ears."

Bobby remained quiet. He honestly didn't know how to respond to her statement. She seemed genuinely concerned about her brother being in and around criminal activity. But since he was living that lifestyle, Bobby couldn't speak on it. From their prior conversations, Bobby knew that Tammy knew of his street life, but he respected that she didn't want her brother to start a life of crime.

Sensing what Bobby was thinking, Tammy altered her statement. "No disrespect to you, Bobby. I know you do what you have to, but I just pictured a different lifestyle for him."

"No disrespect taken. Not everybody can be a hustler."

Bobby thought that it was funny how Tammy talked so proper. He wanted to clown her about it but knew that now wasn't the time.

"I just can't understand how my mother can put a man she basically just met above her children."

"This punk-ass nigga didn't put his hands on you, did he?"

"He's not that fucking stupid. My brother almost choked his ass out one time."

"A nigga after my own heart," Bobby said, smiling. "What happened that made him put dude in a sleeper hold?"

Tammy took a deep sigh. She really didn't feel like revisiting the incident, but she figured that since Bobby was helping her, she could at least give him the full story of what had gone down. Tammy started from the beginning and told Bobby the entire situation. By the time they got to Bobby's place, he was heated. Just hearing about how Tammy's mother's boyfriend was trying to get a look at Tammy naked when he hadn't even seen her goodies yet had Bobby ready to bust his gun. There was no doubt in his mind that the guy was a pervert.

"I'm sorry to impose on you like this. I just needed to get away from that house for the night."

"You ain't imposing at all," Bobby said, licking his lips. "Matter of fact, I'm glad you called, 'cause there's something I want you to do for me anyway."

Tammy cut her eyes at Bobby. "I don't know what you're expecting, but if you're thinking what I think you're thinking, then you can take me to a hotel."

"Hold up! Ain't nobody suggesting anything like that! I've just got something that I want you to check out. A li'l something I've been working on."

"Oh, okay. Sorry."

Bobby just looked at Tammy and smiled. He loved that she was so feisty.

"What?" she asked when she caught Bobby looking at her.

"Nothing. Just tripping on you," he said. He led her out of his truck and into his place of residence.

"Whateva," Tammy said as she rolled her eyes.

Bobby let out a loud laugh as he walked into his living room and plopped down on the couch.

"What the hell is so funny?" she asked with a slight attitude.

"Nothing," he said, shaking his head. "That's just the first time I heard you say anything that didn't sound so proper."

"Whatever," Tammy said, throwing her hands on her hips and making sure that she enunciated the word. "What is it that you want me to check out?"

Bobby smiled again and walked out of the living room. A few seconds later, he returned with a notebook.

"Oh, that must be the book of stories that you told me about earlier." Tammy took the book from him and flipped through the pages. "You want me to read all of this?" she asked, holding up the thick notebook.

"Just a couple of chapters. I need somebody's opinion on it."

Tammy sat on the couch and started to read the first page. While she was doing that, Bobby went into the kitchen and poured himself a shot of Hennessy. After downing the liquor, he went into his bedroom, opened his nightstand drawer, and took out a blunt. He quickly lit the tip and took a puff. He then walked back into the living room, where Tammy was thoroughly engrossed in his manuscript. He stood there for a minute and watched as she flipped to the next page.

"Do you like what you read so far?"

"It's actually pretty good. Is this the first thing you've ever written?"

"Nope. But it is the most pages I've ever written." Bobby took another pull from the blunt.

"Let me hit that," Tammy said when she got a whiff of the potent smoke.

"I don't know if you can handle this chest breaka here."

"Boy, please," she said as she got up and snatched the blunt out of his mouth. "I'm a professional weed smoker."

"Hey, I ain't questioning ya smoking skills, but that shit there will knock you on yo' ass."

"Whatever," Tammy said as she inhaled deeply. She nodded as she let the smoke ease out of her nostrils. "I can't front, though. This is some good-ass weed."

"Damn straight it is. I don't fuck with nothing but the best, li'l mama."

"Why do you keep calling me that?" Tammy asked, blushing.

"I don't know. It just feels right." The two of them stood there for a few awkward seconds.

"You wanna watch a movie or something?" Bobby asked.

"That's cool. What kind of movies do you have?"

"Come check it out," Bobby said as he motioned for her to come over to his movie case. "What kind of movie do you wanna watch?"

"Let me see first," she said as she pushed him out of the way. Tammy skimmed the movie collection until she saw *Boyz n the Hood*. She pulled it out and handed it to him.

"What do you know about that movie?" he asked.

"Excuse me? You are tripping. This is one of my favorite movies." As Bobby put the DVD in, Tammy got comfortable on the couch. "And after this goes off, you can put in *Brown Sugar*."

"You ain't gotta go to work tomorrow?"

"I'm actually off for the next three days."

"Cool. We can watch movies all night then."

"Are you sure you can hang with me?" Tammy asked. "I'm legendary for pulling all-nighters when it comes to watching movies."

"Whatever. You can't see me on the movie-watching tip."

"Well, let's get this movie-watching challenge going then, Mr. Man."

For the next few hours, Bobby and Tammy watched movies, ate popcorn, and enjoyed each other's company. Then they fell asleep in each other's arms.

Ivory's cell phone went off at three in the morning, waking her out of a peaceful sleep. Hakim had left her more than satisfied. But although she was supremely fulfilled by the youngster's cock game, she knew it was probably a one-time deal. Tammy's friendship was much too precious to her to let it be destroyed by a one-night stand. With a pissed-off attitude, Ivory snatched her phone off the nightstand. The fact that the screen said private ticked her off even more.

"Who the fuck is this?" she screamed.

"Ma'am, do you know a Darnell Grayson?" the person on the other end asked, ignoring Ivory's rudeness.

Ivory got quiet for a few seconds. An eerie feeling crept into her stomach. She didn't know what the caller was about to say, but by the tone of his voice, she knew that it wasn't going to be good news. "Yeah, I know him. Why?"

"I'm Officer Peter Baker with the New York Police Department. I'm calling you because this is the last number called from this phone. What relation was Mr. Grayson to you?"

Ivory's stomach tightened up a little bit more. It wasn't lost on her that the officer used the word "was" instead of "is." "My boyfriend."

"Oh, I see. Well, miss, I hate to have to be the one to inform you that Mr. Grayson was arrested by an undercover officer for drug trafficking. I also have to inform you that while he was incarcerated, Mr. Grayson got into a fight and was stabbed to death."

Ivory dropped the phone. Her body went numb. She wanted to pinch herself to see if this was all just a bad dream. Tears flooded her eyes. She fell back onto the bed and balled into a knot. For five full minutes, she cried her eyes out. Then she picked the phone back up. The caller on the other end had hung up, so she called the first person to come to her mind: Tammy. When the call went to voicemail, she called twice more with the same result.

Not knowing what else to do, Ivory grabbed the bag of weed she'd gotten from Darnell and rolled an extra-large blunt. Because she couldn't get in touch with Tammy, she found solace in the only other thing that could calm her nerves. Ivory was so upset that the first blunt didn't seem to do a thing for her. But by the time she was halfway through the second one, the first one started kicking in, and it took her straight to another planet.

Chapter 26

Janice's chest heaved up and down. A satisfied smile seemed to be etched permanently on her face. Steve had just given her the most powerful orgasm of her life. Her leg trembled as he teased her by reaching down between her legs and flicking his middle finger back and forth across her clit.

"Oooo, baby, you gon' make me come again if you don't stop," she moaned.

Steve chuckled lightly. "Well, you know what they say. An early morning nut is the best kind of nut you can have," he said.

Janice wiped the sweat from her forehead. She was so upset when Tammy walked out of the house that she called Steve and asked him to come over and spend the night with her. Of course, one thing turned to another, and the two of them ended up in the sack.

Steve then got up and went to the bathroom. When he came back into the bedroom, he sat down on the edge of the bed and told Janice that he had something to tell her.

"What is it?" she said, stroking the back of his head.

"This shit just ain't working for me," he said coldly.

Janice felt all the air leave her lungs. "Huh? Not working? What are you talking about?"

"I'm just saying that this shit is too fucking boring for me. We don't never do nothing adventurous or exciting."

Janice was floored. In her mind, everything had been going great between her and Steve. She was thoroughly enjoying his conversation as well as his company. "But . . . but what do you want to do? I thought you liked—"

Steve held his hand up to silence Janice. "And there's someone else."

"What? Someone else? What the hell do you mean, there's someone else? Who the hell else are you fucking besides me?"

"Does it really matter?"

"You got-damn right it matters," Janice screamed. "You low-down, dirty muthafucka! How the fuck you gon' do some bullshit like this to me?"

Steve stood still and suppressed a smirk while Janice went completely off. He had her right where he wanted her. He could tell from the look in her eyes that he'd hurt her deeply. He also knew that he'd put the dick on her so good, no matter what she said, she wasn't going to break up with him.

"You know what?" he said when he got tired of hearing her talk. "I don't need this shit! I'm out this bitch!"

"Where the fuck are you going?" Janice yelled.

"To have some fun wit' my other bitch! It's over, and don't fucking call me no more!"

Steve hadn't taken two steps before Janice was begging him not to leave. "No, Steve, please don't go! What do I have to do? What do I have to do to get you to stay with me?"

"Well . . . You know what? Never mind. A boring-ass broad like you is too scared to have some real fun." Steve took another step toward the door.

"No! Please, just tell me what you want me to do!" Janice knew that she was playing herself, but she couldn't help it. She was sprung. Steve had done much more than just make love to her body. He'd tapped the inner regions of her soul.

"You wanna know what you can do for me?" he asked. Before she could answer, Steve walked over to his coat, reached inside his coat pocket, and pulled out a small bag of cocaine and a small mirror. Then, after sprinkling some on the mirror and chopping it into lines, he reached into his pocket and took out a dollar bill. With no hesitation whatsoever, Steve leaned down and sniffed a line up into his nostril. Then he switched sides and sniffed into the other nostril. After holding his head back for a few seconds, Steve smiled and looked at Janice.

"Now, this is how you have fucking fun." Steve held out the mirror for Janice to take.

Janice stared at it as if it were a snake. For the first time in her life, she came face-to-face with something she was afraid of. She despised drugs and drug dealers. But the fear of losing a man whom she had fallen in love with was pushing her toward a place she didn't want to go.

"That's what I thought," Steve said as he put the contents of the dope back into his coat pocket. Steve grabbed the doorknob and opened the door.

"No! Okay, I'll try it," Janice said in a defeated manner.

As soon as Steve set up again, he was pushing the mirror into Janice's face. Janice swallowed hard. She stalled while she was trying to think of a way out of her current predicament.

"You know I wouldn't do anything to hurt you. And besides, I ain't asking you to do this all the time. I just wanted to do a little something different tonight, that's all."

After taking a deep breath, Janice looked up at Steve. "If I do this for you, are you gonna stop fucking that other bitch you been messing around with?"

"I told you," he said, avoiding the question, "the only reason I was even messing around with her in the first place is because she likes to have the kind of fun that I like to have. If it weren't for that, I would have nothing to do wit' her."

Maybe it won't be so bad, Janice thought, trying to pump herself up. *If I only have to do it every once in a while, then I should be able to handle that.*

Janice took a look at the bulge in Steve's pants and knew that in order to keep getting dicked down, she had no choice. She promised herself that she would do whatever it took to break the hold that Steve had on her. Unfortunately for her, the grip of cocaine had a hold ten times as strong as Steve.

Stone woke up feeling like the lowest scum on the earth. Lying on his back with his fingers interlocked behind his head, he stared blankly at the ceiling. It was bad enough that he'd been suckered into letting his partner's daughter give him a blowjob. But to be so weak that he allowed himself to be wooed into climbing into her bed was just wrong.

Stone was almost to his car the previous night when he realized that he didn't have his keys. He'd only meant to go back into the house, find his keys, and leave. That all went out the window when he walked through the front door, and Nancy's naked body took hold of his eyes.

In the blink of an eye, she had taken off her clothes and was getting ready to get into the shower. But then she spotted Stone's keys. Knowing that he would come back for them, Nancy stood there in her birthday suit, dangling his keys.

Stone couldn't stop his pecker from growing inside his pants. He'd already violated her once. He didn't want to do it again, but his loins had a mind of their own. His legs soon followed as he walked over to Nancy and tried to kiss her. Nancy turned her head and made it clear that there would be no screwing without a price. Stone wanted to tell her to go fuck herself, but Nancy's body and willingness to give it up presented too much temptation for him to resist.

Nancy got him all fired up and then stopped him cold.

"What? What's wrong?" he asked.

"Nothing. It's just that if I do something for you, then you're gonna have to do something for me," she said as she backed away from him.

Heated up with a rock-hard dick, there was no way in the world he could resist Nancy. "Dammit, Nancy, what the fuck do you want from me?" he screamed at her. His brow had become sweaty, and his breathing was heavy. He wanted her in the worst way, and he was going to have her, no matter the cost.

"Well, I could use about fifty dollars."

Stone gritted his teeth as he reached into his pants pocket and pulled out his wallet. In his heart, he knew that he was dead wrong. His lust for his partner's daughter was pushing both of them down a path to destruction. He took the money out of his wallet and looked at it. He hesitated for a few seconds before Nancy squeezed her bare nipple and turned him completely on.

Three hours and three nuts later, Stone was exhausted and passed out. Now here he was about to go to work and stare into the face of his partner, knowing that he'd just committed the ultimate injustice.

No matter how hard she tried, Ivory just couldn't go back to sleep. She'd been awake for the last hour, practically begging the sandman to pull her back into the world of slumber. She'd only slept a total of two hours the entire night, but even then, a dream spooked her, causing her to wake up in a cold sweat.

The dream, in which her mother was brutally beaten and raped, caused her to put some things in perspective. She hadn't seen or spoken to her mother since running away from home at the age of 16. Thinking of her mother caused Ivory to smirk at the irony of what she was now doing, which was dealing drugs. It was her mother's weakness toward them that caused her mother to do the unthinkable to her when she was a child. Ivory cringed at the thought of what happened to her that fateful night.

She was all of 11 years old as she sat on the edge of the bed, trying to understand why her mother was asking her to sacrifice herself.

"I know you don't understand, sweetheart. I know. But please do this for Mama. He's going to give me extra medicine if you do. Don't let your mama down. Don't let your mama suffer."

Ivory was frozen stiff. She didn't know what to do. She had a feeling what her mother was asking her to do, but she didn't want to do it. "Do I have to? Can't you just—"

"Ivory, please," she said as she grabbed her daughter by the shoulders. "If you don't do this, I could die! You don't want your mama to die, do you?"

Ivory opened her mouth, but nothing came out. Sensing that her daughter was weakening, Loraine went in for the kill. "Ivory, you do remember all the shit I bought you for Christmas, don't you? I didn't even get mad when you didn't get me anything."

Guilt surged through Ivory's body. She dared not bring up that her mother had to sell the same Christmas gifts to keep them from getting evicted. At least, that was what her mother had told her. Feeling an obligation to save her mother's life, Ivory asked her mother what she wanted her to do. Loraine told her all she had to do was get naked, lie back, and spread her legs.

"I'm scared."

"Do you want me to die? Do you?" she asked as she grabbed her daughter's shoulders and shook them slightly.

"No, but—"

"But nothing! Please just do what I ask!" Loraine got up, turned around, and walked out of the room.

That night, Ivory experienced pain beyond belief. She'd hated her mother ever since.

Chapter 27

Steve leaned back on his couch and smoked a victory cigar. His plan was going along just like he thought it would. He had many women in his stable, and he was making a fortune off of their bodies. But the one man who was paying the most told Steve that he was tired of the young girls who didn't know what they were doing. He wanted a vet. He wanted a woman who was experienced, not some tenderoni who was wet behind the ears and scared to fuck. He wanted someone like Janice. And he was willing to pay top dollar for her. When Steve asked him how much he was willing to spend, the client told him upwards of $1,500. Steve's mouth watered at the amount of money that was presented to him.

He immediately went on a search mission for some seasoned meat. The second he met Janice, he could tell by her quick interest in him that she had been dick deprived for a long time. Being the pimp he was, it didn't take him long to sweet-talk her and get inside her pants.

"Hey, handsome. Can I buy you a drink?" she asked when she first met him at a bar.

"Yeah, why not?" he responded. *"Let me get a gin and juice."*

Janice flagged down the bartender and ordered drinks for both of them. She had no idea that Steve had been watching her for about ten minutes before coming to sit next to her. She'd already hit on a couple of guys, but for some strange reason, they'd turned her down. As their conversation grew deeper, Steve found out why

"You here by yourself?"

"Yep. Just enjoying the night out. What about you?" he asked.

"Well, to be honest about it, I'm looking for a man."

And there it was. Whereas the men she'd been trying to pick up were just looking to have a good time, Janice was looking for something more serious. That was what had undoubtedly chased them away. But for what Steve was looking for, Janice was just right.

"Is that right? What a coincidence. I just happen to be looking for someone special myself," Steve lied. "What's your name, pretty lady?"

"Janice, and yours?"

"Steve. Nice to meet you," he said.

That night, after taking her back to his place and fucking her brains out, she was his for the taking. He didn't anticipate having the problems that he was having with her children, but that was fixable, especially since he planned to kill her son and make her daughter a part of his stable as soon as he got her mother in the fold. He was highly pissed that her son had put his hands on him, and he promised himself that he was going to make him pay dearly for it.

The first part of his plan was to get Janice strung out on cocaine, which he was well on his way to doing. He smiled as he thought about the look on Janice's face when the cocaine took effect on her system. He chuckled lightly and almost wanted to hop up and pound his chest when he thought about how loudly he made Janice scream his name before he left. Steve's dick got harder as he thought about how he'd hit the bottom of Janice's pussy, causing her to beg for mercy.

Thinking that she was the cause of his hardening love muscle, the young girl who was sucking Steve off started moaning with pleasure. As Steve thought back to the nut he'd busted inside of Janice, he came in the young lady's mouth. After getting rid of his plaything, Steve looked at his phone and cracked up. Janice had texted him twice, asking him if he had any more of the powder that made her feel so good.

When Tammy woke up, she was surprised to find herself lying on the couch alone. She rubbed her eyes and looked around. It took her a second to remember that she had spent the night at Bobby's place. She didn't know where Bobby was, but she had to use the bathroom in the worst way. She hopped off the couch and made her way to the bathroom. When she came back out, she was greeted by the smell of sausage biscuits and hash browns from McDonald's.

"Hey, sleepyhead," Bobby said, smiling at her.

Still half asleep, Tammy waved her hand and walked over to him, smiling. "Thank you," she said, taking the bag from him.

"How did you sleep?" Bobby asked.

"I slept okay. I'm surprised you didn't try to take me into the bedroom and take advantage of me."

"What? See, now you done offended a nigga. What type of dude do you think I am?"

"The kind who likes pussy." Tammy wanted to kick her own ass after noticing the offended look on Bobby's face. "Hey, I'm sorry about that. I didn't mean to imply that—"

"That I was a fucking dawg?" Bobby said, cutting her off.

Tammy froze. She didn't know what to say. Seeing the look on Bobby's face told her that it would probably be better if she left. All of a sudden, Bobby started laughing.

"I'm just fucking with you, li'l mama. And you're right. I am the kind of dude who likes pussy. But the thing about it is I wanna get to know you on a whole 'notha level. I wanna know about ya interests and about ya likes and dislikes and all that corny-ass shit."

"Corny? Why does it have to be corny?"

"Come on with that. You know that shit sounds corny as fuck," Bobby said, laughing.

"Whatever," Tammy said as she dug into the bag to get her food.

The two of them talked over their breakfast and thoroughly enjoyed each other's company. All of a sudden, Tammy realized that she hadn't checked her phone. She was so caught up in being with Bobby that she hadn't even bothered to check if her brother or mother had tried to get in touch with her.

"I have to check my phone," she told Bobby as she got up and walked over toward the couch. A look of concern came over her face when she saw that she had an urgent text message.

When Bobby saw the change of expression on Tammy's face, he walked over to her. "Everything a'ight?"

"Oh, my God," she said as she looked at her phone. Holding up one finger to ask Bobby to give her a second before answering his question, Tammy dialed Ivory's number. When she didn't get an answer, she left a message.

"Ivory, this is Tammy. I'm just now getting your message about Darnell. I'm so sorry, girl. Call me back when you get a chance." After hanging up, Tammy told Bobby what had happened.

"Damn, that's fucked up," he said. "You okay?"

"I'm okay. I'm just worried about my girl. She and Darnell had an off-and-on relationship, but she did care about him."

Tammy looked at her watch and decided that it was time for her to go home. She just hoped that she could go into her house without having to deal with the never-ending drama that seemed to always take place in her household.

Ivory parked in front of the house she grew up in and stared at it. It had been close to fifteen years since she'd last seen the place she'd been partially raised in. Now here she was about to go and visit the person who had caused her the most pain in this world. Ivory got out of her car and nervously walked toward the house. The closer she got to it, the more her legs threatened to give way. Ivory had to fight back tears as she approached. Her head was clouded with memories of neglect by her father and drug abuse by her mother. She was almost to the fence when she heard a voice call out to her from the street.

"Ivory! Ivory! Girl, is that you?"

Ivory turned around to see one of her mother's friends walking toward her at a fast pace.

"Where the hell you been? I ain't seen you since forever."

"I been around," Ivory answered. She looked at the old crackhead woman with her bottom row of teeth missing and instantly felt sorry for her. Ivory remembered when the woman used to come over to their house and play spades with her mother. The woman, whose name was Jamie, used to give Ivory money when her mother claimed she didn't have any.

"How you been, Ms. Jamie?"

"I just been trying to live out here." Jamie looked at the house and then back at Ivory. It didn't take her long to figure out that Ivory didn't know what happened to her mother.

"What?" Ivory asked after seeing the look on Jamie's face.

"Uh, when is the last time you talked to your mother?"

"I ain't talked to her in a long while. Why?"

"Well, I don't know if you've heard, but about six months ago, your mother had a stroke."

Ivory's heart skipped a beat. Guilt suddenly washed over her. Even though her mother had pawned her for a hit of crack, she was still her mother. She suddenly started to wonder if she was wrong for holding a grudge against her mother all these years.

"Is she—"

"Oh, no, she's still with us. She's in that nursing home on the west side. It's called Simpkins. You need me to write the address down for you?"

"Nah, I'll just use the navigation system on my phone."

"Okay. But if you plan on going to see her, you betta prepare ya'self. She don't look too good. Yo' mama ain't never been a big woman, but now she really look small. I ain't got to tell you what she was doing before you left. Hell, I got caught up in it my damn self. But when they put yo' mama in that home after she had that stroke, she got depressed as hell. She wouldn't even eat for the first two weeks, and then she started having crack withdrawals. She was already upset about being paralyzed on her left side, and the fact that she couldn't get dope no more almost caused her to commit suicide. One of them nurses went into her room one day and caught her trying to cut her wrists with a butter knife. I'm telling you, if that knife were just a li'l bit sharper, yo' mama wouldn't be here today. She ended up having to get a couple of stitches as it was."

Water formed in the corners of Ivory's eyes. At that moment, she stopped hating her mother. All the hurt and pain that her mother had ever caused her rolled down her cheeks.

Jamie looked at the house where she used to visit her best friend. "Ah, Ivory, we need to move from in front of this house. It ain't the same house you grew up in."

Just as Ivory was about to ask Jamie what she meant by that, the door swung open. The man standing in the doorway looked almost the same as he did when she last saw him. His beard had grayed a little, and he had gained a little weight, but his facial features remained the same.

"Hey, Jamie! You got my fucking money?"

"Huh?"

"Huh, my ass! I asked you if you had my fucking money, 'cause if you don't, you might as well get ready to get on yo' knees, dirty girl!" Drake smiled and grabbed his crotch as he stared at Jamie. He never even looked Ivory's way. "You got fifteen minutes to bring me my money, or you can get ready to put yo' jaws to work!" Drake went back in and slammed the door.

"I'm sorry, Ivory. I gotta go. He don't play about his money. Tell yo' mother I said hi, okay?"

Jamie scurried back across the street. Although Drake didn't pay Ivory any attention when he went back into the house, she knew exactly who he was. Her first thought was to rush into the house and attack him, but she was smart enough to know that would've been a death sentence.

"One day, muthafucka, one day," she said to herself as she got back into the car. "Fuck," she screamed after snatching the phone off of her hip and seeing that the battery was dead. She had been wondering why Tammy hadn't called her back after she'd texted her the news about Darnell.

After she plugged her phone into the cigarette lighter, it immediately came to life. When it did, she saw that she had a message from her friend. She smiled and thought to herself how lucky she was to have a friend like Tammy.

She decided that she would wait until after she'd visited her mother to call Tammy back. She set the navigation system for the nursing home that her mother was in and was on her way.

By the time James dropped him off in front of his house, Hakim was exhausted. He'd been on the block all night, and while his body yearned for sleep, his pockets were filled with money.

"Ay yo, we killed the block tonight," James bragged.

"I bet we made over five Gs."

"You think so?" Hakim asked doubtfully.

"I know so! You see how fast them fiends was coming through? I'm telling you, we slaughtered that shit!" James peeled off $1,000 and passed it to Hakim. "Here you go. Shit, another few months of this hustling and we can start copping weight. Dru told me yesterday that when he get in good with his new contact, he gon' see if he can get him to front us a couple of keys. Then we can all be eating real good."

Hakim liked the sound of that. He'd already made close to $3,500 since he'd been hustling.

"I'm gonna call Dru and let him know that we need to re-up. If I get something, I'll text you and let you know what time I'm gonna set up shop. You down to work tonight?"

"Let's make this chedda," Hakim said as he gave James dap.

Hakim jumped out of James's car and headed for the house. He looked at his watch and smirked, knowing that he was supposed to be at work in less than an hour. He also knew that he wasn't going.

"Fuck that punk-ass job," he mumbled to himself as he walked up the steps. With his nuts drained from screwing

Ivory and his pockets full from grinding all night, the only thing on Hakim's mind was getting some sleep in case he had to hit the block the coming night.

Just before he stuck his key into the door, Hakim turned his head toward the street and saw a truck pulling up in front of his house. His first thought was that it was Steve coming back with some of his cronies to get revenge. He breathed a sigh of relief when he saw Tammy get out of the passenger's side door. It hadn't occurred to him until that very moment that, between his beef with Steve and his hustling activities, he probably needed to purchase a gun.

After seeing Tammy hang an overnight bag over her shoulder, another thought occurred to him. *Where the fuck she been all night that she need an overnight bag?* Hakim tried to see who was behind the wheel, but Tammy closed the door too quickly. He knew damn well that Ivory wasn't pushing nothing like that, so he figured that it had to be a dude.

"Who the fuck was that?" he asked as he walked down the steps and up to his sister.

"Why do you want to know?" she asked with an attitude.

Hakim ignored her as he watched Bobby bend the corner. "Well, whoever that nigga is, don't get his ass fucked up."

"Whatever," she said, dismissing him with a hand wave. "What are you doing up so early anyway? Wait a minute," she said after thinking about it for a second. "Aren't you supposed to be at work?"

Hakim just looked at his big sister and shrugged his shoulders. It was then that Tammy noticed the tired look in his eyes.

"Are you just now getting home?"

"Yeah, so what?"

"Please don't tell me that you've been out there hustling with those derelicts I saw you with the other day."

"Then don't ask," Hakim said as he turned and headed back up the steps.

"Oh, my God. Why won't you listen?"

"Don't start that bullshit again."

"I'm just saying—"

"I don't wanna hear it! Matter of fact," he said as he turned and faced his sister, "that nigga who dropped you off? Where does he work?"

Tammy froze like a deer caught in headlights. She didn't expect her little brother to come at her like that.

"Yeah, that's what I thought," he said.

Before their conversation could continue, Janice walked down the stairs, looking a hot mess. Her nose was swollen, and her hair looked like it hadn't been combed in a month. She had a dreamy look in her eyes and a goofy smile on her face.

"Good morning," she said as she passed between her two children. Hakim and Tammy looked at each other, totally confused.

Hakim lifted his finger to say something but shook his head. "Nah, couldn't be," he said.

"Well, she damn sure looks like she is," Tammy said, knowing exactly what her brother was thinking.

"We need to talk to Mama. Ever since that bitch-ass nigga been coming around, she ain't been acting the same. It's almost like she love that nigga more than she love us."

Hakim sounded angry, but Tammy could see the hurt in his eyes. She figured now was the perfect time to show her mother how much her actions were bothering them.

"I agree. Come on." Both of them walked to the kitchen where their mother was making coffee. Tammy said, "Mama, we need to talk to you."

"About what?"

"I think you know."

Janice walked over to the table and sat down at the table. "Look, you two, I don't know how much clearer I can make this. Steve is my man, and I love him."

"And we don't have a problem with that—"

"Speak for ya'self," Hakim interrupted.

"Anyway," Tammy said, giving Hakim the evil eye, "like I was saying, we don't have a problem with that. But it seems like, now that you've met this Steve guy, you're treating us like dirt." Truth be told, Tammy did have a problem with it. She just didn't want to get their conversation with their mother off on the wrong foot.

"Dirt my ass, sis. She's been treating us like shit!"

"Hakim, calm the hell down!"

"Fuck that!" he exploded. "She needs to decide who she loves more: us or that Johnny-come-lately muthafucka!"

Tammy shook her head at her brother and looked at her mother. A bad feeling crept into the pit of her stomach as an eerie silence hung in the air.

"You're right," Janice said. "I do need to make a choice. Please feel free to leave your keys on the table on your way out."

Janice then stood up and went back upstairs, leaving Hakim and Tammy staring at each other, stunned beyond belief.

Chapter 28

"Bitch, hurry up. I ain't got all day," Red yelled into the phone. He ended the call, leaned back in his seat, and wondered why he was up so early in the morning. A sly smile formed on his face after remembering the reason. After spending half the night getting high and drunk with Hank, Dru, and Cedric, Red was even more pissed when his cell phone woke him up. He was still surprised that he could even hear it, considering the state he was in. As soon as he picked the phone up, he wanted to jump through it and strangle Nancy.

Here he was trying to sleep off the events of the previous night, only to have this broad call him, asking him to take her to work. His anger turned to elation when she told him that she would suck him off on the way there. Red wasn't a fool, though. He knew that as soon as he got her to work, Nancy was going to start begging for some dope. He thought about the vicious head she'd given him before and agreed to pick her up and figured that it was more than a fair tradeoff.

Red was about to get out of his whip and go bang on her door when Nancy came out of the house. "What the fuck took yo' ass so long?" Red asked her.

"I had to get ready."

"Get ready? Yo' ass shoulda been ready! And the next time you wanna get in touch with me, send me a fucking text message instead of calling my muthafucking phone! What if my bitch had answered this damn thing?"

"I'm sorry, big daddy," Nancy said, speaking like a child being admonished by her parents.

"Well, come on and show big daddy how sorry you are, girl."

After pulling off into traffic, Red grabbed the back of Nancy's head and pushed it down toward his lap. His dick was already out, waiting to be serviced. Nancy wrapped her lips around his Johnson and did her thing. Red almost crashed his whip twice while Nancy was showing him her deep throating skills. Just as Red pulled into the parking lot of the mall, he came.

"You holding something?" she asked as she came up, wiping her mouth.

"I'm always holding something. What you need?" he asked as he zipped his pants back up.

Nancy dug into her pocket and pulled out the $50 she'd gotten from Stone. "Let me get fifty dollars' worth."

"Oh, shit, you got money this time," Red said, surprised. After putting the money in his pocket, Red reached into his console and pulled out a bag of dope. Nancy took the bag out of his hand and dipped her pinky finger in it. Then she put it up to her nose and sniffed.

"Thanks, big daddy," she said as she opened the door to get out.

"Next time, text me," Red told her.

"Okay," Nancy said and headed for the mall.

Ray-Ray sat on the edge of the bed, puffing on a Newport. He had mixed feelings over what he'd just done. Red and Hank were his boys. He couldn't believe that he'd just fucked both of their women. He also knew that he had to talk to both of the women and tell them to keep this affair a secret. Neither Red nor Hank was the jealous type, but they did value loyalty, and what he'd just done was the ultimate sign of disrespect. He did smile as he thought about how good April and Cookie had sexed him up. He wasn't in the bar ten minutes before April approached him and invited him to come over and have a drink with them.

He was just there to get his mind off his missing cousin, but he ended up having a good time with the two vixens. He wondered why they kept buying him shots of vodka, and now he knew why. They were fattening him up for the kill. Ray-Ray wasn't stupid, though. He had a feeling they were only doing this because they were mad at Red and Hank. As the night continued, each woman took turns with him on the dance floor. They made sure to grind on him as much as possible.

Then, as the bar closed down, April suggested that they go home and blow some trees. They weren't finished with one blunt before Cookie went to the bathroom and came back out naked. April followed suit as she got up and stripped down to her bra and panties. Ray-Ray couldn't get one word out of his mouth before they sexually attacked him. For the remainder of the night, the three of them engaged in every carnal action they could think of.

Ray-Ray leaned back on the bed and smiled. " I can't believe these two hoes let me smash." Although Ray-Ray did feel bad about screwing his boys' women, he simply chalked it up to all things being fair in love and war. He'd told the two ladies that he was going to be gone by the time they got back from the store, but he was so tired from screwing the two of them that he lay back on the bed and fell asleep.

Cookie and April walked into the corner store, laughing like hyenas. You would think that they'd just heard the funniest joke in the world. Both women felt pretty good about themselves. Vindication filled their hearts as the revenge that they'd just extracted on their men had them feeling themselves.

"Now that's what the fuck I call payback," Cookie bellowed as she gave April a high five. "Now I don't feel so damn stupid!" Cookie noticed the half-hearted high five that April had given her. She also noticed the worried look on her cousin's face. "What the fuck is wrong with you?"

April just shrugged her shoulders. Truthfully, she was starting to regret what she and Cookie had done. In her mind, it made them seem like whores. It made them no better than Red or Hank. Plus, she really didn't want to end up having a major fight with Hank because she let Cookie drag her into something that she wouldn't normally do.

"Spill it," Cookie pressed.

"I'm just saying, I don't know if we shoulda done that shit. What if those niggas find out?"

"How the fuck they gon' find out? Ray-Ray damn sure ain't gonna tell 'em. Unless he wanna end up with a bullet in his head. Stop acting so muthafucking scared!"

After purchasing their items, Cookie and April headed back to Cookie's car.

"I'm still horny," Cookie admitted. "When we get back to the house, I might just give that nigga some more of the good-good."

"Damn slut," April said, laughing.

As Cookie weaved through traffic, April reached into her pocket and took out a dime bag of weed. She normally didn't smoke before three in the afternoon, but for some reason, she was feeling a strong urge to blaze up. It took her less than five minutes to slice the Dutch Master open, empty its contents, replace it with weed, and seal it back up. After lighting it, she took a deep pull and held it in. She smiled as she blew the smoke into the air. The get-high stick instantly relaxed her.

"Damn, stop babysitting and pass that shit," Cookie fussed. After taking one more hit, April passed it to Cookie. Cookie then took a long pull and held it in. "Yeaaahh, that's that shit right there," she said, letting a stream of smoke slide through her nostrils. Cookie then blew her horn three times at a familiar car that was going in the opposite direction.

"Hey, bitch," she shouted out the window.

"Girl, what the hell you doing?"

"That was Kat's ass."

"So?" April asked, confused.

"So my ass! That bitch owes me ten dollars!"

"You can chalk that. That ho been owing me twenty for over a year now. Is she still sniffing up Bobby's ass?"

"Hell yeah. She was tryin'a holla at that nigga at my party, but he gave her ass the brush-off."

April tried to think of something to say real quick. Cookie had already let her have it about skipping her party. Truth be told, she didn't feel like being bothered with her cousin and faked being sick that night. "I heard Bobby got him a young tenderoni now."

"Yeah, I think her name is Tammy. She's friends with my girl Ivory."

"Who?"

"The one I told you about who jumped on the supervisor at work."

"Oh, okay."

"Anyway, that bitch Kat better cough up my dough or it's gon' be on!"

April looked at her like she was crazy.

"What?" Cookie asked when she noticed April's expression.

"Let me get this straight. You gonna jump on yo' own flesh and blood over ten dollars? Heifer, you owe me thirty."

Cookie opened her mouth to protest but then remembered that she did owe April. "Oh, but that's different," she said. The two of them burst out laughing. They continued to laugh all the way back to Cookie's house and up to the front door. They were so engrossed in their giggling, they never even noticed the truck parked two doors down.

Ivory sat in front of the nursing home, staring at it. She'd been sitting there for twenty-five minutes and had yet to make a move to get out of her car. She never imagined that it would be this hard building up the courage to go and visit her mother. After sitting there for five more minutes, Ivory figured she'd stalled enough. Ever so slowly, she climbed out of her car and headed toward the building. A knot formed in her stomach as she walked through the glass double doors of the front entrance. Ivory decided to pick up the pace, knowing that there was a greater chance of her turning around if she didn't. Before she lost her nerve, Ivory rushed up to the counter.

"May I help you?" asked the light-skinned receptionist.

"Yes, I'm here to see Ms. Loraine Moore, please."

"Sign here, please."

After signing in and being told what room her mother was in, Ivory proceeded down the hallway. She felt her knees weaken as she came to her mother's room. Her hand trembled as she reached for the doorknob. Feeling that she might back out if she didn't hurry, Ivory pushed the door open and barged in. Her heart broke as she looked at her mother. The woman lying in bed was Loraine Moore, but she looked nothing like the vibrant woman who had birthed her.

Hair that was once full of bounce and shine was now brittle and dry. Her once-radiant skin was now ashy and pale. She was so thin that Ivory wondered if they were feeding her. A light snore emitted from her nostrils, letting Ivory know that she was asleep. Ivory tried to fight back the flood that was building up in her eyes, but it was no use. Seeing her mother lying there in such a state was too much for Ivory to handle. With tears rushing down her face like waterfalls, Ivory sat down beside the bed and held her mother's hand.

After only ten minutes in the room, she couldn't take it anymore. She got up to walk out of the room and got as far as the door when she heard a faint voice call out to her. Ivory turned around and slowly walked back over to the bed.

"Hey, Ivory," her mother weakly said. "I'm . . . glad to see you," she said to her child.

"I'm glad to see you too, Mama," Ivory said through tear-soaked eyes.

"I just want you to know . . . that I'm sorry for what I did to you."

"Shhh, it's okay."

"No, it's not. I mistreated you in the worst way. And I will never be able to forgive myself."

Ivory grabbed her mother's hand and stroked it gently. "I forgive you, Mama."

Ivory's mother smiled and fell back asleep. While she was sleeping, Ivory sat there and stared at her mother, remembering the good times they shared when she was much, much younger.

Chapter 29

The second Cookie stepped into her crib, all the color drained out of her face. "Oh, my God," April said, as she saw the blood pouring from Ray-Ray's mouth. Standing behind him with a gun trained on the back of his head was Cedric. Dru was seated on the couch, drinking a bottle of Heineken.

"Oh, baby, I see you back," Red said as he walked in from the kitchen with a glass of vodka in his hand.

"Red, what the hell are you doing here? Shouldn't you be somewhere fucking yo' nasty-ass ex?"

"You know I don't care nothing about that ho," Red said, trying to make amends with Cookie. He knew that of all the women he messed around with, Cookie was his main girl and by far the one who had his back the most. He told his boys that Cookie wasn't his girl, but she was as close to it as being someone's girl can get.

"You are and always will be my main bit . . . girl. And oh, April, Hank told me to tell you that if you over here, get yo' ass home."

Dru and Cedric cracked up laughing.

"What the fuck y'all niggas laughin' at? Y'all need to take y'all asses somewhere and do some fucking homework, young-ass niggas," April said, dissing the two youngsters.

"Yo, who the fuck you think you talking to?" Dru said, taking two steps toward April.

Red put his arm out to stop him from going any farther. Then he walked up to April and put his finger in her face. "Make that the last time you disrespect somebody in my damn crew. Y'all getting a little too liberal with that bull-shit."

April rolled her eyes and walked out the door. Red walked up to Cookie and reached into his pocket. He pulled out a roll of bills, peeled off $1,000, and handed it to her.

"Here ya go, baby. A little peace offerin'."

Cookie looked at the money then back at Red. "Thanks," she said as she stuffed the money into her pocket. Then without warning, Red backhanded Cookie to the floor. With a busted lip, Cookie looked up at Red with a stunned look on her face.

"Did you really think I was gonna let you just give up the pussy to one of my boys and not have to pay for that shit? You lucky I don't kill yo' muthafucking ass behind some disrespectful shit like that! Which is more than I can say for this backstabbing-ass nigga," he said as he stared heatedly at Ray-Ray. "I guess killing yo' punk-ass cousin wasn't enough! Now I gotta body yo' bitch ass too!"

"What?" Ray-Ray screamed. "You killed my cousin?"

"Shut yo' bitch ass up," Cedric yelled as he cracked Ray-Ray upside the head with his gun.

"Cedric, take this nigga on a li'l ride somewhere."

Feeling a little slighted because Red asked Cedric and not him, Dru tried to prove his worth. "Ay yo, Red, I can do that shit if you want me to."

"Did I ask yo' ass? Damn!" The two youngsters were starting to get on Red's nerves. His plan to pawn them off to Bobby was backfiring.

"Cookie, go in the kitchen and fix me a sandwich," he ordered her. Cookie dragged herself off the floor and went into the kitchen. She knew that she was out of bounds by sleeping with Ray-Ray, but the pain she felt when she caught Red and his ex drove her to revenge.

"Cedric, I don't know if yo' ass is hooked on phonics, but I thought I told you to take this punk-ass nigga on a ride."

Cedric took his gun and pushed Ray-Ray in the back of the head. "Let's go, muthafucka."

"Come on, Red. Don't do this to me," Ray-Ray begged.

"Miss me with that bullshit! All these muthafucking hoes in Cleveland, and you gotta violate by fucking with mine? You wanna go against the code like that? Fuck you! Get this punk muthafucka the fuck out of my face!"

Cedric put his gun against Ray-Ray's back and guided him toward the door. As soon as they were out the door, Red stuck his hand inside the couch and pulled out a large package of cocaine, which was the only reason he went over to Cookie's in the first place. After calling one of his customers to confirm the transaction that was supposed to go down later, he called Bobby and told him that he needed him to come by later that night to get the dope ready.

Ray-Ray racked his brain, trying to think of a way out of the mess he was in. He didn't know where Cedric was taking him, but if he didn't find a way to get out of that car, he was a dead man riding. "Yo, Cedric—"

"Shut up! I don't wanna hear shit you gotta say!"

After riding in silence for a few more seconds, Cedric looked at Ray-Ray and shook his head. "How the fuck you gonna stick dick to ya homeboy's girl? That's the foulest shit a nigga can do!"

"I don't know. We just started drinking at the bar, and the shit just escalated from there."

"And that little piece of pussy about to cost yo' ass big time."

Ray-Ray started sweating profusely. While he was trying to think of a way out of his current predicament, Cedric was busy texting on his phone. Ray-Ray's prayers were answered when Cedric dropped his phone, and it bounced under the seat. "Shit," he said as he reached down to get it. Ray-Ray glanced at the bent-over Cedric and saw his opportunity.

Foolishly, Cedric placed the gun in his right hand, making it impossible to get off a good shot in the event that he had to take one. Feeling this was his only chance at freedom, Ray-Ray slammed on the brakes hard. Cedric's head hit the front of the glove compartment with a loud thud.

"Ah shit," Cedric screamed. Although he still had possession of the gun, he couldn't get off a shot because his own body was in the way as a result of his body being twisted. As soon as the car came to a stop, Ray-Ray jumped out and sprinted across the street.

He heard two shots ring out but kept running. The man whose car was rear-ended jumped out to say something to Cedric but froze when he saw the smoking pistol in the young man's hand.

"Fuck! Fuck! Fuck," Cedric shouted as he jumped back in the car. He hit a U-turn in the middle of the street, causing other drivers to slam on their brakes. He looked around for his prey as he drove down the street, but it was too late. Ray-Ray was long gone.

Nancy walked into JCPenney like she owned the joint. She knew that the other women who worked there hated her because they felt that she got special treatment, but she didn't give a fuck. All she was concerned about was keeping enough money in her pocket to feed her habit. And with the boss in her hip pocket, all she had to do was show up every now and then and her job was safe. Her coworkers giggled and pointed as she strolled toward the back of the store. She didn't know what they were laughing at, and she didn't care. As soon as she got to the back, Nancy went into the bathroom and took out her bag of dope.

While sitting on the toilet, she rolled up a dollar bill that she'd taken out of her pocket and stuck it into the bag. Then, after sniffing into each nostril, she sat back and allowed the drug to take effect on her system. Her nose got numb as she got up off of the commode and wiped herself. Nancy washed her hands and walked out of the bathroom, sniffing. Knowing that she would probably snort up the dope before the day was half gone, Nancy decided to go and visit her personal bank, Mr. James.

She ignored the stares of her coworkers and continued walking toward where her boss's office was located. "Damn, that bitch look high as fuck," she heard one of the women say. "She ain't gon' be gettin' no special treatment no more," she heard another say. Nancy didn't know what she meant by that, but she was more than prepared to pull her trump card if she had to. She still had the recording of her and her boss, so if he wanted to resist, she would use it to blow his marriage out of the water.

Nancy walked into her boss's office without knocking. She was surprised to see him packing up his things.

"Mr. James? What's going on? Why are you packing up your things?" Before he could answer Nancy's question, his wife came out of the back. As soon as she saw Nancy, she went into a rage.

"Is this her? Is this the bitch you've been fucking behind my back? Is this the bitch I saw coming out of this office when I popped in to surprise your trifling ass last week? Bitch, you been fucking my husband? I'm about to fuck your ass up!"

The woman moved toward Nancy at lightning speed. Before Nancy could even open her mouth to protest or throw up her hands to defend herself, the woman attacked her. Mr. James stood there, stunned as his wife grabbed a handful of Nancy's hair and slung her to the ground.

"Get her off me!" Nancy cried out to her boss.

"Baby, please, let her go. You're gonna get us arrested." Mr. James pulled his wife off of Nancy and received a hard slap to the face for his troubles.

"Get the fuck off of me! This bitch is the reason your stupid ass is being fired, and you wanna tell me to stop?" Mrs. James looked at her husband with a blend of tears and rage in her eyes. "How the fuck could you be the manager of this store and not know that they had put security cameras in your office, you stupid muthafucka?"

Just then, Mr. James's boss, Darlene, as well as the security guard came in. "Is everything okay in here?" Darlene asked.

"Oh, everything's fine. I'm just about to beat blood outta this tramp right here!"

The security guard quickly grabbed Mr. James's wife as she made another lunge for Nancy. Nancy instinctively threw up her hands to protect herself.

"Come with me, Nancy. We need to talk," Darlene said to her. Nancy followed her into the office. She ignored the nosy coworkers who had rushed to the scene to find out what the commotion was all about. "Have a seat."

Nancy plopped down in the chair as if she knew what was about to happen. It had never entered her mind that the store might institute surveillance cameras. But instead of being worried about her job, Nancy was already thinking that she wasn't going to be able to get any more money from Mr. James to buy more dope.

"I'm not going to beat around the bush with this. On an anonymous tip, I was informed that I should look into the relationship status of you and Mr. James. Upon acting on this tip, the company decided to install two cameras in Mr. James's office. Imagine our shock when we looked at the video and saw you and Mr. James engaging in sexual misconduct here in the workplace. Now I know that I do not have to tell you of the seriousness of this situation. We simply cannot have this type of thing going on in the workplace. Therefore, Ms. Dryer, we have no choice but to terminate you. We will mail your check. Please see yourself out. Goodbye."

Nancy walked out of the office amid the giggles and stares of her now-former coworkers. She was certain that it was one of them who'd dropped a dime on her. She looked down toward the end of the hall at Mr. James's office. The door was open. Mr. James was finishing up packing his things, and his wife was standing there, shaking her head and tapping her foot. As soon as she saw Nancy, she reached for the door. "Keep it moving!" Mrs. James slammed the door so loud it almost broke.

Nancy walked into her living room and plopped down on the couch. She was stunned. It never crossed her mind that when she went to work, she would be getting fired. All the way home, she worried not only about how she was going to survive, but about how she'd support her habit. Nancy knew that she needed help to overcome the addiction that had slowly but surely taken over her life. But the shock and depression of losing her job caused her to slowly reach into her pocket and take out the remaining dope she had on her. Nancy stuck the rolled-up dollar into the bag and sniffed away. She didn't stop until she had sniffed it all up. Tears ran down her face as her nose burned. Needing to talk to someone, she picked up the phone and called Tammy.

Tammy sat on the edge of her bed, feeling numb. She couldn't believe that her mother was willing to put her and her brother out in order to please a man she barely knew. She didn't know if her mother was serious, but she didn't want to be anyplace she wasn't wanted, and that included the house she grew up in.

Tammy heard her cell phone chirping but ignored it. Whoever it was would just have to call her back. After twenty minutes had passed, she got up, walked to her closet, and pulled out a large duffle bag and a backpack. She fought hard to hold back the tears threatening to roll down her face.

Her feelings were a mixture of anger and hurt. After packing her duffle bag with enough clothes to last her a week, she went into the bathroom and stuffed her backpack with toiletries. She then walked to her brother's room to check on him. Shortly after Janice told them to leave and walked up the stairs, Hakim gave her the finger behind her back, went into his room, and slammed the door. Tammy suspected that he left quickly so she wouldn't see the tears that he unsuccessfully tried to hold back.

"Hakim, you okay?" she asked as she knocked on his door lightly. "Hakim?" When Hakim didn't respond to her knocks, Tammy opened the door and walked in. There she found Hakim balled up on the bed, crying his eyes out, his heart crushed by the one person he thought would always protect him. Tammy walked over to the bed and sat on the edge. Her heart broke as she saw the hurt in her little brother's eyes.

"Why is she treating us like this, sis? Why is she acting like she don't give a fuck about us?"

Tammy opened her mouth, but nothing came out. She had no idea what to say to him. All she could do was rub his back and try to comfort him. Tammy went back into the bathroom to get some tissue so her brother could wipe his tears away. On her way there, she looked downstairs and saw the front door close. Tammy ran down to her mother's room and knocked on her door. After not getting an answer, she pushed the door open and confirmed what she already suspected. Her mother was gone. She got downstairs just in time to look out the door and see Steve's car pulling off down the street. Tammy went back upstairs to check on her brother.

When she got back to his room, he was packing his clothes. He had a scowl on his face that scared her. Gone were the tears she'd seen fall from his face a few seconds ago. "What are you doing?"

"I'm packing my muthafucking shit! If that bitch don't want me here, then I ain't gotta be in this punk-ass house!"

"Wait."

"Wait for what? You heard what the fuck she said! She want us the fuck outta here!"

"You're seventeen years old. You don't have to go anywhere! She cannot legally put you out!"

"I don't wanna fucking be here if she gon' be fucking around with that punk muthafucka!"

Silence hung in the air as Hakim continued to pack. Right then, Tammy knew that whatever Hakim was about to do, she wouldn't be able to stop him. She couldn't say that she blamed him for wanting to leave if he felt like he wasn't welcome there, but that wasn't going to stop her from worrying about him.

"Where are you going to go?" she asked with concern in her voice.

"Over to Nikki's house."

"Nikki? When did y'all get back together?"

"I don't know if I wanna say that we're back together."

"If you're going to live with that girl, then you'd better want to say that you two are back together. She's not going to just let you move into her house as a damn guest."

"Yeah, I know," he said.

"Do you think her mother is going to be okay with that?"

Hakim looked at his sister and smiled. "Somehow, I don't think she is going to mind."

Tammy stared at her brother for a few seconds. "Uh, why are you looking like that? Wait, never mind. I don't even want to know." Tammy then walked over to her brother and gave him a hug. She looked up into his eyes and caressed his face.

"Look, Hakim. I know it seems like Mama doesn't care about us. But I have to believe that this is just a phase she's going through right now. I mean—"

"Mama is too damn old to be going through a fucking phase," Hakim said, cutting her off. "We gotta just face the facts that Mama is sprung off this nigga, and she loves him more than she loves us."

Tammy hated to admit it, but her little brother was right. And the simple fact of the matter was that there was nothing they could do about it.

"Just make sure you call me and let me know that you're all right from time to time," Tammy said as she hugged Hakim again.

"You make sure you do the same."

Tammy turned and headed for the door.

"Hold up, sis. You never did tell me where you was going."

Tammy stopped in her tracks. She really hadn't thought about it. "To a hotel, I guess," she said as she shrugged her shoulders. "I might put off school for another year, though, because I'm going to look for an apartment tomorrow." Tammy had assumed that she was going to stay at home and commute back and forth to school, but now that plan was up in smoke.

Hakim walked over to his sister and placed his hand on her shoulder. "Hold off on that. Going to college has been a dream of yours since we were little, so don't give up on that."

"I don't want you to—"

"Ain't nothing you can do to change my mind on that one. Whateva I got to do, yo' ass is goin' to school."

Hakim turned around and continued to pack his clothes. Tammy turned around and walked out the door, sadly realizing right then and there that her little brother had married the streets.

Chapter 30

Janice felt like the lowest scum on the earth. She had just chosen a man over her children. As she walked to Steve's house, she couldn't help but wonder if her kids were going to hate her for the decision she'd made. She tried to rationalize that Tammy and Hakim were grown and that it was time for them to leave the nest, but deep in her heart, she knew that was bullshit. While it takes some addicts some time to get addicted to a drug, it only took one sniff for Janice to get hooked on the white lady.

Right after she'd left her kids sitting at the table searching for answers, she went upstairs and called Steve. She'd practically begged him for the stuff that made her feel like she could leave the world behind. Steve told her to come on over, but if she wanted the white lady, then it was going to cost her. Janice smiled as she thought about that. She knew exactly what Steve meant. She could almost feel his python working its way between her legs.

She had thought about asking Steve to come and pick her up, but the last thing she wanted was for Hakim to go crazy and attack her man again. She felt bad about putting her son in jail, but she didn't want him to think that he could just jump on Steve whenever he got upset. She didn't feel like waiting for the bus, so she just chose to walk.

Her feet started to hurt slightly as she bent the corner. Before Janice knew it, she was walking up on Steve's porch. He must've been looking out the window, because before she could knock on the door, he opened it.

Janice smiled as she followed Steve into his living room. Her smile soon turned into a confused look when she saw a strange man sitting on the couch with his shirt off. There were also two very young-looking women sitting beside him, sharing a blunt.

Noticing the strange look on her face, Steve draped his arm around Janice's shoulders. "Come on in, baby. Let me introduce you to a couple of friends of mine."

Janice became slightly unnerved as Steve guided her into the room.

"This here is my man Camp. And the two ladies sitting over there having a little fun are Tracy and Bird."

"Hello," Janice spoke to them as they absentmindedly waved back. "Honey, can I talk to you in the kitchen for a minute?"

Steve smiled sinisterly as he followed Janice into the kitchen.

"Steve, what's going on? I thought we were going to be together tonight."

"We are together. I just thought I would call a couple of friends over so we could have a li'l party. It's a'ight, ain't it?" Steve said with a stern look on his face.

"Uh, yeah, it's okay."

"Good," Steve said as he turned to go back onto the living room.

"Uh, do you have any more of that stuff you gave me the other night?"

"In due time, baby. In due time," he said, smiling.

"What time you talking 'bout linking up?" Bobby asked Red over the phone. After listening for a few seconds, Bobby said okay and hung up the phone.

He smiled as he thought about how Tammy had read his story and was seemingly impressed. He couldn't help but wonder if she really liked it or if she was just being nice. As if she knew that he was thinking about her, the phone rang with her on the other end. Bobby smiled. His heart started to warm as he rushed to press the button and see what his newfound love had to say. His heart sank when, for the second time, he answered the phone, and she was in tears.

"Bobby, can you come and get me, please? I need to go to a hotel."

"A hotel? The fuck you need to go to a hotel for? What the hell is going on?"

"I really don't want to go into it over the phone. Can you please just come and get me?"

"I'm on my way," Bobby said as he hit a U-turn in the middle of the street. Bobby didn't know what was going on, but after reaching up under the seat and grabbing his gun, he punched the gas and sped toward Tammy's house. When he got there, he saw Tammy sitting on the steps. Her elbows were resting on her knees, and her hands were covering her face. She was so distraught and deep in her thoughts that she didn't hear or see Bobby pull up.

Bobby got out of his truck as quickly as he could and ran over to his boo. "What's up? You okay?"

Without saying a word, Tammy jumped up and jumped directly into Bobby's arms. She wrapped her arms around him and held on as if someone were trying to abduct her.

"It's okay, li'l mama. I'm here now." Bobby noticed the duffle bag and backpack sitting on the ground.

"Will you take me to the Marriott downtown, please? I'll explain what happened on the way down there."

Bobby didn't say a word. He simply picked up her bags and carried them to the truck. He knew that she was going to tell him what was going on anyway, so all he had to do was wait for her to feel like talking about it. After putting the bags in the truck, Bobby went back, grabbed Tammy's hand, and escorted her to the truck. He helped her get inside and drove off.

After ten minutes of silence, Bobby couldn't take it anymore. He had to know what was going on, and since it was clear that Tammy wasn't in a hurry to give him any information, he figured the only way that he was going to get anywhere was to ask her straight out. "Okay, you gotta tell a nigga something. What's going on with you?"

Tammy opened her mouth to speak, but instead of words coming out of her mouth, they were replaced with tears streaming down her face. Bobby lifted his arm and put it around Tammy's shoulders. With no hesitation, she leaned her head over and laid it on his shoulder.

Tammy then proceeded to tell Bobby what happened. Bobby just shook his head at the entire situation. He wanted to go find Steve and put a bullet in his head for being the cause of Tammy's family being broken apart.

Tammy sat up and stared out the window. Up until that moment, it hadn't hit her that they were going in the opposite direction of downtown Cleveland. "Where are we going?"

"Well, first, we gon' swing by Rally's and get you something to eat. While you were lying on me, I heard ya stomach growling. When is the last time you had some grub?"

Tammy thought about it and couldn't remember. She didn't know how hungry she was until Bobby said something. All she could do was hunch her shoulders up.

"And then I'm gonna take you back to my place. Fuck that hotel bullshit. There's plenty of room at my crib."

Although Tammy was grateful, she didn't know if she wanted to accept Bobby's hospitality. It wasn't that she felt that she wasn't going to be comfortable in his place. She just wanted to be alone at the moment.

"And don't worry. I ain't gonna bother you," he said as if he could read her mind. "I know you probably want to be alone right now."

"Thank you. I don't know how I can ever repay you."

"Don't worry about that. I just wanna make sure you a'ight."

Bobby was paying such close attention to Tammy that, for the moment, he forgot all about having to meet up with Red.

Hakim sat on the bus, fighting to hold back the tears stinging the insides of his eyes. His emotions were more mixed up than a Rubik's Cube. He didn't know whether he was coming or going. All he wanted to do was find Steve and snap his neck in four places. He didn't know whether to feel sorry for his mother or hate her ever-living guts. She'd turned her back on them for a piece of dick.

Hakim started to think that his initial thought about his mother being on drugs was correct. In his mind, there was just no way that his mom could've gone from a loving, drug-hating woman to someone who was willing to toss her own kids out unless she was smoking or snorting something. Hakim hoped that Nikki was at home when he got there. He'd tried to call her twice, but she didn't answer either time. Just as he lifted his cell phone to call her again, it vibrated.

"Hey," she said as soon as he answered the phone. "What you getting into tonight?"

"Not much," he answered. He wanted to see what she was going to say before he asked her if he could stay there. He fully expected her to say yes, and quite frankly, he didn't know where he was going to go if she said no.

"I was thinking that you could come over tonight and spend the night with me, if you ain't too busy."

"Well, to tell you the truth, I was on my way over there now. I wanted to surprise you," he lied.

"Oh, for real? I'm about to get ready for you. I'm gonna leave the door unlocked while I take a shower, so let yourself in, okay?"

"That's cool."

After hanging up, Hakim's dick immediately got hard. Picturing Nikki in the shower had him literally running to her house. Either her mother and sister weren't at home, or Nikki just didn't give a fuck. And if she didn't care about boning while her mother and family were at home, then neither did he.

It didn't take him long to get to her house, considering his pace. Hakim walked in the house and looked around. He half expected Nikki's mother to come out and start either cussing him out or sucking him off. When he didn't see either her mother or her sister, he crept down the hallway to the bathroom and slowly pushed the door open.

He was instantly turned on by the sight of Nikki sitting in the tub, fondling one of her breasts. He almost came on himself right then. Hakim eased out of the bathroom and tiptoed down to her bedroom, where he stripped naked. With his dick sticking straight up in the air, he made his way back down the hallway.

When he opened the bathroom door, he was surprised to see Nikki sitting on the edge of the tub staring at him. She had a devilish smile on her face. "Did you actually think you could creep up on me in my own house and I wouldn't hear yo' ass? You know damn well I got that ghetto hearing."

"Damn, I guess you do," Hakim said.

"Sooo, what have we there?" Nikki asked, eyeing his penis. "Looks like somebody is very happy to see me."

Nikki walked over to Hakim, reached down, and grabbed his manhood. Hakim's eyes rolled to the back of his head as she stroked it to maximum hardness. After kissing his chest, Nikki led Hakim into her bedroom.

"Where is yo' moms and sister at?"

"I don't know, and right now, I don't give a fuck. Hell, I ain't seen them two skanks in a couple of days."

Hakim felt guilty as thoughts of Nikki's mother popped into his head. Nikki walked him over to the bed and sat down on it with Hakim in front of her. She then took him into her mouth.

"Oh, shit," he said as Nikki worked her magic.

"Mhhhm," she moaned as she savored the taste of Hakim's sex element. Just when he was about to bust, Nikki took her mouth off of it and scooted back toward the head of the bed. She then spread her legs and blew Hakim a kiss.

"Come and get it." Hakim's dick pulled the rest of his body into the warm confines of Nikki's sex.

"Ooo, yes, baby," Nikki said as she wrapped her legs around his waist. Hakim started off slow, but after a while, the two of them were going at it hot and heavy. Thirty-five minutes later, both of them were snoring like goats.

Chapter 31

The second Cedric walked back through Cookie's door, Dru knew something had gone wrong. The two of them had been friends since the first grade, so he knew the shifty look and nervous movements Cedric was exhibiting all too well.

"Ay yo, you take care of that?" Red asked him without even looking up. He was in the middle of rolling a blunt.

"Fo sho. That nigga sleeping wit' the fishes," Cedric said as he shifted his weight from side to side.

"Good, 'cause I ain't got time for no untrustworthy-ass niggas in my camp. Y'all feel me?" he asked, looking both of them directly in the eyes. Both of them nodded in agreement.

"Now let me tell you two young-ass niggas something. I didn't body that nigga 'cause he fucked my bitch. I would never catch a case over a broad. I did it 'cause he disrespected me. Never let a muthafucka disrespect you out here. 'Cause if you do, everybody gonna try to do it."

Red studied the faces of his two young protégés. He wanted to make sure that they understood the repercussions of crossing a man like him.

"A'ight, I'm gonna go back here and holla at this broad for a second. When I come back, we gon' break this shit down. Dru, how yo' li'l niggas out there coming along with that pack?"

Before Dru could answer, the Lil Wayne ring tone went off on his cell phone.

"Yo, tell it," he answered. After listening for a few seconds, Dru started smiling. "A'ight, bet. I'm gonna see what's up and hit you back in a few." He said to Red, "Them niggas been out there in the trap getting it in. My boy James said the new kid we got on our team be holding it down like a G."

"Who you talkin' 'bout, that nigga Hakim?" Cedric chimed in.

"Hakim? Y'all talkin' 'bout that young-ass nigga who works at the shoe store?" Red asked, laughing.

"I'm telling you that kid ain't no joke out there. James said he be holding it down all night. They say they ready to re-up and shit."

Red rubbed his chin and nodded in satisfaction. He hadn't expected the soldiers on the block to sell out so soon. He figured that if they were slinging like that, he should get them all together see what was up.

"Tell you what. Go pick up both of them li'l niggas and bring 'em to my spot in about an hour."

As Red headed toward Cookie's bedroom, Dru did some quick thinking. He'd followed Red over to Cookie's house, and they hadn't stopped anywhere, and when Red got out of the car, he was empty-handed. Right then, he deduced that Red had dope stashed at Cookie's place. Whether she knew it, Dru was unsure, but he did know one thing. If there was dope in the house, he was going to do his best to steal it.

Seeing the smirk on Dru's face, Cedric couldn't help but wonder what larcenous thoughts swam around in his partner's head.

With tears in her eyes, Cookie sat on the bed, picking at her fingernails. She couldn't believe Red had the audacity to slap her in front of his friends like she was a piece of trash. She knew she had taken it too far by sleeping with Ray-Ray, and now her attempt to gain revenge on Red not only ended with her getting a black eye, but more importantly, it ended up costing a man his life. It didn't matter that she wasn't too fond of Ray-Ray. She still felt bad that her antics caused his death. She jumped when Red came into the bedroom and sat beside her. He reached out to touch her face, but she turned away.

"I know you ain't still mad about that other bitch. I told you, I'm through with that ho. It's just you and me from now on."

Cookie knew that Red was just telling her what he thought she wanted to hear. Still, she wanted to believe him. She started to soften until the mirror reminded her why she was mad in the first place. "Did you have to hit me in front of your friends?"

"Look, my bad on that. But how the fuck you think it made me feel seeing that nigga lying in this fucking bed buck-naked? What was I s'posed to do, let that shit ride? Nah, fuck that. I ain't letting no nigga disrespect me like that."

Cookie wanted so badly to ask him why it was different for him. But the truth of the matter was that she'd known the rules when she got in the game. There was no way in the world she should have ever expected a dope-dealing baller like Red to be faithful.

His hearty laughter interrupted her thoughts. She was about to ask him what was so funny until she looked at the television and saw Red's favorite show, *Sanford and Son,* on the screen.

"Fred be tripping me the fuck out. Hey, baby, go get me a beer out of the fridge."

Cookie rolled her eyes but got up to go and get it. On the way back, it took everything in her power to keep from spitting in it.

***

After convincing Cookie to give him a quick blowjob before he left, Red drove back to his place. On the way there, he stopped at IHOP, where he met up with his connect and purchased two kilos of cocaine. He was going to chop up the product that he'd gotten from Cookie's house and distribute it to Dru and Cedric, but he changed his mind when he heard about how James and Hakim were working the trap. Now he wanted to gather everyone together and designate some kind of order to the situation.

When he left IHOP, Red stopped at the store to grab himself a pack of smokes. While there, he ran into Tick.

"Yo, Red, wassup? Let a brother hold something."

"Nigga, if you don't get the fuck away from me, I'm gonna let you hold something all right, but it ain't gon' be what you wanna hold."

Tick frowned and walked away. "That bastard ain't nothing like his cousin," Tick mumbled.

When Red finally did get back to his house, Dru, Cedric, and James were sitting in Dru's car, waiting for him. After the three of them went into the house, Red asked about the whereabouts of Hakim. "Ay yo, where that other nigga at?"

"I don't know," James said. "I called his cell and didn't get no—" James held up a finger and answered his cell. "Where the fuck you at?" James listened for a few seconds and then told Hakim to hold on. "He's at his girl's house. He says he was asleep when I called at first."

"Tell him that you 'bout to come pick him up if he wanna make some real bread."

"Yo, man, I'm 'bout to come scoop you in ten minutes. It's 'bout to be on and poppin' in this bitch."

James used Dru's car to go pick Hakim up. Dru and Red passed a blunt back and forth while waiting.

Hakim rolled out of the bed quietly. He didn't want to wake Nikki after the bomb sex she'd just put on him.

He'd actually been awake for the past ten minutes, trying to think of a way to ask Nikki to let him move in without it costing him a whole lot. He was certain that she would let him stay there, but what it would cost him remained to be seen, especially with her mother's and sister's hands out. After getting dressed, he eased out of the bedroom and the front door. James had just pulled up when he walked outside.

As he turned to close the door, a smile crept across his face. He no longer had to worry about what it would cost him to stay. Once Nikki and the rest of her family saw the eviction notice taped on their door, they would be begging him to live there.

Tammy opened her eyes, slightly confused. For a split second, she had no idea where she was. The arm wrapped around her shoulders brought the memories flooding back to her. She turned her head to the left and smiled. Once again, Bobby had been her knight in shining armor. Tammy leaned over and kissed Bobby on the neck. His scent started making her moist as she gently sucked on his earlobe. Then she ran her hand down his chest and almost exploded on herself when she reached up under his shirt and felt his rock-hard six-pack.

Bobby woke up to a pleasant surprise as Tammy ran her tongue down the side of his neck. "Uhmmm, what are you doing?"

Instead of answering his question, Tammy reached down and started unbuckling his belt.

"Damn, you sure you wanna do this?"

Tammy didn't answer him with words. Instead, she reached inside of his jeans and pulled out his throbbing member. Bobby almost released right then and there as her smooth hands rubbed and caressed his shaft to maximum hardness.

Tammy looked deep into Bobby's eyes. She wanted to make sure that what she was about to do wouldn't come back to haunt her later on. Throwing caution to the wind, Tammy did something that she'd only heard about or seen in a porno movie. She lowered her head to his shaft and started sucking gently. She'd always told herself that if she ever got up the nerve to give a guy head, it would have to be someone special, and in her book, Bobby qualified as that someone.

"Oh God," he moaned as she took her time and pleased him with skills that belied a first-timer.

I guess watching porno movies does pay off. "You like that?" she asked when she came up for air.

"Oooo, hell yeah."

Wanting this to be a special night for himself as well, Bobby stood and picked Tammy up into both of his arms. He carried her into his bedroom and laid her down. Tammy panted as Bobby kissed her inner thigh. She shuddered as his tongue traveled up toward her sweet mound. She thought she was going to lose all control when he blew into her vagina and followed it up by kissing it and then gently sucking on her clit.

After five minutes of foreplay, Tammy was practically begging Bobby to enter her. Bobby was more than willing to oblige her as he mounted her tender frame with care. Normally, Bobby would be balls deep into a girl by now, but there just something about Tammy that made him want to enjoy her. That made him want to please her just as much as he wanted to be pleased himself. She whimpered softly as he entered her. Bobby lost himself in the sweetness of Tammy as she called his name repeatedly. His massive yet tender strokes caused her to melt into his world, just as her softness caused her to mesh with his.

The two of them made love into the wee hours of the morning, until Bobby's cell phone awakened him and reminded him that he was supposed to be at Red's an hour and a half ago.

"Fuck," he said softly as he got out of his bed and slipped back into his clothes. He hoped that Tammy wouldn't be mad at him for handling his business, but this was something he had to do to keep his pockets fat.

By the time two o'clock in the morning rolled around, Janice had learned the hard way that the man of her dreams was a certified nightmare. The monkey named cocaine had grown so large on her back that she had shamefully agreed to let one of the women suck one of her titties for a snort. High as a kite, with tears in her eyes, Janice looked at Steve as the other woman fingered her. Janice felt embarrassed and ashamed.

She became even more disgusted at herself for not being able to stop the orgasm that threatened to erupt as the woman continued to pinch and flick at her clit. Janice tried to stop herself, but she just couldn't. Tears flowed from her eyes as hot, sticky cum ran down her leg.

"I thought you loved me. Why would you make me do this?"

"Love you? What the fuck ever made you thought I loved you?"

Janice's heart broke in half. If she had a razor, she would have slit her wrists right then and there. She couldn't believe that this was the man she'd abandoned her kids for. Now she was beginning to wonder if Steve really was trying to spy on Tammy. As her high started wearing off, the monkey on her back started pounding. The woman who'd been fingering her earlier had disappeared. Janice had thought that she'd seen her leave with someone, but she wasn't sure. At that point, Janice realized that she was in the room alone.

She was just about to call out for Steve when his friend walked into the room with nothing on but a wife beater. His limp dick hung eight inches past his balls as he walked in and sat in the leather recliner adjacent from her. Janice was mortified. She couldn't believe that some man she'd just met would do such a thing. She jumped off the couch at lightning speed and ran to Steve's bedroom. She tried to open the door, but to her surprise, it was locked.

"Steve! Steve," she shouted as she struggled to turn the knob.

"What the hell do you what?"

Janice was beyond shocked that Steve was talking to her that way, but she ignored it for the moment. "I need to talk to you!"

"I'm kinda busy in here, so you're just gonna have to take yo' ass back in the living room and wait until I'm done!"

Janice was so mad she had a good mind to leave. But then she thought about how good Steve was giving the dick to her and didn't want to piss him off. Plus, her high was starting to wear off, and she needed him to hook her up with more dope. Like a small child who'd just been chastised, Janice slunk back into the living room, where the man was now drinking a glass of vodka and snorting lines of cocaine from a mirror.

He had taken off his wife beater and was now totally nude. Janice cringed when she noticed how his now-semi-erect penis seemed to be pointing at her. The man set the mirror down on the table and started sipping his drink. He remained silent, with a sinister smirk on his face, as he watched Janice sniff and rub her nose. He knew that she wanted some in the worst way. All he had to do was wait, and he would get whatever he wanted from her. He knew that once Steve's main customer got a hold of her, she'd be lost, so he figured that he may as well fuck her while he had the chance.

"Excuse me," Janice said, not being able to take it any longer, "but do you think you could share your candy with me?"

"If I give you some of this, what you gon' do for me?"

Janice knew what he was getting at, but she tried to buy it with money instead.

He laughed at her. "Sweetheart, I don't want ya money. I wanna see how good you can suck a dick."

Janice wanted to scream. Suicidal thoughts popped in and out of her head. "I don't want to do that," she said.

"Suit ya'self," he said as he got up. He reached down and grabbed the mirror and attempted to walk past her.

Instinctively, she reached out and grabbed his arm. "No, wait," she begged. "Okay. Okay," she conceded as she eyed the white demon.

The man extended his arm so that the mirror was just inches from Janice's face. Then he pulled it back, shook his head, and pointed at his penis. He sat down on the couch and told Janice to get on her knees. Janice did as she was told and put the head in her mouth. She hated what she was doing but knew if she did a subpar job, she would get stiffed on the dope.

For a woman who just two weeks ago despised drugs, Janice felt like the biggest hypocrite in the world. It wasn't until she felt a sharp pain in her anal area that she realized Steve had crept up behind her and started fucking her in the ass. Janice wanted to cry a river, but sadly she had no more tears to give.

Chapter 32

Tammy woke up feeling like a new woman. Although the pain of her mother choosing a man over her still resonated within her soul, the shock was slowly starting to wear off. She hated that Bobby had to leave and, more importantly, hadn't come back yet, but she'd known what kind of man he was when she'd gotten involved with him.

Tammy smiled as she thought about her newfound love. Her spine tingled as she thought about the toe-curling lovemaking session she'd had with Bobby. After relieving her bladder, Tammy decided to call Hakim and see if he was okay. She became a little concerned when he didn't answer.

She didn't want to jump to conclusions and assume that he'd gone back to their mother's house and caused trouble. Since she hadn't gotten a phone call saying that he'd been locked up again, she shrugged it off and figured that he was probably busy with his new street job. Although she disapproved, Tammy knew that there was nothing she could do about it. Plus, she would look like a total hypocrite for looking down on Hakim when Bobby was in the streets even deeper than he was.

She returned the call she'd missed from Nancy, but after several rings, it went it voicemail. She thought about returning Ivory's call but decided to do it later. She didn't feel like hearing about her friend's drama at the moment. Tammy went into the bathroom and jumped in the shower. She wanted to be fresh and clean for Bobby, whatever time he got back home. After getting clean, Tammy dried herself off and got back in the bed. She turned on the TV and flicked through the channels. She quickly became bored and started wondering what she was going to do until Bobby returned. An idea quickly formed in her head, and she got up and walked into the front room.

Bobby pulled into his driveway and took a deep breath. He didn't want to take his anger out on Tammy, so he decided to sit in his truck and listen to music for a minute until he had a chance to calm down. Red had pissed him off so bad. Bobby didn't know how long he would stay mad. If he thought that he was going to treat Bobby like one of them young cats helping them bag up the dope, then he had another think coming. Blood or no blood, Bobby wasn't going to be disrespected. Although it was early, Bobby needed a blunt to calm his nerves. He reached into the glove compartment of his whip and took out a sack of weed and a box of Dutch Masters. After lacing the Dutch, he slowly took pull after pull as he sat back and thought about what had transpired between him and his cousin.

Bobby pulled up in front of Red's house. He knew his cousin was going to be pissed that he was late, but he really didn't give a fuck. All he knew was he was happier than he'd been in a long time. He was a thug, but he was a thug with a heart. He jumped out of his truck and walked up to the door. Red must've looked out of the window and seen him coming, because before he even knocked, the door was opened by Dru. The two of them exchanged unpleasant stares as Bobby walked in. Dru was still pissed at Bobby for pistol-whipping him.

Dru walked sideways so he could keep his eyes on Bobby as the two of them headed down the foyer and into the living room. Red stared hard at Bobby. Bobby stared right back. Dru, Hakim, and Cedric looked on as Bobby and Red continued their staring contest. The tension was as thick as fog.

Finally, Red made the first move. "You late."

"I ain't on no damn clock."

"I didn't say you was on no fucking clock, but damn, man. We trying to make this paper. This shit ain't gonna cut itself," Red said as he pointed at the two keys of dope that lay on the table.

"A'ight. My bad," Bobby said as he sat down at the table.

"Maybe you need to cut that bitch loose if she gon' be causing you to slack on ya game," Red mumbled.

"Hold up. That's the second time you done called my girl a bitch. You gon' have to ease up on that bullshit."

Red started laughing until he looked up again and noticed that Bobby was serious. "You serious? I know damn well you ain't trying to flex up on me over no broad. We blood."

"Then show me some damn respect."

"Ain't that a bitch?" Red said with a surprised look on his face. "Yeah, a'ight. My bad, cousin."

The way Red said the word "cousin" let Bobby know that Red didn't appreciate him putting a woman in front of their kinship. Whether Red knew it or not, that wasn't what Bobby was doing. All he wanted was for Red to respect Tammy, and everything would be fine.

Hakim was amused by the whole scene. He, too, couldn't understand why Bobby was putting a woman before his own flesh and blood. Little did he know that the woman was his sister.

"Yo, where that nigga Ray-Ray at? Ain't he s'posed to be here too?" Bobby asked

*"Nah, he called me and told me that he had an emer-
gency going on with one of his baby mamas," Red lied.
He didn't feel like explaining what had gone down with
Ray-Ray. He decided he would just let Bobby think that
one of their rivals snuffed Ray-Ray out when his body
was found.*

Bobby shook the earlier events from his mind and
hopped out of his truck. The closer he got to his front
door, the better he felt. Bobby had smashed many wom-
en over the years, but being with Tammy felt different to
him. It just felt right. Bobby walked in the door quietly
just in case Tammy was still asleep. When he walked into
his living room, a large smile fell across his face. Tammy
was so engrossed in his manuscript, she didn't even hear
him come in. Bobby cleared his throat to get her attention.

"Oh, hey. I was wondering when you were going to get
home," she said in a sweet voice that nearly caused his
heart to melt.

Bobby's stomach rumbled, reminding him that he
hadn't had anything to eat since early yesterday.

"Damn, sounds like you're starving," Tammy teased.

Bobby chuckled and shook his head. He just couldn't
get over how proper Tammy was talking.

"What's so funny?" she asked, sensing that he wasn't
laughing over her remark about him being hungry.

"Nothing, just thinking about something. You know
what, li'l mama? Let's go get something to eat. I know this
place that got the bomb-ass breakfast."

"You're not tired?" she asked, reminding him that he'd
just gotten in a few minutes ago.

"Nah, I'm straight," he lied. He was tired as hell, but he
knew that he needed to put something on his stomach.
Plus, he wanted to take Tammy out to breakfast.

"Okay, boo. Let me go put some clothes on."

As Tammy walked back toward Bobby's bedroom, he got a hard-on watching her ass switch from side to side. As she disappeared down the hallway, Bobby started wondering where he was going to take her. He wanted to take her to Maria's soul food restaurant, but because Kat worked there, he ruled that out immediately. The last thing he wanted or needed was for his ex to cause drama and throw salt in his game. Bobby decided to take Tammy to Pancake Heaven. It wasn't as good as Maria's, but he was confident that she would enjoy it.

Tammy came back out dressed in tight jeans and a gold Cleveland Cavaliers T-shirt. "I'm ready, boo."

Bobby frowned. That was the second time she'd called him boo. He wasn't sure if he liked it. In his mind, it made him sound soft.

"What's wrong?" she asked, noticing the wrinkles in his brow.

"Nothing really. I mean, it's just you calling me boo. What grown man wants to be called that bullshit?"

"Ah, come on. You know you're my boo," she said as she ran up to him and threw her arms around his neck. Once again, his heart melted. Tammy and Bobby were falling for each other, hard.

The two of them walked hand in hand out of the house. Tammy got confused when they passed Bobby's truck. "What, are we walking or something?" she asked.

"Nope." Bobby led her to a white Nissan Maxima that was parked directly in front of his house.

"Is this your car too? Why don't you ever drive it?"

"I do sometimes, but I like my truck better." Bobby opened the door for Tammy and held it until she got in.

"Then why did you even buy a car if you like the truck better?" she asked once they headed toward their destination.

"I actually had the car first. But now that I have the truck, I like it better."

"Oh, so when you get tired of something, you just go out and get something new to take its place, huh?"

Bobby knew where this conversation was going, and he wanted no part of it. He was relieved when Tammy's cell phone started ringing. As she answered her phone, she wagged her finger back and forth at him, letting him know that their conversation on the subject was not over.

"Where the hell are you?" she screamed into the phone at Hakim as soon as she answered it.

"Stop tripping. I'm handling business."

"Oh, is that right? Look—"

"No, you look. I didn't call you for you to start the dumb shit. I was just returning ya call and to let you know that I was good. I gotta go. I'm gonna call you later, a'ight?"

Before Tammy could protest, Hakim had hung up on her. Tammy just shook her head. In her mind, she partially blamed herself for the way her brother was turning out.

Bobby seemingly read her thoughts as he patted her leg. "Stop worrying about it. I know that's ya brother and all, but if he wants to be in the streets, there really ain't too much you can do about it."

"Yeah, I know," she conceded. "That doesn't mean I have to like it, though."

Bobby remained quiet as he pulled into Pancake Heaven. His stomach had been growling ever since they'd left. He couldn't wait to sink his teeth into some good food. The two of them were seated in a booth right next to the window. When the waitress came over to take their order, Bobby instantly got a headache.

"Hello, Bobby," she said as she rudely and unprofessionally popped gum.

Tammy looked at Bobby and then at the waitress, who refused to even acknowledge that Tammy was in the room.

"Sup, Rita."

Instead of taking their order, Rita stood there for a few seconds and just stared at Bobby.

I know Bobby didn't used to date this overweight heifer. Tammy cleared her throat to let Bobby know that she was still there, in case he'd forgotten.

"Oh, I'm sorry, baby. This is Rita. Rita, this is my girl, Tammy."

Tammy nodded in agreement. She wondered how Bobby was going to introduce her. "Hello," Tammy said, trying to be cordial.

"Yo' girl?" Rita asked as if she found that hard to believe.

"Yes, his girl," Tammy chimed in.

Rita stared at Tammy like she was a piece of shit before saying, "Anyway, Bobby, have you talked to my girl Kat?" Rita wanted to make sure that Tammy knew who Kat was.

"Hell nah! You know damn well we broke up."

"Yeah, right," she snickered, trying to make it look as if Bobby were lying. "What y'all having?" she said, rolling her eyes at Tammy.

"Not a damn thing from here," Tammy said as she started to get up.

"Sir, is there a problem over here?" asked a thin man with a receding hairline. The crisp shirt and starched khakis suggested that he was probably the manager. The conversation among the three of them had gotten louder than they thought.

"Your rude-ass worker won't take our order, and unless we get another server, we are not eating here," Tammy said before Bobby had a chance to respond.

"I'm sorry, ma'am. I will send someone else over here right away." The manager dismissed Rita and called another waitress over to serve them. He also assured them that the situation would be handled accordingly and even agreed to give them their meal for free. When the manager walked away, Tammy's neck snapped around like in *The Exorcist*.

"Who the fuck was that bitch?" she asked with attitude.

Bobby wanted to go to the back of the restaurant, find Rita, and break her neck. He had no idea that one of Kat's friends was now working there. Bobby didn't want to lie to Tammy about the situation, so he told her the truth. "Okay, look. That was the best friend of a girl I used to mess around with. As you can tell, she'd petty as fuck, so let's just ignore her ass and get our eat on."

Tammy listened intently while keeping her eyes trained on Bobby the entire time. It only took him a few seconds to explain to her who Rita and Kat were. Tammy rolled her eyes and snorted. She believed him, but she decided that she would make him suffer a little. After ordering her food, Tammy looked at Bobby.

"And what will you have, sir?"

"Yes, what will you have, lover boy?" Tammy said.

The waitress let out a light chuckle as Bobby sighed and placed his order. From the sound of Tammy's voice, Bobby figured it was going to be a long day.

Tammy smiled on the inside, giddy over the fact that Bobby had introduced her as his girl. Bobby didn't know it, but he was in for a treat that night.

Meanwhile, as Bobby and Tammy enjoyed their meal, a cold set of eyes was trained on them from behind a newspaper. Detective Dryer had been given a week off from work because of his injury sustained during the fight with Hank. Knowing that if he'd told his boss the truth, he would be disciplined, Dryer lied to his captain and told him that he'd gotten the injury by falling down the stairs. For the past two days, he'd been trying to come up with a plan that would take down Red and his crew once and for all. Seeing the way Bobby seemingly felt about Tammy caused his mind to race. A devious plan unfolded in the corner of his mind.

Shortly after leaving the nursing home, Ivory decided to go shopping. She felt really proud of herself for having the ability to forgive her mother after all these years, so she figured that she'd reward herself by splurging a little. Ivory had already put the word out that she was holding the weed tip, so she figured it was just a matter of time before she made back the money she'd spent.

When Ivory got home that night, the joy and warmth that had occupied her soul turned to anger. The eviction notice on her door had her wanting to choke her landlord. She'd accidentally erased the recording that she'd made earlier, so she had no leverage to use. The only thing she could think of to keep herself from getting kicked out into the street was to try to use weed as payment.

Ivory awakened from her deep sleep feeling refreshed. She looked at the four bags of clothes she'd bought, which cost close to $1,200, and she thought seriously about taking them back. The eviction notice was starting to hit home. But before she took them back, she had one last trick up her sleeve. Even though she knew it was a scandalous, trifling thing to do, she made plans to go over to Darnell's place and search his house for cash and weed.

She was still upset that her lover was dead, but there was no sense in letting the money and marijuana go to waste. Ivory got up and hopped in the shower. The more she thought about it, the more she was convinced that Darnell had stashed a few dollars in his house. As she lathered her body up, Ivory tried to remember if there was a place in particular that Darnell didn't want her to go when she visited him. Then it hit her. His bedroom closet. He always made it a point to tell her not to go in there.

Even if she didn't bring it up, he did, using excuses like he thought there was a rat in there and he was embarrassed because it was so junky. Ivory started smiling, figuring that she'd just hit the jackpot. She quickly jumped out of the shower and got dressed. The notice said that she had three days to pay her rent or she, along with her belongings, would be tossed into the street. She cursed herself, thinking that if she hadn't accidentally erased that recording of her weed-smoking landlord, she wouldn't be in this mess. She picked out one of the outfits she'd purchased and slipped into it.

She sure as hell wasn't going to take the clothes back now that she was about to get paid. After getting dressed, Ivory quickly rolled a blunt, stuffed it in her pocket, and headed for the door, grabbing her keys off the kitchen table as she went by. She opened the door to leave and was greeted by a tall, thin black man with a short Afro and sideburns.

Who the fuck is this Shaft-lookin' nigga? "May I help you?" she asked.

"Is yo' name Ivory?"

"Who the fuck wants to know?" Ivory responded defiantly. The words had barely left her lips before the man's bony right hand backhanded her to the floor.

"I'm askin' the muthafucking questions up in here, if you don't mind."

Ivory was dazed. She shook her head twice in an attempt to clear the cobwebs. Then she heard the door slam. She looked up and saw the man who'd hit her being flanked by two other men. One of them, the larger of the two, stood slightly slumped over, as if his back were hurting him. He was a brute of a man who easily stood over six feet two inches and weighed in the neighborhood of 300 pounds.

The other gentleman was significantly smaller, at around 180 pounds. His long, angular face and oversized ears made him look like he something you would visit at the zoo.

"Oh, excuse my manners," the man said sarcastically. "These two gentlemen are my, uh, associates, Rilla and Monk. My name is Bo," he said as he walked slowly over to Ivory. He leaned down and got face-to-face with her. "Now I'm gonna ask you one more time and one more time only. Is yo' name Ivory?"

Not seeing any other way out of the predicament she was in, Ivory answered, "Yes," through gritted teeth. She could've kicked herself in the ass for not following her first mind and grabbing her pistol on the way out the door. She would've surely shot this asshole in the face if she had it on her.

"Now we getting somewhere." Bo stood up and reached down to help Ivory up. She looked at him like he'd lost his mind. With a sinister scowl on her face, Ivory got up and wiped blood from the corner of her mouth. Bo shrugged his shoulders and smiled at Ivory's attempt to act brave. The smile then slowly disappeared from his face. His brown eyes turned to narrow slits, and his cold stare gave her the chills.

"I'm gonna make this short and sweet. Darnell owes me ten thousand dollars, and since I can't seem to locate him and you're his next of kin, you assume the debt."

"Next of kin? What the hell are you talking about, next of kin?"

"Ain't you his fucking wife?"

"Wife?" Ivory broke out in laughter. "If I were his wife, why the fuck would we be living in separate places, genius?" Ivory continued to laugh until Bo quickly walked up on her and wrapped a bony hand around her throat. Ivory raised her hands to scratch his face but was stopped cold by the .45 he pressed against her temple.

"You better watch how the fuck you talk to me! I ain't Darnell, and I damn sho' ain't none of these li'l niggas you be fucking around with who are wet behind the ears and pissing on they self! I don't give a fuck if you're his wife, girlfriend, or muthafucking concubine. The last time I talked to that nigga, he told us that if we couldn't find him, then we could come see you! And from the look on yo' face, I guess he fucked you too. But I gave him that shit on consignment. All he had to do was sell that shit and gimme my cut! Apparently, his ass didn't sell it, 'cause you ain't got my money . . . or do you?"

"No."

"Well, since you got played too, I'm gonna give you some time to come up with my dough. I'm gonna be back here in two weeks."

"Wait a minute! That shit ain't right! You expect me to pay for a debt his ass made?"

"Yep," Bo said as he walked out and slammed the door.

Ivory was tight. She couldn't believe that Darnell had put her in such a fucked-up position. She ran into her bedroom and opened up the duffle bag that contained the weed he'd left. To her surprise, there was nowhere near the amount of weed that was in there before. *Damn, have I been smoking that damn much?* She quickly closed the bag back up.

Ivory then grabbed her gun out of the nightstand. She wasn't going to get caught slipping again. Ivory jetted out the door and down the hallway. Just before she ran out the front of the building, she heard her landlord screaming about the rent. Ivory ignored her and continued on her way, hoping like hell that Darnell had enough money stashed in his house to pay off the debt.

Ivory repeatedly and angrily banged her fists on the steering wheel. From her vantage point, she could tell that someone had broken into his house. It didn't take a genius to quickly figure out that whoever broke in had more than likely ransacked the place, too. Ivory slowly got out of her car and walked toward the front door. With her knuckles, she pushed the already-open door and eased in the house. Her temperature rose immediately as her eyes focused on the trashed house.

Ivory quickly ran into the bedroom and went straight to Darnell's closet. Although she felt bad about him getting killed, she was pissed that he involved her in his bullshit. She opened the closet door and started hyperventilating. Right there on the floor was a safe that looked as if it had been pried open some kind of way. The only thing in it was air.

Ivory stormed back out of the house, mad as fuck. She knew that there was no need to look anywhere else in the house. Whoever had looted Darnell's house had probably gone through every room in there, and Ivory saw no reason to put herself through the aggravation. During her drive home, Ivory tried to figure out what she was going to do. Not only did she not have a way to pay back the dudes who had come to collect Darnell's debt, but she also didn't have any way to pay her rent. In her mind, there was only one thing she could do

As soon as Ivory got home, she started packing. She needed to leave town, and she needed to leave fast. There was no way she was going to be able to come up with the money. Staying with Tammy was out, not only because her mother didn't like her, but also because she didn't want to extend her problems to her friend.

When she was done packing, Ivory walked out the front door and ripped the eviction notice off the door. She crumpled it up, threw it on the ground, and spat on it. Sentimental value didn't mean anything to her, so she didn't give a shit about anything that was in the place. She was going to miss Tammy, and as soon as she got to her destination, she was going to call her and explain what went down. With two suitcases, an overnight bag, the duffle bag of what was left of the weed, and $2,000 in her pocket, Ivory headed for Solon, Ohio, to stay with the only other person in the world other than Tammy who she truly believed cared about her.

Chapter 33

Hakim's introduction into the dope was turning into a tedious chore. He was up all night at Red's learning how to cook, cut, and bag dope. This was the part of the game he hadn't thought about. All he envisioned were cars, flashy jewelry, and lots of money in his pocket. Hakim thought about how they had worked him like a plow mule and shrugged his shoulders. If this was what it took for him to become a kingpin, then he would just have to bear it. *Besides, it ain't like I'm flipping burgers or no fucked-up shit like that.*

Hakim suddenly had a thought. He had to find somewhere to hide his product while he was living at Nikki's. He knew damn well that he couldn't leave it out in the open, especially with Nikki's dopefiend mother and sister lurking around.

"Damn, nigga, you gon' get out or stare into fucking space?" James asked him, breaking his train of thought.

"Oh, my bad, dawg," Hakim said as he thanked James for the ride.

"Yo, hold up a second," James said just as Hakim was getting out of his car. James reached under his seat and pulled out a .45-caliber handgun and handed it to Hakim. "You gon' need one of these if you gon' be in the game."

Hakim grabbed the cold piece of steel and immediately felt like a big shot. Visions of Steve lying in a pool of his own blood flashed through his mind, but he quickly dismissed them, knowing that his mother would never forgive him if Steve met his demise by his hand. "Thanks, dawg."

Seeing the look in Hakim's eyes, James figured he'd better say something to the youngster. "Don't be pulling that muthafucka unless you plan on popping something for real. They play for keeps out here in these streets. You gotta protect yo'self at all times, but don't be a fool with it."

Hakim nodded as he got out of the car. Walking up to the front door, he smiled. He saw that the eviction notice had been taken down, so he knew what to expect once he got inside the house. As soon as he walked through the front door, he heard sobs coming from Nikki's bedroom. He slowly walked down the corridor and pushed the door open. Nikki was sitting on the edge of her bed with her head in her hands. Tears trickled down her arms and fell off the points of her elbows.

"What's goin' on?" he asked as if he didn't know.

"I just found out that my mother hasn't been paying the fucking rent! And that bitch-ass landlord put a damn eviction notice on our door, talking about if the rent ain't caught up by Friday, I gotta get out."

Hakim noticed that Nikki said "I" and not "we." "Damn, that's fucked up. What did yo' moms say about that shit?"

"I don't even know where the fuck she at! I ain't seen her or my sister in three damn days! They probably somewhere sucking somebody's dick for a hit of crack! I ain't got no money. How the fuck am I gonna pay seven hundred fifty dollars by Friday?"

Nikki then fell back on her bed and covered her face with the pillow. Hakim's hustle profits were now up to $5,000, so he could afford to pay it, but first, he was going to set some ground rules. He went over to Nikki and sat down beside her.

"I'll tell you what," he started. "I can help you out, but if I do that, then I'm gonna have to stay here. I ain't paying rent in a place where I ain't laying my head." Hakim smiled on the inside because he knew that there was no way Nikki was going to be able to turn him down. Plus, he would have in-house pussy whenever he wanted.

"You would do that for me?" she asked as Hakim easily misled her.

"Of course. I'm ready to get up outta my mom's house anyway. But check it. If I'm gonna pay the rent up in this piece, then I got a few rules that have to be followed. I don't know how yo' sis and moms gon' feel about that, though."

"Don't worry about them," she said as she hugged him. "As long as you paying the bills, my mom's ain't gon' give a fuck what you do."

"That's what's up," Hakim said as he grabbed her ass. This was going along just as he'd planned. And if he was lucky, he thought, he might just get to fuck Nikki's mom after all.

Dryer's mood had changed dramatically since he'd walked into the restaurant to grab a meal. He smiled sinisterly while he watched Bobby and Tammy walk out the front door of Pancake Heaven. He hadn't talked to his partner for a couple of days, so he had no idea if Stone was at work, but he was so giddy about his plan to get at Red that he decided to call him and run it past him. The first time he called, it went to voicemail. He called again five minutes later, and Stone picked up on the second ring.

"Hey, what's up, partner?" Dryer said after Stone answered the phone.

"Not much, just enjoying my day off," Stone answered

"Well, let me run this idea by you right fast."

Stone held the phone, completely disinterested in what Dryer was talking about. He had more important things on his mind at the time. When Dryer was done, he tried to get Stone on board with his plan. Stone accepted for no other reason than to get Dryer off the phone. After hanging up, Stone went back to enjoying the head that Nancy was giving him.

Even though Nancy liked dealing with blacks on the sex tip, Stone was giving her money to support her habit. Knowing his partner's fiery temper and penchant for violence, he had a choice to make at that point. He could either stop messing around with Nancy, or be more careful. And since Nancy had the ability to make him come twice in less than five minutes, he decided that he would just have to be more careful.

Chapter 34

Six Weeks Later

Tammy sat on the couch and sighed. She had just come from the doctor and was having mixed feelings. Getting pregnant right before she was scheduled to start school was not in the plan. Now she had to decide if she was going to attend classes while pregnant or put her schooling on hold.

The only time they were ever separated was when Bobby was in the street doing his thing. Over the last few weeks, she and Bobby grown closer and closer.

The fact that he and Tammy were so close irked the hell out of Red. In his mind, Tammy was costing him money because Bobby had missed a few meetings while kicking it with her.

Although Tammy and Ivory conversed on a regular basis, Tammy hated that her homegirl stayed in a different city. She resisted the urge to say, "I told you so" when Ivory told her about the sheisty way Darnell had put her life in danger. She was just glad that her friend was okay.

Tammy thought back to that night she moved in with Bobby. That had to be the night she got pregnant, because every other time after that, they made sure to use protection. Tammy was very nervous. She had no idea how he would react. She wanted to call her mother and tell her that she was going to be a grandmother, but due to the fact that she'd hardly talked to her since she'd put her and Hakim out, she didn't know if she should try to call her again. She'd only talked to her a couple of times since then, and even then, Janice would rush her off the phone.

It hurt Tammy to her soul that her mother didn't want to be bothered with her children anymore. She would have to give some thought to whether she would call her mother.

She still hadn't worked up the nerve to ask Bobby if her brother could visit them. Bobby was very apprehensive about letting people he didn't know visit him, and even though Hakim was Tammy's brother, she wanted to make sure that it was okay with Bobby before she invited him over. To this day, she hadn't called Hakim by his name in front of Bobby. She always referred to him as "my brother" when she talked to Bobby.

Tammy rubbed her stomach and wondered if she had made the biggest mistake of her life by getting pregnant. To keep her mind off of things, Tammy picked up another one of Bobby's manuscripts. His writing was really starting to look authentic. She'd been trying to get him to send it off and see if he could get it published, but he didn't think it was good enough. Tammy shook her head and laughed. It seemed that Bobby was confident in everything except the one thing that he should've been confident in.

Bobby and Red sat on Red's couch playing Xbox. They'd had a strained relationship ever since Tammy came in the picture. It was funny how Tammy was never mentioned by name. Whenever anyone in the crew said anything about Tammy, they referred to her as "broad" or "chick." Bobby didn't like it, but he decided that he wasn't going to give them the satisfaction of knowing that it bothered him.

He was on his way out of the game anyway. Bobby had socked away a cool $500,000 and had plans to start his own publishing house. Tammy didn't know it, but Bobby had been spending a lot of time reading up on the business, and he'd learned a lot in a short period of time.

Red held out a blunt he was smoking so Bobby could take it.

Sensing the tension between the two of them, Dru asked about a meeting that Bobby had missed. "Yo, Bobby, how long you think it took for us to bag that shit up last time?"

Bobby turned his head and glared at him.

"How the fuck he know? He wasn't here," Red laughed.

Bobby knew exactly what Dru was doing. Looking like Joe Pesci in the movie *Goodfellas,* Bobby pulled out his gun and fired a shot in Dru's direction.

"Shit!" Cedric and Hakim screamed in unison as the two of them ducked for cover. The bullet ripped through Dru's ear and lodged in the loveseat.

"Nigga, what the fuck wrong with you?" Red yelled as Dru fell on the floor and squirmed around. Dru immediately reached for the .22 that was on his hip.

"Go ahead, so I can put a muthafucking part in ya head."

Seeing that Bobby had the drop on him, Dru eased his hand off of his weapon. Bobby then backed up until he passed Red.

"Bobby, what the hell is wrong with you?" Red asked.

"Ain't shit wrong wit' me! I'm just tired of that punk muthafucka over there trying to talk slick all the damn time!"

"That nigga just playing with you!"

"He plays too muthafucking much! I know exactly what the fuck he's tryin' ta do, even if yo' blind ass don't! But you know what? Fuck you, that bitch-ass nigga over there, and this punk-ass operation! From now on, I'm through with this shit!"

"What the fuck you talking about? All this muthafucking cheese we making, and you wanna just bounce like that?" The two of them stared at each other for a few seconds. "Oh, I know what it is," Red said, snapping his fingers. "You catering to that bitch you been fucking around with for the last couple of months."

Without even thinking about it, Bobby punched Red in the mouth. Blood and spit flew on the floor.

"Muthafucka, is you crazy?"

"I told you to stop disrespecting my lady," Bobby said as he stared Red down. Then he stormed toward the door and slammed it on the way out.

Red stood there, stunned that his blood cousin would trip like that over a woman. Although Dru's ear was killing him, he was as happy as a mouse in a cheese factory. The fact that Bobby was now out of the picture brought him one step closer to being the new king.

"See, that's what happens when you go crazy over a bitch," Red spat as he plopped back down on the couch and lit a blunt. "Tammy got that nigga's head all fucked up."

Hakim's eyes got wide. That was the first time he'd heard Red refer to Bobby's girl by name. He immediately became concerned.

Tammy looked up at the clock and saw that she'd been reading Bobby's manuscript for almost an hour and a half. She'd meant to suggest to Bobby that he get a computer to type his work on. Her train of thought was broken by her ringing cell phone. She looked at the number and, after seeing that it was her mother's house, quickly answered it. A funny feeling came over her when she said hello and no one spoke.

"Mama?"

Still, no one answered. The line went dead, and Tammy's stomach started to turn. She didn't know what was going on, but she aimed to find out. She dialed her mother's number, and when someone picked up, she started to say hello only to have someone hang up in her face. She tried to call again, and it went straight to voicemail.

Tammy jumped up from her seat on the couch, grabbed the keys to Bobby's car, and headed out the door. To keep from driving her around every day, Bobby simply gave her the keys to his Maxima. She peeled rubber down the street, trying to get to her mother's house. Thinking that something sinister may be going on, Tammy flipped open her phone and called Hakim. After getting a busy signal, she hung up and pressed the gas.

Detective Dryer woke up just in time to see Tammy pull off down the street. "Shit," he said as he tried to hurry up and start the ignition. He pulled off in a hurry only to have to slam on the brakes when two cars backed out of back-to-back driveways and blocked him. "Fuck," he screamed. Dryer had been following Tammy for several weeks now. He was just about ready to spring his trap to bring Red and Bobby to their knees.

Hakim tried hard to convince himself that his sister wasn't the same Tammy who Bobby was talking about. Tammy didn't even like him selling drugs, so he couldn't fathom that she would be dating someone who was selling them. Hakim didn't know a lot about Bobby. He didn't know where he stayed, what kind of car he drove, or even his last name. All he knew was that he was Red's cousin. Hakim had noticed that Bobby wasn't coming around as much as did when he first got in the game. It really didn't matter to him, because he was making paper, and in his mind, the more people involved, the more money came out of his pocket.

Hakim had even saved enough to but himself a car. It was a doo-doo brown Chevy Caprice Classic. Hakim didn't even have his license yet, but once he showed the salesman at the used car lot the dead presidents, it was a wrap. He pulled up in front of his and Nikki's house and called his sister. He got frustrated when her line was busy. He changed his mind about going in the house. He wanted and needed to know if Red's cousin Bobby was the same one his sister was sweet on. His thoughts were interrupted by his vibrating cell phone. Hakim sped off down the road.

Tammy ran up on the porch with her keys in her hand. As fast as she could, she inserted them into the front door and let herself in.

"Ma! Ma," she yelled as she walked into the house. The house was eerily quiet. Tammy walked up the steps and toward her mother's room. She could have sworn that she heard someone inside the room. "Ma, you in there?" When no one answered, Tammy opened the door and started to walk in. She stopped suddenly, and her eyes bucked at the sight before her. Steve's friend Camp was sitting on the edge of the bed, sniffing cocaine off of a small mirror.

"Who the hell are you?" Tammy spat.

"Who the fuck are you?" Camp shot back.

Tammy ignored him and stepped inside the room. "Ma, you in here?" she asked again.

"Ma? Oh, you must be that Tammy bitch Steve's been telling me about."

"Bitch? Muthafucka, who in the fuck are you calling a bitch?"

Camp smiled as he looked behind her.

"What the fuck are you looking at me like that—"

All of a sudden, Tammy felt a hard push in her back. The impact catapulted her across the room. Camp laughed out loud as Tammy hit the floor with a loud thud. Tammy looked up and saw Steve standing there in a pair of boxers and his shirt off. All of a sudden, it hit Tammy like a ton of bricks. Her mind flashed back to where she'd saw Steve before. It was in the grocery store, where Tammy and Ivory had gone the day before Ivory got fired from her job at Rite Aid. Right on a "1-800-Crime-Stoppers" poster was a picture of Steven Bowers.

He'd changed his appearance by cutting his hair and shaving his mustache, but Tammy knew beyond a shadow of a doubt it was him. She even remembered what he was wanted for: armed robbery, drug abuse, attempted murder, and rape.

"Time for you to take care of daddy."

"You'd better get the fuck away from me!" Tammy got up and went for the door but was quickly blocked from leaving.

"Where the fuck you think you going?" Steve screamed.

"Get the fuck out of my way!"

Tammy tried to push her way past Steve, but she wasn't quite strong enough. Steve roughly grabbed her and slung her onto the bed. Camp reached down and took hold of her shirt, ripping it to shreds. Steve smiled as he walked toward the bed. His dick was now sticking out of his boxers.

"You gon' give me some of that pussy today," Steve said with conviction.

Tammy was terrified. Camp held her down while Steve started ripping off her pants. "Get off of me!" Tammy screamed. She fought back as hard as she could, but no to avail. In no time at all, Steve had her pants completely off. Tammy knew right then that she'd been set up. It wasn't her mother who had called her from that house. It was

Steve. She didn't know how he'd gotten her phone number. She'd hate to think that her own mother had sold her out. Two thoughts suddenly occurred to her: where the hell was her mother, and why wasn't she coming to her rescue?

Tammy fought for all she was worth until Camp elbowed her in the side of the face, dazing her. Then he pinned her arms above her head while Steve grabbed her knees and pushed her legs open. With his dick rock hard, Steve climbed on top of Tammy.

"No. Please don't," Tammy yelled in panic. All the fight had left her. The thought of Steve penetrating her was making her nauseated. Just as he was about to plunge inside of her, Steve screamed out in pain. His body slumped to the side as a result of being hit on the side of the head by Hakim's pistol.

"Get the fuck off my sister!"

Seeing the gun in Hakim's hand caused Camp to release Tammy's arms and back up against the wall.

"Hey, man, this shit was his idea," Camp said when Hakim pointed the gun in his direction.

Tammy jumped up from the bed as fast as she could. On wobbly legs, she struggled to get her clothes back on. "What took you so long to get here?" Tammy had sent Hakim a text message telling him that something wasn't right over at their mother's house.

Blood poured from the side of Steve's head. Hakim walked up on him and, without saying a word, hit him in the head again. Steve blacked out instantly. Camp was scared to death. He didn't know Hakim, so he didn't know what the youngster was prone to do.

"Take it easy, young blood."

"Shut the fuck up! Where the fuck is my mother?" Hakim yelled as he pointed the gun in Camp's face.

"She at one of Steve's cribs. He told her to stay there until we got back."

"And where the fuck is that?"

Camp sang like a canary as Hakim cocked his pistol. After getting the information he needed, Hakim lowered his gun. Camp thought he was home free until Hakim cracked him upside the head as well. The man slumped down on the floor and passed out.

"Let's get the fuck outta here, sis."

"But what about Mama?"

"I'm taking you to get cleaned up first. Then we can go over there and get her."

Hakim found two extension cords in the house and tied both of them up as tight as he could. "Now, even if they asses wake up, they can't get to her before we do."

Tammy and Hakim headed out the door. Hakim followed Tammy back to her residence. Bobby hadn't gotten there yet, so she invited Hakim inside. That's when she told him that she finally realized where she'd recognized Steve from.

Each one of them took turns trying to call their mother's cell phone, and each time their calls went directly to voicemail. Tammy went to the bathroom to get cleaned up. She couldn't wait to get to her mother. If this didn't convince her to leave Steve's no-good ass alone, nothing would.

While she was in the bathroom, she heard the front door close. After hearing two people yelling, she heard a gun cock. Tammy's eyes got wide as she ran toward the living room as fast as she could.

Bobby had pulled up in front of his house. His senses immediately went on high alert. Sitting directly in front of his house was the same Chevy he'd noticed when he left Red's house. He hadn't come straight home because he was angry and didn't want to take it out on Tammy, so he decided to toss back a couple of beers at the bar. When he felt that he'd cooled off enough, he went home.

Bobby had gotten out of his car, cocked his pistol, and hidden it behind his back. In broad daylight, he crept up to his door and let himself in. His jaw had dropped when he saw Hakim sitting on his couch. Before Hakim could even open his mouth, Bobby had pointed his gun in Hakim's face.

"What the fuck you doing in my house?"

"Yo' house? My sister stay here! Oh, you know what? Hold up a second," Hakim said when he remembered he'd heard Tammy's name earlier.

"Fuck that! I know what the fuck up! Red sent yo' ass over here to do something to a nigga, didn't he? Well, I got a message for my bitch-ass cousin!"

Hakim's eyes got wide as Bobby pulled back the hammer. Tammy suddenly ran into the room, screaming.

"Bobby, wait. Hakim is my brother!"

"This li'l nigga yo' brother?"

"Yes, he is," she said as she jumped between Bobby and Hakim. Bobby lowered his gun and stuck it back in the small of his back.

"That's what I was trying to tell you," said Hakim.

"My bad. I thought that bitch-ass cousin of mine sent you to my house to do some wicked shit."

"Wait, you two know each other?" Tammy asked.

"You could say that," Bobby said, smiling. "We used to, ah, work together."

"Used to?"

"I wasn't bullshitting when I told Red to go to hell. I got other things on my mind." Bobby walked over to Tammy and hugged her. "What brought on this visit, li'l nigga?"

Hakim looked at Tammy, who held her hand up. Bobby noticed the exchange between the two. "What's going on?" he asked.

Tammy gave Bobby the short, altered version. She told Bobby that she went to her mother's house after receiving a call from there and that she and Steve got into it. She left out the part about Steve trying to rape her. The last thing she wanted was for Bobby to kill Steve and for her to end up having to raise her baby alone. He was already pissed about Steve playing games like that anyway.

"I need a fucking drink," he said, walking into the kitchen.

Hakim looked at Tammy, who put her finger over her lips, letting him know to be quiet about the attempted rape.

"I gotta run to the store, Tammy. Come on, li'l nigga, let's roll."

Hakim followed Bobby out of the door. "All this time, I didn't know you was kicking it with my sister."

"Yeah, man. I like yo' sister a lot. You ain't got to worry about me fucking her over."

This made Hakim feel better. He did wonder how in the hell Bobby pulled her though, seeing that Tammy hated that he was selling drugs. As soon as they got into the car, Hakim spilled the beans on what went down at their mother's house. Bobby instantly saw red.

"And you let them muthafuckas live? What the fuck is wrong with you? You got a lot to learn about the street life. You wanna hang out in the streets, you better learn how to put in work when it's time to put in work."

Bobby mashed the gas. It didn't take him long to get to his Janice's house. With Hakim behind him, Bobby held up his gun as he entered the house. Hakim led him to his mother's room, where Steve and Camp were still tied up. The two men looked up in horror as Bobby walked over with malice in his eyes.

"Which one of these niggas tried to rape Tammy?"

"I think it was this nigga right here," Hakim said as he kicked Steve in the ribs.

"You like to rape women, huh?"

"Hold up. You got it all—"

Pow!

Steve screamed as Bobby stuck the barrel of his gun into Steve's crotch and pulled the trigger.

Camp's eyes got as big as saucers when he saw the blood pouring out from between Steve's legs. Bobby stomped Steve viciously in the head. He continued to do so until Steve was no longer breathing. "Bitch-ass nigga," he said, and he spat on Steve's corpse. He passed his gun to Hakim.

"Put in work. Show me you a G."

Hakim took the gun and pointed it at Camp. His hand trembled as he held the cold steel in his palm. This was the first time he'd ever pointed a gun at a human being.

"Do that shit! This muthafucka played a part in yo' sister being hurt! For all you know, he and this other dead muthafucka here could've been raping yo' mom! If you wanna be a G, then pull that muthafucking trigger!" Bobby may have liked Tammy, but there was no way he was going to let Hakim leave the house without putting in some real work. If he did that, he would be opening himself up to blackmail by the youngster at some point.

"Do that shit! Don't be a pussy-ass nigga! Pull that muthafucking trigga!"

Hakim closed his eyes and squeezed. He quickly discovered that actually killing someone was totally different than just thinking about it. When he opened them back up, Camp had a hole in the middle of his forehead.

"A'ight, let's go."

"What about them niggas?"

"Don't worry 'bout them. I got some niggas who'll come by here, scoop them niggas up, and dump 'em somewhere for a small fee. Let's be out."

Bobby and Hakim walked out of the house, leaving two dead bodies lying on the floor.

Chapter 35

Tammy stood in front of the living room window with her arms folded. Impatiently, she tapped her feet while waiting for Bobby and Hakim to return from the store. *What the hell is taking them so long?* Tammy couldn't wait for them to get back. As soon as they hit the door, she was going to grab Hakim by his hand, and they were going to see their mother. If Bobby wanted to come along, then fine. But if he didn't, then that was fine too.

Hell, if she had to go alone, then she was going to go. Tammy looked at her watch and saw that they'd been gone almost thirty minutes. She cocked her head and started to think. She knew that it shouldn't have taken them that long. She had a sneaking suspicion of where they may have gone, but she prayed it wasn't true. Even though Steve and Camp had tried to rape her, she didn't want her man and her brother to do something stupid and end up having to face murder charges. After another five minutes, Tammy couldn't wait any longer.

Throwing caution to the wind, Tammy grabbed the .38 handgun that Bobby had bought for her two weeks earlier, and she headed for the door. She didn't know a lot about guns, but Bobby had taught her enough about them to protect herself. Tammy sprinted out the door and straight for the car. She was in such a hurry that she never even noticed Detective Dryer staring at her from behind the wheel of his unmarked police car.

Dryer felt that his luck was about to change. After being sidetracked from following Tammy earlier, he'd gone to get something to eat and made a beeline right back to his stakeout spot. He'd been waiting all of ten minutes before Tammy came rushing out the door.

Sure looks like she's in a hurry.

This time, there were no interruptions of cars as he got behind Tammy and followed her to her destination. When she reached it, he parked half a block away. Dryer smiled wickedly as he watched Tammy make her way up the steps of a large two-story house.

Tammy looked at the door and took a deep breath. Although she was a little nervous about what she might see when she went inside, she was more afraid of what might happen to her mother if she didn't. She knocked on the door twice and peeked in as it eased open.

"Ma? Ma, you in here?" Tammy tiptoed into the living room and stopped dead in her tracks. Her mouth flew open, and she dropped to her knees. She couldn't believe her eyes. Right there in the middle of the floor was her mother on her knees, sucking some strange man's penis. Tammy was mortified. "What the hell are you doing?"

The man who was being serviced looked at Tammy liked she had just stopped him from hitting the lotto.

"Oh, my God," Janice said as she scooted away from the man.

"Hold up," he said. "I don't know who the fuck you is, but I done paid this bitch a lotta money to suck and swallow, so unless you gon' join the party, I suggest you get the fuck outta here!"

The man roughly grabbed Janice by her hair and yanked her head back down on his dick. Reluctantly, Janice started back to her business. After a few seconds, Janice heard a click.

"I know damn well you ain't pulled no fucking gun on me!"

"Get the fuck off of my mother," Tammy yelled, ignoring him.

"Tammy, what the hell are you doing?"

"Me? What am I doing? What the hell are you doing? Who in the fuck is this sorry son of a bitch standing in front of you with his dick in your mouth?"

"I'm sorry," Janice said as she dropped her head in shame. "There are a lot of things you don't know about me."

"Yeah, I see," Tammy said. She was getting angrier by the second. "You kicked me and Hakim to the curb so you can hang out with trash like this!"

"Please, you don't understand," Janice cried out.

"Then tell me! Explain it to me so that I understand it!" Tammy wasn't a fool. She knew damn well that if her mother was doing this sort of thing, Steve had probably pushed her to it.

Meanwhile, as Tammy and her mother went back and forth with each other, the man took the opportunity to ease toward Tammy. When he was sure that she wasn't paying enough attention, he rushed her and tackled her to the floor. The gun flew from Tammy's hand and landed over by the door.

"I'm gonna teach yo' ass to pull a fucking gun on me," he screamed.

He drew back his fist and brought it crashing down. Tammy barely moved her head in time as the punch grazed the side of her face. Pain shot through her temple as she reached up in an attempt to ward him off. The man grabbed both of her wrists and slammed them down to the floor, over her head. He went into his pocket and came out with a switchblade knife.

"Let's see how many niggas wanna be with yo' ass after I carve up that pretty little face of yours!" As soon as he popped the knife open to cut Tammy, hot pain seared through the left side of his body.

"Muthafucka, get the fuck off of my child!"

The barrel of Tammy's gun was still smoking when the man took his last breath and slumped to the floor. After nearly two months of wondering if her mother truly loved her, Tammy found out that she did in one breathtaking moment. Janice helped Tammy off the floor, and for a moment that seemed to last forever, they stood there and looked at the dead body.

"Mama, we gotta get outta here," Tammy said, grabbing her mother by the hand and pulling her to the door.

"But what about him?"

"Fuck him! Let's roll," Tammy said, pulling on her arm even harder.

Chapter 36

Ray-Ray sat behind the wheel of a stolen Ford Taurus. A mask of anger occupied his face as he observed James standing on the corner serving the fiends. Knowing that he couldn't get at Red and his crew without help, Ray-Ray enlisted some assistance to help him get revenge on the people who'd tried to kill him. Red, Bobby, James, Cedric, and Dru all had to die. It didn't matter to him that James and Bobby weren't even around when Red tried to have him snuffed out. They were part of Red's crew and therefore had to be eliminated. He couldn't believe that Red had the nerve to try to have him killed over a broad he didn't even give a shit about. After checking the clip of his .40-caliber handgun, Ray-Ray smiled as he watched his sinister plan unfold.

James followed the sexy vixen into the alleyway. It was hard to believe that a woman this fine could be a crackhead, but after selling enough drugs in his young life to start a pharmacy, James knew better than most that fiends came in all shapes, sizes, and colors. The woman quickly got down on her knees and started fumbling with James's zipper.

"Damn, baby, you don't waste no time, do you?"

The woman shook her head slowly from side to side. She caressed his manhood and watched as he leaned back against the brick wall and closed his eyes. "You ready for this?"

"Oh, hell yeah," he said with his eyes still closed.

James started to get antsy. In his opinion, she seemed to be taking a long time to take him into her mouth. Then all of a sudden, he didn't feel anything anymore. When he opened his eyes, Ray-Ray and Cookie were both standing there, giving him a death stare. James was so scared he pissed on himself.

The minute he saw Ray-Ray standing there holding his gun, he knew that he was in a world of trouble. Before he could even begin to explain to Ray-Ray that he had nothing to do with the attempt on his life, Ray-Ray shot him between the eyes. Brain matter and blood painted the wall behind him like graffiti. *One down, four to go,* thought Ray-Ray.

Dryer was so tired it only took him a few seconds to nod off while waiting for Tammy to come out of the house. His head snapped up at what he thought was a gunshot. Had he been awake, he could have easily identified what it was. He looked around for a minute to see if any suspicious activity was going to happen, but none did. Dryer was getting tired of waiting. He was going to give Tammy a few more minutes, and then he was going to knock on the door and make up some bogus reason to take her in.

Just as he was about to get out of the car, Tammy and another woman came walking out of the house. Dryer perked up as the two women hopped inside the car Tammy was driving and headed up the street. Dryer let them get a half block up the street and pulled them over.

Janice had to do a quick job of calming her daughter down. Tammy's bowels almost released when she saw the man in the dark suit walk toward the car. She was sure he was coming to arrest them for killing a man.

Dryer knocked on the window and smiled when Tammy rolled the window down. "Good afternoon, ma'am," he said with a fake smile on his face.

Tammy and Janice looked at him like the devil he was.

Dryer leaned into the car and looked in the direction of the back seat. As soon as the two women looked back to see what he was looking at, he dropped a bag of cocaine between the floor and the driver's side door.

"What the hell are you looking at?" Tammy asked.

"Ma'am, I'm not looking at anything back there, but I am looking at that bag of a powdery white substance right there."

"What the fuck? You planted that shit there," Tammy screamed.

"Yeah, yeah, that's what they all say. Get out of the car, ma'am." Dryer snatched the door open and pulled Tammy out of the car.

"You're just going to pull on a pregnant woman like that, huh, asshole?"

"Pregnant? Tammy, why you ain't tell me that I was gonna be a grandmother?"

"'Cause I haven't seen you, that's why."

Pregnant, Dryer thought. *My day just keeps getting better and better.* Dryer eased up, but just slightly. "I'm sorry about you being knocked up and all, but you're going to have to get up against the car and spread your legs."

Dryer did a quick search of Tammy and then told her to wait there. Dryer then walked away and called Stone. He knew that Stone was on vacation, but this was his chance to bring Red down. When Stone answered the phone, Dryer told him exactly what he needed him to do. Then he arrested Tammy and took her to jail.

Right before getting into the police car, Tammy told her mother to get in touch with either Hakim or Bobby. Janice noticed Tammy's phone in the cup holder and picked it up. She immediately started looking for Bobby's number.

After Hakim left, Bobby kicked back on his couch and lit a blunt. He didn't know if Tammy had gone to see her mother, but since he and Hakim had taken care of Steve and his friend, he felt that Tammy was safe. He wanted to get to know Hakim somewhat, since Hakim was going to be in his life now.

His cell phone rang, annoying him slightly, so he chose to ignore it. It rang two more times, irritating him, so he picked it up with an attitude that quickly disappeared when he saw Tammy's number. "Hey, li'l mama. Where you at?" he asked, smiling.

"Bobby! This is Tammy's mother, Janice!"

Bobby's heart sank. He knew that if someone other than Tammy was calling him with her phone, then something was terribly wrong. "What's going on?" he asked.

"Tammy has been arrested! Some punk-ass detective planted some dope in the car she was driving."

Bobby knew right then that Dryer was the culprit. He'd been trying to get at him and Red for quite some time. "Yo, where'd they take her?"

"I think they took her to the sixth district."

"A'ight, I'm on it." Bobby hung up and called his lawyer. He had one on retainer, just in case some shit popped off. He was pissed that it went straight to voicemail. "What the fuck am I paying this muthafucka for?" he screamed. He grabbed his keys and headed out the door. Bobby opened the door and saw a note taped to it.

If you don't want that little bitch of yours to re-main in jail, meet me at Tiko's in thirty minutes.
Dryer

Tiko's was a small diner known for its juicy cheese-burgers. Bobby had no idea why Dryer wanted to meet there, but he had no choice but to go.

Bobby ran to his car and jumped in. He raced over to the diner, ignoring any and all traffic laws.

Meanwhile, Ray-Ray got behind Bobby and followed him the entire way. He didn't know why Bobby was driving so fast, and he didn't care. His original plan was to wait for Bobby to come out of the house, catch him slipping, and blast him. But when he got to Bobby's house, Bobby was just pulling off.

Dryer smiled as Bobby walked into the diner. He was finally going to bring Red down, and Bobby was going to do all the work. "Why, Robert, nice of you to show up," Dryer mocked.

Bobby gave him a death stare as he sat across the table. "The fuck is this shit all about? You can't touch me, so you wanna fuck with my girl?"

"Well, it's like I told you before. We want that piece of shit cousin of yours. Now you can either play ball with us, or your little bitch and that bastard child of yours will rot in jail. I'll make sure of it."

"Bastard child? What the hell are you talking about?"

Dryer smiled. "Ooohh, you didn't know, huh? Your girl is pregnant," Dryer said as he leaned across the table.

Bobby was stunned. Tammy hadn't said a thing to him about being pregnant.

"Make up your mind, Bulletproof Bobby. You either help me take down Red, or by the time I'm finished, your little girlfriend will look like Scarface."

Bobby seethed. He wanted to reach behind his back, pull out his gun, and blow Dryer's brains out. He knew Dryer hated him, and he really had it in for Red. As fate would have it, a young couple walked past the diner, pushing a stroller. Bobby glanced out the window and took a deep breath. He was caught between a rock and a hard place. No man wants his girl locked up, especially while she is pregnant with his child. What if Dryer made good on his threat? What if he really could get her locked up for a long period of time? Bobby leaned back and looked into Dryer's wicked eyes. If Bobby had any doubt that he would do that to a pregnant woman, the look in Dryer's dark pupils erased it. Bobby was torn. Dryer was asking him to break one of the most sacred street codes of all. He was asking him to snitch.

"What's it going to be, Mr. Walker?"

Bobby took a deep breath. He leaned forward and looked Dryer directly in his eyes. "I'll tell you what," Bobby started.

Before he could get any other words out of his mouth, the glass beside him shattered. Bullet after bullet flew through the window as Ray-Ray cut loose with his pistol. He didn't know who the white man was with Bobby, but he was in such a rage over Red and his crew trying to kill him that he was willing to lay down anybody in his way. The first shot barely missed Bobby's head and sent him scurrying to the floor.

Dryer wasn't as lucky. One of the bullets caught him in the temple. He collapsed right on top of Bobby. Customers and workers alike were all screaming and ducking for cover. An elderly couple both caught slugs to the face and died instantly. One waitress was struck in the knee, leaving her with a nasty scar and a permanent limp.

After pushing a dead Dryer off of him, Bobby crawled along the floor until he got to the door. He peeked out and saw a deranged-looking Ray-Ray reloading his gun. This was all the time he needed.

Bobby pulled out his own gun and pointed it at Ray-Ray. "Ray, what the fuck are you doing?"

"You know what the fuck I'm doing! Don't act like you ain't have shit to do with trying to have me clipped!"

"What? I don't know what the fuck you talking about!"

"You lying," Ray-Ray shouted as he lifted his heat and pointed it in Bobby's direction.

Bobby had no choice but to pull the trigger. He didn't know what was going on, and he wasn't about to get shot over some shit he didn't know anything about. Bullets ripped through Ray-Ray's body like a hot knife through butter. Bobby quickly hopped to his feet, ran to his car, and peeled off down the street.

Chapter 37

It had been two months since Bobby had been involved in the shootout at the diner. With Dryer dying from his injuries, the police had no case against Tammy, so they had no choice but to let her go. She and Bobby had started talking about starting a family together. Bobby had no idea that the lawyer he had on retainer was also a literary agent and would be able to help Bobby get his publishing house off the ground. Bobby had talked Tammy into letting him pay for her schooling.

Even though she was pregnant, she decided that she would attend school until it got to be too much for her, and then she would take a little time off. To keep money coming in while his company was being put together, Bobby started dabbling in real estate, flipping houses.

Hakim was still in the streets, putting in work. Although he continued to work for Red, he kept quiet about Bobby and his sister being an item.

Janice entered a drug rehabilitation program and swore on her life that she would never again let a man control her to the point where she mistreated her children.

Ivory was still in Solon. She still talked to Tammy on the phone, but for the most part, she was enjoying her new life and had no intention of moving back to Cleveland. Every so often, she would sneak back in to chill with Tammy, but with those thugs still looking for her, she never stayed too long.

Sadly, the news of her father being fatally wounded was too much for Nancy to bear, and she overdosed on cocaine a week after he died. On that particular day, Bobby was at a meeting with his lawyer to go over the papers that would make him the owner of Bulletproof Publishing. Tammy was at home, eating a bowl of ice cream and waiting for Hakim to come over. He'd told her on the phone that he had a surprise for her and would be over in twenty minutes. After ten minutes, the doorbell rang.

"Damn, he's early." Tammy got up, walked toward the front door, and slung it open.

"Hello," said a woman dressed in tight jeans with her hair wrapped in a purple bandana. "Are you Tammy?" she asked with a smile.

"Yes. May I help you?"

Without saying another word, Kat pulled out a knife and stabbed Tammy in the stomach. Tammy fell back onto the floor, screaming in pain.

"He'll always belong to me, bitch." Kat then put the knife back in her purse and walked away.

Epilogue

Bobby sat in the hospital chair with his face in his hands. From the moment Hakim had called him and told him what had happened, he started blaming himself. He figured if he had just told Tammy about Kat, then maybe she would have been on guard. Whoever said thugs don't cry had never felt the pain of potentially losing not one, but two people he cared about at the same time.

Janice put her hand on Bobby's shoulder and tried to assure him that everything was going to be all right. She didn't know that for sure, but she really liked Bobby and wanted to be there for him as well as her daughter.

Hakim stomped around the hospital an emotionally confused young man. One minute he would scream of revenge, and the next, he would break down like a newborn baby.

Although he and Bobby hadn't spoken to each other since their falling out, even Red showed up to give his support. He didn't stay long, though. Just enough to show concern for his cousin.

Bobby had been there for the past four hours while Tammy was in surgery, and if he had to, he would stay there four more. Tammy had captured his heart. He loved her, and if he could trade places with her right now, he would do it in a heartbeat.

Bobby was just about to get up and go to the bathroom when the doctor came out. He was an elderly gentleman with thinning hair that was graying on the sides.

"Family for Tammy—"

"Yes," Bobby jumped up and said before the doctor could say her last name. With Janice and Hakim by Bobby's side, the doctor walked over and placed his hand on Bobby's shoulder.

Red sat in his car in the parking lot of the emergency room smoking a blunt. He looked intently as the doctor walked up to Bobby and placed his hand on his shoulder. Red had never forgiven Tammy. He blamed her for getting inside Bobby's head and capturing his heart. In his mind, it cost him a ton of money.

Red went into his pocket and pulled out a wad of hundreds. He handed the money, which totaled $5,000, to Kat. Red wanted Bobby to come back to the organization, and he figured the only way he could make that happen was to eliminate Tammy from the equation. So he devised a devilish plan to murder Tammy.

Kat smiled as she got out of Red's car and walked back to hers $5,000 richer. Little did she know that Dru was waiting in the back seat to cut her throat. Red laughed out loud as he watched Bobby and the rest of Tammy's family break down and cry.

The End